"Gray, I'

"You'd be her, both w what he di

He dropped his head forward so his brow rested on hers. She'd never before thought of him as a man who needed to lean on others, but in that moment, she felt as though they were propping each other up.

"Gray?" she said, the single word a question that encompassed all the thoughts inside her head. *What's going on?* she wanted to ask. *Do you feel it, too?* But she didn't have the guts.

"I'll protect you," he said. The words of the heartfelt vow punched through her because she instinctively knew he wasn't just promising to protect a witness. He was promising to protect *her*.

"I know you will," she said, trying not to make more of this than it really was. "Because it's your job."

"And because of this," he replied. Then he tipped her face up and touched his lips to hers.

COLORADO MOUNTAIN ESCAPE

JESSICA ANDERSEN

&

USA TODAY Bestselling Author

CASSIE MILES

Previously published as *Mountain Investigation*
and *Unforgettable*

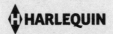

ISBN-13: 978-1-335-42478-5

Colorado Mountain Escape

Copyright © 2021 by Harlequin Books S.A.

Mountain Investigation
First published in 2009. This edition published in 2021.
Copyright © 2009 by Dr. Jessica S. Andersen

Unforgettable
First published in 2011. This edition published in 2021.
Copyright © 2011 by Kay Bergstrom

Recycling programs
for this product may
not exist in your area.

Harlequin Enterprises ULC
22 Adelaide St. West, 40th Floor
Toronto, Ontario M5H 4E3, Canada
www.Harlequin.com

Printed in U.S.A.

CONTENTS

Jessica Andersen has worked as a geneticist, scientific editor, animal trainer and landscaper...but she's happiest when she's combining all of her many interests into writing romantic adventures that always have a twist of the unusual to them. Born and raised in the Boston area (Go, Sox!), Jessica can usually be found somewhere in New England, hard at work on her next happily-ever-after.

Books by Jessica Andersen

Harlequin Intrigue

Dr. Bodyguard
Secret Witness
Intensive Care
Body Search
Covert M.D.
The Sheriff's Daughter

Bear Claw Creek Crime Lab

Ricochet
At Close Range
Rapid Fire
Twin Targets
Manhunt in the Wild West

Visit the Author Profile page
at Harlequin.com for more titles.

MOUNTAIN INVESTIGATION

Jessica Andersen

Chapter 1

Mariah Shore paused on the ridgeline about a half mile from her isolated cabin. Standing in the lee of a sturdy pine, she scanned the woods around her with a photographer's sharp eye. She wasn't looking for a subject for her old, beloved Canon 35 mm, though. The camera was stowed safely in her backpack for the hike home.

No, she was looking for a target for the Remington double-aught shotgun she held across her body.

"There's nobody there," she told herself, willing it to be true. But the woods were quieter than she liked, and the day was rapidly dimming toward the too-early springtime dusk.

With her curvy figure swathed in lined pants, a flannel shirt, a wool sweater and a down parka, and her dark curls tucked under a thick knit cap, she'd be warm enough if she stayed put. But her hurry to get home wasn't about the warmth. It was about the cabin's thick walls and sturdy locks, the line of electric fencing near the trees, and the motion-sensitive lights and alarms that formed a protective perimeter around the clear-cut yard.

The cabin was safe. Outside was a crapshoot.

She needed to keep moving, would've been nearly home if she hadn't heard a crackle of underbrush and seen a flash of movement directly in her path. She'd tried to tell herself it was just an animal, but she'd spent the best weeks of her childhood following her grandfather through Colorado woods like these, and she'd lived in the cabin thirty miles north of Bear Claw City for more than a year now. She'd hiked out nearly every day since arriving, first for peace and more recently for some actual work, as she'd started to feel the stirrings of the creativity she'd thought was gone for good. She knew the forest, knew the rhythms and inhabitants of the ridgeline. Whatever was between her and the cabin, her sense of the woods told her it wasn't a bear or wildcat. Her gut said it was two-legged danger.

Her ex-husband. Lee Mawadi.

Or was it?

"He's not there," she told herself. "He's long gone."

She'd kept tabs on the investigation, listening to the infrequent follow-ups on her small radio, and asking careful questions during her rare trips into the city for supplies. Because of that, she knew there had been no sign of Lee in the nearly six months since he and three other men had escaped from the ARX Supermax Prison, located on the other side of the ridge. She also knew—or logic dictated, anyway—that her ex-husband had no real reason to come back to the area, and every reason to stay away.

After a long moment, when nothing could be heard but the muted sounds of the sun-loving animals powering down and the nocturnal creatures revving up as dusk fell along the ridgeline, she even managed to believe her own words.

"You're talking yourself into being scared," she muttered, slinging the double-aught over her shoulder and heading for home. "There's no way he's coming back here."

Lee might be a terrorist, a murderer and a liar, but he wasn't stupid.

Still, she stayed alert as she walked, relaxing only slightly when it seemed like the forest noises got a little louder, as though whatever menace the woodland creatures had sensed—if anything—had passed through and gone.

When Mariah reached the fifty-foot perimeter around the cabin, the motion-sensitive lights snapped on. The bright illumination showed a wide swath of stumps in stark relief, mute evidence of the terror that had driven her to chainsaw every tree within a fifty-foot radius of the cabin, and install a low-lying, solar-powered electric fence to keep the animals away.

In the center of the clear-cut zone sat the cabin. It was sturdy and thick-walled, its proportions slightly off, a bit top-heavy, and if she'd thought a time or two that she and the cabin were very much alike, there was nobody around to agree or disagree with her. She lived alone, and was grateful for the solitude. She used to think she wanted the hustle and bustle of a city, and the mob of friends she'd lacked during childhood. Now she knew better. Once a loner, always a loner.

Reaching into her pocket for the small remote control she carried with her at all times, she deactivated the motion-sensitive alarms. The security system wasn't wired to call for any sort of outside response, first because she was too far off the beaten track for the police to do her any good, and second because she didn't have much use for cops. That wasn't why she'd installed the system; she'd wanted it as a warning, pure and simple. If she was in the cabin and trouble appeared, she'd know it was time to get out—or dig in and defend herself. If she was somewhere in the forest, she'd have a head start on escaping.

The Bear Claw cops and the Feds had offered her protection, of course, first when Lee had been arrested for his terrorist activities, and again when he'd escaped. But those offers had all come with questions and sidelong looks, and the threat of people in her space, watching her every move, making it clear that she was as much a suspect as a victim.

Victim. Oh, how she hated the word, hated knowing she'd been one. Not as much a victim as the people Lee had killed, or the families who mourned the dead, but a victim nonetheless. Worse, she'd been selfish and blind, not looking beyond the problems in her marriage to see the larger threat. She had to live with that, would do so until the day she died. But that didn't mean she had to live with strangers—worse, cops and FBI agents—reminding her of it, and hounding her and her parents. Not when there wasn't anything she could do to help them find her ex-husband.

"There's no way he's coming back here," she repeated, shifting the shotgun farther back on her shoulder so she could fumble in her pocket for the keys to the log cabin's front door. "He'd be an idiot to even try."

She unlocked the door and pushed through into the cabin, starting to relax as she keyed the remote to bring the motion-sensitive alarms back online.

They shrieked, warning that something—or some-*one*— had breached the perimeter in the short moment the alarms had been off.

A split second later, a blur came at her from the side and a heavy hand clamped on her arm, bringing a sharp pricking pain. Jolting, Mariah screamed and spun, but the spin turned into a sideways lurch as her legs went watery and her muscles gave out.

Drugs, she thought, realizing that a syringe had been the source of the prick, drugs the source of the spinning disconnection that seized her, dampening her ability to fight or flee. The tranquilizer didn't blunt her panic, though, or the sick knowledge that she was in serious trouble. Her heart hammered and her soul screamed, *No!*

She fell, and a man grabbed her on the way down, his fingers digging into the flesh of her upper arms. His face was blurred by whatever he'd given her, but she knew it was Lee. She recognized the shape of her ex's body, the pain of his hard grasp and the way her skin crawled beneath his touch.

He took the remote control from her, and used it to kill the alarm. Then he leaned in close, and his features became sharp and familiar: close-cropped, white-blond hair; smooth, elegant skin; and blue eyes that could go from friendly to murderous in a snap.

Born to an upper-class Boston family, the second son of loving parents with a strong marriage, Lee Chisholm had been sent to the best schools and given all the opportunities a child could've asked for. Logic said he should have matured into the cultured, successful man he'd looked like when Mariah had met him. And on one level, he'd been that man. On another, he'd been a spoiled monster whose parents had hidden the fact that he'd had a taste for arson and violence. That nasty child had grown into a man in search of a cause, an excuse to indulge his evil appetites. He'd found that cause during his years at an exclusive, expensive college, where he'd been recruited into the anti-American crusade.

As part of a terrorist cell, under the leadership of mastermind al-Jihad, he'd gone by the name of Lee Mawadi, and had arranged to meet Mariah because of her father's connections to one of al-Jihad's targets. Lee had wooed her, courted her, pretended to love her…and then he'd used her and set her up to die.

She hadn't died, but in the years since, she hadn't really lived, either. And now, seeing her own death in her ex-husband's face, she cringed from him, her heart hammering against her ribs, tears leaking from her eyes.

Lee, no. Don't! she tried to say, but the words didn't come, and the scream stayed locked in her throat because she couldn't move, couldn't struggle, couldn't do anything other than hang limply in his grasp and suck in a thin trickle of air.

Then he let go of her. She fell to the floor at the threshold of the cabin and landed hard, winding up in a tangled heap of arms and legs, lax muscles and terror.

He crouched over her, gloating as he held up the small styrette he'd used to drug her. "This is to shut you up and keep you where you belong," he said. Then he stood, drew back his foot and kicked her in the stomach. Pain sang through her, radiating from the soft place where the blow landed. She would've curled around the agony, but she couldn't do even that. She could only lie there, tears running down her face as he said, "That was for forgetting where you belong, *wife*. Which is by my side, no matter what."

He grabbed her by the hood of her parka and dragged her inside, kicking the door shut.

The sound of it closing was a death knell, because Mariah knew one thing for certain: the man she'd once promised to love, honor and obey didn't intend to let her leave the cabin alive.

Five days later

Michael Grayson was a man on a mission, and he didn't intend to let inconsequential details like due process or official sanction interfere. Which was why, just shy of six months after he'd nearly been booted out of the FBI for sidestepping protocol, Gray was back on the edge of the line between agent and renegade, between law officer and vigilante. Only this time he was well aware of it and knew the consequences; his superiors had put him on notice, loud and clear.

The threats didn't stop him from taking his day off to drive up through the heart of Bear Claw Canyon State Forest to the hills beyond, though, and they didn't keep him from using a pair of bolt cutters on the padlocked gate that barred entry to a narrow access road leading up the ridgeline. Up to *her* house.

He drove into the forest as far as he dared, just past a fire access road that marked the two-thirds point of the journey. He tucked his four-by-four into the trees, off the main track so it couldn't be seen easily from the road, pointing it downhill in the event that he needed to get out of there fast.

Then he started walking, staying off the main road and out of sight, just in case. As he did so, he tried to tell himself that it was recon, nothing more, that he just wanted to get a look at Lee Mawadi's ex-wife six months after the prison break. But he couldn't make the lie play, even inside his own skull. His gut said that Mariah Shore had secrets. There had to be a reason she'd moved into a cabin on a ridgeline that, on a clear day, provided views of both Bear Claw City and the ARX Supermax Prison.

His coworkers and superiors in the Denver field office had put zero stock in Gray's gut feelings—which admittedly had a bit of a hit-or-miss reputation. The higher-ups had written Mariah off as nothing more than she seemed: a pretty, dark-haired woman who'd married a man in good faith, not realizing that he was using her twice over, once to create the illusion of middle-American normalcy and disguise his ties to al-Jihad's terrorist network, and a second time to gain entrée to her family.

When the newlyweds moved to a suburb north of Bear Claw City to be close to her parents, Mariah had leaned on her father to find a job for her engineering-trained husband within the American Mall Group, where her father had been an upper-level manager. It wasn't until after the attacks and subsequent arrests, when the story had started coming together, that it became clear Lee had manipulated Mariah into getting him the job, just as he'd manipulated her into serving as his alibi through the first few rounds of the investigation.

Or so she had claimed. Gray hadn't fully bought her protestations of innocence two years earlier during the original investigation, and he sure as hell hadn't believed them more recently, when her husband had escaped. There were only so many times he could hear "I don't know anything" before it started to wear thin, especially when the suspect's actions said otherwise.

Mariah Chisholm, who had gone back to using her maiden name of Shore after the divorce, knew more than she was admitting. Gray was positive of it…he just couldn't convince his jackass, rules-are-God boss, Special Agent in Charge Johnson, to lean on her harder.

Then again, SAC Johnson was in this investigation to make his career and avoid stepping on any political toes. Gray was in it for justice.

The horrific terror attacks two and a half years earlier, dubbed the "Santa Bombings," had targeted the start of the holiday season, when families with young children had gathered at each of the American Malls to welcome the mall Santas. The bombs had been concealed in building stress points near the elaborate thrones where the Santas had sat for whispered consultations with hundreds of hopeful, holiday-crazed kids. The explosives had all gone off simultaneously, in six malls across the state. Hundreds had been killed—families destroyed in a flash—during the most joyous of seasons.

It had been an inhuman attack, directed solely at the most innocent of innocents. Terrorism in the truest sense of the word.

In the investigation immediately afterwards, a couple of sales receipts and a glitchy security camera had led the FBI agents to Lee Chisholm—who called himself Mawadi among his "real" family within the terror network—along with his co-conspirator, Muhammad Feyd, and the mastermind himself, al-Jihad. The evidence had been enough to convict the men—barely—and get them

sentenced to life-plus at the ARX Supermax. The clues
hadn't seemed to point to the involvement of Mawadi's
wife, who at the time had been dealing with bad press,
a quickie divorce and her father's forced retirement and
subsequent near-fatal heart attack. In the end, Mariah
Chisholm, née Shore, had been cleared of suspicion as
far as the higher-ups were concerned.

As far as Gray was concerned, though, they'd missed
something.

He'd been part of the initial interviews of Mariah and
her father, and he'd memorized all the reports—both
the official file and the assembled news stories. The
reports from two years earlier, during the time when
Lee Mawadi had been arrested, tried and convicted,
had described Mariah as "shocked," "devastated" and
"grief-stricken." One Shakespeare of a journalist had
even called her a "doe-eyed innocent played false by
the man she thought she knew."

The pictures and film clips had backed up those
descriptions, showing a lovely, sad-eyed woman with
curly, dark-brown hair and full lips that had trembled
at all the right moments. For the most part she'd tried to
avoid the cameras. On the few occasions she'd spoken
publicly, she'd read prepared statements in which she
had apologized for not having seen her husband of six
months for what he'd been—a monster—and had urged
swift justice for Mawadi, Feyd and al-Jihad. Even Gray,
an admitted cynic, had bought the routine, all but forgetting about her once Mawadi and the others were behind
bars. He'd shifted his attention away from them and focused on tracking down more of al-Jihad's terror cells.

All that had changed the previous fall, though, when
Mawadi, Feyd and al-Jihad had escaped from the ARX

Supermax with the help of fellow prisoner Jonah Fairfax. Fairfax had proven to be a deep undercover Fed who'd been charged with flushing out al-Jihad's contacts within U.S. law enforcement, and had planned to do so by facilitating the escape and then netting all the conspirators when they made their move. But the setup had backfired badly when it turned out that Fairfax's superior, who had progressively isolated him over the previous two years, had turned, becoming one of al-Jihad's assets.

In the end, Fairfax had helped al-Jihad escape, and the only conspirator he'd flushed out was his own boss, code-named Jane Doe, who had vanished in the aftermath of a foiled attack on a local stadium. The Feds and local cops had managed to recapture Muhammad Feyd, but so far he had refused to talk, which left the authorities pretty much chasing their own tails.

Worse, in the immediate aftermath of the thwarted stadium attack, Gray himself had wound up as a suspect in the conspiracy. Which was just plain stupid.

Yes, he'd failed to pass along a potentially crucial message, but that wasn't because he'd been working for al-Jihad. He'd made the decision in a split second of distraction, a moment when his version of justice and the law had clashed and he'd gotten caught up in his own head, stuck in memories. And yeah, maybe there'd been other factors, too, but they were nothing he couldn't handle. He could—and would—bring the bastards down. No way he was letting the Santa Bombers go free. Not now, not ever. Not after what they'd done.

The thought brought a flash of memory, of concussion and screams, and the rapid flutter of a dying child's chest in the sterile confines of an ICU.

Shaking off the image, Gray forced his mind to

focus on the task at hand. Moving silently he worked his way through the thick forest, headed for Mariah Shore's cabin. He had no orders, no official sanction. Hell, he was on probation. He was supposed to be riding a desk, monitoring transcribed chatter and helping with the tip lines.

"I'm just out for a hike," he murmured, keeping his voice very low, even though he hadn't seen or heard anything to indicate that he had company. "Is it my fault I just happened to wander out of the state park and stumble on her cabin?"

It wasn't much as plausible deniability went, but he was done with waiting around for a break that wasn't coming. He'd helped jail Lee Mawadi, Muhammad Feyd and al-Jihad in the first place, using slightly less than orthodox methods in his zeal to gain some measure of justice for the victims of the Santa Bombings. He'd do the same thing again, even if it meant the end of his career.

"Well, well. Will you look at that?" he said, whistling quietly under his breath as the ex-wife's isolated cabin came into view. He stopped amid the cover of a thick stand of trees and scrubby underbrush, and peered through, scoping out the scene.

It looked like Mariah had been doing some landscaping.

Originally, the cabin had been tucked into the woods, with trees very near the structure, shielding it even from satellite view. Now there was a clear-cut swath a good fifty feet in all directions, with raw stumps giving mute testimony to where trees had once stood. In one corner of the lot, a huge pile of cut and split logs sat beside a gas-powered wood splitter. A thin wisp of smoke rose from the cabin's central chimney, indicating that someone was home, as did the vehicles parked in the side yard. One was the banged-up Jeep Mariah had registered in her name. The other was unfamiliar, a nondescript, dark-blue four-by-four SUV.

Two cars. Two people, maybe more? Gray thought, tensing further as a quiver of instinct ran through him.

When he'd asked Mariah Shore point-blank why she'd bought the forest-locked cabin no more than thirty miles from the ARX Supermax Prison, she'd claimed it was a sort of penance. She'd said she wanted to be able to see the prison on one side of her, the city of Bear Claw on the other, that she wanted to be reminded of how many lives had been destroyed because she hadn't recognized her husband for what he was.

And maybe that explanation would've worked for him if she'd come off as the grief-stricken victim she'd played two years earlier. But the newer reports—some of which Gray had written himself—described her as "closed off," "detached," "unfriendly," and "nervous"… which weren't the kind of words he typically associated with innocence. They were more in line with the behavior of a woman who had something to hide.

Unfortunately—as far as Gray was concerned, anyway—a detailed check of her activities since Mawadi's incarceration hadn't turned up any indication that she was in contact with her ex. Heck, she'd kept almost entirely to herself, not even visiting her parents when her father had been hospitalized again a few months ago for his recurring heart problems.

In the absence of evidence to the contrary, and with all the available information suggesting that Mawadi, al-Jihad and Jane Doe had fled the country, SAC Johnson had ended all surveillance of Mariah Shore, despite

Gray's protests that she was one of their few remaining local links to the terrorists.

In retrospect, Gray knew he probably should've kept his mouth shut. Rather than making his boss take a second look at the decision, his opinion had only made Johnson dig in harder, to the point that he'd ordered Gray to stay the hell away from Mawadi's ex-wife. But Johnson hadn't known that she had clear-cut the area around her cabin and strung up what looked to be some serious motion-activated lights and alarms, along with a low electric fence that was no doubt intended to keep deer and other critters out of the monitored zone, lest they trigger the alarms.

She'd turned the place into a fortress.

Question was, why?

"And won't Johnson be glad I just happened to be hiking this way?" Gray murmured, having taken up the dubious habit of talking to himself over the last few years, ever since he and Stacy had split up.

Refusing to think of his ex-wife, or how things had gone so wrong so fast after their so-called "trial" separation just before the bombings, Gray moved out of the concealing brush and eased closer to the cabin, his senses on the highest alert.

He hadn't gone more than two paces before the door swung open, and Lee Mawadi himself stepped out onto the rustic porch. Gray froze, adrenaline shooting through him alongside a surge of vindication and the hard, hot jolt of knowing he'd been right all along.

Mariah Shore was in this conspiracy right up to her pretty little neck.

Chapter 2

Gray stayed very still. He was wearing camouflage and stood hidden behind a screening layer of trees and underbrush; as long as he didn't move, Mawadi shouldn't be able to see him. Gray wasn't totally motionless, though: his blood raced through his veins and his heart pumped furiously, beating in his ears on a rhythm that said he was right, the ex-wife was part of it, after all.

And Lee Mawadi had very definitely *not* fled the country, as all the reports had indicated.

The bastard stood there—blond and Nordic, loose-limbed and relaxed, cradling a Remington shotgun in the crook of one arm as he scanned the forest. Then he headed for the corner of the porch, shouldered the shotgun, unzipped and urinated, all the while scanning the forest. He seemed to be looking for something, but what? Had he seen Gray skulking in the trees? Was he expecting company?

Mawadi finished and rezipped, then turned toward the still-open door, calling, "You said they'd be here at five, right?"

Gray didn't hear the answer, couldn't tell if the responding voice belonged to a man or a woman. His brain raced, trying to parse the tiny nugget of information. It was just past four o'clock, which meant the meeting was an hour away. And if he could figure out who was coming for the meeting, it could be a huge break in the case, allowing them to identify more of the terrorists, maybe even the traitors they suspected might be working within the Bear Claw Police Department, and maybe even the FBI itself. For half a second, excitement zinged through him at the thought of al-Jihad himself showing up. Gray would give anything to be the one to subdue all of them, the terrorists and the ex-wife, and put them where they belonged—in the ARX Supermax or a grave, either way was fine with him.

Then Gray cursed, realizing that if the newcomers were driving up the mountain, he could be in serious trouble. The only way up the ridgeline to the cabin was the narrow track he'd come up, or the fire-access road that merged with the track just below where he'd parked. His four-by-four was off the road and somewhat hidden, but the concealment was far from foolproof. A driver coming up the lane might see the vehicle, even in the gathering dusk.

Which meant he had two choices. One, he could retrace his path, pronto, in hopes of making it down the ridge and hiding the truck before the other vehicle turned up the road. Then he could boogie down the mountain, get into cell range and call for backup. Or two, he could stay put and hope his four-by-four escaped detection while he cobbled together some sort of a plan to subdue Mawadi and whoever else was in the cabin, then capture the others when they arrived.

Gray wasn't a glory seeker by a long shot, but for both personal and professional reasons, he liked the image of dragging in the murdering bastards himself. Not to mention that there was a good chance that even if he made it to cell range, SAC Johnson and the others would give him a less than enthusiastic response. Gray had cried "wolf" before and it had come to nothing, and then he'd dropped the ball on that damn message during the festival, with the result that al-Jihad and the others had very nearly succeeded in their aim of destroying a stadium filled with tens of thousands of city residents awaiting a benefit concert. Which meant that Gray wasn't exactly the go-to guy for anything these days. For all he knew, Johnson would ignore his report and put him back on administrative leave for going near the cabin in the first place.

All of which is one big, fat rationalization, Gray admitted inwardly, staying quiet because Mawadi was still on the porch. But spoken aloud or not, it was the truth. He was making up excuses for doing what he fully intended to do, whether or not it was reasonable. He was going in now and alone, not just because he didn't trust Johnson and the other special agents in the Denver office, but because he didn't trust the system itself. Not anymore.

The system hadn't stopped pampered rich-boy Lee Chisholm from taking his love of violence and his knee-jerk hatred of his father's politics and turning it into terrorism. The system hadn't been able to pin any one of a half-dozen other crimes on al-Jihad in the years between the 9/11 terror attacks and the Santa Bombings. The system had let down all the men, women and children who'd died in the attacks; it had failed them and their families twice over—once by not preventing the bombings and again by not keeping the terrorists behind bars. All of which meant the system couldn't be trusted this time, either.

That was why Gray had taken his day off to hike up the ridgeline, and it was why, even though he knew he should focus on returning Mawadi and the others to prison, in reality he wanted a far more permanent solution, and eye for an eye, a tooth for a tooth. Justice.

An image flashed in his head, a baby in a PICU incubator, her tiny hands clinging to her breathing tube just as tenaciously as she'd clung to life for twenty-two endless hours.

Keeping her memory in the forefront of his mind, Gray unclipped his holster and withdrew the 9 mm he'd carried on this little "hunting" trip, and started working his way through the trees, skirting the electric fence and the range of the motion detectors, heading for the back of the cabin.

The last of the surveillance reports, filed a few months earlier, had noted a rear exit, one that looked new, as though Mariah had put it in after she'd bought the cabin. Sure enough, there was a door at one end of the back of the building, with two windows beside it, blinds drawn to the sills. The rear exit was definitely a point in his favor, Gray decided. Mawadi and the others would have to power down the motion sensors when their company arrived. In that small window of opportunity, Gray planned to slip in through the back.

If he could take Lee and his ex-wife alive, he would. If not, dead was fine. He'd take his revenge however he could get it.

Mariah fought her way through fuzzy, drugged layers of consciousness and awoke to heart-pounding panic. Twisting wildly against her bonds, she looked around and found herself where she'd been the last time she'd awakened: tied to her own bed in her otherwise stripped-down bedroom. The nightstand and bureau were gone, as were all her books and personal things. That wasn't the worst of it, though. The worst was knowing that although she'd woken up this time, it didn't guarantee that she'd wake up the next.

Whenever she'd regained blurry consciousness over the past few days, she'd seen Lee's face crowding close. And she'd seen the murder in his eyes.

When the time came for her to die, she knew, he would kill her himself, and he'd relish the process. He'd delight in punishing her for having testified against him, for helping break his alibi and for divorcing him while he'd sat in jail. No doubt he would've already killed her by now if it'd been up to him. It apparently wasn't up to him, though. A second man had stood behind him each time she'd awakened, his figure blurry with distance and the drugs they had pumped into her to keep her sedated for hours, maybe days.

Broad-shouldered and muscular, the second man had dark, vaguely reptilian eyes. Lee had called him Brisbane, though she didn't know if that was a first or last name, didn't think it mattered. The big man had arrived

sometime between when Lee had drugged her unconscious and when she'd awakened the first time, lying
on the floor in a pool of her own filth, still wearing the
heavy layers and parka she'd had on when Lee attacked
her. She must've made some noise when she'd regained
consciousness, because she'd heard voices soon after,
and Brisbane had come into the room.

At first she'd been terrified of the dark-eyed stranger
with the faint accent, sure he was there to kill her. Instead, he'd been the one to keep Lee away from her—
mostly, anyway—and he'd been the one who, when
she'd begged, had untied her and let her shower and
change her clothes. He'd watched her, cradling her shotgun in clear threat, but she'd forced herself through the
process, shaking and crying, and weak with the
drugs as she'd gulped shower water in a painful effort
to slake her thirst.

She'd been almost grateful to collapse back onto her
bed, have him retie her hands and feet, and let herself
sink back into oblivion. She'd surfaced a few times after
that; each time one of the men had untied her and let her
use the bathroom, and once or twice she'd been given
some sort of liquid protein shake that had made her
gag as she'd forced it down. She'd been vaguely aware
of questions and threats, aware of refusing to answer.

The last time, Lee had stayed behind after Brisbane
left the room. She'd been seriously out of it, but had
been aware enough to see the hatred in her ex-husband's
eyes when he'd leaned over her. He'd wrapped one big,
hurtful hand around her neck, squeezing lightly at first,
then harder and harder, all the while staring down at her
with those beautiful clear blue eyes of his, which made
him look like a good guy, when he was anything but.

"I'll kill you for betraying me," he said, his voice as calm as if he'd been discussing the weather. "And for making me look bad. You should've answered questions when you had the chance. Now he's coming to *make* you talk." His eyes had slid to the door, and the quiet woods beyond. "As soon as we get what he needs from you, you're dead."

She hadn't needed to ask who *he* was; she'd known instinctively that it was al-Jihad. The terrorist leader was the one who'd given Lee a sense of purpose, though she hadn't known it at the time of their marriage. Al-Jihad was the one who'd told Lee to ingratiate himself into her life and use her father to gain inside information. Al-Jihad was also the one who'd told her husband to make sure she died in the bombings. And apparently he needed something more from her now. But what?

In a way, it didn't matter, because as Lee had leaned over her in her cabin bedroom, she'd seen her own murder in his eyes. One way or the other, she was dead.

She'd thought he was going to kill her right then, just choke the life out of her. He hadn't, though, and now she'd awakened yet again, bound to the wall, lying on her stripped-bare mattress. She thought it had been four, maybe five days since they'd imprisoned her. Five days that they'd kept her alive, feeding and watching over her because al-Jihad himself wanted something from her. She couldn't conceive of what it might be, though, couldn't remember the questions the men had asked her.

The cops and the Feds had taken everything that had belonged to Lee during their marriage, and she'd been glad to see it go. She'd given the rest of their things to charity, keeping only the few items she'd brought with her into the marriage, all keepsakes from her childhood.

Nothing of any real value, and certainly nothing that would interest someone like al-Jihad. What could the terrorists possibly want?

The more her thoughts churned, the more Mariah's head cleared and the room sharpened around her. Her arms and legs tingled and nausea pounded low in her gut, but the rest of her felt nearly normal, suggesting that she was coming out of her drug-induced daze. Which was good news. But it was also bad news. Lee was too smart to let her regain consciousness unless he'd meant to, and she couldn't imagine that Brisbane was any less shrewd. So they'd intentionally let the drugs wear off, which suggested things were about the change. Was al-Jihad on his way up the mountain to question her personally? The idea was beyond terrifying. Al-Jihad was said to be an expert interrogator.

Nausea surged through Mariah, along with a rising buzz of adrenaline and the certainty that unless she got away now, she wouldn't be waking up ever again.

Stirring, she tried twisting on the bed. Her head spun, but her arms and legs moved when and where she told them to before hitting the ends of her bonds. Her ankles were crossed and tied with nylon rope, her hands bound behind her. A loop of rope ran from her feet to her wrists, and was threaded through an eyebolt screwed into one of the heavily varnished logs that made up the cabin wall.

She'd been lying in the same position for so long that her shoulders and hips had all but stopped aching, and had gone numb instead. As she moved, though, the tingling numbness started to recede, and pins and needles took over, making her hiss in pain. She gritted her teeth and kept going, pulling against her bonds, searching for some hint of give. The eyebolt and beam were solid, the bonds on her ankles tight enough to cut her skin. But after a few moments, she thought she felt the ropes on her wrists yield a little.

Excitement propelled her to work harder, and she yanked at the ropes, starting to breathe faster with the exertion. Blood moved through her veins with increasing force, and hope built alongside the panic that came at the thought that she was so close, but still might not get free in time.

"Come on, come on!" she muttered under her breath, working the ropes while straining to hear through the closed bedroom door. Was that a voice? A conversation? Or just the radio the men had been playing each time she'd awakened? Was that a footstep? Were they coming for her? Was it already too late?

The doorknob rattled and turned.

Mariah froze, holding her breath. The door opened a crack.

"Not yet," Brisbane said sharply from the other room. "They won't be here for another hour or so."

Lee's voice spoke from the doorway. "But I was just going to—"

"I know what you were going to do, and you're not doing it. You had your chance to question her, and it didn't work. Leave her be. We need her for another few hours. After al-Jihad's done with her, you can do whatever you want."

Mariah barely heard Lee's soft curse over the hammering of the pulse in her ears. But the door shut once again, and the footsteps moved away. She was saved—for the moment, anyway.

But time was running out.

Hurrying, nearly sobbing with terror, she fought against her bonds, yanking at the loosening ropes around her wrists and twisting against the tie connecting her hands and feet together. Slowly, ever so slowly, she worked her hands free from underneath the first layer of rope, then the second. The nylon strands cut into her skin and blood slicked her wrists, but she kept going, kept fighting, refusing to give up.

She'd given up before, accepting her marriage for what it was. Maybe she hadn't completely given up, but she'd certainly given in for too long, letting herself be blinded to the truth about her husband.

Not again, she vowed inwardly. *Not this time.*

On that thought, she gave a sharp jerk. Her left hand came free with a slash of pain as the nylon fibers tore into her skin. But she didn't care about the injury. She was free!

Working faster now, sobbing with fear, relief and excitement, she undid her other hand, then her feet. Rolling off the bed, she stood, barefoot and wobbly, wearing only the fleece sweatshirt and yoga pants Brisbane had tossed at her after her last shower. Within seconds, the crisp air inside the cabin cut through the single layer of material and chilled her skin, waking her further.

Trying not to think of how much colder it was going to be outside in the cool Colorado springtime, especially come nightfall, she headed for the door, keeping herself from passing out through sheer force of will. Two years ago she'd been too weak to deal with the downward spiral of her life. Now, hardened by time and Lee's betrayal, she was stronger. But was she strong enough?

"You're going to have to be," she whispered, saying

the words aloud because the volume gave her growing resolution form and substance.

Brave words weren't going to get her out of the cabin, though. Not with the bedroom window nailed shut and two armed men in the front room, not to mention the motion detectors she'd so carefully wired in the woods around her home. They'd been meant to keep her safe. Now they would warn Lee and Brisbane if she managed to sneak out the back door. She didn't have her shotgun, didn't have the remote control to the security system, didn't have anything going for her except the knowledge that the men wanted her alive for another hour or two. They needed some sort of information from her, something important enough that they'd kept her alive and untouched for however many days it had been.

They might shoot at her, but they'd be aiming to wound, not kill. And everything she'd learned about firearms since this whole mess began suggested that it was very difficult to purposefully wound a fleeing target. During the trial it had come out that Lee had serious skill in bombmaking, but he'd claimed not to have any experience with guns. If she were lucky, Brisbane wouldn't be a sharpshooter, either. Even if he were, what was the difference, really?

Better to die trying to escape than let the terrorists use her to kill more innocents.

Mariah paused just shy of the doorway, feeling very small and alone. Raised by parents who'd met as rock band roadies and liked to keep moving, she'd lived in ten different places before her tenth birthday. Even after her parents had finally settled down in Bear Claw and her father had gone into engineering, landing a good job at the American Mall Group, Mariah had remained a private person, a loner who had to make a real effort when it came to meeting people. Her few forays into couplehood—including her disaster of a marriage—had only proved that she was the sort of person who was better off alone. Problem was, she wasn't always strong enough, smart enough, or just plain *enough* to do the things that needed to be done.

You have no choice, she told herself, clamping her lips together and fighting to be as silent as possible as she reached for the doorknob. Putting her ear to the panel, she listened intently but heard nothing, not even the radio. Did that mean both men were outside, maybe preparing for the arrival of the others? Or were they somewhere inside the cabin, just being quiet?

She didn't know, but she wasn't going to figure it out by listening at the door, either.

Blowing out a shallow, frightened breath, she eased the panel open and paused, tense and listening. Still no sound. She slipped through, unsteady on her numb legs, her heart beating so loud in her ears she was sure Lee and Brisbane would hear it all the way out front and come running.

But there was no shout of discovery as she slipped around the corner to the other back room, where she'd installed a rear door several months earlier. The room had served as her office; now it was overstuffed with the furniture Lee and Brisbane had pulled out of her bedroom, along with her usual office clutter. She glanced at her bureau, but it was facing the wall, which meant there was no way she could pull out clothes or shoes with any sort of stealth.

Crossing the room, barely breathing, she unlatched the dead bolt, wincing when the loud click cut through the silence. Then she opened the door and paused on the threshold, stalled by the sight of the fifty feet of raw-edged stumps between her and the relative safety of the forest.

Her heart thumped in her ears. She couldn't stay in the cabin. But crossing the clear-cut zone would trigger the alarms.

They don't want me dead, she reminded herself, although that was little solace as she drew a deep breath, plucked up her thin courage and plunged through the door.

She hit the ground running. Splinters and woodchips from the clear-cutting bit into her feet, but she kept going. Seconds later, the alarms went off, emitting a mechanized buzz that sliced through the air and straight through to her soul.

She wanted to scream but held the sound in, hoping to delay discovery as long as possible. Maybe they weren't even home. Maybe they'd gone to meet—

"She's out. Get her!" Lee's shout warned that she wasn't that lucky.

Moments later, a shotgun blasted behind her, and a full pellet load blew out the top of a nearby stump as she ran past it. The next shot hit the ground behind her, stinging the backs of her calves with dirt spray.

The pain worried Mariah that she'd miscalculated, badly. Apparently, they'd rather have her dead than free.

She screamed once in fear, but then clamped her lips on further cries. She wouldn't give up! Sobbing, she flung herself the rest of the way across the clear-cut zone and hurdled the low electric line with ill grace.

She landed hard, stumbled and went to her knees, her legs burning with injury and exertion. As she fell, the shotgun roared, and tree bark exploded right where her head had just been.

Blubbering, she rolled and scrambled back up, then ran for her life as Lee and Brisbane bolted across the clearing and plunged into the forest after her. The alarms cut out abruptly. She heard the men's curses and their heavy, crashing footsteps. They were close. Too close!

She didn't dare loop around to the vehicles at the front of the cabin; she couldn't trust that the keys would be in plain sight or that her captors hadn't created some sort of roadblock farther down the lane. So she ran the other way, deeper into the forest, limping on her badly abraded feet, but unable to slow down for her injuries. Her breath sobbed in her lungs, burning with each inhalation, and wetness streamed down her face, a mix of tears, sweat and panic.

"There!" Brisbane shouted from her right. "Over there! For crap's sake, get her!"

Brush crashed, the noises closer now and gaining on her. Mariah kept going, but her body was weak; her legs had gone to jelly and her feet and calves screamed in pain. She stumbled, dragged herself up and stumbled again. This time she went down and hit the ground hard. For a second, she lay there, stunned.

Before she could recover, rough hands grabbed her.

Panic assailed her and she started to struggle, inhaled to scream, but someone clapped a hand across her mouth and hissed, "Quiet!"

Then the world lurched and he was dragging her, lifting her and wrestling her into what looked like a solid wall of thorny brush from a distance, but up close proved to be scrub covering a deep depression, where a tree had fallen and the root ball had popped up, forming an earthen cave of sorts.

Excitement speared through Mariah alongside confusion. She looked back and got an impression of a square-jawed soldier wearing a thick woolen cap, heavy, insulated camouflage clothing and no insignia. He wasn't Lee or Brisbane. He was…rescuing her?

He shoved her into the hiding spot and crowded in behind her.

"Down," he whispered tersely, pressing her into the cold, moist earth and following her, rolling partway on top of her so she was beneath him and they were pressed back-to-front, with his heavy weight all but squeezing the breath from her lungs.

The fallen tree had rotted over time, providing nourishment for the profusion of vines and scrub plants that had sprung from it, forming an almost impenetrable thicket. But would it be enough to conceal them fully?

Her rescuer's arms tightened around her, and he breathed in her ear, "Be very still. They'll see us if you move."

Coming from nearby, she heard the sound of footsteps in the undergrowth, and a man's muttered curse. Freezing, Mariah pressed herself flat beneath the soldier, and held her breath, praying they wouldn't be discovered.

The noises stopped ten, maybe fifteen feet away. After a moment, Lee's voice called, "Are you sure you saw her? There's nothing here."

"She was there a second ago. Keep looking." Brisbane's answer came from the other side of the woods, back toward the cabin. After a moment, Lee moved off.

Mariah counted her heartbeats, trying to stay calm

as she exhaled slowly, then risked inhaling a breath. Another. The sounds of the search diminished slightly, suggesting that the men had moved to the other side of the cabin.

Hoping that Lee and Brisbane were walking into one hell of an ambush, she rolled her eyes back, trying to get a look at her rescuer as she mouthed, "Where are the others hiding?"

He must be part of a coordinated attack, right? Somehow, someone had learned that she was in trouble and had sent help.

Most likely, the FBI agents—particularly the cold, gray-eyed bastard who'd kept questioning her father even after he'd started complaining of chest pains—had been keeping watch on the cabin. They'd probably identified Lee days ago and were just now moving in, knowing al-Jihad was on his way. The thought that they'd known she was in there and hadn't bothered to mount a rescue beforehand brought a kick of resentment, but it was no more than she'd come to expect from the Feds. They carried out their own plans on their own timetable, and to hell with the people they hurt in the process.

But the soldier shook his head slightly. "I'm alone," he breathed in her ear. "Quiet now. They're coming back."

What? Mariah's thoughts churned. It didn't make any sense that he'd be up on the ridgeline alone, but she couldn't deny the physical reality of him, either. She would've demanded an explanation, but just then, Brisbane and Lee returned, stopping very close to the thick copse where Mariah and the soldier were hidden. The two men conferred in low voices.

Breathing shallowly through her mouth, Mariah flattened herself against the moist, partially rotted leaves and twigs beneath her. She was acutely aware of the man pressed against her. The solid weight of him was more reassuring than it probably should have been, and she fought the urge to huddle her chilled body into his heavy warmth as her mind continued to race.

What sort of soldier worked alone?

"I'll call down and have the boss bring up more men," Lee said. "We'll fan out, search every rock and tree until we find her. The bitch has to be hiding somewhere nearby—there's no way she got away that fast with no shoes."

"I told you to keep her drugged," Brisbane spat, disgusted. "Told you she was smarter than you gave her credit for."

Lee's voice edged toward a whine. "I thought al-Jihad would prefer her awake."

"Awake doesn't do us any good if she's gone. This was your idea. At this point, you'd better hope to hell she doesn't make it down the ridge, or your ass is toast."

"Al-Jihad wouldn't do anything to me. He needs me."

"Al-Jihad doesn't need anybody," Brisbane countered. "Come on, let's keep looking. I'll start over here while you call down and tell the others we need a full-fledged search party. Have them bring up infrared, night vision, the whole works. They'll want to watch the roads, too. The bitch is bound to turn up somewhere."

Despite the warm weight of the man pressed against her, Mariah began to shiver, fear and confusion warring within her. What did they want from her? Whatever they wanted, the men were right about one thing: in the absence of help, it seemed highly unlikely that she'd make it to safety—the nights were too cold, the trails difficult to manage without proper climbing equipment, never mind without shoes of any kind. If she had help, though, she might very well make it off the ridge and into the city safely.

Question was, did the man who held her count as help?

As Lee and Brisbane moved off in opposite directions, the sounds of their steps fading to forest silence, she stirred beneath the stranger, twisting around to get a good look at him. "Who are—" She bit off the question with a quiet hiss when she recognized the cool gray eyes beneath the woolen cap, recognized the suit-clad monster in the man she'd thought was a soldier. *"Grayson!"* She spat the word out like a curse.

It was Special Agent Michael Grayson, the FBI agent who'd made her life a living hell and nearly killed her father in his efforts to get at a truth that had existed only in his mind.

And now she was at his mercy.

Chapter 3

"I prefer to be called Gray. Not that it matters much to you, I'm guessing," he said, seeing displeasure flood her face, no doubt due to the way he'd treated her and her family during the investigation. Which was too bad, because as far as he was concerned he'd done what needed to be done.

Besides, it wasn't as if he was thrilled to see her, either. He hadn't been about to let Mawadi grab her and drag her back inside, but rescuing her had complicated the hell out of the situation. He'd planned to wait for the five o'clock meet and move in then, when the motion detectors were down, but now there were going to be more men, and they would be searching the damn forest, which shot that plan to shreds.

No, the best thing for him to do now would be to get the woman down to the city and hand her over to

Johnson and his crew. The SAC would be furious that Gray had disobeyed orders, but he'd be forced to send a team up to the cabin. Gray knew damn well that by the time they got up to the ridgeline, Mawadi and the others would be long gone. But, unfortunately, as tough as Gray might be, he was just was one man with a 9 mm, and that was no match for a terrorist cell on high alert.

Muttering a curse, he rolled off the woman, banishing the sensory memory of how she'd felt beneath him—all soft, curvy and female. He so wasn't going there.

Once this was all over and al-Jihad and the others had been brought to justice, he'd allow himself to live again. But at the moment he had no intention of letting himself be distracted by a woman. Besides, even if he had the inclination, there was no way in hell he'd be going for this woman. There was a physical connection, yes—it had been there from the first moment he saw her. But she was a witness at best, a conspirator at worst, and she'd been married to one of the bombers.

She was a means to an end, nothing more. The fact that her glare suggested that she hated his guts made it that much easier to ignore the fine buzz of tension running through his body as they faced each other in their small hiding space.

Her eyes were dark and bruised in her pale face, her full lips trembling, though whether from fear or cold or a combination of the two, he didn't know. It didn't much matter, either, because he needed to focus on getting them the hell away from the cabin and down to cell phone range ASAP.

Shucking out of his camo jacket, he shoved it at the woman. "There are mittens in the pocket. Put them on your feet and follow me. And for crap's sake, don't make any noise."

She started to snap in response, but shut her mouth when he pulled his gun from where he'd tucked it at the small of his back, and racked the action to the ready position, just in case.

He waited for a second, watching to see what she was going to do. When she pulled on the jacket without comment, then felt in the pocket and covered her bloody feet as best she could with the mittens, he nodded grimly. "Good call."

Then he turned his back on her and led the way out of the small copse, moving as silently as he could, but traveling fast because the light was fading. Already, the sky had gone gray-blue, and the world around them had turned colorless with the approaching spring dusk. So he jog-trotted downhill, hoping to hell they'd get lucky and make it down the ridgeline undetected.

The first half mile was tough going through a hilly section of deadfall-choked forest, made more difficult by the fading light. At first Mariah moved quietly, but as they kept going, Gray heard her breathing start to labor, heard her miss her footing more and more often.

He turned back, ready to snap at her to be quiet if she wanted to live. But one look at her waxy, pale face, which had gone nearly white in the fading light, had him biting back the oath and cursing himself instead.

He crossed the small gap between them and caught her as she crumpled, sweeping her up against his chest.

She was feather-light in his arms, though his memory said she'd been solid, bordering on sturdy before. The change nagged at him, making him wonder exactly how long she'd been bound in that cabin, and what Mawadi and the other man had done to her.

Guilt pinched, but Gray quickly shoved it aside, into the mental refuse bin where he consigned his other useless emotions, few and far between though they might be.

After only a few seconds of unconsciousness, she roused against him, pushing feebly at his chest. Her eyes fluttered open. The dusk robbed them of their color, but he knew they were amber, just as he knew he couldn't trust the stealthy twist of heat that curled through his midsection when their gazes locked. She moistened her lips and swallowed, and he was far too aware of those simple actions, just as he was far too susceptible to the tremor in her voice when she whispered, "Put me down. I can walk."

"Don't be stupid," he said, the words coming out more roughly than he'd intended. He yanked his gaze from hers and pressed her closer, not in comfort, but so he wouldn't be looking at her face, wouldn't be thinking of how her body felt against his, flaring unwanted heat at the points of contact.

Gritting his teeth, he shifted his grip so he could shove the 9 mm back in the small of his spine, then took hold of her once again and headed downhill, moving as fast as he could while still keeping quiet. His four-by-four was maybe another mile farther down, and as he hiked, he forced himself to focus on the case, not the woman. The case was important. The woman wasn't.

By now, Mawadi and the second man would have gotten in touch with the other members of their cell. If Gray could talk SAC Johnson into sending choppers and search teams up to the cabin, they might get lucky. They wouldn't get al-Jihad, of course; he was too smart to come up the mountain now. But they might get Mawadi, might get some idea of why the terrorists had returned to the area.

As Gray put one boot in front of the other and his back and arms began to ache, though, it wasn't the terrorists, his boss or even revenge that occupied his mind—it was the woman in his arms. And that could become a problem if he let it.

Mariah would have held herself away from Gray, but she lacked the strength to do anything but cling, with one arm looped over his neck and her face pressed into the warm hollow at his throat. She despised surrendering control to him, hated that her safety was in the hands of the FBI special agent who had been a large part of making her life a living hell more than two years earlier, and whose relentless questions had put her father in the hospital, nearly in his grave.

But at the same time, the man who held her easily, walking with long, powerful strides, was so unlike the picture in her mind, it was causing her brain to jam. This man was warm to the touch rather than cold, and when their eyes had met, his had blazed with an emotion that she couldn't define, but had been far from the detached, sardonic chill he'd projected during the investigation.

His warmth and steady masculine scent surrounded her now, coming from the jacket he'd given her and from the solid wall of his body against hers. She'd hated the man who had interrogated her, hated what he stood for and how he treated people. But she didn't know how to feel about the man he'd turned out to be—the soldier who'd come up to her cabin alone and had been there when she'd needed him in a way that nobody else had for a long, long time.

Confused, weak with drugs and exhaustion, she was unable to do anything but give in to circumstances beyond her immediate control. Closing her eyes, she leaned into her rescuer, anchoring herself to his warmth and strength.

She must've dozed—or maybe passed out—after that. She was vaguely aware of Gray loading her into a large vehicle and strapping her in tightly. Through the fuzzed-out fog her brain had become, she knew that he was white-knuckle tense as he pulled the vehicle out of its hiding spot and headed it down the road. It was full dark; he wore a pair of night-vision goggles he'd retrieved from the glove compartment and drove with the truck's headlights off, muttering a string of curses under his breath as he kept the gas pedal down and steered the vehicle along the fire-access road leading down from her cabin. Then they flew through the gate, which hung open, and turned onto the paved road headed toward Bear Claw.

He decelerated, shucked off the goggles and flipped on the headlights before glancing over at her. "We got lucky. No sign of your husband's reinforcements."

"Ex-husband," she corrected him, the faint echoes of warmth and gratitude dispelled by irritation because he'd made the same mistake a handful of times during the initial investigation into the prison break. It annoyed her that he kept insisting on the undoubtedly deliberate gaffe, and that she couldn't stop herself from correcting him each time.

He nodded, his eyes not quite the cold steel of Special Agent Grayson, not quite the fiery resolve of the soldier he'd been up on the ridgeline. When his gaze met hers, she felt a click of unwanted connection and a shimmer of fear. *What next?* she wanted to ask him, but didn't, because she wasn't sure she wanted to know what his answer would be.

So, instead, she turned away from him, settling into her seat as the truck accelerated, heading for the city. While he drove, he made a call on his cell, tersely reporting the situation, and what he'd seen and done. Mariah didn't add anything to the conversation. There was nothing she could do to change her situation; she was too weak, too confused. And, bottom line: whether it was logical or not, she was heart-sore.

Being around Lee again hadn't only been terrifying, it had also brought to the surface of her mind things that she'd thought she'd managed to bury years ago. Seeing him had reminded her of the good times—or at least the times she'd thought were good ones, when Lee had courted her. He'd brought her flowers and silly gifts; he'd made her feel as though she were the center of his universe, that she was special. And when he'd proposed, dropping to one knee and promising that they would be together forever, she'd believed him.

But those memories were overlaid now with the pain of remembering the months after their marriage, when he'd gradually changed, growing cold and distant. After a while, his petty cruelties and outright manipulations had made her grateful for the nights he didn't come home, and had made her start to think she was losing her mind. It was only later that she realized that he'd purposely broken her down, little by little, undermining the defenses she'd built up over a lifetime of being an outsider. Then, once he'd made her completely vulnerable by promising her forever, he'd started beating her down further, stripping her of her worth until she'd been nothing but his wife, his plaything. Simply because he could, because it amused him.

She knew the authorities thought of Lee as a follower, a patsy. She knew different; he might follow al-Jihad's orders, but when it had come to their marriage, he'd been the one in control.

Despite the months of subtle torment, though, she'd retained a tiny core of strength. It had been too little, too late back then. Would it be enough to see her through whatever came next?

The bang of a car door startled her, jolting her awake, though she hadn't realized that she'd been dozing.

She squinted against the sudden glare of lights. When she finally focused on the scene, she recognized the walled-in parking lot of the main police station in Bear Claw City. A tingle of unease and ill will shimmered through her at the memories of being interrogated in the station, then rushing her father to the nearby hospital, where he'd nearly died, not just because of Gray's heavy-handed questioning, but because of the decisions Mariah herself had made, the horror she'd brought into her parents' lives.

That was her shame. One of many.

There was a crowd gathering outside the truck; it seemed to be made up of equal parts cops and suited-up Feds, with the latter group gathering around Gray as he climbed from the vehicle. In his flannel shirt and camouflage pants, with his short brown hair bristled on end and his face and clothing streaked with dirt and sweat, mute testimony of their harrowing escape, he should've looked at a disadvantage compared to the other agents, neat and clean in their dark suits. To Mariah's eye, though, he looked like a man of action, one who could break the others in half, and might do just that, given the provocation.

She saw him visibly brace himself as he squared off opposite a salt-and-pepper-haired agent who wore an air of command and a deep scowl. It took Mariah a moment to place the other man, but when she did, nerves bunched in her midsection.

SAC Johnson, the FBI special agent in charge of the federal arm of the jailbreak investigation, had struck her as a pompous ass far more concerned with his own on-camera image than the actual investigation. There was no way she wanted him calling the shots when it came to her cabin…and potentially her life. Because that was one of the things that seemed painfully clear: she didn't need to protect herself simply from Lee's personal revenge. The terrorists apparently wanted something from her, which meant she was going to need help staying safe, whether she liked it or not.

Not liking it one bit, she pushed open the truck door, unclipped her seat belt and dropped down from the vehicle, hissing in pain when she landed on her injured feet.

A young, uniformed Bear Claw City cop appeared at her side almost instantly, and took her arm. "This way, ma'am. Agent Grayson said you're wounded. We have an EMT-trained officer who'll take a look at you while we wait for the paramedics."

"Not yet." She pulled away, focused on the group of FBI special agents, where Gray and SAC Johnson were arguing in low voices, their faces set in stone.

She took a couple of hobbling steps toward the knot

of suits, pulling Gray's camouflage jacket more tightly around her shoulders. As she came closer, she heard Johnson snarl, "Were my orders somehow unclear?"

"No, sir." Gray's square jaw was locked, his eyes cool. But underneath that coolness, Mariah thought she sensed an undercurrent of hot anger. For the first time, she started to wonder whether the chill of his demeanor was designed to hide something entirely different, something more in line with the soldier he'd been up on the ridgeline.

And you so shouldn't be thinking about that right now, Mariah told herself as she moved to join the men.

Johnson glared at his subordinate. "So my orders were clear, yet you deliberately disobeyed them by performing reconnaissance near Ms. Shore's cabin."

Gray nodded. "Yes, sir."

Which explained why he'd been alone. It also reinforced her initial impression that Johnson was more focused on protocol than results, whereas Gray was... well, she didn't know what he was, but he wasn't anything like his boss.

"If Agent Grayson hadn't been up at the cabin, acting on orders or not, I'd probably be dead by now," Mariah said, coming up beside Gray. "And you wouldn't have a clue that Lee and the others are back in the area, would you?" When the older man's attention locked on her and his scowl deepened, Mariah lifted her chin and met his glare.

Johnson must've seen something in her eyes, because he brought his attitude down a notch, nodding and holding out a hand. "You may not remember me, Ms. Shore. I'm Special Agent in Charge Johnson."

"I remember." She shook because there was no reason not to, then said, "Please tell me that you have men on their way to my cabin."

"They're already on scene. The cabin shows signs of having been abandoned in a hurry."

Gray bit off a curse. "You searched the woods?"

"Of course. Mawadi and the others are gone."

"What about—" Gray began.

"The investigation is proceeding appropriately," Johnson interrupted with a sharp look in Gray's direction. "That's all Ms. Shore needs to know." He returned his attention to Mariah. "Obviously, we'll need to ask you some questions."

Mariah nodded. "Of course."

She hoped none of them could tell how much she dreaded the next few hours, how much she wished she could rewind time by a week, to when she'd been at home in her cabin, safe in her delusion that Lee couldn't get at her there. But she wasn't back in her cabin. She was smack in the middle of the city, in enemy territory.

She'd dealt with the FBI's idea of "some questions" twice before. The first time, she'd been weak and soft, and they'd bullied her and her parents until they'd nearly broken. The second time, just after the jailbreak, she'd been in shock, dazed and disconnected, and her flat affect had put her under suspicion, making them think she was hiding something, maybe even that she'd been in contact with Lee. In the aftermath of that second round of questioning, she'd vowed never to make those mistakes again, never to be the victim again.

Lee might have captured and victimized her, but she wasn't his victim, wasn't anyone's victim. If the agents wanted something from her, they could damn well give something back this time.

So she met Johnson's eyes and said, "I'll tell you everything I know, but I have conditions."

Beside her, Gray muttered a bitter oath, but she couldn't take her eyes off his boss, couldn't correct what she suspected was a deep misapprehension. There would be time for that later. Maybe.

There was no humor to the wry twist of Johnson's lips. "Of course you do." He paused, waving over two uniformed officers.

Mariah stiffened when they flanked her and urged her away from the agents, away from Gray. "Wait!" she cried, unconsciously reaching for him.

Gray drew away, and when he looked down at her, his eyes had gone even colder than before. He said, "They're taking you inside where it's safer, and where they can clean up your injuries, find you some shoes and socks, and something else to wear. They'll get you some food, something to drink. I'd advise you to take them up on the offer. I have a feeling it's going to be a long night for all of us."

Even wearing camouflage, he'd gone back to being the no-nonsense agent she remembered, and she hated the change. But in a way it was a good thing, because it forced her to step away from him, made her remember that they weren't friends, that there was no real connection between them. He might have gotten her off the ridgeline, but that didn't make him her white knight.

She nodded and took a big step back. "Thanks for the rescue," she said, which didn't even begin to encompass what she was feeling just then.

His eyes went hooded. "Sorry I didn't get there a couple of days earlier." He turned away before she could process the flicker of emotion she thought she'd seen in his eyes, the one that suggested she wasn't alone in feeling a spark of attraction where none should exist.

Part of her wanted to ask him to stay with her, but what sense did that make? He might have rescued her, and he might have disobeyed orders in the process, but that didn't mean he was on her side. Far from it, in fact. Because how could she forget what he'd done to her father? Gray had hammered at him with the same questions over and over again, implying that her father had known about Lee's plan, that she and her whole family had knowingly helped the terrorists. Which was so wrong it should've sounded preposterous, only it hadn't, coming from him. And as the first hour had turned to three, he hadn't eased up, hadn't given up, even when her father's color had started to fade. Eventually, he'd let them go, but not without a stern warning to stay available, that there would be more questions to come.

By nightfall, her father had been in the cardiac ICU. By the next day, he'd been undergoing bypass surgery. All because of a not-so-civil servant on a mission to uncover an imaginary conspiracy. In the same vein, Gray had been up on the ridgeline, not to rescue her, but because he'd been suspicious of her. Again.

She couldn't trust him, couldn't lean on him. And she'd do well to remember that.

Chest aching with a hollow sense of disappointment she knew she shouldn't feel, Mariah turned to Johnson. "As I said, I'll cooperate, but I've got conditions."

"We'll see." He gestured to the men flanking her. "Take her inside, let her clean up and call counsel. I'll be there in fifteen."

The uniformed cops escorted her to a small, spare room where a pair of paramedics waited for her, equipment at the ready. One was a pretty, light-haired woman with kind eyes; the other an older, heavyset man who looked like he'd rather be napping.

Mariah held up both hands. "It's not all that bad, really. Just some cuts on my feet, and a pellet-burn on my calves." And a hell of a headache, and some serious room spins, thanks to the residue of whatever Lee and Brisbane had been pumping into her system. When she listed it like that, she started to feel worse by the second.

The light-haired woman shook her head apologetically. "We'll treat your injuries, for sure. But first the CSIs want to collect your clothes and photograph you. We'll need a blood sample, too."

Two and a half years earlier, Mariah would have— and had—done whatever the cops had asked. Older and wiser now out of necessity, she said, "Then I'm going to want to call my lawyer first."

She was done being a pushover.

Over the next eighteen hours, Gray fought to get himself put back on the case and lost, fought to keep his active-duty status and lost that battle, too. Johnson was furious that he'd disobeyed orders. More importantly, the SAC was embarrassed that Gray's breach of protocol had yielded a badly needed break in the case. As far as Johnson was concerned, the new intel didn't cancel out Gray's insubordination, not after he'd been specifically warned to stay away from Mariah.

Those conversations took place in snatches, amid the information storm that followed the new developments. The response team reported back with little new information from the cabin, and the infrared helicopter sweeps failed to turn up anything but wildlife and a few hardy preseason campers up on the ridgeline. There was no sign of Lee Mawadi or the other man, whom Mariah hadn't yet identified from among al-Jihad's known associates. More, although Mariah was convinced Lee had tried to question her, and had called al-Jihad for help when she'd proven resistant, she claimed to have no idea what they wanted from her.

It was possible that the forthcoming detailed forensic analysis of the cabin might yield some clue as to where the terrorists were going, where they'd come from or what they wanted with Mariah. However, it would be days at the earliest—more likely weeks—before the relevant clues were teased out from among the normal detritus of a lived-in home. The Bear Claw crime scene analysts were excellent, and had strong ties to the federal investigators, but they weren't miracle workers.

Meanwhile, the members of the prison break task force, who had scattered over the past months when the investigation had moved away from Bear Claw, were being reassembled. As before, the investigation would be headquartered partly at the FBI's Denver field office, partly at the Bear Claw City PD. However, Gray wouldn't be part of the task force at either location. Johnson had made it crystal clear that he didn't want to work with a renegade, couldn't afford to risk a court appeal if one of his agents used questionable methods during an investigation. The SAC had offered Gray a transfer or a desk to ride, but they both knew he wouldn't take either. The offer had been an empty formality, nothing more.

Which was why, at just past noon on the day after he'd rescued Mariah and broken the news that Lee Mawadi was back in town, Gray was in his Denver office, packing his personal effects. His service weapon and badge were on the desk, weighting down his letter of resignation.

He didn't feel grief at the decision, didn't feel relief. He felt hollow. Determined. He might be off the task force, but he wasn't off the case. Not by a long shot.

He piled his things haphazardly into a box, leaving the official stuff behind and taking only the few items he cared about. The first was a bifold frame containing a picture of his parents and him at his academy graduation a decade earlier on one side, opposite a more recent shot of his whole extended family, cousins and all, taken last Christmas. The latter photo brought a spear of the pain he suspected would always accompany thoughts of the holidays, but he hadn't let that keep him away from family doings. Christmas was important to his parents, and therefore it was important to him. He'd gone to the annual get-together and pretended to enjoy himself, and had ducked the inevitable questions about his love life, reminding himself that his family members meant no harm. Even though most of them were cops or married to cops, they didn't fully understand that he had things to take care of before he could move on.

Thinking of those things, he set the bifold frame in the box and picked up a smaller photo of a laughing man grinning up at the camera, his arms wrapped around a flushed-faced woman who held a small baby.

"Grayson," SAC Johnson's voice barked from the doorway, stanching the impending flood of memories and setting Gray's teeth on edge.

Gray didn't even look over at his soon-to-be-ex boss, just placed the photo in the cardboard box and gestured to the pile of papers on his desk. "The letter of resignation's right there. Go away."

"I want you to reconsider."

Of all the things Gray might've expected, that didn't even make the list. Frowning, he turned toward Johnson.

And saw Mariah standing behind him.

She looked very different than she had the day before. Her dark hair fell to her shoulders in soft waves, and she wore a green turtleneck sweater, jeans and boots that made her look like a model out of an upscale outdoorsy catalog, simultaneously sexy and practical.

Although he'd always before gravitated to fussy, feminine women, Gray felt something inside him go very still and hushed, the way it did just before he got the "go" signal on a major op, when his body was poised equally between fight and flight, his blood surging with adrenaline and survival instincts. This wasn't an op or a fight, he knew, but he had a feeling that if he let it, his association with Mariah could become just as messy. So it was up to him not to let it go there.

Straightening, he nodded to her. "Mariah."

"Gray," she acknowledged, her expression giving away nothing. She pushed past Johnson, then hesitated just inside the office doorway. "I need to talk to you." She threw a look over her shoulder and said pointedly, "Alone."

Johnson muttered something under his breath, but nodded. He shot Gray a warning look, one that said, "For crap's sake, don't screw this up," then retreated, shutting the door at Mariah's back.

A tense, anticipatory silence filled the small room until Gray broke it by grabbing the box top off his desk and fitting it into place, sealing in the memories. "I expect Johnson told you that I don't work here anymore."

"Yes. Right after I told him I'd let the FBI use me to set a trap for Lee, but only if you act as my bodyguard."

Gray had thought he was beyond surprise when it came to this case. Apparently, he was wrong. "Why me?"

"Because you don't play Johnson's game."

That got his attention. "What game would that be?"

She was still standing just inside the door, as though she might slip away at any moment. She didn't leave, though, didn't move a muscle. She just stood there, her eyes locked with his, as though she were trying to figure out how much to tell him, how much to trust him. After a short pause, she said, "The game where he does and says exactly the right thing, the defensible, by-the-book thing, even when it's the wrong choice under the circumstances. Let me guess…he wants to be governor some day."

"Actually, I'm pretty sure he's got his sights set on Congress." Gray was reluctantly impressed, though. Not too many people saw through the SAC's act, at least not until they'd known him for a while. Moving around the desk, he crossed the room to stand very near her, close enough that he could see the flutter of her pulse at her throat. "You want me guarding you because my boss doesn't like me. Any other reason? Not to pry, but I didn't get the impression you liked me very much, either, especially after what happened with your father two years ago."

"That wasn't your fault," she said, surprising him again. At his startled look, she glanced away. "I didn't get much sleep last night, for obvious reasons. It gave me an opportunity to think a few things through. One of the conclusions I came to was that the outcome would've been the same even if you'd been all sweetness and light in the interview. My father was furious with himself for not seeing Lee for what he was. He was in the process of being forcibly retired from his company because of his involvement in the bombings, and he was trying to deal with a boatload of guilt. The interrogation just brought all that to the forefront at once, and his heart couldn't take it."

Something in her voice suggested that wasn't the whole story, but Gray didn't call her on it. Instead, he cleared his throat and waited for her to focus on him. Then he said, "For what it's worth, I'm sorry about how it played out." He'd called the hospital to check on her father, but didn't think she needed to know that. In a way it'd probably be better if she saw him as the enemy, especially since he was getting the idea that they hadn't yet seen the last of each other. Still, he found himself asking, "How's he doing?"

That earned him a sharp look, but she must've seen that his question was sincere, because she answered civilly enough. "He had a second surgery a few months ago. I guess he's doing okay now."

"You guess?" When she didn't respond, he pressed, "Are you afraid that this is going to set his recovery back?" By *this,* he meant her imprisonment and the continued situation with Mawadi, and indicated as much by sketching a wave around his office, ending with his badge, which lay on his desk beside his resignation letter.

She shook her head. "My parents moved away last year, said they were done with Colorado." The way she said it made it sound like Colorado wasn't the only thing they'd turned their backs on.

"I'm sorry."

"Not your fault."

They fell silent, and in the quiet he became aware of how close he and Mariah were standing. He could feel her warmth reaching out to him, making him itch to be even closer still, to lift a hand to her face and touch her. To kiss her.

Before the mad impulse could supersede his better judgment, he said, "What, exactly, do you want from me?"

"Johnson is going to arrange to have me hospitalized, and let it leak that I was found on the ridgeline. I want you to be in charge of surveillance, and when Lee comes for me, I want you to take care of him."

"Take care of him?" The idea of killing Mawadi in cold blood didn't bother Gray nearly as much as it probably should have.

"Get him off the streets and out of my life," she said, which wasn't really a clarification. "And in the process, I want you to do your best to keep me alive." There was a new thread of steel in her voice when she said, "I know you'll do whatever it takes—rules or no rules. Since that's the way Lee thinks, it's the only way you're going to be able to take him down before he gets what he wants from me, and undoubtedly uses it to kill again. Your boss doesn't understand that, which is why I want you involved." She held out her hand. "What do you say?"

He looked at her for a long moment, seeing her outstretched hand and the delicate bones of her wrist, which he could break one-handed if he wanted to. But though her bone structure might be more delicate than he'd remembered—made especially prominent now by her days in captivity—the woman herself was far stronger than he'd thought. He saw it in her eyes and heard it in her voice.

The part of him that still spent the holidays with his family, knowing it mattered to them, said he should decline, that he should put Mariah into protective custody, stay on the job and do whatever he could—or rather whatever Johnson would let him do—to bring Lee Mawadi, al-Jihad and the others to justice through official means.

But the other part of him, the part that awakened from nightmares drenched in sweat, seized with killing rage and the need for revenge—that part had him reaching out and gripping her hand. As he shook on it, he felt a twinge of guilt and regret, a premonition that pretty Mariah Shore would be the one to suffer the most from her choices.

In the end, though, he knew that nothing else mattered but getting justice for the dead. He was a little surprised to find that she knew it, too.

"Okay," he said softly. "I'll do it."

Chapter 4

Over the next two days, Mariah learned that it was far easier to say "Use me as bait" than it was to actually *be* the so-called bait.

Gray and the others had installed her in a square private hospital room that embodied the word *drab*. The furniture was cheap prefab; the upholstery, paint and uninspired wall art were all variations on the same theme of beige, mauve and mossy green. The single window overlooked the parking lot and was on a low floor, so she couldn't even see beyond the neighboring buildings to the mountains in the distance. Not that she'd even seen much of the parking lot, because Gray had ordered her to stay in bed, aside from necessary trips to the small bathroom located in a walled-off corner of the room. They had no way of knowing the sophistication level of al-Jihad's local network, so she had to play the part of an invalid.

Round-the-clock guards stood outside her door, but they were mostly for the show of protective custody, and were on orders to let their vigilance slip now and then for a bathroom break or conversation. Mariah's real security came from electronic surveillance that had been installed in secret by a team dressed to look like a maintenance crew. Thanks to them, she was constantly being monitored by both video and audio. Hello, Big Brother.

Five years earlier, when she'd moved to New York, full of hope and enthusiasm, bursting with plans to launch herself into the world of fashion photography while becoming part of the "in" crowd, she might've seen the hidden cameras and microphones as no big deal; she'd tried out for that reality show, hadn't she? But that period of her life had been a fluke, an aberration. She'd been trying to make herself into someone bright, glittering and interesting, someone very unlike the shy, uprooted loner she'd been throughout high school and college.

And for a time, she'd succeeded.

It had been during that time that she'd met Lee—or rather, he'd arranged to meet her. For the months he'd been courting her, she'd truly felt like the bright, glittering, interesting person she was trying to be. But she hadn't been bright and interesting, she'd been desperate for attention, and so gullible that she'd bought his act right down to the last "I love you." She'd thought it was her idea to move to Bear Claw in an effort to forge a better relationship with her parents, her idea for her father to help Lee get a job. In reality, she'd been played, and played badly.

She hadn't been glittery or interesting. Worse, she'd been stupid. In retrospect, it seemed ludicrous that she'd ever believed that a man like the one Lee had portrayed could have been interested in her, never mind being smitten, as he'd claimed to be. She simply wasn't the type to inspire strong emotions in other people. Not her parents, not men, not anyone.

Drifting in her hospital bed, dozing in that half-aware state between sleeping and waking, she thought of the hopes and dreams she'd brought into her marriage, and how Lee had extinguished them one by one.

As if summoned by the memories, she heard his voice in her mind, low and beguiling. *You're going to help us whether you like it or not,* he'd whispered against her cheek, his breath feathering the hair at her temple as she'd lain bound and helpless, slipping into drugged oblivion. *It's simple, really, all you have to do is tell me where—*

"Deep thoughts?" Gray's low, masculine voice said, breaking the reverie.

Mariah jolted alert, yanking her attention to the doorway of her drab hospital room even as she scrambled to hold on to the memory. Or had it even been a memory? She wasn't sure, didn't know if it would help even if it had been real. Confusion churned through her, and it didn't dissipate one iota at the sight of Gray standing there. If anything, her tension increased, not because she was afraid of him, or even because of the misplaced resentment she'd harbored against him for far too long.

No, this tension was purely a product of the situation and the man.

Deciding to keep the partially remembered whisper to herself for the moment, she shook her head and answered his question with a neutral, "Just resting."

His gray suit hung on him a little, disguising the

broad shoulders, flat waist and strong legs she now knew were part of the package. He looked as though he'd lost weight since he'd bought the clothes, making her think that in the past he might have carried some softness that was no longer evident in his tough, honed frame. That same toughness edged the sharp planes of his face and lent intensity to his expression as he crossed the room and took the visitor's chair beside her bed.

Mariah was unable to keep herself from noting the smooth, almost feral grace of his actions. She was equally unable to squelch her body's unexpectedly sharp yearn in his direction when he sat. She wanted to move closer, wanted to lean into his heat and steadying strength. Because she did, and because she knew she didn't dare, she scooted away a few inches instead.

Ever since he'd rescued her in soldier's guise, she'd been unable to go back to thinking of him as the cold, uncaring man she'd thought he was before. If he'd been motivated solely by the needs of his job, he would have tried to capture Lee and Brisbane as they'd chased her from her cabin. Or he could've let them recapture her, waiting until al-Jihad arrived to make his move. Instead, he'd sheltered her with his own body and carried her down the mountain when she'd been unable to walk. And now he was doing everything in his power to keep her safe. Granted, that was part of the job—it was *all* part of the job—but she couldn't help thinking there was something more there, something personal. Something that hummed in the air between them as silence lingered. Some of it was because they didn't dare speak freely, due to all the FBI surveillance equipment, as well as the surveillance they assumed Lee and his terrorist colleagues were using. That meant they were careful to act as though he was nothing more to her than a federal agent assigned to the case. Not the man who'd saved her life, and not a bodyguard awaiting Lee's next move.

That awareness, though, hung heavy between them.

Finally, she broke the quiet to ask, "Do you have more pictures?"

Several times during her hospital stay, he'd brought mug shots of men the FBI thought might be Brisbane, none of which had been a match. Other times, he'd stopped by to see if she needed anything, or to update her on the progress of the investigation. Granted, the latter snippets were undoubtedly doctored to avoid giving away anything to potential listeners, but she still appreciated knowing that her cabin had been released by the crime-scene techs, and that the intelligence community believed that al-Jihad was still out of the country. There had been no word on Lee, though, and the sense of creeping dread that stayed firmly rooted in her stomach made her positive that he was somewhere nearby, watching her.

She shivered involuntarily when Gray handed her a computer printout bearing a dozen photographs, some candids, some mug shots, all of different men with cold, killer's eyes. A jolt of icy fear shot through her when she finally saw the man who had played the curious role of keeping her safe from Lee, while holding her prisoner for some other purpose. She touched his photograph. "That's Brisbane."

"You're sure?"

"Positive."

Gray nodded as though he'd expected the answer,

and took the printout from her, but he didn't seem pleased about the break in the case.

"Who is he?" Mariah asked, knowing Gray would only tell her as much as he wanted the terrorists to know.

"He was a guy we know of but don't know much about, a ghost who called himself Felix Smith. He's a midlevel thug we looked at in connection with the Santa Bombings, but didn't pursue. Apparently, that was a mistake." But she sensed that more than just the mistake was bothering him.

"He *was* a ghost?" Mariah pressed. "As in, he's not anymore?"

Gray fixed her with a hard look. "Depends on your definition of *ghost*. His body turned up in a Dumpster this morning." He paused. "Al-Jihad doesn't take failure lightly."

"Oh." A shudder started in her gut and worked its way to her extremities. "Was there…" She faltered, then fell silent.

"There's still no sign of your ex." Though Gray was sitting close to her, he seemed very far away, his expression remote and businesslike.

Mariah pinched the bridge of her nose, trying to force back an incipient headache. "Is that good news or bad?" Without waiting for him to answer, she continued, "From my perspective it's bad news. If he was dead, I wouldn't have to worry about him coming after me for revenge."

Gray's eyes lost their distance as he zeroed in on her. "You think he'd come after you even if al-Jihad didn't need something from you?"

"I know he would. Lee took the 'till death do us

part' thing literally." She paused. "You've seen the letter, right?"

Several weeks after Lee and the others had been incarcerated, she'd picked up her mail from her post office box and found a large manila envelope addressed to her in block print, along with a badly smudged return address and a Denver postmark. Inside had been another envelope, blank. Inside that had been a three-page letter in her ex-husband's elegant script, a cutting missive that could be summarized simply as: "When I get out of here, you're dead. Nobody leaves me." The Feds had tracked the letter as best they could, but the lead had dead-ended quickly. Somehow, Lee had smuggled it out of the ARX Supermax, and another member of the terrorist network had made sure she got it.

Gray's jaw tightened. "Yeah. I've seen it. I wondered whether it was part of something else, though. Word is that your ex is more of a follower than an independent thinker."

"I didn't know that side of him," Mariah said slowly. "The man I married was a golden boy. He was the captain of the football team, class valedictorian, the nice boy my mother always wanted me to meet. He was handsome, charming and persistent, and it seemed to me that he always knew the right thing to say."

"He did," Gray said bluntly. "Someone in al-Jihad's network studied you and drew up a game plan."

"I know." Lee had said as much to her, jeering from the witness stand. She tangled her fingers together and held on tight as she forced herself to continue, "And I fell for it, hook, line and sinker. Pathetic, really."

If Gray had tried to soothe her, she would've shut down. If he'd tried to tell her she wasn't pathetic at all when they both knew that she—or at least her actions back then—had been exactly that, she would've snapped at him. Instead, he sat in silence, watching her with cool gray eyes that she now suspected hid far more emotion than she'd initially given him credit for.

She hesitated, torn. Her inner loner said that the details weren't pertinent to the case, that there was nothing between her and Gray except the investigation. But another, less familiar part of her wanted him to know about her past, wanted him to know *her*. She wasn't sure what she was looking to get back from him—absolution, perhaps? Understanding? Or maybe just a moment of feeling as though she weren't alone in this mess. She, who almost always wanted to be alone.

"My parents were roadies with a heavy-metal band when they met each other," she said, still not entirely sure where the words were coming from, or whether telling him was such a good idea. "My mom was an artist—still is—and my dad was taking some time to 'find himself' after spending nearly a decade getting an advanced degree in structural engineering. He was burned out, she was looking for something more in life… It was love at first sight, and they married and got pregnant within the year. As soon as I was old enough to travel, they went back out onto the road, sometimes crewing for bands, sometimes working carnivals, sometimes just driving their RV from place to place, picking up work where they could and experiencing life to the fullest." She paused. "That was what they called it. Experiencing life."

"What did you call it?"

"It was what I knew. I just called it life." But when he just sat there, looking at her as though he knew that was an evasion, she said, "Okay, maybe I saw the kids who came to the carnivals, how they hung together and knew each other so well, and maybe I wished I could have that." This time her pause was longer, as old resentments banged up against newer guilt. "Sometimes my parents were so wrapped up in each other, there didn't seem to be room for me. They knew I wanted to stay in one place for a while and go to a real school rather than being homeschooled, but that wasn't in their game plan. When they finally did decide to put down roots in Bear Claw, I was applying for college." She lifted a shoulder. "My dorm room was the first place I'd ever stayed for more than a couple of months."

"That must've been a big change," Gray said.

His comment reminded her of something she'd noticed about him before, back during the first two investigations. He didn't ask questions as much as prompt with comments, and then let the silence hang between them until the other person filled the airspace. Before, the tactic had grated on her, making her feel as though he considered himself the maestro, that he had only to gesture and his suspect would tell all. Now, though, it felt different, more personal, as though he wanted to hear her life story. And yeah, he probably did. But was that because he hoped it would give him some new insight into Lee, or because he was interested in her for her own sake? Did he feel the faint hum in the air, the faint tingle of warmth that zinged from him to her and back again?

"You don't want to hear this," she said, going for practical rather than coy. "It has nothing to do with the case."

He tipped his head slightly. "Like it or not, you're part

of the case, which makes everything about you relevant. Besides, we're still trying to figure out what Lee and al-Jihad want from you. Any small detail could help."

"I can't imagine you'll learn much hearing about my years of college angst."

"You never know." His voice and expression were impassive, giving away nothing.

From nowhere, sudden frustration bubbled through Mariah. Or maybe it didn't come out of the blue, she realized after a moment of surprise. On some level the irritation had been humming beneath the surface for longer than she'd known, even before Lee had breached the defensive electronic wall around her cabin and taken her hostage. In the months leading up to that, as she'd slowly come awake from the shock of the disaster her life had become, she'd found a kernel of angry impatience growing inside her.

Propelled by that hot irritation, she sat up and faced Gray in her hospital bed, leaning toward him in an effort to make her point, and maybe to see if she could find a crack or two in that cool façade.

"Then what, exactly, do you want to hear?" Her voice rose beyond the sick-sounding whisper she'd been affecting as part of her hospital-bound role, but she didn't care. She'd been lying there, waiting, for nearly two full days; surely Lee would've come for her by now if he were planning on taking her from the hospital. For all they knew, he'd left the country, slipping the noose once again.

That fear, and the knowledge that she wouldn't be safe as long as he was on the loose, sharpened her voice further as she said, "Okay, then. What part of my college angst do you want to hear about? Do you want to know how hard it was to finally be in a position to hang with a group of friends, and realize I didn't want to, that I didn't fit in with the uncool kids, never mind the cool ones? Or maybe how the only way I could really be a part of things was by hiding behind my camera, using it as an excuse to talk to people who forgot me the moment the frame was shot? Oh, wait. I bet you want to know that the reason I moved to New York after I graduated was because I hoped I'd fit in better with an artsy crowd. And how when I got there, when I got my dream job as the lowest of the low in a fashion photog's shop, *that* was when I got to be a part of the cool crowd. That was when I got invited to the clubs, and partied until dawn without the damn camera in my hands."

Gray leaned in and touched one of her hands, where she'd balled it into a fist. "Mariah—"

"I'm not done," she snapped, barreling over him. "Because you probably want to hear about how I met Lee, not in one of those clubs, but in a coffee shop near my apartment. I was sitting at a sidewalk table reading a travel book about Paris—a girl can dream, right?— when someone reaches past me, taps the page I'm on, and a man's voice says, 'I've been there. It's the most beautiful place on earth.' The next thing I know, this absolutely gorgeous guy sits down opposite me and starts telling me about his trip to Paris. Only he doesn't just tell me about himself, he asks me questions, too, and he listens as if he really cared about the answers, like he's really into *me*."

She thumped herself on the chest with one hand, barely registering that the other had somehow become tangled with Gray's, that he'd turned to face her so they were practically knee-to-knee, nose-to-nose.

He drew breath to say something, but she beat him to it, knowing what he was undoubtedly going to remind her. "Of course, I know it was a setup. I didn't back then, though. Back then, I thought it was love at first sight, just like it'd been for my parents." She stared down at her hands, unconsciously tightening her grip on Gray's fingers. "I may not have wanted the childhood I got, but I wanted what they had. I wanted that connection, the sort of landslide love that swept away everything else and made the rest of the world less important than what the two of them had together." Her voice broke on tears she hadn't even realized were threatening. "I thought I'd found it with Lee. He made me believe in him, in *us,* but it wasn't real. Everything I thought and felt was a lie. Worse, I was so blind, so stupid, that I didn't see him for what he was. You've got to believe me," she said urgently, leaning in closer. "I didn't know. I didn't suspect. If I did, I swear I would've done something before those bombs went off."

And for the first time since three days after the Santa Bombings, when dark-suited men and women had appeared on her doorstep with a search-and-seizure warrant and had asked her to come with them, she thought there might be a chance that the person she was speaking to might finally believe her. She'd lived so long under a cloud of suspicion and self-recrimination that she'd thought she'd never find her way out. But somehow, in that moment, she saw a glimmer of hope, a small clear spot in the dark fog. At its center was a pair of cool eyes.

Gray's face was very close to hers, making her aware of small details she'd been oblivious to before. Fine creases ran from the corners of his mouth and eyes, suggesting that he'd once smiled far more than he seemed to now. The touches of silver at his temples made him seem older than his years; she guessed he was in his late thirties. He projected a tough, battle-ready demeanor, but in his eyes, she thought she saw another man—not the soldier or the special agent, but a younger, softer version of both.

"It wasn't your fault, Mariah," he said, gripping both her hands now, as though trying to make her believe.

For a moment she thought he was talking about whatever had happened to make him the cool, cynical character whose façade he presented to the world. Then, realizing he was talking about Lee, she blushed slightly. Inside her, a coil of uncertainty loosened, even as something else drew tighter. "I lived with him. I was married to him." *He was my first and only lover,* she thought, but didn't say that because that was the one thing she'd never shared with another human being, aside from her ex.

Since Lee hadn't mentioned that fact, either to sneer about it in the courtroom or gloat over it in his letter, she prayed he'd forgotten that detail as inconsequential. But knowing him—or rather knowing the man he'd turned out to be, she feared that he was saving that information for the moment when it would inflict the maximum amount of pain. That was the sort of man he was.

She didn't tell Gray any of that, though. Not because he was a Fed, but because he was holding her hands as though he could keep her safe through that simple contact, and because he was looking at her with a new heat in his eyes, one that sparked something deep inside her, something she thought had died the day she'd learned that Lee had been lying to her from the first moment they'd met.

"He never loved me," she said matter-of-factly, having come to terms with that. "And he'd never been to Paris." It wasn't the most important thing, but it seemed to encapsulate their entire relationship. The first words he'd ever said to her had been a well-researched lie.

Gray's lips twitched. "Bastard."

And though she knew full well that the agent's main purpose in life was bringing down people like Lee, she liked that Gray played along with her in that moment. Incredibly, impossibly, she began to laugh—a deep, belly laugh, tinged with hysteria. Within moments, though, the laughter threatened to turn to sobs as everything started pressing in on her.

It was all too much—the guilt she'd lived with for too long, the fear of captivity, the complications that had arisen in the wake of her escape…once again she was trapped in a life she didn't want, one that kept her from feeling safe and at ease in her own skin.

Face burning from the embarrassment of Gray—of anyone—seeing her on the verge of losing it, she tried to pull away from him. "I'm sorry. You're going to have to give me a moment here."

He didn't leave, though, and he didn't let her withdraw. Instead, he held on to her hands, squeezing tight in support. "Don't beat yourself up," he said. "You didn't ask for any of this."

Tears filming her vision, she shook her head. "But I didn't do anything to stop it."

"You are now."

She blinked, surprised at the intensity in his eyes, and at the warm rush that surged through her at his words, a knife-edge combination of fear and unexpected heat. "I'm scared," she said, the words coming out very small and thin, and shaming her with the weakness they revealed.

"You'd be an idiot not to be." He surprised her, both with the low fervency of his words and by what he did next.

He dropped his head forward so his brow rested on hers. She'd never before thought of him as a man who needed to lean, but in that moment, she felt as though they were propping each other up.

"Gray?" she said, the single word a question that encompassed all the thoughts suddenly jammed inside her head. *What's going on?* she wanted to ask, *Do you feel it, too?* But she didn't have the guts, had never had the guts to do what mattered.

"I'll protect you," he said, the three words punching through her in a heartfelt vow, because she instinctively knew he wasn't just promising to protect a witness, or potential asset. He was promising to protect *her*.

"I know you will," she said, trying not to make more of this than it really was. He was tired; they both were. The situation had thrown them together, and it had broken down barriers that perhaps would've been better left in place. Trying to resurrect some of those barriers, she said, "Because it's your job."

"And because of this," he replied. Then he tipped his face up, and touched his lips to hers.

Chapter 5

Mariah froze as heat raced through her veins and an unexpected flare of connection threatened to unlock a torrent of wants and needs too long denied. Her rational brain screamed that there was a cop at the door, and though Gray was the only one watching the in-room surveillance, everything was undoubtedly being caught on tape. More, experience had taught her that desire could make her do very stupid things.

But as his mouth slanted against hers and his lips exerted subtle suction, teasing hers apart for a touch of tongue, a nip of teeth, she couldn't find the strength to pull away.

She hadn't expected him to kiss her. Or at least not now, not under these circumstances. It seemed out of character for a man like Gray, who might push the boundaries of his position and his boss, but was always aware of himself, always on the job. Yet at the same time she could understand it, had felt—and denied—the chemistry from that first moment they'd met during her initial interrogations, and again when he'd rescued her from the cabin and shielded her with his own body.

Now, realizing from the urgent press of his lips that he felt the same sharp, greedy attraction, she leaned into him, opened to him. And if a piece of her wondered whether this was another layer of manipulation, she told herself to enjoy now, analyze later.

He groaned when her tongue touched his, a harsh rattle at the back of his throat, and he held himself tense for a moment, as though fighting the mad impulse that had roared up and was riding them both, spurring them on. Mariah knew she should pull away, knew they both should, but she couldn't make herself break their partial embrace any more than she could force herself to assess his motives.

Gray's lips were clever and agile, and far softer than she would have expected, based on what she knew of the man. His skin was cool to the touch, which was definitely what she would've expected, but it heated rapidly, bringing an unfamiliar sizzle of feminine power surging through Mariah.

Going with that power, which made her feel as though she were in control, in charge, she changed the angle of the kiss and added a light scrape of teeth, then feathered a breath along his jaw, and into the soft place behind his ear, where she herself was supersensitive.

His breath caught on a second groan and he shuddered against her, then retaliated, dragging his lips across her throat, taking her earlobe between his teeth and biting down gently.

Mariah angled her head, baring herself to the sensuous torture and moaning when he obliged. Then his lips returned to hers and she gave herself over to the kiss, losing her edge of control in the heat that rose up to surround them, consume them. She was vaguely conscious that she'd shifted, uncrossing her legs and leaning back as he stood and followed her down, so they were almost—but not quite—wrapped together on the narrow hospital bed. Still, though, their fingers were tangled together, a last hold on sanity.

Wanting to touch the big, masculine body that rose above her, she released his hands at the same moment he let go of hers. They reached for each other. Touched each other. And froze.

Reality returned with a cold, hard slap that did little to temper the burning heat rocketing through Mariah's body. What the hell was she doing? What was she thinking?

She eased away from him and he from her, so their lips were no longer touching. Still, they were wrapped in an almost-embrace, with her palms pressed flat against the hard planes of his chest, and his hands cupping her waist in a caress that had perhaps been intended to help soothe away the danger and complications that had brought them together in the first place.

It was precisely those issues that rose up now, and had Mariah saying, "Bad idea."

She could feel the hammer of his heart beneath her palms, and hear passion in the rasp of his breath. A mad part of her wanted him to argue, wanted him to take the decision away from her, simply wanted him to *take* her, there on the hospital bed, with a cop standing guard just outside the swinging door and the video cameras taping away. The daringness of it surged through her blood-stream, a heady mix of heat and temptation. But instead of moving in to kiss away her reservations, Gray released her and stood up, stood back, his color draining.

Feeling exposed, though she was wearing yoga pants and a T-shirt, Mariah sat up and drew the thin hospital sheet around her waist. She focused on those small tasks, giving them both a moment to recover. But when she glanced back at Gray, she found that he still stood there, looking shell-shocked.

Then she saw him retreat behind his cool agent's façade; she could all but see the shields slam down, separating her from what little emotion he'd allowed to leak out during the kiss. When he spoke, his voice grated. "That can't happen again."

Mariah buried a small slice of hurt and nodded. "You were comforting me, and it got out of hand. That's not a federal crime."

"Got out of hand is an understatement." He grimaced, raking a hand through his brown hair, mussing it. The result made him look younger, like the man she'd thought she'd seen just before their kiss. His eyes, though, were hard and uncompromising, very much those of the soldier, or the special agent. "Look," he said, seeming to make an effort to soften his tone, "this isn't going to work. I'll deal with the tapes of the last few minutes' worth of surveillance, then find someone else to take over this part of the case."

"You're quitting?" The thought brought a clutch of fear. She hated the idea of losing the one person she'd considered even partially an ally. And that, she realized, had been a mistake. Gray wasn't her friend or her ally, and he certainly wasn't going to be her lover. When had she lost track of that? How had she let herself be so foolish based on a spark of chemistry and the fact that he'd rescued her?

"It'll be safer for you if the agent protecting you isn't emotionally involved in the case."

She felt a shimmer of warmth at that, but squelched it and said, "We can agree to keep our distance from each other." She would've reached out to him, but didn't dare touch him, not with the residual hum of their kisses still speeding through her bloodstream. So, instead, she curled her fingers into the hospital sheet, trying not to let his answer matter. "Please don't leave because of what just happened." There was a faint tremor in her voice, warning that her emotions were suddenly too close to the surface when she'd successfully kept them buried for so long.

"I'm not leaving because of what just happened, or at least not the way I think you mean." He paused, and in his eyes she thought she saw a flash of regret. But there was none of that in his voice, which went cool and remote, very much that of Special Agent Grayson when he said, "The emotions I was talking about, the ones that don't have any place in an official investigation…they don't have anything to do with you, or what just happened."

Ouch. That was direct, she thought. But even so, it took a moment before she got it. When she did, she sucked in a quiet breath and let it out again on a slow sound of pain. "You lost someone in the bombings."

She didn't need his slow nod of confirmation to know she had it right. It explained so many things, from his cold, almost brutal demeanor during the first investigation and his insistence on being involved in the jailbreak case, to his disobeying orders to sneak up and spy on her cabin for no other reason than because he suspected that she might still be involved with Lee.

"So you'll understand why you'd be better off with someone else," he said, his expression implacable.

"No, actually, I don't," she said, fighting to keep her voice level, and conscious of the others who might be listening. "We both want the same thing. We both want Lee, al-Jihad and everyone associated with them either dead or behind bars, right? There's no difference."

"There's one very important difference." Gray surprised her by moving into her space again, and leaning down so she could feel the heat of him.

"Oh?" she said, damning herself for the weakness of her voice, which had gone nearly to a husky whisper. "What would that be?"

"You want your ex off the streets so you'll be safe. I just want him off the streets." His eyes bored into hers. In case she'd missed his message, he spelled it out: "In the second scenario, you're expendable."

"Yet you kissed me." It wasn't the most important point, perhaps, but it was the one she wanted out there.

"It shouldn't have happened. Chemistry can make us imagine things that aren't real. It can complicate things that shouldn't be complicated."

But all of this is complicated! she wanted to snap at him, but didn't, because she saw a flicker of something in his expression—a hint of wariness, maybe, or a crack in his armor.

She wanted to lean in and touch her lips to his, and see if she could turn the crack into a split, and get him to tell her what was really going on inside his head. But who was she to presume to know what a man was thinking? Maybe it was exactly as he'd said. Maybe she was a means to an end—nothing more—and the kiss had been, just as they'd both said, a mistake.

So instead of leaning in, she stayed put. "Please reconsider, Gray. I don't trust Johnson to do the right thing."

He didn't argue that point. He did, however, straighten and move away, saying over his shoulder, "I'll take care of it. It's the least I can do."

He pushed through the door and was gone before she could ask what he meant by that. Did he mean he owed her because he'd rescued her, and therefore felt partially responsible for her safety? Was it because he and his coworkers hadn't yet brought the escapees to justice? Or, in the end, was it because of the kiss?

Mariah touched her lips, feeling the phantom press of his mouth against hers. "Leave it," she whispered, trying not to dwell on what had just happened, and what it had made her feel, a response that had been so much stronger than she'd expected or wanted. But unexpectedly, the words brought a new urge, strong and fierce. *Leave it.* She should just go, take off, disappear someplace where neither Lee nor the Feds could find her.

The thought was so liberating, the desire so strong, that she was on her feet before she was even aware of having moved. She was halfway across the room when the door swung open again. She looked up, her heart kicking at the thought that Gray had come back to argue some more, or maybe apologize, though he didn't seem like the sort of man to apologize for telling the truth, hurtful or not.

It wasn't Gray, though. It was a uniformed officer,

presumably the one who'd been guarding her out in the hallway.

He blocked the door and avoided her eyes, making her wonder how much of her and Gray's exchange he'd heard, and what else Gray had told him. But the cop said only, "Special Agent Grayson said I should guard you eyes-on until he gets back with his replacement."

"Oh," she said faintly. "I was just…" She trailed off. "Never mind."

She got back in bed and lay on her side, facing away from the officer, who ducked through the door to pull his chair inside the room. She knew it was rude of her to all but ignore him, knew she'd feel bad about that later, but she didn't care right then. She was tired, sad and hurting, and just wanted to be left alone with the realization that Gray hadn't agreed to protect her because of the attraction that snapped between them or because he was a good guy at heart. He'd agreed to the plan because, like his boss, he'd seen the value in using her. She'd been right—the kiss had been another layer of manipulation, though seemingly not a calculated one. There had been nothing personal about it at all. Worse, the cop inside the room was proof positive that Gray didn't trust her one bit.

Which is fine, she told herself. *Because I don't trust him, either.* They'd moved from what she'd thought was the beginning of a truce that might've become more, to…nothing. He was gone and she had a feeling that he wasn't coming back.

More important, she wasn't sure she wanted him to.

With Mariah safely guarded by the officer on duty, Gray found an empty room down the hall and snagged a landline to dial out. When the phone rang for the fourth time on the other end, he started cursing under his breath. "Come on, come on. Pick up."

The line clicked live, and a familiar voice said, "Jonah Fairfax here."

"It's Gray. I need your help."

"Anything," the other agent said without a moment's hesitation. "What can I do?"

It still surprised Gray how quickly the two of them had become allies, especially given that the first time they'd met, Gray had arrested Fax none too gently. Granted, at the time Gray had not known that Fax was undercover, and that the prison break had been a setup. Fax had gone into the ARX Supermax Prison undercover on the orders of his boss, Jane Doe, and hadn't realized that she'd turned and was working for al-Jihad until too late—after the jailbreak and subsequent chaos. He'd managed to avoid totally compromising the mission by hooking up with Bear Claw Medical Examiner Chelsea Swan and several of her friends. The small group, which had included a few trusted members of the FBI and the Bear Claw PD, had averted a disaster and captured one of the escaped convicts, al-Jihad's closest lieutenant, Muhammad Feyd.

In the aftermath, Fax and Chelsea had paired up and eventually gotten engaged, though they had put off the wedding until Chelsea was finished with her FBI training. She'd pursued FBI training as part of a long-delayed dream. Until then, Fax was committed to chasing down al-Jihad and the others, while doing his bit for the wedding plans—which, he'd admitted to Gray privately, had so far consisted mostly of staying out of Chelsea's way. Gray had nodded and tried to grin, but as with the subject of holidays, the topic of weddings and marriages made him cringe.

He and Fax might have met as adversaries, but in the months since then they'd become cautious and somewhat unlikely friends, drawn together because both of them were viewed with serious suspicion by the bulk of the local and federal law-enforcement professionals. Fax was distrusted because no matter how much evidence proved that he'd been acting on orders, the fact remained that he'd helped al-Jihad and the others escape from prison. Heck, even Gray would've probably mistrusted the other agent, if he himself hadn't come under a similar cloud of suspicion not long after he'd arrested Fax. Back then, when Johnson had accused him of colluding with al-Jihad, Gray's only and best defense had been to blame his personal problems for the choices he'd made, when, in reality, he'd gone with his gut and had been wrong.

Well, after what had just happened with Mariah, his gut was 0-for-2. He'd thought he could use her without letting things get complicated. He'd been dead wrong.

"From your utter silence, I'm guessing that whatever's going on, it's complicated," Fax said. "Are you in the hospital?"

"Yeah. Why?"

"I just hit the parking lot, and I'm about to get in the elevator. See you in a couple of minutes." Fax hung up.

At least something was going his way, Gray thought. If Fax was already there, he could take over Mariah's protection immediately. That'd be better for everyone involved. And if the decision kindled an acid burn in Gray's gut, nobody else needed to know about it.

Gray was standing by the elevators when Fax stepped

out. Just shy of six feet, with close-clipped black hair, hard blue eyes and the faint thread of a scar running through one dark eyebrow, the other agent was a tough, no-nonsense scrapper from a police family, not unlike Gray's own. Fax kept his own counsel, went outside the box when the situation called for it and had only one vulnerability Gray was aware of—namely Chelsea.

Fax was one of the few men Gray would trust at his back in a firefight, which made him the man for this particular job, too. And if a small voice at the back of Gray's head pointed out that he'd just put Mariah's safety on a par with his own, when he'd been so careful to tell her that wasn't the case, then he ignored it just as he'd ignored the sense of disquiet that had poked at him when he'd put the cop in her room and abandoned his surveillance post. Those were gut-level twinges, and his gut had been less than reliable of late.

Fax nodded in greeting. "Hey. What's up?"

"Any news?" Gray asked, though he had little hope that the case had broken in the thirty minutes since his last update.

"More of the same," Fax replied. "There's a good chance that al-Jihad is out of the country, and there's been no word on Mawadi, Jane Doe or the others. The Bear Claw PD's Internal Affairs Department is taking a look at the local cops, trying to figure out whether there's an in-house conspirator, and, if so, who it might be. The investigation's being led by Romo Sampson. Career cop, has the reputation of being a hard-ass, but usually he calls it right. At the moment, he's looking long and hard at the coroner's office. I guess the head coroner has both friends and enemies in high places, and she and Romo have a past."

"None of which gets us any closer to Mawadi," Gray said, frustration riding him hard. Aware that they were exposed even with the normal hospital bustle swirling around them, Gray moved them into a nearby alcove and kept his voice pitched low. "I need you to take over the protection detail. I've got to get out of here."

Fax's scarred eyebrow rose, but he said only, "You've got another angle to work?"

If he said yes, Fax would accept that without further explanation, Gray knew. But it would be a lie. Shaking his head he said, "I've got to get out of here. This assignment's making me crazy."

"The assignment or the woman?"

Gray shot his friend a quick look. "Why? What have you heard?"

"Nothing. I saw the two of you together in the interview tapes, and again the other day when you pulled her down off the ridgeline. From the way you were acting with each other, I thought there might be something going on. Sparks, at the very least."

Scowling, Gray muttered, "I think all that wedding planning has fried your brain. She and I weren't sparking, we were arguing."

Fax snorted. "Whatever. Are you trying to tell me it's my imagination?"

Gray started to…and then exhaled on a curse, scrubbing both hands across his face in a vain effort to relieve some of the tension—and wipe away the memory of a very big mistake that had felt like something else entirely. "I kissed her. Just now, in her room, under the damn surveillance cameras. We were fighting over something—I don't even remember what. One second we were going at it, and then we were…" He trailed off.

"Going at it?" Fax offered, looking devilishly amused.

"You're not helping." Gray shook his head. "Anybody could've come in gunning for her, and I would've been beyond useless. What kind of an agent does something like that?"

Fax shot him a level look. "This one, for starters. Been there, done that, bought the diamond ring. Not that I'm advocating that method of courtship, but if you're looking for someone to warn you off, you've come to the wrong guy."

"I'm. Not. Courting." Realizing he was clenching his jaw hard enough to crack a molar, Gray consciously relaxed his suddenly strung-tight body. "And if I were, Mariah wouldn't be where I'd be headed. She's closed-off, short-tempered and stubborn as an ox."

"So are you," Fax retorted. "And I don't think too many oxen look like her. Then again, I'm a city boy. What do I know?"

Gray glared because Fax knew damn well he was another city boy, straight from the rough side of Chicago. Yeah, maybe he was the first in his cop family to go to a big college out of state, the first to take the plunge and go federal, but still. Even city boys knew it worked best to keep policework in the family. Cops understood other cops. People on the outside—people like photographers, or whatever Mariah would be when this was all over—didn't understand the life, didn't grasp the dangers and demands. His ex-wife, Stacy, had come from a cop family, and even her familiarity with the demands of policework hadn't been enough to overcome the difficulties created by his job.

That, and the fact that they might've had lust going for them, but when the sex had mellowed, they had belatedly realized they didn't have a damn thing in common.

"None of it matters right now," Gray said, as much to himself as to Fax. "I'm out. I'm done. I want you to take over the surveillance detail while I do what needs to be done." The frustrated anger inside him needed an outlet. He was stirred up, churned up, and he wasn't going to do anybody any good in that state. And when it came right down to it, he was tired of playing by the rules. Forget due process—he was looking for results.

This time, he was damn well turning in his resignation and making it stick.

Fax took a good long look at him, then shook his head. "All indications say that al-Jihad's not even in the country anymore."

"Maybe not. But Mawadi is." And if Gray's need to hunt the bastard had suddenly become far stronger than before, and far more personal, nobody but him needed to know it.

"If we can't find him," Fax said, meaning the FBI, "then how do you expect to?" He shot Gray a sidelong look. "If you're serious about this, I'd think you'd be looking to use the woman, not leave her behind."

Gray growled, but Fax had a point. He was being inconsistent and reactive, neither of which were good traits when it came to doing the job. But that was exactly why he needed to get away from the hospital, away from Mariah. She was stirring him up, distracting him. When he was near her, he wasn't focused on the case—he was thinking about her, looking at her. Wondering how she would feel against him, how she would taste on his lips.

Now that he knew, it would only be worse, because

he couldn't pursue the attraction without risking her safety and the vow he'd made on a tiny grave.

"The dead deserve my full attention," he finally said. "And Mariah needs a bodyguard who's protecting her, not climbing all over her."

"The dead are gone," Fax said quietly. "You're not." He held up a hand to forestall Gray's knee-jerk response. "That's not to say the dead don't deserve justice—of course they do. But their being dead doesn't mean that you don't get to have a life."

"She's not what I want," Gray said starkly, though there was so much more to it than that.

Fax looked at him for a long moment before he nodded slowly. "Okay, then. I'll watch out for her. You want to introduce me? The changeover might come easier from you."

"I doubt it," Gray said, largely because he was too tempted to see her one last time. "You go ahead. She'll understand."

"If you're sure." Fax stuck out his hand. "I'll keep her alive. You keep yourself alive. Deal?"

"Deal." Gray was reaching to shake when all hell broke loose.

Chapter 6

Gray was sprinting for the source of the alarmed cries—Mariah's room—before he was even aware of having moved. Fax pounded at his heels. The hospital staffers' shouts of "Where is she?" and "She was there a minute ago!" warned him that they were already too late.

A uniformed cop stood in the doorway, wild-eyed. It wasn't the officer who'd been on duty when Gray had left her, maybe five minutes earlier, which was a very bad sign. When the cop saw Gray, he snapped, "What the hell happened?"

Gray didn't answer. He pushed past the cop into Mariah's hospital room, expecting to see signs of a struggle, and the officer on duty injured, maybe down for good. Instead, he found the room nearly pristine. The bed was badly rumpled, though he suspected he was at least part of the cause of that—and the memory brought a kick of heat and anger. He was furious at himself for letting emotion override duty. He'd been sulking in the hallway when he should've been in the surveillance room, doing his damn job.

Which was exactly why he'd wanted Fax to take over, because his growing attraction to Mariah was distracting him, churning him up and causing him to make mistakes, perhaps even fatal ones. But the heat eating at him didn't emerge as rage; it turned to ice. He felt the change, felt himself closing off and going killer-cold.

"Call it in and seal the room," he said to the cop, then spun away, gesturing for Fax to follow as he jogged to the surveillance room. "Come on. The bastard is bound to be on tape. That'll give us a starting point, and information."

They would see whether the cop had taken her, or been taken along with her, and where they'd gone. The tapes would tell Gray where to start looking, and what he was looking for. That was the upside of being part of a well-stocked organization like the FBI.

Gray and Fax grabbed chairs, and Gray started running back the tapes, first taking a few precious seconds to erase the part where he had kissed Mariah and then working forward, moving as fast as he could, knowing every second counted.

Gray scanned the film, muttering curses under his breath as his blood beat with the need to find her. Mariah was his. Or rather, he corrected himself, she was *his responsibility.* And if she suffered—or worse, died—because he'd fouled up, then it would be on his soul. Again.

* * *

Mariah awoke in darkness, swathed mummylike in sheets and gagged with a towel jammed in her mouth. She fought to struggle but could barely move; she was strapped down to something hard and flat, bound by restricting strips that crossed her chest, waist and ankles.

Panic seized her, as she felt the vertigo of motion and heard the growl of engine noise. She inhaled to scream, and nearly choked on the heavy, chemical smell suffusing the air around her. The fumes had her nasal passages closing, making her gag and fight for breath. When lack of oxygen made her even more terrified, threatening to send her over the edge, she told herself to calm down, to think. Focus.

It wasn't easy, but she managed it. Her heart still hammered and tears leaked from the corners of her eyes, but she slowed her breathing through sheer force of will. She could get enough air—barely—through her nostrils, and suck some through the towel. She wouldn't suffocate, at least not immediately. But that was small comfort as she began to suspect that she was bound to a backboard and zipped inside a coroner's body bag. She could feel the heavy plastic with the tips of her fingers, and it stood to reason. Lee and the others had escaped from the ARX Supermax in body bags, on gurneys transported out of the jail in a coroner's van. If she had to guess, from the tip and sway as the vehicle transporting her rounded a corner, that was exactly what had been done with her as well.

It fit with Lee's twisted sense of irony. Knowing him, she was probably lying in the very body bag he planned to use to dispose of her when the time came.

Revulsion tore at her, alongside despair, but she

fought both with the hard practicality she'd been forced to learn over the past two years. If she vomited with a gag in her mouth, she'd aspirate and die. If she despaired and gave up, then Lee had already won, and that wasn't acceptable. Over the past few months, as she'd reawakened to herself as a person, she'd begun to see beauty once again in the dawn and dusk, and the woods around her home. She'd discovered a new sense of purpose, of determination. And she'd kissed a man and felt the burn of lust. Maybe he hadn't been the right man, maybe it hadn't been the right time, but the kiss had proved that she was able to respond sexually. She'd worried now and then, late at night when her brain insisted on replaying hurtful segments of her marriage, that that capability had died. She was still alive, dammit. Kissing Gray had proved that, if nothing else.

The burn of remembered heat hardened her resolve. She wasn't giving up without a fight. Not this time. But what could she do from where she was? She was trapped. Helpless.

Panic washed through her at the thought, but she forced it away, made herself think and remember what had happened, how she'd gotten where she'd wound up.

The cop, she thought, remembering that she'd rolled onto her side so the officer sitting just inside the door couldn't see her tears, which had been mostly out of frustration and anger, and a bit of self-pity following Gray's precipitous exit.

Her eyes filmed again, and a desperate wish shimmered through her. *Please find me,* she thought, as though her brain waves could magically reach inside his thick skull. *I don't care how you feel about me, or whether you walk away afterwards, as long as you get me out of this before Lee does...whatever he's going to do.*

The thought brought a shudder of dread, one that threatened to undermine her sense of purpose. But she fought not to give in to the terror.

Lee needs something from me, she reminded herself, trying to breathe through the panic. *Otherwise, I'd already be dead.* But how long would that logic hold? At what point would the terrorists decide that keeping her alive was too much of an effort and just kill her?

As if answering her question, the driver swerved, hit the brakes and brought the vehicle to a skidding halt. Inertia made Mariah's insides slosh sickeningly, but the flat surface beneath her didn't move, except to give a metallic rattle, adding weight to her suspicion that she was strapped to a gurney that'd been locked into place in a coroner's van. Lee would've liked the convenience, as well as the psychological torture, of her waking up inside her own shroud.

Bastard, Mariah thought, fanning the anger and hatred because both were better than fear.

Then she heard muffled footsteps approaching the rear of the vehicle, and the fear took over. She whimpered involuntarily behind the gag, hoping against hope that the footsteps belonged to a savior but knowing deep down inside that they didn't.

The door locks popped and she heard a door open. A man's voice asked, "Did anyone see you take her?"

It was Lee.

Sick dread rolled through Mariah in waves at the sound of her ex's too-familiar tones, draining her resolve in an instant.

"No." The second voice, coming from very close to

her, was thick with emotion. She thought it was the cop from her room and became sure of it when he said, "I did what I was told. You said you'd tell me where my wife—"

"Help me switch her to the other car," Lee interrupted. "Someone will call and tell you where to find your family."

That explained the abduction, Mariah thought, her heart clutching for the cop. The terrorists had gotten to the officer, using the best leverage of all. Family.

A slice of despair suddenly surfaced as Mariah inwardly acknowledged that she might never see her parents again, that she should have tried to fix that relationship when she'd had the chance. She hadn't understood why they'd needed to move away any more than they'd understood why she needed to stay. That, combined with Mariah's awful guilt over knowing she'd brought Lee into their lives only to have him destroy her father's career and self-respect, had driven a wedge into their already estranged family unit.

She should've apologized a thousand times over, should've done more to help them start over. Instead, she'd walled herself away in her isolated cabin.

Mariah felt sick, then even sicker still when the men climbed into the back of the van with her. The vehicle shuddered under their weight. Moments later, she felt the men approach her and pause. She held herself still, trapped and terrified.

An unzipping noise reverberated through the dark space that enclosed her, and suddenly there was light again, she could see again. But that wasn't a relief, because what she saw was Lee's face as he bent over her, wrinkling his nose at the smell coming from the bag's lining. His beautiful blue eyes were lit with unholy satisfaction and excitement.

"Hello, Mariah," he said, his voice sounding as cultured and urbane as ever, his whole demeanor giving no evidence that he was talking to a woman bound in a body bag. "This shouldn't take long at all. A short drive, a little session with al-Jihad where you'll tell us what we want to know, and after that…well, we'll see what happens after that, won't we, sweetheart?"

The Feds had said Lee was a follower, with the undercover agent, Fairfax, even going as far as to call him a lemming, a weak personality who chased the leader. But they didn't know him the way Mariah did. When it came to his wife—or the woman he perceived as still being his wife despite the paperwork that said otherwise—Lee was no follower. He went his own way, and didn't give a damn what anyone else said, least of all her.

She'd married him thinking she was in love. But she'd found herself in hell. And now he was going to do everything in his power to put her right back there, or worse.

Heart pounding with fear and rage, Mariah narrowed her eyes, not caring that tears leaked from their corners as she screamed against her gag, telling him how much she hated him, and that she wasn't afraid of him, not anymore. She struggled against the straps, wanting to rake her nails across his lying face, needing to do something, anything, to prove that she wasn't the doormat she'd become while she was married to him.

He smiled and leaned in to kiss her cheek, though she struggled and turned her face away. "I missed you, too. This time I'll be very certain not to let you get away from me. We can't have the others thinking I'm unable to control my wife, can we?"

Refusing to look at him anymore, Mariah focused on the second man. The cop stood nearby, tense and unhappy, and coated in the stink of fear. His eyes were unfocused, turned inward, as though he were picturing what the terrorists were doing to his family.

Mariah could relate, but she felt no sympathy. She felt only anger. *How could you?* she wanted to shout at him. *You're one of the good guys!*

Then, in the distance, she heard the rattle of an engine being driven too hard, too fast. Fear seized her. Was it al-Jihad?

But Lee jolted and cursed at the sound, suggesting that the other car was unexpected. "Come on. Let's get her transferred to the minivan."

The cop obeyed, but his expression didn't change; it was as though he were acting on autopilot, beyond himself with fear and shock.

The two men unlatched the gurney and started muscling it off the van, but had difficulty with the folding legs in their haste. Mariah's pulse pounded and her thoughts raced as the surface she was bound to lurched this way and that. She saw forest on either side of her, and caught a glimpse of a brown sign that told her she was somewhere within Bear Claw Canyon State Park. The park, which covered thousands of wilderness acres, offered a steady stream of tourist income, along with the perfect hiding place for nefarious deeds, ranging from teenagers sneaking time alone, to drug deals and even murder and body dumps.

That was what Lee and the others had used it for the day they had escaped from prison, disposing of the bodies of four slain guards and an assistant coroner in a small cave off the main drag. Mariah whimpered at the back of her throat, wondering if this was the same place.

Once they had the gurney off the van, they started hustling it toward a second vehicle, this one a minivan with its back deck wide open and the engine running. Another figure was visible in the driver's seat, though Mariah saw him only briefly as the men approached the minivan.

"Hurry up, damn it," Lee snapped. "If you don't help me get the bitch out of here, your family's dead."

"They're already dead, aren't they?" the cop asked in a dull monotone, his face hardening from shock and grief to a mask of rage.

"Of course not. They're fine." But Lee's answer was too quick, and his eyes showed the lie.

Cursing, the cop exploded into action, shoving the gurney straight into Lee, trapping him against the minivan's back deck. Lee swore as the gurney yawed in his grasp, threatening to tip over.

Surprise and vertigo seized Mariah for a second before she saw her chance to escape. Once she saw it, though, she grabbed on to it, knowing it might be the only shot at freedom she had. Shouting inwardly, she threw her weight in the direction in which she was tipping, hoping against hope that would be enough.

It was. Lee yelled profanities as the gurney flipped and Mariah plummeted to the ground.

She landed hard, banging her head and exhaling in a rush when the metal gurney came down with its full weight on top of her. It took her a second to realize that the jolt had popped the strap securing her arms. She was partway free!

Struggling to breathe through her gag, she tried to free herself from the confines of the body bag. She was in darkness again, having fallen face forward, but she managed to roll onto her side. Working quickly, sobbing with fear, she ripped open the bag, then yanked at the strap binding her chest. Almost clear!

Lee was shouting. She heard him curse, and heard another man's voice join in, followed by the sound of running footsteps and the cry of, "The cop's taking off. *Shoot him!*"

Mariah screamed behind her gag when gunfire cracked above her, three times in quick succession. She didn't know if the cop had run in order to escape, to draw the attention of the incoming vehicle, which sounded as though it were nearly on top of them, or to buy her time to get free of her bonds, but she'd take the distraction no matter what the reason. She yanked the towel out of her mouth, tearing her parched lips in the process but not caring about the pain because it meant she could finally breathe.

Sucking in deep, wrenching breaths and sobbing in relief, she reached for her ankles, which were strapped to each other, but not attached to the backboard she'd been secured to. Before she could get to them, though, the gurney was lifted off her and Lee rasped, "You're not going anywhere without me."

He shifted his gun to his other hand and reached down to grab her. Screaming, she struck back, fisting her hands together and swinging them at his face. The blow was a solid connection that reverberated up her arm and sent Lee reeling back, roaring obscenities through split and bleeding lips. Fury lit his eyes as he switched the gun to his dominant hand and leveled it at her. "You're going to regret that, *wife*."

The man still in the minivan lurched halfway out, snapping something that, even in a foreign language, sounded like, "We're leaving, *now!*"

Lee's finger tightened on the trigger. Mariah thought it was over. She was dead.

Then gunfire split the air, but it came from the tree line, not Lee's gun. Bullets glanced off the minivan, one shattering the back window. The driver shouted, leaped back into the minivan and hit the gas. Lee dove in the open back deck, yelling, "Go, go, go!"

The vehicle peeled out, spraying Mariah with sand and debris, but she didn't protect herself. She was staring slack-jawed in shock as Gray burst from the tree line, running flat-out after the minivan.

She screamed, "Gray, no!" but he didn't hear her. Or if he heard her, he paid no heed.

He flung himself through the open back deck, tackling Lee and hammering a punch into her ex's jaw as the vehicle flew down a dirt access road and disappeared.

A scant second later, four official vehicles burst from the tree line in the direction Gray had come from. Two skidded to a stop near Mariah and the hospital van. The other two raced in pursuit of the minivan.

"Are you okay?" The cop was back, fresh grief and remorse in his eyes. "I flagged them down, but—"

"Don't say anything more," said a big, brown-haired man as he emerged from one of the official vehicles. He had wide-palmed hands, uncompromising features and a local PD badge. "As your friendly local Internal Affairs stiff, I'm advising you to shut the hell up now." He cuffed the cop, who went with him, unresisting.

Mariah simply stared, uncomprehending, as too many things happened around her at once, seemingly unconnected in her brain. Time passed in a fog…yet there was no sign of Gray. The chase cars hadn't come back, and for all the agents and cops piling out of the two big black SUVs and the cruisers pulling up behind them, not a single radio relayed news of Gray's safe return.

"Hey." A man squatted down in front of her and held out a hand. "Can I help you up?"

He had black hair and dark blue eyes, and he looked familiar, though Mariah didn't think they'd been officially introduced. "You're Fairfax."

"That's right. I'm also Gray's friend." Moving slowly, as though he were afraid she would panic if he went too quickly, he eased her feet out of the body bag and undid the straps that were the last things holding her down.

Still, though, even once she was free, she couldn't seem to stand. She just stared up at Fairfax. "Where is he?"

Gray had come for her. The realization shimmered through her. Whether or not he wanted her, or wanted to want her, he'd come for her. He'd chased Lee, had been fighting him as the car disappeared. Then the gunshots. What had happened? Was he alive? Dead?

"We're working on that. Come on. Let's get you out of there." Fairfax hauled her to her feet. He used the bulk of his own body to block her view of the scene, but she caught sight of the corner of the gurney and the still-idling van, and shuddered.

If Lee hadn't arranged to transfer her to the second vehicle…if Gray and the others hadn't figured out where they would be…

Frowning, she glanced at Gray's friend. "How did you find me?"

"GPS." The agent nodded back at the van. "Hospital property."

Mariah shuddered. "Lucky me."

"Maybe not." Fairfax sounded seriously grim. "Especially when you consider that they knew to disable the transponder on the prison van they stole during the jailbreak."

She wrapped her arms around herself as the sharp air cut through her yoga pants and thin T-shirt, and she became aware of the cold ground beneath her sock-clad feet. "Maybe Lee forgot."

"Maybe. Or maybe this was meant as a distraction. Maybe we were supposed to chase the van out here and find it abandoned, while other members of the cell do something else. But what?" Fairfax glanced down, seeming to notice for the first time that she was shivering against him. "Sorry. I'm thinking out loud. Let's get you into a squad car."

But before they'd gone two steps, the big black chase cars reappeared through the trees. Mariah stopped dead, almost afraid to hope. Then the rear door of the first SUV swung open and Gray emerged, looking bruised and battered, with one suit coat sleeve torn most of the way off and scratches along the side of his face. But he was alive. He was up and moving.

He straightened and scanned the crowd, and his eyes locked on her.

Mariah's heart jolted, then started pounding in her ears as he strode toward her, looking simultaneously furious and implacable, and very much like the soldier who had saved her life twice now, once up on the mountain and again just now. When he reached her, he stopped a few feet away, and flicked a glance at Fairfax.

"I'll take her," Gray said, and he exchanged a look with his friend that conveyed a great deal more than those three small words.

Mariah knew she should be offended by the idea of being passed from one man to the next. And she would be, as soon as she stopped shaking. "Did you get him?" she asked, her voice barely above a whisper.

Gray shook his head. "Bastard booted me out of the minivan. Chase car nearly ran me over before I rolled into some scrub." Before Mariah could react to that—if she could even figure out how—he raked her from head to toe with a cool-eyed inspection. But there was heat in his voice when he said, "Are you okay?"

I am now, she meant to say, just as she meant to hold it together and be the practical, no-nonsense woman she prided herself on being these days.

Instead, she shook her head as tears filmed her vision. "I hate this," she whispered. "I hate all of it." She meant the fear and the danger, and maybe—even a little bit—she meant him, and the emotions he stirred in her, emotions she couldn't deal with. Not now. Maybe not ever.

"I know," he said gruffly. "I'm sorry." And again, the few words he spoke were loaded with meaning. He approached her, and Fairfax stepped away, leaving the two of them to face each other.

Gray would've held her if she'd wanted it; she could see it in his eyes. He would've let her pretend that the embrace meant as much to him as it did to her. But he'd made his position crystal clear back at the hospital—he wasn't in this for her, and he didn't intend to let their connection interfere with his priority, which was bringing the bombers to justice. Well, she told herself, that was just fine with her, because she wouldn't be safe until Lee and the others were off the street. Gray wanted nothing but business between them? Fine, that was what she'd give him. And, frankly, the sooner he and the others did their jobs and she was free to go back to rebuilding her life, the better.

So she leaned away from him and said, "What now?"

He looked at her long and hard, and after a moment his expression went cool and took on an edge she hadn't seen before, one that she couldn't quite place. "Now we debrief, and figure out if this was a planned distraction, or simply a case of your ex figuring he'd be faster than we were."

"I'm very glad he wasn't," Mariah said. "Thank you for getting here so quickly."

"He shouldn't have gotten you out in the first place." Scowling, Gray glanced over at one of the SUVs, where the cop from Internal Affairs was standing guard over the turncoat officer, preventing anyone from talking to him. "Looks like the problems in the Bear Claw PD go deeper than we suspected."

"They took his family," Mariah said, her heart aching. "And in the end, he did the right thing."

"I would've found you even if he hadn't flagged me down," Gray said, transferring his attention to her, and she got the sense that he was saying more than that, whether he knew it or not.

In her heart, his words resonated as *I would've done whatever it took to find you.* And if that were simply her delusion—her needy, greedy wish to feel as though someone in this insane mess cared for her as a person rather than as a witness or an asset—then she acknowledged the weakness and kept it to herself.

Crossing her arms over her chest, she hugged herself. "You should look for his family."

"We already found them." His flat tone confirmed what the poor cop had guessed. Al-Jihad hadn't left them alive as potential witnesses. When the news brought another shiver, Gray scowled and shucked out of his ripped suit jacket. He tossed it to her. "Here. You're freezing."

She didn't argue. Nor did she take his gesture as a sign of anything but expediency. "Thanks." She pulled on the jacket, which was way too big for her but felt like heaven. Resisting the urge to snuggle, she took a deep breath and steadied herself to do something she knew she should've done before. "I need to go back up to the cabin."

That got his attention. "Why?"

"Because it's my home."

He shook his head. "You're smarter than that. They got in once, they can do it again."

She wrapped the suit coat tighter around her torso. "Not if you're there to protect me."

"I'm not a babysitter, and I'm not wasting my time playing bodyguard when I could be doing something more productive." He paused, eyes narrowing. "And you know that. Which means you think returning to the cabin will be productive."

She liked that he gave her credit, hated that he saw through her so easily. The transparency made her feel vulnerable, exposed. But she dipped her chin in a faint nod. "Earlier today, before you came into my room and…you know." She waved away what had happened between them, determined to play it as no big deal, although the depth of her response had been a very big deal to her. She continued, "Anyway, earlier, I was just dozing, drifting, and I heard Lee's voice whisper something about me helping them. And I'm pretty sure I remember him asking me about something, hounding me to tell him where something was. I'm not sure what."

Gray went still. "I thought you couldn't remember anything."

"I think it's coming back. I remember being tied up in the cabin, with him leaning over me."

"You were drugged. Your mind could be playing tricks on you."

"I'm convinced it was a real memory."

His eyes narrowed. "One that didn't surface during your debriefing? That's convenient."

Frustration sparked. The six hours she'd been questioned in a secure room deep within the Bear Claw PD prior to her transfer to the hospital had been difficult. With her lawyer present, she'd told the Feds everything she could remember about her captivity. She'd submitted to their blood tests, worked with a sketch artist to capture Brisbane's—or rather Felix Smith's—face, and even allowed Thorne Radcliffe, an FBI profiler with more than a touch of otherworldliness to his technique, to try hypnotizing her. "It's not my fault Thorne couldn't put me under. I told him before he started that I don't hypnotize well."

Actually, the mentalist had dubbed her "blocked" and "closed off," but Gray didn't call her on it. Instead, he shoved his hands into his pockets and rocked back on his heels, giving her the impression that she was finally getting through to him. "You didn't go under during hypnosis, yet you think visiting your cabin is going to shake the memories loose?"

"Not visiting. Staying there." She lifted her chin. "What happened today changes nothing. Unless al-Jihad has another source for whatever he wants from me. I still need protection. The cabin is a fortress. Lee only got to me last time because I shut down the perimeter in order to get back inside. You've got access to more men and better equipment."

"That's not a guarantee," he muttered.

"There aren't any guarantees here," she agreed. "You may not be able to keep me safe. I may not be able to figure out what Lee wants from me. But I think it's worth a try." Seeing that Gray was giving the idea serious consideration, she pressed, "What have you got to lose?"

That earned her a sharp look, but then his expression blanked. After a moment, he nodded. "Fine. We'll do it your way. I'll get Fax to help me clear it with Johnson, and collect the manpower and equipment we'll need to secure the cabin beyond your Mickey Mouse system."

Within twenty minutes, Gray got his superior's okay and preparations were underway.

Later that evening, almost seventy-two hours to the minute after Gray had driven Mariah down off the ridgeline, he drove her back up again.

The air in the truck was tense, and there was little conversation as the vehicle bumped up the access trail, followed by a chase car containing additional FBI agents and supplies. The knowledge that she and Gray weren't going to be alone up at the cabin should've been a relief to Mariah. Instead, she found herself wishing the other agents were gone, wishing Gray were gone, wishing she were alone and everything was back to normal. Which was impossible.

As the night-darkened woods passed on either side of the truck, she tried vainly to remember what Lee had said. What did the bombers want from her? They'd already taken so much from her. Why wasn't that enough?

Think, she told herself. *Focus!* But the memory eluded her, staying stubbornly out of reach.

She told herself that her failure to remember was the source of the leaden lump at the pit of her stomach. But as Gray turned his truck into the parking area beside her cabin and pulled up beside her Jeep, she couldn't help thinking that the sick feeling was more than her inability to recall what Lee had said.

"You ready?" Gray said, killing the engine and pocketing his keys.

She was tempted to tell him no, that she wasn't ready, that they should return to the city and try something else—questioning, more hypnosis, whatever it took. But they'd already tried those things and they hadn't worked. So rather than calling off the plan, as her instincts were clamoring for her to do, she nodded. "Ready."

At his signal she dropped down from the truck, then paused when the front door swung open and Fairfax stepped out onto the porch. The dark-haired agent looked past her and nodded to Gray. "All clear."

Gray urged her forward. "Let's get you inside."

She wanted to balk. Instead, she forced herself up the stairs and through the door into her cabin, her certainty growing with every step.

This had been a very bad idea.

Chapter 7

The moment he stepped through the front door he'd seen Lee step through only four days earlier, Gray found that Mariah's cabin might have been "all clear," but it still bore evidence of the recent siege.

The main room was a wide sweep running the length of the front of the cabin, with a sitting area to the right and a small kitchen to the left, separated by an island that doubled as both counter space and a dining table. The wall opposite the front door was broken up by two doors and a short hallway. From Mariah's description of her escape, he knew her bedroom was to the right, her spare room and bath to the left. The walls were polyurethaned logs intended to look far more rustic than they actually were, and the faux log-cabin theme was carried through in exposed beams and wide pine on the floor. The décor, such as it was, leaned toward

the practical and comfortable. The main room had
club-footed chairs and a cushionless sofa, upholstered
in forest green, along with two rustic end tables, and
several plain, functional lamps that lit the front rooms
with stark yellow light. In the kitchen, the shelves stood
empty. The floor was bare, the windows uncurtained,
though the advance team had covered them with plain,
functional blinds that would shield the cabin's occupants
from view. On the counter rested several grocery bags,
also courtesy of the advance team.

There were no personal touches, no hints of femi-
ninity, but Gray knew from the reports—and his own
instincts—that those touches had been there before
Lee's arrival. More, he knew in his gut that Mariah
would've made her space a home, a nest.

He'd seen the way she'd maintained order even in
her hospital room. She had kept the items on her bed-
side table and in the bathroom each in the place she'd
assigned them. She was neat and organized, not in the
way of someone who was obsessed with it, but more
like someone who'd had so many upheavals in her life
that she'd learned to control what pieces of it she could.

He imagined that she'd taken care with her small living space. He could only assume that seeing her home
stripped bare, as it was now, would hurt her.

He was tempted to block her from entering, to take
her back down to the city and watch over her there—
or, even better, lock her into a safe house until Mawadi
and the others had been dealt with.

But that was the irrational part of him talking, the
part that had gotten so caught up in guilting himself
over their kiss that he hadn't been at his post when the
turncoat cop had abducted her from the hospital. And

although that situation had worked out, thanks to a GPS and some major strokes of luck, it only confirmed what his rational, trained side had been telling him since that first moment he'd kissed her and nearly lost himself. Or hell, since the moment he'd plastered himself atop her out in the woods beyond the cabin, shielding her from discovery, and had been all but derailed by the feel of her body beneath his.

She was trouble, and the two of them together were a bad mix.

There was chemistry, yes—a whole lot of chemistry, though she was nothing like the soft, feminine women he was typically drawn to. And he was even tempted to like her from time to time, when he didn't want to strangle her for being stubborn and insisting on challenging him at every turn. But none of that was pertinent to the case at hand, was it? He had to think like a special agent on this one. She was an asset, nothing more. The next time he forgot that and let her distract him, she could very well end up dead. And if she died without remembering what Lee wanted from her, then the next terror attack, and the hundreds—maybe even thousands—of lives lost, would be on his head.

So instead of sparing her the sight of what her ex had done to her home, he stepped aside and beckoned her inside. "Come on. Let's do this."

She moved through the front door and stopped short. Her eyes went blank for a second, then flooded with emotion. "Oh. It's so…empty." She looked around, her breath catching. "Where are all my pictures? The rugs are gone, the pillows, everything." She turned to him. "Did the CSIs really need to take everything?"

"They didn't." His voice came out flat as he forced

himself to keep the necessary distance. "I had a cleaning crew come in and clear out everything that Lee and Brisbane wrecked while they were staying here. The damaged stuff is bagged and tagged outside." According to the reports, that accounted for just about everything in the cabin except the furniture. "You can go through it later, but the cleaners said almost all of it was beyond salvage."

The men—or, most likely, in Gray's opinion, Lee—had used the sofa cushions for target practice, smashed the photographs, urinated on the rugs, torn through her clothing and photographic equipment, and wrecked almost everything else that could be wrecked. The couch and chairs had taken some hits, too, but the cleaners had been able to remove the worst of the stains. It would be up to Mariah whether she wanted to keep those pieces.

Not that she needed to know those details right now. The violation she was feeling showed in her eyes, and in the stiff tension in her body. She was wearing jeans and a pale amber sweater that earlier in the day had picked up the color in her eyes and the highlights in her dark, curly hair. Now, though, the color only served to emphasize the deathly pallor of her face, giving her an air of fragile vulnerability, and he was used to her being neither fragile nor vulnerable.

For a second she looked small and delicate, which kicked at every protective urge Gray had ever possessed, threatening to override his better judgment. He'd actually taken two steps toward her before she turned and pinned him with a look.

"No." The word was soft, but underlaid with steel. Tears glistened in her eyes, but her voice held only determination when she said, "You don't get to have it both ways. You don't get to touch me when you feel like it, then turn around and tell me it's all about the case. You don't want to be attracted to me, don't want to be with me. I get that. Well, guess what? Given a choice in the matter, I wouldn't pick you, either. Which should make this much easier than it would've been otherwise." She looked past him to the open door. "Are the others coming in?"

He reached back without looking and swung the door shut. "Nope. They'll form a perimeter outside." It wasn't SOP, but it was what Gray had insisted on. Not because he wanted to spend time alone with her in the small cabin, but because he'd thought it would be easier for her that way, without five other agents lurking in the cabin.

She looked at him for a long moment, then surprised him by nodding. "Thanks. Good call. The more space I've got to myself, the more likely I'll be able to remember what Lee said."

That was pretty much what Gray had been thinking, which made him wish he didn't understand her as well as he was coming to. In his business, detachment was key.

Needing some crucial distance, he pulled out his cell and checked the time. "It's nearly midnight. We should move some furniture, get some sleep." He prowled across the main room to check out the two back bedrooms. They were both equally small, but one was crammed full of furniture, while the other held only a bare mattress on a bed frame that was pushed up against the wall, right below a shiny new eyebolt that'd been screwed deep into one of the polyurethaned logs.

Gray went rigid with raw fury as he pictured Mariah

lying there, bound, terrified and chained to the wall, terrorized by the man she'd thought she loved.

This time, he gave in to the urge to block the doorway. He turned and found Mariah close behind him. Scowling, he said, "You'll sleep in the main room or the other bedroom."

He halfway expected an argument, halfway expected relief. He hadn't expected her eyes to soften just a hint, or her lips to turn up at the corners in a sad smile.

"I appreciate the thought. Seriously. But we both know the best way for me to remember is to put myself in the same situation I was in when I heard Lee the first time." She nudged him aside, and Gray gave way because she was right, dammit.

She moved to the center of the room, then stopped and stood, staring at the bed. The overhead bulb illuminated the scene in stark yellow light that did nothing to blunt the impact of a bedroom that had been turned into a cell.

When she turned and looked at him, Gray saw the memories in her eyes, and the despair. "Mariah," he began, but then stopped, because what could he say? She was right about a number of things, not the least of them that she needed to stay in that bed, and he needed to keep his hands off her if he didn't intend to follow through on what was—or could be—between them.

She nodded as if he'd said those things aloud. "Yeah. I know." Squaring her shoulders, she said, "Did he leave me any sheets and pillows?"

"I had an agent pick up supplies, bedding included. The advance team left the bags in the spare room."

"In other words, no, he didn't leave me anything except the walls and some furniture." She nodded as if she'd expected the answer, though her expression was bleak and her voice very soft and sad when she said, "Lee has a mean streak. Heck, that's practically all he is—one big mean streak. I didn't see it until after we were married. That's going to haunt me, I expect, until the day I die. If I had seen it, if I had done something—"

"Don't," Gray interrupted. He moved in closer to her, not to soothe, but so she would know that he meant every word. "First off, there was no way you could've known; he was playing a role, and he's smart and ruthless enough to pull it off." Gray knew that for a fact, having watched the bastard nearly charm a jury into acquitting him. "Second, if your gut had warned you off him in the beginning, he would've just moved on to someone else, used someone else. That would've changed your life, yes, but it wouldn't have stopped the bombing. Al-Jihad doesn't open himself to risk by having just one plan—he has backups upon backups. You were one piece of a larger whole. And third, if you'd figured it out and turned Lee in, there's no telling what would have happened. Maybe the authorities would've traced him back to al-Jihad before the bombing. Probably not, though. And you know what one thing you can be sure of? If you'd turned him in, you wouldn't be here right now."

He hadn't meant to put it so bluntly, but there it was. She'd survived her marriage only because she'd withdrawn into herself and presented such a minimal threat to Mawadi's plans that it hadn't been necessary to kill her beforehand. And then she'd gotten very, very lucky. On the day of the bombing, Lee had arranged to meet her at one of the Santa's thrones. She'd been delayed by traffic just long enough so that she arrived at the mall late. She'd been in the parking lot when the bombs went off.

"You're right." She nodded, pale but determined. "And I'm going to make him sorry he ever pulled me into this. I'd like to say he's going to be sorry for what he's done, but I don't think he's capable of that." Features set, she headed out of the room. "I'm going to make the bed, at least. I may have to sleep in here, but I don't have to do it on a bare mattress." She turned back in the doorway. "You want the foldout in the spare room or the couch in the living room? If you want the foldout, we'll have to shift some furniture around in the office. They certainly jammed stuff in there." Her tone was matter-of-fact, but he could see the effort it took her to maintain that practical, no-nonsense front. He sensed that she needed to crumble, but she'd be damned if she'd do it in front of him.

He wanted to soothe, but he didn't have the right. So he dipped his chin, acknowledging all of it, and said, "I'll bunk down on the couch."

Not that he'd be sleeping much. He could go days without sleep on assignment and intended to do exactly that on this job. It wasn't that he distrusted the perimeter the other agents had set up, per se. It was more that he'd stayed alive up to that point by virtue of not trusting anyone but himself. According to Stacy, that was one of the things that had torpedoed their marriage, which by extension meant it had begun the domino effect that had put him and the others in Colorado for the bombings. But so what? His lack of trust might have indirectly put him in the current situation, but it was going to damn well get him out of it intact, and he was bringing Mariah out safely with him.

Although she'd seemed to read his thoughts from his expressions a few times before, this time she took his words at face value, simply nodding and turning away. "I'll go see what your agents left us."

Gray didn't follow her out. He crossed the room, shoved her bed out of the way and went to work on the eyebolt. Cursing Mawadi to hell and back, he used the spare clip from his 9 mm as leverage to unscrew the hardware from its bite in the heavy log wall. The bolt resisted at first; it'd been driven deep with what he imagined had been Mawadi's desire for revenge against the woman who'd dared to divorce him.

But Gray was fueled by an equal measure of anger, and hatred for men like Mawadi, who killed because it entertained them, or like al-Jihad, who killed because their own warped, twisted sense of right and wrong demanded it. And, as the bolt finally came free of the wood and clattered to the floor beneath the bed, Gray knew he was currently being compelled by another, equally hot emotion.

He needed to know that Mariah wouldn't be staring at that damn eyebolt as she tried to remember what her ex had said to her.

Stirred up, ticked off and feeling as though he were about to explode, Gray swept up the bolt from under the bed and stalked through the crowded spare room to the back exit, through which Mariah had escaped four days ago—four days that seemed like so much longer. He was aware of her watching him, wide-eyed, as he yanked open the door, waved for the perimeter guards to stand down, and hurled the eyebolt outside.

Then he slammed and locked the door, and headed back out into the main room. Edgy, greedy need licked along his nerve endings like fire, and he knew if he didn't get some space, he wasn't going to like what happened next. But where the hell was he supposed to get space when he was locked in with just the person he needed to get away from?

"Gray," she said from behind him.

He held up a hand to forestall whatever was coming next, but didn't look back at her because he wasn't sure what would happen if she kept talking. "Not now. Please, Mariah, not now. Just go to sleep. We'll talk in the morning."

He expected an argument, and a hard, hot piece of him might have welcomed it. But for the first time since he'd met her, she took the coward's way out, saying only, "Good night, then."

He held himself still, standing rigid in the center of the main room until he heard her bedroom door close.

Then he dropped down onto the sofa, put his head in his hands, and tried to remember his damn priorities. He wasn't there for her. She was there to help him bring down Mawadi and the others, nothing more. There couldn't be anything more, he reminded himself. Not until he'd taken care of the business at hand. And then? Well, then he and Mariah would go their separate ways.

He knew from personal experience that physical attraction didn't make a solid foundation for a lasting relationship when the two people involved had nothing but chemistry in common.

Mariah slept fitfully, her slumber broken up by dream fragments and nightmares. Each time she awakened, she tried to relax, tried to lull herself into a state where she could call forth Lee's questions, but to no avail. Maybe she was trying too hard. Who knew? All she knew for sure was that she was wide awake before dawn, physically exhausted but mentally restless.

The knowledge that Gray was out in the main room kept her in bed for longer than she would've stayed there otherwise, partly because she didn't want to wake him if he were sleeping, and partly because she didn't want to deal with him, period. He made her feel so many contradictory things all at once, in one big messy knot of uncertainty. She felt safe with him, yet vulnerable; empowered yet weak; sometimes needy and feminine, other times practical and unsexy. She didn't know who she was around him, didn't know how to act.

She lay in her bare bedroom, replaying the kiss they had shared, remembering the sensations he'd sparked, and the emotions.

She had come into her marriage relatively inexperienced, and while sex with Lee had been pleasant at first, even exciting at times, those good times had quickly shifted to power plays and manipulation. It had taken her months to figure out what had changed, and longer than that after the bombings and her quickie divorce to separate out the guilt from the sex and rationally work through what he'd done to her, and how. She'd consulted a therapist, and though it had profoundly unsettled her to share intimate details with a stranger, the sessions had helped her find her center and her balance.

She didn't fear sex, she'd decided, but neither had she desired it for some time. The therapist had assured her that her libido would return eventually. It was just her luck the damn thing had decided to come back online now, and with a totally unsuitable man. Still, she couldn't escape the memory of how his mouth had felt against hers, how his lips had felt on her skin. As they'd kissed, he'd been focused only on her, and on the heat they'd made together.

And she so wasn't getting any closer to remembering what Lee wanted from her, lying there thinking of another, far better—though no less complicated—man.

Muttering under her breath, she got up, got dressed in yesterday's clothes, used the bathroom and then headed for the kitchen, in need of a serious caffeine hit to counteract the effects of the long night and the preceding days.

A light was on in the main room, though Gray appeared to be asleep, lying on his back in a sprawl of leashed male strength. He'd swapped his ruined suit for worn jeans and a long-sleeved shirt that gapped open at the throat, and he wore thick socks against the snap in the mountain air. His boots sat close at hand and his holstered weapon rested on an end table. The sight was more reassuring than intimidating, though Mariah found it a bit of both.

"Bad dreams?" he said, sounding wide awake, though he didn't open his eyes or otherwise move.

She was grateful he'd kept his eyes closed; she didn't want to start the day by being caught staring. Then again, the fact that she'd stopped dead in the middle of the living room had probably been a good clue.

"I wouldn't mind the bad dreams if they were at all productive," she answered. Forcing herself to get moving rather than watching him any longer, she tossed over her shoulder, "You want coffee?"

His jaw went tight, and something that looked like anger flashed in his eyes when they opened. "I'll fend for myself." He rose and headed for the bathroom, seeming to have come fully awake in an instant. When he returned to the main room, he pulled on his boots, donned his holster and grabbed the jacket he'd hung near the front door. "I'm going to check in with the others. Be back in a few."

"Will it bother you if I make enough breakfast for everyone?" she asked, having gotten a definite edge off his tone when he'd turned down her offer of coffee.

"Suit yourself." He didn't look at her as he unlocked the front door, snapped a quick radio check at the team outside and left, closing the door behind him with an emphatic thunk of wood on wood.

When he was gone, the air should've felt softer and less tense to Mariah. She should've welcomed the few minutes of privacy, the moment to be alone. Instead, the cabin felt empty, and the atmosphere hummed with the same tension as before, only worse now, as though her psyche were determined to make her acknowledge that things had changed, that maybe being alone wasn't what she wanted anymore.

But she'd fallen into that trap once before, following the urges to New York, and from there into marriage. She'd learned her lesson, hadn't she?

Working on autopilot, she made coffee, grimacing when she pawed through the grocery bags and checked the refrigerator. The brands weren't the ones she would have chosen, the selection somewhat haphazard, serving to drive home the reality she'd been trying to avoid facing since the previous night, when she'd stepped inside the cabin and felt like the space wasn't hers anymore. Lee had destroyed her photos and knickknacks. He'd eaten her food, sat on her furniture and done heaven only knew what else to her personal space. And whatever the crime-scene analysts hadn't needed, the cleaners had taken care of. Her home had been stripped of character, her touch erased, leaving her to start over yet again.

But when tears threatened to blur her vision, she dashed them away, irritated with herself. "They're just things. Get over it."

Except Lee hadn't taken only her things. He'd also taken a big chunk of her self-respect and her ability to trust, and he'd driven a deeper wedge between her and her parents. They hadn't left because they'd needed to get away from Bear Claw. They'd left because they'd wanted to get away from her and the intrusive media presence she'd brought into their lives. She'd tried not to blame them, but just as they'd stayed on the road when she'd wanted to settle down, and settled down just as she was ready to leave the nest, her parents had done what they needed for each other, not what she'd needed from them.

That wasn't news, or even much of a surprise, but it had stung nonetheless. Was it so much to ask that someone care for her for her own sake?

"And aren't we feeling self-pitying this morning?" she said aloud. "Get over it. You're alive and in protective custody, and sooner or later this thing is going to break." God willing. And when it did, when Lee and al-Jihad and the rest of them were all off the street, then she'd be free to start over. Again.

Needing to keep busy while her brain churned, she pulled together a basic breakfast from the supplies at hand, and refilled the coffeemaker after she'd downed her second cup. By the time Gray returned, she had prepared scrambled eggs and toasted bagels, and found paper plates and plastic utensils among the bagged supplies. She was trying not to think about what Lee had probably done to her dishes. They had been inexpensive warehouse-store purchases, but she'd liked the repeating motifs of birds and pinecones.

Gesturing with the package of plates, she said, "Can I impose on you to take these outside, or can the agents take turns coming in or something?

Gray scowled, temper lighting his eyes. "I told you we'd fend for ourselves."

She would've snapped in response, except that she thought she caught a thread of something else beneath the anger, a hint that looked almost like desperation, and told her this wasn't about eggs, or even the case. Setting down the plates, she crossed to the coffeepot, very deliberately poured a second mug and carried it over to him. She held it out, partly a peace offering, partly a dare. "No," she said, keeping her tone reasonable, "you said I should suit myself, which I did, by making breakfast for everyone."

He stared down at her for a long moment. Then he muttered something under his breath, and took the coffee. "Seriously, it's not your responsibility to feed us."

"I need to do something, or I'll go insane," she said reasonably. At least she thought it was reasonable.

He dipped his head in a half nod. "That much I get. Okay. Thanks. I'll let them know they can come in on a rotation." But he didn't leave, didn't turn away, just stood there holding the mug of coffee, staring down at her.

Mariah held her ground, refusing the sudden urge to fuss with her hair or check if she had a smattering of bagel crumbs on her cheek. The damn electricity that had gotten them in trouble before sparked in the air between them now, as his expression went from fierce and annoyed to something softer. The sight of it brought a warm twist low in her belly, and her voice threatened to shake when she said, "If you're trying to come up with an apology for being an ass, don't worry about it. This isn't exactly a normal situation."

"Not an apology," he said, "an explanation for why I'm not comfortable with the whole breakfast thing."

"You've got a lifelong bacheloresque fear of having a woman cook you breakfast?" she asked, and for the first time she realized that while he knew some of the most intimate details of her life, she knew almost nothing about his.

"I was married," he said, surprising her because she'd pegged him as the "never been married, never wanted to be married" type. He continued, "More than that, I liked being married. I liked coming down and smelling coffee and toast, or getting up first and putting something together for the two of us. That's something I miss." He paused. "The last time anyone made me breakfast was the morning of the bombings."

Mariah sucked in a breath as the world closed in around her. "Your wife was in one of the malls?"

He shook his head, but his expression didn't clear. "No, Stacy's alive and well, remarried and living in L.A. We'd just gotten separated—it was her idea, though I think we both knew it wasn't working. I went to stay with friends out here in Colorado—my college roommate, Ken, his wife, Trish, and their six-month-old baby, Catherine. My goddaughter." He paused. Mariah would've said something, but all of the air seemed to have been sucked from her lungs, rendering her silent as he continued, "They wanted to cheer me up, so Trish made a big breakfast late that morning, we went and picked out a Christmas tree and then we headed over to the local mall so they could take Catherine's picture with Santa." He broke off then and took a long swallow of the scalding-hot coffee, but didn't seem to notice the heat.

"Gray," Mariah began.

"I was standing in line with them," he continued as if she hadn't spoken, "and God help me, I was frustrated as hell, and getting mean. I was jealous of Ken—the guy who'd been my wingman in college, my good friend in the years since. He was so damn happy, he and Trish were so good together, and baby Catherine was so perfect… I couldn't take it anymore. I said something to them—I don't even remember what—and I took off. I just needed a minute alone, needed to find a way to stop hating my buddy for having everything that I wanted." He spread his hands away from his body and looked at her, hollow-eyed. "I was sitting on a bench near this fountain, maybe a few hundred yards away, when the bomb went off."

Mariah would've touched him, would've soothed him if she could've figured out how. But he looked so closed off, standing there with pain in his eyes and his body language telling her to keep away, that he didn't want sympathy or understanding, didn't want anything but to punish himself.

"Gray," she said again.

This time he heard her. He looked at her, seeming to see her now, and his voice went harsh when he said, "So yeah, that's an apology for my being less than gracious over your offer of breakfast. And it's an explanation for a whole bunch of other things, isn't it?"

"You're not going to move on until you're sure your friends have gotten justice," she said, making it a statement rather than a question. Her chest ached for a family she hadn't known, and Gray who'd suffered one blow on top of another, for no other reason than he'd been in the wrong place at the wrong time.

In that, she thought, they finally had something in common. Neither of them had done the wrong thing to begin with, but the domino effect of decisions they'd made had led to terrible consequences nonetheless.

"The baby was partly shielded by her parents' bodies," he said, his voice raw. "I got her out and pulled rank to get her on the first ambulance out of there, triage be damned. They tried... I know they tried. I was sitting outside the PICU when she passed twenty-two hours later. I've been trying to wipe al-Jihad and his network off the face of the planet ever since, and I don't intend to stop until I do it, or die trying."

He said the latter so matter-of-factly that she believed, with absolute certainty, that he would willingly lose his own life if he could be sure of taking the terrorists with him.

What would it be like, she wondered, to be the focus of an emotion that intense, coming from a man capable of such feeling?

"I'm sorry," he said, "that was probably way more than you wanted or needed to know." He turned away, heading for the door. "I'll tell the others to come in and get food. Stay put for an hour and don't give them any grief, okay? I need to walk."

She told herself to let him go, that it would be better for both of them if she did. Instead, she said, "Wait."

He paused, glancing back. "Yeah?"

"I'm coming with you. You don't know these woods they way I do."

His eyes went unreadable. "Thanks for the concern, but I found my way up here just fine the other day. Trust me, I won't get lost."

"No, but you won't find what you're looking for, either."

"Which is what?"

"Peace," she said simply. "A place where you can sit and think, or clear your mind and just let yourself forget for a little while." She almost held out a hand to him, but thought better of it and walked past him to grab a jacket and shove her feet into a pair of hiking boots.

"You're not leaving the cabin," he said, but it was a weak protest.

"Bring the others if you want, or bring some of them and leave the rest here to guard our backs," she said, suddenly realizing that she needed to make the visit for her own purposes as well. "I really think we should go. I think... I'm sure that if I can just clear my head, I'll be able to remember what Lee said. I can't do that here after all. Maybe I'll be able to do it where we're going."

"Where is that?" he asked, and she knew she had him.

Now she did hold out a hand to him. "Come on. I'll show you."

Chapter 8

Protocol said they should stay in the cabin, but as far as Gray was concerned, protocol—or rather Johnson's stubborn adherence to protocol regardless of the situation—had hampered the investigation too much for too long.

Besides, Johnson was off chasing other leads. The SAC hadn't said as much, but Gray knew his boss held little hope of Mariah being able to help at this point. That was why Johnson had agreed so readily to the op up at the ridgeline cabin, and why he'd assigned a handful of relatively junior agents to the protective detail. Which was just fine as far as Gray was concerned, because it gave him greater leeway than he would've had otherwise—including the leverage to fall in with Mariah's plan of hiking out into the woods to meditate. If they were lucky, it'd smooth out the edges they were both feeling, allowing her to relax and access her memories of being incarcerated.

He was rationalizing—he knew it. Logic dictated that they should stay put in the cabin, that Mariah should try working with the self-hypnosis protocols the profiler, Thorne, had given her. Instead, they were going for a damn walk, not just because Mariah thought it would help her remember, but because he'd dumped his story on her, and in the aftermath she'd recognized that if he didn't get out of the cabin, didn't burn off some of the restless, edgy energy that always gathered when he thought about the day of the bombing, the consequences could be dire.

He'd thought he had the memories and the rage under control. Apparently, he'd been dead wrong.

Mariah led the way along the narrow, wooded trail, which was on a slight upgrade that headed up the mountain. Gray hiked immediately behind and off to the right of her, keeping a sharp eye on the scene ahead of them, ready to shield her if necessary. Behind him ranged three of the junior agents, one of whom had clearly let his gym time lag. Gray could hear the guy puffing with the effort of the climb, and felt zero sympathy.

They were all on high alert, though there had been no sign of anyone else in the woods. They'd barely seen any wildlife, either, just trees and more trees, with glimpses of the leaden gray sky becoming more frequent as they climbed higher and the forest thinned slightly.

Gray's blood hummed with tension and exertion, clearing his mind and sharpening his senses.

The dull snap of the damp leaves and twigs beneath their boots was a rhythmic counterpoint to the rasp of their breaths, occasionally highlighted by the cry of a gliding hawk or eagle. The air moved through the tree-tops in a steady flow, forming a whisper of background noise that took the edges off the churned-up feelings inside him. The air smelled of pine and rain, with an overtone of rot from the fallen trees that littered the forest floor, slowly returning to the soil they'd sprung from. And though Gray knew it was his imagination, or wishful thinking that everything could've been different between them, as he walked, he swore he could taste Mariah on his lips. They'd only kissed once, but her feel and flavor were locked into his sensory memory.

Ahead of him, she walked with loose, swinging strides. She didn't look around, keeping her attention fixed on the root-strewn trail, but somehow he knew she was completely aware of her surroundings, fully tuned in to the forest.

After a half hour or so, she turned off the path and picked her way up a steep incline, using gnarled pine roots as footholds. When Gray followed, he saw that the roots she'd used were worn smooth. And when she paused on a narrow ledge and waited for him to catch up, he found that she'd led him to a small cave that had been invisible from below, shielded by overgrown scrub and a trick of light and angles.

"The others should wait here," she said. "It's tight quarters in the cave. It'll be too crowded and distract-ing with five of us in there."

Gray couldn't argue, especially after the three ju-nior agents had reached the ledge, forcing him to crowd her practically into the cave mouth. But he frowned. "There's no way your ex could know about this place?"

She shook her head. "I moved here after he was locked up, and this cave isn't on any of the maps that

I'm aware of. It's not part of any of the old mine systems, and we're way off the beaten tourist path."

"You found it," he pointed out.

She glanced at him and hesitated a moment, as if weighing her answer. Then she said, "I told you how my parents were always moving around? Well, my grandfather didn't—he lived in Montana, in a set of woods not unlike these. I spent as much time there as my folks would let me, and whenever I visited, Grandpa took me out hiking. In part, I think he was trying to wear me out so I'd stop talking—I loved to talk to him, because it felt like he really listened." She paused and flicked a glance beyond Gray to the other agents. Lifting a shoulder in a self-conscious half shrug, she finished, "Anyway, he was a woodsman from way back, sometimes hunting wildlife, though mostly shooting with his camera by the time I came along. He taught me how to read the woods, and how to find my way home."

Gray wanted to tell her to clue him in on that last part, because it had been a long time since he'd been someplace that felt like home. That had been a large part of his snappishness that morning—the realization that coming into her cabin and finding her in the kitchen, surrounded by the smells of morning and warmth, had felt far too natural, bringing a wistful ache.

They were different in more ways than he could count. So why did it sometimes seem as if they clicked on levels he hadn't even known would get to him?

"It's not safe," one of the junior agents said from behind him. It took Gray a moment to figure out that the other man was talking about the cave.

"We'll be fine," Gray said, before he realized that he'd made the decision. He glanced back at the others.

"Stay here and keep watch. I doubt the radios will work in the cave, so if we get in trouble, we'll fire a couple of warning shots. If we're not back in three hours, come in after us." He fixed the third, lagging agent with a look. "And while you're waiting, maybe you can talk to these guys about joining a damn gym." When he turned back to Mariah, he caught the hint of a grin. "What?"

"For a second there, you sounded like your boss."

Gray shuddered. "Please." Gesturing to the cave, he said, "Lead on."

She pulled a midsized flashlight out of her back pocket. Snapping it on, she directed the yellow cone of light into the cave. "Follow me."

With a final warning look at the junior agents, whom he suspected had also been tasked with keeping tabs on him for Johnson's benefit, Gray ducked through the scrub guarding the cave mouth and moved inside.

The temperature immediately dropped a good ten degrees and the air dampened, sending a shiver down the back of his neck. The cave walls were raw and uneven, arching up and over him by a foot or so. The floor was a craggy mix of stone and dirt, the latter of which had been flattened in places by a woman's footprints, suggesting that Mariah came here often.

In a dozen long strides, he caught up with her as she forged ahead down the narrow arcade formed by the cave. "No offense, but this isn't exactly my idea of a meditation spot." He pitched his voice low, but the sound bounced off the rock walls, making it seem as though he'd shouted.

"Patience, Grasshopper. And silence is a virtue."

It surprised him to realize that he, a man who most often kept his own counsel, wanted to talk, the words coming from the fine hum of energy that ran through him. He didn't think it was nerves, exactly, but he didn't know what else to call it. Awareness, maybe, or the gut-deep sense that something important was about to happen.

He'd felt the same way once or twice on assignment, when his instincts had warned him that things were going south. He hadn't had any premonition the day of the bombing, though, or the day he'd ignored another agent's message and had nearly gotten a stadium full of innocents killed. Was it any wonder he didn't trust his own instincts? They sure as hell hadn't proven themselves when it counted.

"Through here," Mariah said, poking her head into what looked like a crack in the wall of the main cave. "Watch your head."

A hint of claustrophobia kicked in. "I don't know—"

"It opens up a short way in," she called back, her voice echoing strangely from within the small niche.

"I don't like feeling trapped."

"Who does? It's worth it, I promise. Trust me."

He wondered if she understood how rarely he trusted anything but rock-solid evidence. He didn't even trust himself half the time. Yet still, he ducked and followed, crab-walking toward the faint yellow glow of her flashlight, hoping to hell she'd considered the fact that he was considerably larger than she was.

The tight fit brought a second, stronger surge of claustrophobia, but he kept going, ignoring the way the rock touched him on all sides and snagged at his clothing. Moments later, he realized that he wasn't following the flashlight at all. He was headed toward daylight. Beyond, he could hear the sound of running water and the trill of a songbird.

The cave opening became clear, partly blocked by Mariah's body, which was silhouetted against the light. When he reached her, she took his hand, the gesture somehow managing not to bump up against the boundaries they'd set, seeming friendly rather than sexual, as if saying they were in this together. "Come on," she urged. "Take a look."

She drew him through the opening, onto another stone ledge like the one they'd come from. Only this one didn't overlook a forest path, he saw when he straightened to his full height. It overlooked a mountain paradise.

The small bowl of grass-covered earth was bounded on all sides by high rock walls, though dark niches here and there suggested that their particular cave wasn't the only way in or out. In almost the exact center of the bowl, a pool of water formed a nearly perfect circle, fed by a tall, cascading waterfall that accounted for the roaring noise. At the opposite side, a narrow outflow disappeared between a pair of rock slabs that leaned into each other, forming a small triangular gap at their bases.

The ledge where Mariah and Gray stood was twenty, maybe thirty feet up from the grassy floor, giving them a breathtaking vantage point without distancing them from the splendor of the view.

"What do you think?" Mariah asked softly, not looking at him.

"You promised me peace," he replied, his voice not echoing now that they were back outside. "I'd say you delivered." He could practically feel the tension melt away from him, thought he felt the same from her through their joined hands.

"Come on." She tugged him along the ledge, to where a treacherous-looking path wound down to the grassy floor.

He followed without protest, not feeling trapped anymore, but feeling humbled and somehow insignificant. Human. Very unlike the person he'd become over the past few years, who was more special agent than man, and who walked the thin line between justice and vigilantism.

She led him to the edge of the pool, where a flat rock hung over like a wide diving platform. Instead of the cool of the cave, the air beside the water was mild, and the spray from the cataract felt warm on the exposed skin of his hands and face.

"Is there a hot spring underneath?" he asked, pitching his voice so Mariah could hear him over the thunder of water.

She lifted her free hand in a gesture of "Who knows?" "Either that or the bowl somehow creates a miniclimate of its own. I'm a photographer, not a scientist. The water's warm, that's for sure."

Which reminded him of something that got his gut twinging. "The pictures Lee wrecked. Were they of this place? Could he follow them here?"

She shook her head. "No, those were older pictures, ones I'd taken before I met Lee. Once he and I got married, there never seemed to be time for me to shoot pictures, or I was never in the mood. It wasn't until later that I realized that was another way he was controlling me. Then, after the attacks there was the trial and all the problems with my parents and the media, and there was no way I could see beauty in the world the way I used to." She paused. "I only started taking pictures again a

few months ago, after I found this place. It gave me…
perspective, I guess you could say. Maybe it'll do the
same for you."

And maybe it'll help you remember, he thought about
saying, but didn't because he recognized the urge for
what it was: a cop-out, a pretense that this was about
the case rather than the two of them, and the simpatico
connection that had grown between them whether either of them liked it or not. So rather than deflecting
the moment, he gave in to it, dropping down to sit at
the edge of the warm stone overhang, where a natural
depression formed a place where they could lean back
comfortably. He tugged her down beside him, no words
seeming necessary.

They sat there for a long moment, watching the waterfall. The liquid curtain was both hypnotic in its relentless rhythm and surprising in the endless variety of
patterns that arose from water falling along the exact
same path.

After a while, he said softly, "I don't remember the
last time I talked about Ken, Trish and the baby. I guess
I got tired of everyone telling me their deaths were on
al-Jihad and his people, not on me. But the whole mall
trip was Trish's idea of how to get me out of my own
head. She said she just wanted to see me smile."

"What would they say if they saw you now?"

Gray winced at the question he'd consciously avoided
asking himself more than once before. "Doesn't matter. They're dead."

"You're not."

"Aren't you supposed to be meditating?"

She shot him a "gotcha" look from beneath her

lashes, but fell silent and returned her attention to the waterfall.

Gray watched the patterns of the cataract, and the tumbling swirls of impact where the fall met the pond. The moist, warm air melted into him, relaxing him, and the skimming patterns, coupled with the thunderous white noise of the waterfall, made him dizzy, then slid him toward a light doze.

He didn't mean to fall asleep, didn't know how long he was out, but when he awakened the cloud cover had broken and sunlight was streaming down, lighting the glen and refracting through the mists that gathered where the waterfall hit the pool below. Rainbows grew from the mists, making him think he was still dreaming because in his experience, such beauty was the province of movies and fantasy, not the hard, bloody grit of the real world.

It wasn't just the mist or the scenery, either. It was the woman beside him.

Mariah lay on her side facing him, propped up on one elbow, looking down at him expectantly, as though she'd been the one to wake him. Her dark hair was a riot of moisture-sprung curls, and her lips were wet and full, as they'd been the day before, right after he'd tangled with her in a kiss that they'd both agreed was a mistake, but that had felt like anything but.

When their eyes connected, the sun warmed a degree, and the rainbows gleamed a fraction brighter, which only confirmed what he'd suspected—that this was a dream. And because it was a dream, it was supremely natural for him to reach up to her, and for her to lean down, so they met halfway in a kiss that might not make sense in the real world, but was exactly right in this one.

* * *

Mariah saw the fuzzy warmth in his eyes, and knew he hadn't fully awakened when he reached for her, when he kissed her.

On one level she knew she should stop him, that they had tried this, and it hadn't left either of them in a good place. But the waterfall always left her warm and soft, and sharing this spot with him had wound up feeling far more intimate than she'd expected or intended. She'd meant to offer him a bit of peace to counteract the grief she'd seen in his face when he'd spoken of his dead friends. She'd also meant to find some peace for herself, and maybe use it to dredge up darker memories.

She'd found the peace but not the memory, and maybe it was partly that frustration that had her leaning into him and allowing the kiss. Welcoming it. Returning it. But that was only part of what had her twining her arms around his neck and shifting so they almost touched, so the air between them heated with the promise of that touch.

The rest was simple desire. Which wasn't simple at all.

Need spun through her, spiraling higher when he shifted against her, so his chest dragged against the sensitized tips of her breasts and his strong thighs tangled with her legs. She moaned, the soft sound carrying over the crash of the waterfall and jolting her to new awareness of what they were doing, and where.

More important, she remembered what was waiting for them back out in reality—namely, the knowledge that they weren't a good fit, and the presence of larger stakes, not just for the two of them but for the innocents she'd failed before. And in remembering that, she remembered something else: a happy image of a smiling clown face.

Adrenaline slashed through her. Breaking the kiss, she pulled back, grinning. "I think I know what Lee wants."

As a mood killer, that statement ranked pretty high.

Gray went very still, though she felt the tension in his body and the rapid beat of his pulse. His eyes darkened with something akin to regret. "For a second, I thought this was a hell of a dream."

"Sorry."

"Me, too." He disengaged and rolled away from her to lie on his back for a moment, breathing deeply, his eyes closed in concentration. When he opened them again, she saw not the man, but the soldier. "What did he say to you?"

She shook her head. "I can't remember precisely what he said. But I was sitting here doing some of the breathing exercises that profiler showed me, just letting myself drift, and I started getting panicky, and heard myself saying, 'No, no, no!'"

She didn't realize that she'd balled her hands into fists until she felt him take one in his own and uncurl her fingers to tangle them with his in a gesture that was more supportive than sexual, but brought a warm, steadying glow nonetheless. "I'm here," Gray said simply. "He's not. You're safe."

And because she was safe in this insulated place, with this good-hearted though closed-off man, in this moment in time, she was able to continue. "Just now, I saw an image, and I suddenly knew what he'd been asking me about. It was this little statuette I used to have, a ceramic figurine of a clown I kept in my curio cabinet."

Gray frowned. "Why would he want a piece of china?"

She shook her head, baffled. "I don't know. Maybe because it was one of the few things I ever stood up to him on. He didn't like it, thought it was silly and juvenile. After we got married and moved into the new house—I know, how old-fashioned, that we didn't live together first?—he told me to get rid of it a few times. I argued with him, and he let me keep it. For the longest time, though, I thought that was where the problems started in our marriage, with that damn ceramic clown."

Gray squeezed her fingers, bringing her attention to him. "What, exactly, did he want to know about the clown, and what did you tell him?"

"I didn't tell him anything," she said softly. "You know how they were waiting for someone the night I escaped from the cabin and you helped me get away? Well, something he said yesterday brought that memory, too. Al-Jihad was going to use drugs and torture to force me to talk…then Lee was going to kill me, to make sure I never talked again, ever."

"Mariah," he said, his voice soft of the syllables. "What did they ask, exactly?"

"Lee kept wanting to know where the clown was." The memory hurt, constricting her chest and making it hard to breathe. Bearing down on Gray's grip, letting him anchor her as the water thundered around them and the air sparkled with rainbows, she said, "I couldn't tell him. I already ruined their lives once. I couldn't do it again."

Gray exhaled. "Your parents have it."

She nodded, fighting to breathe. "It was my mother's. My father won it for her a long time ago at one of the carnivals they'd worked. I'd always had my eye on it—that one in particular—over all the other little figurines she'd collected. I played with it whenever I could persuade her to let me take it out of its case. She gave it to me the day I left for college, she said so I'd always remember her and my father, and the life I came from. I almost didn't take it, but I knew it was her way of apologizing, if only a little bit, for us not being the best match."

"Believe me, I know how that is," Gray said softly, and she didn't think he was talking about the case anymore. But then he continued, "How did she end up with the clown?"

"She asked for it." Mariah lifted a shoulder, trying to play it as if she'd understood, though she hadn't really. "Before they moved away, she said she'd like it back, as a reminder of better times. That was why I couldn't tell Lee. He would've gone after her, after both of them." She paused when a terrible thought occurred. "What if he has? Gray, what if—"

"Don't. Mariah, stop!" He shook her, interrupting her building panic. "They're fine, I promise. The FBI does this for a living, remember? We've had a team on your parents since about a half hour after I got you to the city that first night, when we realized you were still involved in this somehow."

"Oh." Mariah blew out a breath, then winced. "Oh. My mother's probably furious with me. If the neighbors find out they're under FBI surveillance and the media circus starts all over again…"

"They'll deal," Gray said firmly. "And so will you." He rose to his feet, drawing her up with him. "First things first, though. We need to have someone pick up that statuette." He paused. "Any idea why your ex wants the clown?"

"Other than to smash it? Not a clue. It's not hollow

or anything, so I can't see him hiding something inside it." But there was some logic to the idea. "He could be pretty sure I wouldn't get rid of it, though—he knew it had major sentimental value to me. Which begs the question of why he never did smash it. That's exactly the sort of thing he would've done—something he knew would hurt me, but that he could make into no biggie if I called him on it. 'It was an accident,' he'd say, or, 'I didn't know it meant that much to you.'"

"Since he didn't ruin it," Gray finished for her, "you have to wonder whether he was counting on you keeping it safe…say, for instance, if he spent some time in jail."

"You're right. Come on." Crouching, filling with new purpose, she scooped up her flashlight and headed for the cave entrance. When she didn't hear his footsteps right behind her, she paused and turned back, only to find Gray standing where she'd left him, staring at the waterfall with an odd look on his face. "What is it?"

When he glanced at her, that expression blanked to neutral. "Nothing. Let's go."

But as she led the way back out to the other special agents, and they began the process of contacting Johnson and having an Albuquerque field agent collect her mother's china clown as evidence, Mariah couldn't help thinking that, for the first time since she'd come to know Gray, he'd lied to her.

Whatever he'd been thinking just then, it hadn't been nothing. And he'd been looking at her when he'd thought it.

Gray spent a good half hour on the phone getting Mariah's parents pulled into protective custody over their apparently rather forceful protests, and seizing the ceramic clown from Mrs. Shore. Since she apparently had several dozen of the things and couldn't seem to remember which one she'd gotten back from Mariah, the field agents had bagged and tagged all of them, and were sending them to Bear Claw so Mariah could make a positive ID on the clown in question. So to speak.

Even as the conversation seesawed from deadly serious to mildly ridiculous and back again, Gray was hyperaware of Mariah's position in the cabin relative to his, conscious of her every move and breath. Maybe it was because he'd opened up to her about having lost what he'd practically considered his second family in the bombings; maybe it was the sense that they were finally on to something with this case, and that maybe, just maybe, they were getting close to nailing Mawadi. Whatever the reason, his perceptions of her—and his feelings toward her—had undergone a radical shift.

When he'd awakened by the waterfall and seen her leaning close, he hadn't been thinking of the case or the past as he'd reached up to kiss her. He'd been thinking only of the present. And in that moment, kissing her had been the most important thing in his universe.

She was nothing like the woman he'd thought she was in the first two sets of interviews, nothing like the woman he'd expected to find—or at least spy on—that day nearly a week earlier when he'd hiked up the ridge to the cabin where he was now headquartered, trying to track down a damn china clown her mother had ungifted her.

It might be unfair, but he wasn't getting a very good picture of her parents. His own hadn't been perfect— whose were?—but he'd never once questioned whether he and his sisters were their priority. Even when he'd disappointed them by splitting with Stacy, his parents had been on his side. Whatever he needed, they would've given him if he'd asked. He hadn't, of course. But it had helped to know that he could. Mariah didn't have that. As far as he could tell, she'd never had that from any source, except maybe from her grandfather.

"You still there?" a voice said in his ear, as the agent he'd been haranguing returned to their telephone conversation, having been scrambling down in the city, trying to get all the necessary facts.

"Waiting on you," Gray said, though he'd also been watching through the open bedroom door as Mariah moved furniture around. Having remembered what her ex was after, she'd declared herself done with sleeping in her erstwhile cell. She'd set about turning it back into a bedroom, at least as much as she could with the decorations and items Mawadi hadn't destroyed. Watching her, Gray didn't have the heart to tell her they wouldn't be staying long.

The agent on the other end of the line rattled off the info Gray had been holding for, which mostly consisted of negatives. No, there hadn't been any evidence that Mariah's abduction the day before had been a subterfuge designed to distract law enforcement from another prong of an attack. No, there hadn't been any indication that al-Jihad had reentered the country, and there had been no further word on Jane Doe. Everything was quiet. Too quiet, to Gray's mind. There was an itch along the center of his spine, a nagging sense that they were missing something, and it was something that was going to come back around and bite them, hard.

"And one last thing," the agent said in closing.

"Yes?"

"Johnson said, and I quote, 'Tell him to get his ass

down the damn mountain with the woman before all these clowns get here,' end quote." There was a thread of laughter in the guy's voice.

Yeah. Gray had a feeling he was never going to hear the end of the clown thing. "Got it," he said curtly. He signed off and clicked the phone shut, knowing that Mariah wasn't going to like the news.

He couldn't say he was a fan, either, though not for any particular reason he could specify. It was more of a vague disquiet, a sense that they shouldn't make the trip down to the city. But that didn't make any sense, either. He'd never been a cabin-in-the-woods kind of guy. The faint urge to stay another few days, or come back up after all this was over… Those were just situational urges. They'd disappear eventually.

Steeling himself, he joined Mariah in her bedroom, which was already looking more like a room than a jail cell. She'd gotten one of the junior agents to help her move a dresser in from the office, along with an end table and a small desk, and then accessorized with a couple of lamps and the few small pieces of bric-a-brac that had escaped her ex's taste for destruction. The bedclothes were new and she didn't have a rug or curtains, but the room already looked better. More important, at least to him, Mariah looked better. She seemed more settled. Steadier.

He hated having to take that away, to take her away. If it were up to him, he would've stayed the night, and… well, it didn't matter now, did it? "I'm sorry, Mariah," he said gruffly. "We've got to get back down to the city."

She surprised him by nodding. "I figured as much. Your boss will want me to ID the statuette, and probably add me to the protective custody my folks are under. Makes sense to guard us all in one place, right?"

He knew he shouldn't touch her. He did it anyway, a glancing caress on her cheek that brought her head up, brought her eyes to his.

"You're okay with this?" he asked, which was a stupid question, but still. He needed more from her than he was getting. He needed… Hell, he didn't know what he wanted, just that she'd awakened feelings in him that he'd never expected to feel again. She made him want, made him dream. Made him desire, though she was nothing like what he'd thought he wanted.

She met his eyes and laid her hand atop his, capturing his fingers against her cheek. Warmth kindled low in his belly, beside the twist in his gut that wouldn't go away. "I'll be okay," she said. "One of these days, I'll be just fine. And so will you."

"Mariah," he began, but she touched a fingertip to his lips, effectively silencing him.

"Not now," she said softly.

He was grateful she'd stopped him, because he didn't have a damn clue what he'd been about to say. So he went with a lame, "Do you want to pack anything for the trip back down?"

She shook her head. "The terrorists ruined the few things I really cared about."

"Join the club," he said, meaning it to come out light, and wincing when the effort fell flat.

They just stood there for a long moment, staring at one another, and the air hummed with the hard, edgy warmth that always surged through him when they were together, only it was sharper and hotter now, because he knew how she tasted and what she sounded like when she moaned into his mouth. He'd begun to know how her body felt against his, and burned to know more.

He wanted to kiss her, wanted to back her up until she sank down on that wide bed of hers. He wanted to touch every inch of her, worship her, take her. And in doing so, he wanted to give her new memories of the room, of her cabin. He wanted to superimpose his own stamp over the ruin her ex had made of her life. He didn't, though, because he knew, even in the throes of lust, that while he'd be a hell of a lot better for her than her ex had been, he still wasn't what she needed.

She deserved someone who would put her first the way nobody else had done before. She should be the center of someone's universe, the lodestone around which the family revolved. And he knew, deep down inside, that even if Lee, al-Jihad and the others were back behind bars—or dead—and the entire terror network dismantled, he couldn't be that man for her. Not because he didn't want to, but because he simply wasn't capable of it.

Stacy had called him cold and detached, and he was. At first she'd accused him of putting his work ahead of his family. Later, when she'd really stepped back and taken a long, hard look at his relationship with his parents, she'd changed that to encompass putting his work ahead of her, and she'd been right. He'd been so determined to find a perfect match, as his parents had—finding a woman from a cop family, one who would get what it meant to be married to a cop—that he hadn't stopped to really think about why his parents' marriage had worked. It wasn't because of the job or how his mother handled things. It was because his parents loved each other. Somehow Gray had lost track of that feeling, of how to find and keep it. He'd thought he loved Stacy, but really she'd simply been a good fit, or what he'd thought was a good fit. And he'd thought he'd loved Ken and Trish, and especially baby Catherine. But if that were the case, why hadn't he managed to catch and put away their killers by now?

Instead, here he was, on the verge of losing his job and obsessed with a woman who was more wrong for him than Stacy had ever been.

But knowing it, knowing how wrong he and Mariah were on paper, even though for some reason they seemed to click in person, he let his hand drop and stepped away. "Then if you're ready, we should get going."

She looked at him long and hard before she nodded. "I'm ready."

She headed for the door without hesitating, without looking back, and Gray got the distinct impression that they'd just agreed to far more than driving back down to the city. He was pretty sure they'd just agreed that it—whatever *it* had been starting to happen between them—was over.

Logic said he should be relieved.

Logic could go to hell.

"Mariah, wait," he said, taking two long strides to catch up to her. "Wait. I think we need to—"

He didn't get a chance to finish his thought, because at that moment the sound of gunfire erupted from the front of the cabin, there was a *whump* of detonation, and the world exploded around him.

Chapter 9

Mariah screamed as the flames engulfed the front room of the cabin. This wasn't happening, she told herself. This couldn't be happening. Only it could and it was.

"This way." Gray grabbed her arm with one hand, his weapon appearing in the other, held with deadly intent. "Out the back."

She started to follow him, then dug in her heels when she heard the crack of gunfire from out front, followed by a cry of pain. "Shouldn't we—"

"No," he said flatly. "We shouldn't. Right now, you're more important than they are." It was the soldier talking now, not the man, but she could tell that it cost him.

Another explosion detonated outside, and when she glanced through a window, she saw the two FBI vehicles in flames.

This time when Gray yanked at her, urging her out the back, she followed without protest, scrambling, stumbling, clinging to him because he was the one sure, solid thing she knew she could hang on to in the midst of chaos.

He stopped at the back door, took a look around the partially cleared office, grabbed a couple of lamps and set them near the door. Then he moved to a ruined coffee table, with two of four legs broken—Lee's handiwork. Made of hardwood, the tabletop was crisscrossed with rusted iron strapping and impregnated with old hand-forged nails, mute testimony that the wood had been reclaimed from one of the local mills.

Using the remaining two legs as handles, Gray lifted the flat wooden slab and nodded with grim satisfaction. "It'll do."

Mariah didn't have to ask for what, because she could guess—as a shield. They had to assume that Lee and the others had the rear exit covered.

Gray glanced back at her, his eyes steely with determination and rage. "Ready?"

No. "Yes."

"Let's go. Keep your head down and *move!*"

He kicked open the door and hurled the lamps out. Gunfire spat from the tree line, coming from two positions, one dead ahead of them, the other slightly to the right.

Holding up their makeshift shield, Gray rushed out the door. Mariah followed and got in the lee of the slab, ducking to stay below the protected level and keeping her feet moving. Gray angled them to the left, away from where the gunfire had come, and charged for the forest.

Grabbing an edge of the table, partly to help and partly to keep herself steady as they hurdled over the stumps she'd clear-cut for her own protection, Mariah ran for her life.

Gunfire chattered and bullets slammed into the heavy wood of the table, some of them pinging as they ricocheted off the embedded metal. A new, larger explosion ripped through the air, and heat scorched her skin.

She didn't look back, didn't need to. Lee had left the cabin standing as bait of his own, knowing how important her home was to her. Now, if he couldn't trap or kill her in it, he would destroy it, knowing how much the loss would hurt.

"No!" she screamed, denying the evil that she'd married.

"Are you hit?" Gray shouted, not looking back as he maneuvered them closer to the trees, shifting his grip to fire a few rounds off to their left, though she didn't know if he'd seen someone or was laying cover fire.

"No, I'm mad. Get us out of here so we can nail these bastards!" That was all that drove her now—less fear for her own safety and more the knowledge that she had to stay alive long enough to identify the statuette and help Gray and his people figure out why Lee had wanted the thing. For the first time, she thought she understood why and how Gray had subsumed his own life and needs for so long beneath the mantle of revenge. She only hoped she lived long enough to do the same.

Gunfire erupted from their unprotected side as they hit the tree line, stitching a line of bullet strikes in the forest floor just as the continued barrage from the other side finally took its toll on the wooden slab, which all but crumbled under the onslaught.

Tossing the tabletop, Gray grabbed Mariah's hand. "Come on!"

Together, they bolted into the woods.

Déjà vu ripped through her, and she had a crazy moment of profound gratitude that she was at least wearing shoes this time, and hadn't spent the previous five days tied to her own bed, drugged and disoriented.

Then again, she also wasn't trying to elude only two men. From the amount of chaos coming from the front of the cabin, where her Jeep and the other vehicles burned, smudging the air with choking smoke and the roar of fire, she knew Lee had come with a team. And, unlike Brisbane, it didn't seem as though they had any compunction about killing her this time.

So, clinging to Gray's hand as her only anchor in a storm of gunfire and insanity, she ran as hard and fast as she could.

Moments later came the sounds of pursuit, and a familiar voice shouting, "Get her! No, go around that way!"

At Gray's glance, she nodded and confirmed, "Lee."

He cursed as the sounds of pursuit intensified. "The others couldn't hold them."

She didn't ask if that meant the agents were dead; she didn't want to know just then. She could feel the guilt later. Right now, she and Gray needed to get out of there and back down to the city.

Realizing that they were running uphill, not down, she said, fitting the words between breaths as she began to labor with the effort, "Should we circle back to the cars?"

"The cars are gone," he reminded her. "What's up this way?"

"Trees."

"Damn."

Back when she'd bought the cabin, its isolation had been a blessing, its location suitable for her self-imposed penance. Now, she found herself wishing that she'd bought a condo in the city, where screaming for help might've gotten her somewhere.

"Let's stop here for a second." Gray pulled her into the lee of a big, lichen-covered boulder, then leaned back against it, breathing hard. "Quiet. I think they've stopped."

They strained to regulate their breathing, listening intently. Mariah could all but picture Lee and his men doing the same thing.

There was only silence. Either Lee and the others had stopped as well, they'd retreated…or they were creeping up on the boulder, soundlessly, aiming to surround her and Gray and gun them down where they stood. That thought brought a huge shiver crawling down Mariah's back, and she unconsciously moved closer to the man who, thus far, had consistently chosen retreat over attack in an effort to keep her safe, despite his claims that he'd turn her over if it meant he'd get justice for his friends and the others.

She was vaguely surprised when Gray curled an arm around her and hugged her to his side. "I've got you," he whispered, not looking at her, but instead scanning the forest around them.

Yes, a small voice whispered inside her, *but who's got you?* He stood alone so often, apart from his so-called teammates. His boss didn't like him; his wife had divorced him; he didn't speak about his family; he felt responsible for the deaths of his closest friends; and his only living friend that she knew of, Jonah Fairfax, was engaged to be married to a special agent-in-training and was off on a vendetta of his own, trying to track down his former boss, agent-turned-traitor Jane Doe.

For a man Mariah had initially thought of as just another cog in the FBI machine that seemed determined to tear her life and family apart, Gray had turned out to be as much of a loner as she was, if not more so, with one main difference: she sought solitude, while he carried his with him.

When there was no sound or movement from the direction of the cabin, Gray eased his arm from around Mariah to dig into his pocket and pull out his long-range cell phone. "Hopefully, one of the other agents got off a mayday and reinforcements are already on their way up." He punched a speed-dial button, then held the phone to his ear. "Won't hurt to follow up, though. Johnson should be able to get a chopper up here."

There were too many *hopefullys* and *ifs* in that statement, Mariah knew. Her fear was confirmed when Gray cursed, stabbed a couple more buttons on the phone, then flipped it shut and shoved it back into his pocket.

"What's wrong?"

"Signal's jammed."

He didn't give her time to process that, or what it might mean. Instead, he pushed away from the boulder and held out a hand. "Come on, we need to—" He broke off when a new sound encroached on the silence: the low thump of helicopter rotors.

"Yours?" Mariah asked hopefully. Was their rescue at hand so quickly?

"Maybe." But he didn't sound optimistic. He glanced at her, and there was worry in his gray eyes. "The timing doesn't quite mesh, unless Johnson had the bird on its way up the ridge already, which he wouldn't have had any reason to do."

A chill settled into her bones. "Then it's al-Jihad's."

"Could be." He took her hand and tugged her along. "Could just be sightseers or flight lessons."

"All the way out here?"

"Yeah. Not likely. And if they're coming after us, we have to assume they're prepared for a forest search this time—infrared, night vision, the works." He took a long look around at their surroundings. "It'll be dark soon, and there's no way we can chance looping back around to the cabin. Better to hole up for the night and try to get to cell range in the morning." He paused. "How far are we from that cave of yours?"

Determined not to panic, not to despair, Mariah took a good look around, followed by a glance at the setting sun, and forced her voice to sound level. "A mile, maybe more. I'm pretty sure there's a river between here and there. It's fordable, but we'll get wet."

"We'll have to chance it," he decided. "The water could be to our benefit if they bring in tracking dogs."

She shivered at the thought. It seemed unbelievable that this could be happening. Less than an hour earlier she'd been under full FBI protection. Now she and Gray were cut off and on their own. "Won't your boss figure out that something's wrong when you guys don't check in on schedule?"

"Of course, but depending on what's going on with the case, he might send a single car up to see if our communications went down, rather than sending in the cavalry right away. That'll take time." Gray lifted a hand and touched her cheek in a gesture that was more reassuring than sensual, though there was heat there, as well. "Can you take me back to your cave?"

She hesitated as something deep inside her warned that that was a bad idea, that too much had changed too quickly between them, but what other choice did she have? His logic was irrefutable; they needed someplace safe to hide for the night. She didn't know anyplace better than the cave system leading to the secret waterfall. Dammit.

Hating the thought of bringing fear and uncertainty into her small zone of peace, hating that Lee was taking that from her, too, she nodded and firmed her chin. "Follow me."

She led the way and he fell in behind her, each of them straining to hear the sounds of pursuit. The chopper noise passed over them and faded, but Mariah knew that was no guarantee either way. Maybe the terrorists were conferring over search plans. Maybe the agents had gotten a message through and reinforcements had already arrived at the burning cabin. They just didn't know, and couldn't risk going back to take a look.

For now, hiding was her and Gray's best and only option. Tomorrow, they'd find some way to fight back, or die trying.

It took them nearly an hour to reach the cave. The river crossing was shallow, but the water current was stronger than Gray would've liked, the flow tugging halfway up his thighs as they fought their way upriver, working to confuse trackers. They were most of the way to where Mariah had indicated they should climb out, when the chopper's rotor thump returned.

Without a word, working in the strange synchrony

that kept developing between them when he least expected it, they both dropped down into the water, submerging themselves almost completely.

The cold water killed their heat signatures instantly, and the helicopter passed overhead without incident. In the last of the fading light, Gray looked up at the passing bird and got a glimpse of a sleek-nosed shape with regulation FAA tail numbers but no official seal. Not FBI, then. Maybe rented, maybe private. Almost certainly al-Jihad.

When the helicopter had moved on, he and Mariah dragged themselves to the riverbank, and up and out of the water, shivering. The night air cut quickly through their wet clothing, making the chill even worse.

"We need to get moving," he said, the words coming out shaky as his jaw chattered.

She nodded, but didn't speak, and she didn't protest when he took her hand and walked at her side rather than bringing up the rear guard. Helping each other, leaning into one another for warmth, they staggered onward. By the time they crawled up the rock face leading to the hidden ledge, it was fully dark and he was all but carrying her, with his arm looped around her waist, hers around his neck. She was shivering and in shock, but she hadn't complained, hadn't given up.

The moon was out, which was a damn good thing, since they didn't have even her small flashlight. When they got inside the cave, he lit the way with his cell phone—stupid thing couldn't call out, but at least it was water-resistant enough that it was still working, and the display light was good for something.

His initial intention had been for them to spend the night in the cave itself, but the dip in the river had changed the direction of his thoughts. They needed to get warm. In the absence of matches, a lighter or any certainty that either of them could start a fire from scratch, and not being sure a campfire was the best idea, even inside the cave, his next best choice was to keep going, all the way to the hidden glen with its strangely warm water.

"Will the pool be warm enough to camouflage us if they fly over?" Mariah asked softly. She'd all but stopped trembling, which was a bad sign, indicating that her body was starting to shut down on her.

The real answer to her question was "We don't have a choice," followed by "If it's warm enough to hide us, it's warm enough to show up on infrared, which could mean they might give it a second or third look." But Gray knew she needed more from him than that, so he said, "Absolutely." And, as they neared the smaller offshoot that would lead them to the hidden canyon, he hoped it wasn't a lie.

"Wait here. I'll be right back." Mariah paused, took the phone and moved away from him, stumbling a little as she walked deeper into the main branch of the cave. Gray did as she'd ordered, but he tracked her progress by the glow of the phone and the small sounds she made, and held himself ready to go after her, if necessary.

He heard the sound of rock shifting against rock, and called out, "What's going on over there? You have this place outfitted with a secret door that leads straight back to the city?"

"Not quite that good, but I think it'll help." She returned, carrying his phone in one hand and a battered, dusty canvas knapsack in the other. "I built a cairn a little farther in and stashed some emergency supplies in case…well, just in case. We've got some energy bars, water, a blanket and a first aid kit. Not exactly the comforts of home, but it'll help."

"Any matches?"

"Yeah, but they're soaked. One of the water bottles leaked."

"Bummer," Gray said, but felt something ease in his chest when she rejoined him. At the same time, something else tightened within him.

This wasn't just the place she'd come for peace, he realized. It had also been her bolt-hole. If she were outside the cabin's perimeter when the alarms sounded, she'd intended to come here and hide. The knowledge wasn't surprising; she'd proven herself a survivor time and again. What was surprising was the hard squeeze that caught him beneath his heart, and the sadness that accompanied it.

The system had failed her so badly that she'd felt the need to protect herself in isolation. Worse, he'd been part of that system. In the process of trying to save the world from the terrorists' threat and gain justice for Ken and his family, Gray had lost sight of some of the other people involved. He'd seen Mariah alternately as an asset or an obstacle. He'd forgotten to remember that she was also one of the innocents he was charged with protecting.

In the blue-white light from the cell phone, her expression shifted to one of worry. "What's wrong?"

"I'm sorry." He took the knapsack from her, let her keep the phone for the dim glow it provided.

She frowned. "For anything in particular?"

For most of it, he realized. He was sorry for how he'd treated her and her family during the first round of the investigation; sorry that al-Jihad and his conspirators had outsmarted some of the country's best and brightest to escape from the ARX Supermax; sorry that once they had, she'd been treated with more suspicion than compassion, and hadn't felt safe in her own home. Hell, she hadn't *been* safe in her own home, and even once she'd gotten free, Gray had turned around and put her right back in harm's way. It didn't matter that she'd volunteered to become bait, he should've been man enough, agent enough, to say *no thanks* and tuck her into protective custody, far away from Bear Claw City. Instead, he'd used her and nearly gotten her killed. More than that, he'd kissed her. He'd known she was growing attached to him and hadn't done anything about it.

But he was too much of a coward to tell her that, so he focused on the matter at hand, on the failure of the system. "I'm sorry the FBI wasn't there for you, and that you figured you were better off alone than under our protection."

Her expression flattened to something he couldn't quite interpret, but she said only, "Come on. I'm freezing."

He ducked and followed her through the narrower offshoot cave, breathing a sigh of relief when they emerged once again out into the open.

The air warmed palpably, and the hidden valley spread out beneath them, the waterfall close enough to touch. Moonlight bathed the scene, a magnificent display of blue-white light that sparkled on the plunging waterfall and the rioting surface of the pool below, all of it cast over by the mist, which had thickened as the night air cooled.

Gray paused, awestruck by the beauty of the scene.

But he knew there were more practical, immediate issues to deal with. They needed to get warm, and quickly.

"Come on." He holstered his weapon, which by his count had a scant four or five rounds left in it, shifted the bulky knapsack onto his shoulder and held out a hand to Mariah.

They helped each other down the narrow path to the flat rock, which was damp and slippery with condensation, and shrouded in mist. The moist air beaded on Gray's hands and face, and the contrast between the warmth of the stone and the damp chill of his clothes made him long for the hot, dry warmth of a fire.

The thought made him flash on his last sight of Mariah's cabin. He'd looked back as they had fled, and had seen flames licking from the front of the log structure, devouring the porch.

He wanted to believe that the other agents had gotten to safety, that the gunfire they'd heard had been a rearguard action, but he feared that wasn't the case. The cabin was gone. His backup was gone. And Lee and the others were on the hunt.

The terrorists had torched the cabin, indicating that they knew full well that the statuette wasn't there. But was that because Lee had searched the place top to bottom while he'd been in residence...or was it because someone privy to the investigation itself had leaked information on the great clown roundup down in Albuquerque? If the latter, what did it mean in terms of the FBI's response when the ridgeline team failed to check in at midnight? Would a conspirator within Johnson's group try to delay their rescue?

"Hey," Mariah said, breaking into his reverie. "Turn it off for a little bit. Right now we need to concentrate on getting warm, having a snack, maybe scouting one of the other caves as an escape route and then bunking down as safely as possible. There's nothing more we can do until daylight."

"Yeah. I know." But he shook his head. "This wasn't how it was supposed to happen, you know?"

"Story of my life." She dropped his hand, and, with her eyes on his, took a couple of steps back until she was all but obscured by the mist. "I'm serious, though. I think we should turn it off and think of something else."

It wasn't until he heard the plop of wet cloth hitting the rock ledge that he realized he was staring at her.

"Mariah," he said, the word coming out on a soft growl. "What are you doing?"

"My clothes are soaked. I'm taking them off and hanging them off the backside of the rock in hopes that they'll dry a little while I'm hot-tubbing it, so to speak." The practicality of the response was somewhat undercut by the faint tremor in her voice, one that spoke more of nerves than chill, and turned her tone husky when she said, "I think you should do the same."

He wanted to, more than he'd wanted to do just about anything else, ever. But hadn't he just been thinking of all the things he'd done wrong when it came to her? He didn't think he could add "took advantage of her at a particularly vulnerable time" to the list and still look himself in the eye afterward.

Though a large part of him wanted to do just that, and damn the consequences.

Keeping his voice gentle when it wanted to go rough, he said, "You've had a hell of a day, on top of a hell of a week. Don't do something you'll regret later on, when all this is over and we go back to our normal lives."

He thought the corners of her mouth turned up in a small, sad smile, though he couldn't be sure in the moonlight and mist. "What's normal? My cabin is gone. Even if part of it is salvageable, I won't be able to live there by myself again and feel safe. Even if Lee's out of the picture, how will I know that another one of al-Jihad's men won't come after me?"

There it was again, her basic, well-earned distrust of the system. Gray wanted to tell her to have some faith, but who was he to talk?

Half the time he went around his boss, trying to do what he thought was best. In that, he and Mariah weren't so different. They were very different in all the other ways that mattered, though. Or, rather, they were too alike to be compatible—both hardheaded and stubborn, and too used to fixing their own problems rather than working as part of a team. Which by all rational inter-pretations of right and wrong meant he should turn away while she finished undressing and slipped beneath the surface of the swirling pool.

But he didn't.

He kept watching as she shimmied out of her shirt and panties, and unhooked her bra, each motion cam-ouflaged by the mist, letting him see impressions but not details, lending romance to something that should have been simple expediency, but had become some-thing more.

"You'll get through this," he said with quiet certainty, even as his blood heated and his heart set an increas-ing tempo. "You're going to get through this and come out the other side, and you're going to make the life you want. Maybe you'll make up with your parents, maybe not. Maybe you'll rebuild the cabin, maybe not. You'll make those choices for yourself, not anyone else, and you'll figure out what comes next. I have faith in that, in you, and I'm not a man who's big on faith."

This time her smile was more genuine. "Yeah. That much I've figured out." She let the bra dangle from her fingertips, then drop to the stone surface. She took one step toward him. Then another.

Gray's breath caught at the moonlight-limned sight of her. He drew his eyes from her gracefully muscled calves up the long, curving sweep of her thighs and hips, along the dip of her waist to the symmetrical globes of her breasts, which were tipped with dark, pouting aureolas and nipples that puckered in the warm moist air, crinkling under his regard.

"Mariah," he said again, this time not in warning but almost as a plea.

Don't ask me to do this, one part of him wanted to say, while another, equally strong part wanted to say, *Don't stop, come closer, let me touch you.*

"Gray," she said in answer, stopping very close to him, so her eyes dominated his vision and his breath came thin in his lungs. "Don't worry, I don't think this is love, or even the beginning of something that will last beyond tonight. But over the past few days, I've had good reason to take stock of my life. I've thought about the things I'd regret doing, and regret *not* doing, if Lee gets me before you get him."

Her words were matter-of-fact, and they brought a deathly chill to his gut. "I won't let that happen."

"Maybe you should." She held up a hand when he started to argue. "I'm not saying I want to die—absolutely not. But you said it yourself—there might come a time when saving me might mean letting him go. If that happens, I hope you'll do the right thing."

"I will," he said, his voice harsh. "I'll get you the hell out of there and stick you in protective custody where you should've been all along. Then I'll get a team back out there, and go after the bastard."

"And what will he have done in the meantime?" Her eyes were sad, but resolute. "How many people died in the bombings? How many would've died if al-Jihad's plan to destroy the stadium hadn't been foiled?"

"But it was."

"We might not be so lucky the next time, and you know it. Tell me I'm wrong."

He wanted to grab her and shake some sense into her. He wanted to protect her, to kiss her, to make love to her, to throw his head back and shout at the moon, railing against the unfairness of it, the cruelty of men who destroyed for nothing more than their own pleasure, though they might disguise it as something else. Men like her ex and al-Jihad.

"Tell me," she pressed.

"You're not wrong," he admitted, though the words laid him bare.

"Then knowing that, knowing what you might have to do in the next couple of days, tell me you'll do me a favor."

"What favor?"

"I don't want my biggest regret to be that Lee was my first and only lover."

Shock rattled through Gray, followed by understanding and a sharp twist of grief for the purity that an evil man had used for his own purposes. "Mariah," he said, voice catching in his throat, "no." He wasn't sure if he was denying her words or the greedy leap inside him, the one that wanted her, that would take her on the thinnest of excuses.

She lifted a shoulder in a half shrug, and though her eyes were full of uncertainty, there was only acceptance in her voice when she said, "Your call, Gray. If the answer is no, your reasons are your own, and I'll respect them, as I've come to respect you." She touched her lips to his, bringing a spike of heat and a thrill of passion to the complicated mix of emotions that tangled together inside him. "Just as I'll still respect you if you say yes."

Her lips left his as she backed off a few steps. Then she turned, dove cleanly into the warm water and was gone, leaving him standing on the stone overlook, trying to figure out what had just happened to turn his world inside out. And what the hell he was going to do, when what he wanted to do conflicted so thoroughly with what he knew was right.

Chapter 10

Mariah told herself she was trembling because of the cold, but even her conscious mind knew that was a crock. She was wired tight, her body humming with nerves as her immediate future hung balanced on the knifepoint of Gray's choice.

She held her breath, hovering beneath the churning water, which warmed her flesh as she tried to guess what he would decide. Would she surface to see him sitting cross-legged at the edge of the stone ledge, watching over her as she bathed, protector but not lover? Or was he even now stripping down to the hard body she'd felt beneath his clothing, preparing to dive into the pool naked, in tacit agreement with her plan?

She stayed under as long as she could, unwilling to surface and learn the answer. She wanted this, wanted him, for all the reasons she'd cited, and because she'd done the wrong thing before in choosing a man who'd seemed so right for her. This time, she was picking one she knew was wrong, and going in with her eyes wide open.

Knowing that even making the choice was part of taking control back from the memory of what Lee had done to her, she rose and broke the surface, sucking in a deep breath of air.

She nearly got a lungful of water as Gray dove in beside her.

The impact of his body rocked the churning waters that surrounded her and brought a flare of heat to her belly, a balm of healing to her soul. They might be wrong for each other, she knew, but in this moment they were exactly right.

He surfaced a few feet away from her, treading water as he smoothed back his short-cut hair, leaving it bristling on end, dark in the silver-blue moonlight. He didn't speak as he sculled toward her, gliding across the distance that separated them.

As he did so, Mariah was acutely aware of the warm press of water on her suddenly sensitized skin. No longer chilled, she burned from within and reveled in the sly touch of watery currents. Mist surrounded them, bringing clinging wetness with every breath, and when she licked her lips, the moisture carried a tang of minerals and a thrill of excitement.

She skimmed gently backward, until she was standing on a submerged outcropping, the water lapping at her collarbones. Gray followed and stopped very near her, not touching her, but close enough that she could touch him if she reached out.

When he didn't say or do anything, just looked at

her, his eyes serious and silver in the moonlight, she said, "I wasn't sure you'd agree to this." She rushed on before he interrupted, "I know we said we couldn't—and shouldn't—do this, but I'm not suggesting that we start something. I just want a new memory—one that's true, rather than tainted." She looked up into the sky, letting her head tip back and her hair dip into the blood-warm water as mist feathered her face like the faintest of kisses. "I want to make love, here under the waterfall, in a place that's brought me peace. And don't worry—I'm using the word *love* in its most generic sense. I want to love life, love our bodies, love what I feel when I'm near you." She straightened to look at him once again. "Did I just scare the hell out of you?"

"No," he said simply. "You've humbled me. And you make me wish I were a better man, one who could let this be the start of something, rather than just a memory." He paused, looking around as she had done moments earlier. "You make me wish I had flowers to give you, or poetry. Something worthy of this place and what we're about to do in it. But I'm not a romantic and I haven't got a way with words, so I'll just say it plainly. This will be a memory for me, too, Mariah. I haven't been with another woman since Stacy. I haven't wanted anyone that way. Then I saw you."

Mariah thought she felt her heart sigh, and maybe break and bleed a little for what she couldn't have. But this was her deal, her terms, so she said only, "I wasn't looking for poetry or romance, but you just gave me enough of both to count as a memory in itself."

There was beauty, too, in the powerful promise of his bare shoulders, the bulge of his biceps and the glistening planes of his upper torso. There was poetry there, whether he knew it or not.

They drew together and kissed then, because it was impossible not to. The attraction that had started as sparks and grown into something more flared from a warm kernel in Mariah's belly to a lick of heat when his lips touched hers.

That was the only point of contact at first—mouth on mouth. Mariah tasted the tang of mineralized water on his lips, and gloried in the press of wetness, of heat. She felt the brush of his bare legs against hers, felt one of his hands skim across her hip.

A bubble of joy burst through her at the caress, and the glint that entered his eyes. His normally closed expression held acceptance, anticipation and blatant male hunger. She touched her lips to his, then sank into the kiss, into the water, and tangled her legs with his. They dipped beneath the surface, lost in each other.

The kiss spun out on a single breath, a single moment, as they came together, skin on skin, with her breasts pressed against his powerfully sculpted chest, and the solid, hard length of his erection nestled between them. Her flesh burned at the points of contact, and the perfection of the fit, the feeling of connectedness, was so acute she shied away from it, afraid she was in over her head, figuratively as well as literally.

With a powerful surge, he sent them back to the surface. Mariah's head was spinning when they broke into the misty air, and she regained her footing. She ended the kiss to suck in a great lungful of air, exhaling it again on a delighted laugh when Gray hooked an arm around her, pulled her from the ledge and started swimming, aiming them at the waterfall.

"You'll drown us!" she exclaimed, though she hung on to his neck, reveling in the coarse friction of masculine hair against her water-softened skin, and the powerful play of muscles as he drew them beneath the thundering stream.

"Then you'd better hang on!" With that scant warning, he dove beneath the waterfall, wrapping his arms around her and taking her with him.

They surfaced, laughing, in the sheltered space behind the waterfall. She'd swum there before, and had explored the small niche where centuries—maybe millennia—of watery friction had carved a soft-edged bowl in the stones behind the cataract. She'd never been there at night, though, never seen it moonlit.

"Oh," she said in a small gasp of pleasure as Gray released her, touched bottom and stood, rising over her to inspect the ledge.

The silvery moonlight cast the waterfall in a brilliant white glow. Against it, Gray was a black silhouette of masculinity as he reached down to take her hand. "Come here," he said, his voice pitched low beneath the waterfall's thunder.

Mariah went. How could she not join him in the shallow niche? How could she not rise from the water with him, and lie with him there, in that place outside reality?

They lay on their sides on the warm, water-smoothed stone, facing each other, and sank into a kiss that spun out endlessly. The water cooled slightly on Mariah's skin, bringing delicious shivers instead of chills as she touched him, tentatively at first, running her hands over his shoulders and down the leashed strength of his arms.

He copied her actions, slicking the water on her skin

and kindling the sparks within her to a flame. She murmured her pleasure and crowded close.

It was all that she'd dreamed of in her premarriage fantasies—a romantic setting with a handsome man, out in the open, though with little threat of discovery. The realization brought a laugh bubbling to the surface, and Gray pulled away to look down at her, his features unreadable in the dark silhouette of his powerful form.

"That tickle?"

"No. Or rather, yes, but in a good way." She paused, then went with the truth. "I was just thinking that before—well, when I was younger—I always imagined doing this outside. I never have until now."

A low growl rumbled in his chest, a mix of amusement and feral sexuality that kicked her pulse a notch higher. "What, exactly, did you imagine?"

She blushed hard and hot. And she told him, embellishing in the places where her innocence had fallen short before marriage. Not that her marital sex had been great, ranging as it had along a descending continuum from pleasant to domineering, but it had given her some ideas of how things were supposed to work.

And oh, boy, did they. Gray took her at her word and then went from there, kissing her, touching her, exploring her body more intimately than she'd imagined in the not-so-wild fantasies that had suddenly become real, and then been exceeded. He licked her, suckled her, made her bow back in ecstasy.

A small orgasm caught her unexpectedly, vising her inner muscles in a long, languid pull of pleasure that had her crying out, her words lost beneath the water-thunder. Then he was shifting onto his back, and lifting her above him.

She stiffened. "I don't know—"

"The stone's worn smooth, but it's still stone. Trust me, this'll work better than me squashing you flat. And...it'll let you work out more of those fantasies. That is, assuming you've had a few of what you'd like to do to your lover."

She didn't miss his use of the generic—he hadn't said "what you'd like to do to me," as though any man would've done once she'd made the decision to take a lover. Though she understood his need for distance, she put a purr in her voice when she said, "I don't know about that, but I've definitely gotten a few ideas over the past week or so."

And she proceeded to show him.

If she fumbled anything, he didn't seem to notice or care, showing her his appreciation with long, possessive strokes down her back and sides, letting her hear it in his groans. When it finally became too much, when they'd driven each other beyond reason and joining wasn't just the next step, it was the only one, he gripped her hips in his powerful hands and shifted her so the long, hard length of his erection was poised for entry.

There, he paused. "Okay?" he asked, his voice a sexy rumble almost the same pitch as the water. "We're condomless, but I'm clean."

"Oh." Positioned there, poised for the most intimate of joinings, she scrambled to collect her thoughts. "Yeah. Yeah, we're good. I got tested after...well, after." After she learned her husband wasn't even close to being the man she'd thought. "As far as the other, I've got an IUD. For medical reasons, not because I sleep around."

"Yeah. I sort of got that from the part where you haven't been with anyone except the ex."

The reminder probably should've been a cold one. Instead, it made the comparison between the two men that much more poignant.

Lee had insisted on being on top, on being in control. Gray had touched her the way she wanted, then put himself on the bottom so he'd be the one with his back to the stone.

Because of that, she found a smile when part of her wanted to weep for the girl she'd been, for the way her life might've gone if she'd chosen better the first time around. "Then that's your answer. Bombs away."

Her words were flip, but there was nothing frivolous about the sensations or emotions when she eased down and back, taking him within her. She couldn't see his face in the darkness behind the waterfall, but she could feel his intensity in the reverence of his touch, hear it in the catch of his breath and his low hiss of pleasure.

He was large inside her, filling her, stretching her, his size magnifying each sensation, every burst of pleasure. Her eyelids eased down, blocking out even the silver glow of moonlight. The sound of the waterfall surrounded her, as did the feel of the man who moved beneath her, urging her, guiding her, touching her as he whispered praise and promises, making her feel every bit of the woman she'd once imagined herself becoming.

She bent to kiss him and he rose to meet her, so they were sitting face-to-face, with her straddling his lap. The position brought new sensations, new heats and desires. She went with them, riding him until they were both groaning and gasping and laughing, partners in pleasure.

Then he dropped them down into the water, still joined, still wrapped together. He pressed her back against the stone wall, pinning her hips in place and driving deep.

Mariah arched back on a strangled gasp, gripping his shoulders as the sensations within her changed from pleasure to blinding heat, from play to something larger and darker, an all-consuming need that threatened to take over and leave her helpless.

Yet even as Gray thrust into her, pressing her against the stone and holding her steady as he pistoned, she knew he was as much in her power as she was in his. This pleasure was a give-and-take, not a domination.

The knowledge, and the strength it brought, gave her the confidence to let go. She strained into him, against him, and touched her lips to his.

The kiss held a sweetness at odds with the rampaging fury of their bodies. She sank into it, into him, and heard him murmur her name as the awesome madness of their pleasure rose up, sweeping her into a pulsing coil of heat and need, and the power they made together.

Her orgasm was a long, throbbing pull of pleasure that bound her to him, and him to her, as he shuddered in her arms and cut loose. She felt him surge within her, felt her inner muscles contract to prolong the spasms—his, hers, theirs. And when she leaned back onto the rock ledge where he'd held her pinned, he followed her down, turning them so they were on their sides, she tucked against him. Then he turned his face into the side of her neck, breathing her in. And whispered her name once again.

Gray's world had gone soft and warm, smoothing out all the edges he'd lived with for so long. Mariah was curled up against him, her back to his front and his hands folded with hers beneath her chin.

Yet, at the same time, she surrounded him as surely as the warm mists and the water that ran from their bodies. He breathed her in, felt her in every cell of his body. He'd just spent himself inside her, yet he wanted her again already. He'd been her first lover in all the ways that mattered, the first to be with her for her own sake, and his, not because of some nefarious plan.

The thought of Lee and al-Jihad brought too much reality into a moment where it didn't belong, so Gray pushed the outside world aside and touched his lips to Mariah's neck, kissing the soft place behind her ear. She shuddered against him, raised their joined hands to her lips, and pressed a kiss into the center of his palm.

The simple gesture, one of love and acceptance, sent a poignant jolt through his system, and a whispered thought: *I wish.* He wished he were a better man with a different life. He wished he could offer her a home and a lifetime. Those wishes were so strong, yet so incompatible with the things that had driven him for so long. And still, part of him said, *What if?*

What if he put aside his drive for revenge and made a new life for himself? For them? He could turn in his gun and badge; they could rebuild the cabin, and then...

And then what? He was a cop from a family of cops. He knew policework, loved it. He didn't have any hobbies, didn't know who or what he'd be without the job. More than that, there were Ken, Trish and Catherine, and all the others al-Jihad and his men had killed. They no longer had their lives or loves. Didn't he owe it to them to put off his own until justice was served?

Still, he wished. And because he wished, because the

desire to make an impossible change was so strong that it nearly consumed him, he eased away from her. "We should swim back out and check the phone. If Lee and the others have left the vicinity, they may have taken the signal scrambler with them." When that came out more coolly practical than he'd meant it to, he consciously softened his tone. "Besides, I could do with one of those energy bars. You just about used me up."

She lay still for a moment, then rolled away from him and sat up, her gloriously naked female form silhouetted against the silver rain. He couldn't see her expression, but her voice was carefully neutral when she said, "Back to reality, then?"

"Back to reality." When that seemed pitifully inadequate, especially considering the undeniable depth of what had just happened between them, he tried to explain. "It's not that—"

"Don't," she said, interrupting with the single, soft word. "Please, don't. I didn't mean for this to complicate things. I just… I wanted a better memory. Which is exactly what you've given me."

"What if I want more than that?" he said. He should've been shocked by his own words. Instead, they felt exactly right.

"Do you?"

"Maybe."

She shifted, and a glint of refracted moonlight allowed him to see her small, sad smile. "Even if that 'maybe' had been a heartfelt 'yes,' my answer would be that I'm flattered, but we both know I'd need and want more from you than you're willing to give." She paused, and when he didn't argue, she nodded. "Yeah. Thought so."

"If it helps at all, I wish things were different."

"But not enough to change them."

Something squeezed tight in his chest. "I can't."

She nodded. "Then there we are." She leaned into him and touched her lips to his, surprising him. The heat gathered, sparked higher. But then she eased back, with that same sad smile in place. "Goodbye, Gray."

Neither of them was going anywhere at that moment, but he knew what she meant, knew that this was the end of anything physical between them, which was something they probably shouldn't have started, but he'd be damned if he'd regret it. She wasn't the only one who'd made new memories just now.

He tipped his head in acknowledgment. "Goodbye, Mariah. And good luck."

Together, they slipped into the warm mineral waters, ducked beneath the waterfall and swam to the flat boulder where they'd left their clothes and supplies. They dressed in awkward silence and she rummaged through her dusty pack for food and water while he checked his phone.

The signal was good, and a text awaited him: *Tracking your GPS; chopper ETA 30 min.* The time stamp said they were down to less than ten minutes.

He showed the message to Mariah, who smiled sadly as water dripped from her hair like tears. "Well, then. Back to reality it is."

"Yeah," Gray said, and turned away, gritting his teeth at the sudden realization that he damn well didn't want to go back to reality. He wanted to stay exactly where he was.

The pickup went smoothly, with no sign of Lee or al-Jihad, which left Mariah wondering whether they should've tried to sneak back to the cabin rather than hiding up at the glen. But, by the same token, she couldn't regret the decision, or what had come after. New memories were precious things.

Not wanting the others to know what had happened between them, she consciously avoided looking at Gray as the helicopter flew them down off the ridge, back to Bear Claw City. Instead, she huddled in the blanket she'd pulled from her knapsack, trying to recapture the warmth of the hot spring without thinking of the things she and Gray had done to each other, the feelings he'd unleashed in her.

It was impossible not to think about the emotions, though. They overwhelmed her, consumed her and made her deeply afraid that she'd done the unthinkable and had once again fallen for the absolute wrong guy.

Realizing that she'd heard someone say her name, she looked to the front of the passenger area of the helicopter, where Gray was huddled with two other agents while talking into a radio headset. He was looking at her, one elegant eyebrow arched to suggest that he'd asked her something. When their eyes met, heat sparked low in her midsection, hotter now than before, because now she knew how it could be with a man like him. Or rather, with *him*.

She cleared her throat. "Sorry, I was zoning out." And then some.

"A car is going to meet us at the landing pad with the statuettes. Once you've pointed out the right one, we'll take it for analysis and the driver will take you to your parents." Gray rapped out the summary, making it clear that what happened next wasn't open to discussion. He wasn't the soldier now, or the man. He was pure, cold federal agent.

"Fine," she said dully, suddenly sick of it all. She'd tried to make the right choices before and she'd been wrong at almost every turn. This time she'd play along with the Feds, and hope for the best. What else could she do? She was tired of fighting when she never actually won.

She must've dozed off after that, because the next thing she knew, the helicopter was landing with a shuddering bump, and she was suddenly surrounded by armed men snapping terse, clipped orders to one another as they hustled her off the aircraft.

Fear kicked in, and she instinctively looked for Gray. He was still talking into his radio headset, but met her eyes and nodded. She couldn't tell if the nod meant "You're okay, go with them and I'll be right behind you," or "It's over."

Knowing they'd said their goodbyes already and it wasn't the time or place to ask for more, if she'd even meant to, she went with her escort. Moments later, she was staring into the trunk of a dark SUV, where her mother's ceramic clowns were arrayed like a small army of terminally cheerful, red-and-white painted gremlins.

"That one," she said, pointing out a floppy-footed guy with green suspenders.

"You're sure?" The question came from Gray's friend, Fairfax, who had hopped out of the SUV as they approached.

"Positive. That's the one Lee kept asking me about when he was holding me prisoner. That's what he wants from me." A stinking clown. There was irony there, she was sure of it. She just couldn't see it through the heartache.

At Fairfax's nod, two of the men guarding her took possession of the statuette, bundling it up and spiriting it away. Fairfax gestured to another man and slammed shut the rear deck of the SUV. When the agent approached, Fairfax gave him low-voiced instructions, then turned to Mariah. "Special Agent Sykes here is going to drive you to your parents'. Do you need anything before you go?" The look in Fairfax's dark blue eyes made the question far less casual than it should have been.

She didn't want to think about what Gray might have told his friend about them, didn't want the pity she thought she saw in Fairfax's expression. "I'm fine," she said tightly, and yanked open the passenger door of the SUV before either of the men could get it for her. She climbed up and moved to slam the door shut, but Fairfax caught it before she could.

"Gray said he'd call you at the safe house," he said, keeping his voice low so it was just between the two of them.

She shook her head. "He doesn't have to. He doesn't owe me anything."

"He seems to feel differently," Fairfax said. "How about you?"

"I just want to get this over with," she said, which they both knew wasn't an answer.

He seemed to accept it, though. He shut the door, tapped the roof of the SUV and moments later Special Agent Sykes hopped into the driver's seat. Sykes was probably in his late twenties, lean to the point of gauntness, with blond hair and pale eyes that looked almost colorless in the glow of the dashboard displays. He didn't say anything, but that was fine with Mariah. She just wanted to be left alone.

The agent drove them away from the airport, through the city and out the other side, into the 'burbs. A sick feeling gathered in Mariah's stomach as the landmarks started looking all too familiar. "Where is this safe house exactly?"

As he rolled to a stop at a red light, Sykes reached out and patted her hand. "In your case, the word *safe* might be an exaggeration."

Before she fully processed the words, before she could pull away or scream or react at all, he grabbed her wrist, yanked her arm across the console, and plunged a needle into the meat of her forearm.

Mariah screamed and tore away, then grabbed for the door handle. But before she could get the door open, the world began to spin, then yaw. Then go black.

The last thing she was conscious of was Sykes putting both hands back on the steering wheel and hitting the gas when the light went green, his lean-featured face impassive and his voice impossibly gentle when he said, "That's right. I'm taking you home where you belong."

Chapter 11

Gray paced the length of the Bear Claw crime lab, which took up most of the basement of the PD. He was keeping an eye on things inside the lab while Fairfax watched the front and rear entrances, making sure their secure investigation stayed that way.

These days, trust was a hard thing to come by. Gray counted himself lucky that Fax and his fiancée, Chelsea, knew and trusted several members of the Bear Claw PD, who had helped them take down Muhammad Feyd and foil the stadium attack the previous year. Those trusted members of the PD, along with FBI forensic investigator Seth Varitek—also a friend of Chelsea and Fax's—were hunched over the ceramic clown statuette in the main room of the three-room lab, a large area filled with machines and long counters. So far they'd been at it twenty minutes, and hadn't yet figured out what made the clown so important.

"This had better not be a decoy," Gray growled under his breath the next time his pacing brought him near Fairfax.

"If it is, we'll deal," Fax said. "At least it'll free us up to do what we've got to do."

"And what is that?" Gray spun on him. "If this clown thing doesn't pan out and give us a solid lead on where the bastards are and what they're planning next, we're not a damn bit further along than we were before—" He broke off, frustration bringing an unfamiliar tightness to his chest.

"Hey." Fax gripped his shoulder. "She's safe, okay? Sykes called in to say he'd made the delivery, that there were hugs and tears all around when she was reunited with her parents."

Gray stopped dead. "What did you say?"

"Sykes called to say—" A shout from the lab interrupted Fax midsentence.

Brain buzzing with dread, Gray spun on the CSIs. "It's not there anymore, is it?"

Varitek's eyes narrowed. "That's right. We found a space chipped out of the statuette and then concealed again—looks like the size and shape of a flash drive, but it's empty. How did you know?"

"Because Mariah isn't close with her parents, not in the slightest. No tears. No happy reunion." Gray headed for the stairs at a dead run. "Call the safe house. Talk to someone *other* than Sykes and confirm that she's there." But in his gut, he knew she wouldn't be.

Sure enough, by the time he arrived at the in-city safe house, the phone and radio traffic had confirmed that Mariah had never arrived at her intended destination, and Sykes's SUV had been found abandoned in the state park north of the city.

Still, Gray continued on to the safe house. Full of cold rage, he checked in with the security detail and let himself into the second-floor condo where Frank and Ada Shore were being protected.

He didn't know precisely what he'd expected them to look like, based on the few, tight-lipped details Mariah had shared, but he hadn't been prepared for the couple he found holding hands on a love seat in the condo's main room.

Mariah's mother was a small, elegantly dressed woman with short, graying hair and kind eyes. Her father was tall and slightly stooped, with the deflated-balloon look of someone who'd gone through a recent weight loss. His expression, however, went hard when he caught sight of Gray. Letting go of his wife's hands, Frank rose to his full height and faced Gray squarely. "What's happening? Where's Mariah?"

Gray didn't answer immediately because he couldn't trust himself to be civil, and insults weren't going to help him find her. Besides, he wanted to be mindful of the older man's heart condition. Still, he needed answers. "Where would Mawadi take her?" he asked, his voice laced with deadly intent.

Frank's eyes went blank, then heated to fury. "He's got her? What the hell are you people doing? What kind of protection is this? We've given you everything you've asked for, and the one thing we've asked for—that you keep our daughter safe—hasn't happened."

Two years earlier, or maybe even as recently as a couple of weeks before, Gray might have responded with a threat, or by telling Mariah's father exactly what he thought of parents who put themselves first, always. But getting to know Mariah had changed him. She'd reminded him that the victims of terrorism weren't the only ones hurt by the bombs and attacks. The effects reached far and wide, and were sometimes mixed with guilt and culpability, but that didn't make them any less real.

So instead of attacking, he laid it out as simply as he could. "They got past us again. I won't apologize for it because I'm not sorry—I'm furious." He paused, and his voice went rough when he said, "Mawadi already had possession of the computer files he'd hid in the statuette—Sykes took them during transport. So we have to assume that Mawadi took Mariah for revenge. She had the guts to leave him, and for that he wants her dead. More than that, he wants her to suffer—she said that was his way. So I'm asking you—I'm begging you—to think. Where would he take her, someplace nearby, if he wanted her to suffer?"

"I don't… I don't know." Mariah's father seemed to sink into himself, deflating further. "I didn't know any of it. She never told us anything was wrong in her marriage, never even hinted at it."

"That might've had something to do with the fact that you never listened to her," Gray said, unable to help himself. "If you'd—" He snapped off the words. "Never mind. Not my business."

"No, I don't think it is," Ada said. She rose to join her husband, standing at his shoulder to form a united front, one that excluded Gray just as he imagined it had excluded Mariah. But then Ada's expression softened, and she reached out to take one of Gray's hands in both of hers. "But it seems like Mariah thought otherwise."

His voice went thick. "She's told me a few things." And she'd given him a gift beyond measure, he was starting to realize. She'd reminded him how to feel.

He'd been numb for so long, he almost couldn't bear all the emotions bombarding him now—fear for her, grief for how he'd left things between them, and anger at the parents who'd made her feel that she had to solve every problem on her own.

"We love her," Ada said simply. "We always have, though we haven't always shown it as we should, and we weren't always the best of parents."

"You took the clown back," he said, which wasn't the most important point by far, but had stuck with him as the crowning injustice. "She defended the damn thing from her bastard of an ex, and you took it away from her."

Ada's eyes filled. "We were moving away. I wanted something that reminded me of her."

"Next time, ask for a damn picture. Or, better yet, stay put and take care of your daughter." Gray knew he was being harsh, and when he saw Frank's color change, going from ruddy to sickly pale, he feared that he'd gone too far, that he'd compromised the older man's health once again in his efforts to do the right thing.

But Frank regained his composure with a visible effort. He gripped his wife's hand as if it were his anchor, and she leaned into him, bumping his arm with her shoulder. The bond between them was palpable; Gray recognized their true, lifelong love, like the partnership his parents had shared, the connection he'd sought but never found.

Until now, he realized. He'd found that connection with Mariah. It wasn't that they were incompatible, it was more that they were very different on the surface, but alike underneath, in the fundamentals. They were both opinionated and stubborn, comfortable being alone, but so much happier when they were with the right friend—or lover. At least he hoped she felt the same way, because at that moment, he realized that he was so much more alive with her than without her, that he wanted her in his life.

"I'm sorry," Ada said, tears spilling over and tracking down her cheeks. "I don't know where he would take her. We lived less than a half hour away from them, but we barely knew them as a couple."

Gray's head came up. "Wait. Where did they live? Where exactly?"

It had been in the investigative files, but he hadn't done much more than glance at the information in passing, because the small house where the couple had moved right after their marriage had been searched extensively and then released from the evidentiary chain. As far as he knew, it had been sold but never occupied, and still stood empty.

What if that had been part of the plan?

Mariah had gone to her marriage bed a virgin, gone into the marriage full of hopes and dreams, only to see them gradually crushed beneath her husband's insidious brand of evil. What better place to make her suffer and die—in Mawadi's twisted brain, anyway—than back at the house where the torture had truly begun?

Frank thought for a moment, then shook his head. "I'm sorry. I don't know exactly, and my address book is back at home. Somewhere north of the city. I remember that much."

They'd found Sykes's abandoned SUV north of the city.

Gray gritted his teeth. His mother could've recited his last three addresses by heart. At one point, when he'd just wanted to be left alone to wallow, that sort of love had felt smothering. Now he realized that it was a gift.

"Never mind. I'll get my people to look it up." He spun and headed for the door, calling for Fairfax to get on the horn to Johnson and have a team meet them at the address.

"Special Agent Grayson," Ada said from behind him. The soft plea in her voice made him stop, even though every fiber of his being said he had to hurry, that each second could be Mariah's last.

He turned back. "What?"

"Please tell her…please tell her we're sorry."

"Tell her yourself when I bring her out," Gray said. Then he turned away and headed for the car at a dead run, praying that he could get her out, that she and her parents would have a chance for reconciliation. And hoping to hell he got that same chance with her.

Mariah awakened disoriented, and for a few seconds thought she was still dreaming—a nightmare of times past, when she'd thought she was losing her mind, seeing a demon inside the skin of the man she'd married.

She was back in the bedroom they'd shared, back to awakening with him staring at her, and with the prickly, sore sensation that he'd been fondling her too hard, pinching her breasts to the point of pain, though he'd always denied touching her while she'd slept so deeply she'd been almost certain he'd drugged her.

Drugged. The thought brought Sykes's image, and the pain of an injection. The memories snapped her to the present, and warned her that she was in serious trouble. She started to struggle, only to find her wrists and ankles bound tightly and affixed to something solid behind her.

The bastard had tied her to the wall again.

"Awake now, Mrs. Mawadi?" Lee asked, though he hadn't used the name *Mawadi* when they'd been married. They'd been Mr. and Mrs. Chisholm. He nodded and smiled his all-American smile. "Good. I've been waiting for you to come around."

He rose to his feet, making her aware that she wasn't on the bed they'd shared, but rather lying on the carpeted floor of what had once been their bedroom. That was more evidence that she was in the present, that this wasn't a dream. She knew the old house had been stripped of furniture because she'd signed the auction papers herself, though she hadn't been back since the day she'd been escorted out by several FBI agents, including Gray.

Gray. The name sighed in her heart, but she didn't say it aloud, didn't want to give Lee the leverage. Instead, she glared at the man she'd once thought she loved. "Revisiting old haunts, Lee? Not very smart of you. The FBI is keeping watch on this place."

He gave her a backhanded slap, his expression never changing from one of polite indifference. "Don't lie to me. Our information indicates the surveillance was lifted months ago." He smiled, and the look in his eyes chilled her blood. "You and I should have a little while longer before the feebs track us down. Plenty of time to get reacquainted."

Mariah tasted blood and her own fear. Her insides trembled and she was sorely tempted to crawl inside herself and pretend none of this was happening. But she wasn't that woman anymore. She was tougher, stronger. So rather than let loose the whimper that wanted to break free, she said, "What did you hide inside the statue, Lee? What didn't you want them to find?"

His face split in a self-congratulatory smile and he drew back, fiddling with a small, flat remote control–like box, tossing it from one hand to the other. "Nothing that'll help you, that's for sure. Those files are part of the larger plan, one we've been working on since well before I picked you up at that crummy coffee bar. And the clown…ah, the clown. It was pretty freaking clever of me, wouldn't you say? I figured if you died, your cold bitch of a mother would take it back. If you lived, I figured you'd keep the stupid thing, even if you ditched the rest of our stuff. Which I knew you'd do, because you're just what al-Jihad said you'd be—a disloyal bitch who ran the second things got tough."

"You tried to kill me. You call that things getting tough?"

He hit her again, then sucked her blood from his knuckles. "You don't leave a man like me, Mariah. I don't believe in divorce. I don't recognize the court's power to do something like that. Which means you're not only still married to me, you're an adulterer."

"How did you know—" She bit off the words, but it was too late.

"I didn't before, but I do now. You just confirmed it, my unfaithful little wife." He leaned in and put his face very close to hers, eyes suddenly blazing. "It was Grayson, wasn't it? I heard about the way the two of you were looking at each other."

The way he said it made it seem as though al-Jihad had people throughout the local and federal arms of the investigation. Mariah knew Gray suspected there were insiders, but didn't think he had any idea of the extent. If she could just get to him...

Who was she kidding? She didn't want to see him to pass along information on al-Jihad's resources and plans, or not really. She wanted to see *him,* to be with him. She wanted to talk to him, to convince him that they weren't so different after all. They clicked. They fit. They made sense.

And she loved him. When she came right down to it, that was the truth in her soul, the emotion she'd been avoiding for too long.

She'd been thinking of herself as a fighter, but she hadn't fought for what mattered most—her future.

Lee smacked her again, this time on the other cheek. "Answer me, bitch! Tell me you spread your legs for some loser FBI agent whose own boss doesn't even trust him not to screw up." He got very close, practically screaming the words into her face. "Tell me!"

"Yes," she said very clearly, speaking through a face gone numb and sore. "I was with Grayson. I love him."

"And the feeling's mutual," Gray's voice said, snapping Mariah's attention to the bedroom doorway. He stood there, coldly furious, his attention fixed on Lee, though she knew he was as acutely aware of her as she was of him.

"Gray." She sighed his name on a whisper of hope and a whole lot of fear, because she'd also seen the flash in Lee's eyes. Not fear, but triumph. He'd planned for this, maybe even intended it. *Lee, don't,* she wanted to say, but didn't because she knew her pleas would only add to his pleasure.

"FBI. Hands up and get the hell away from her," Gray growled, entering the room with his weapon drawn. Other men, including Fairfax, were crowded into the hallway behind him. "We've got the house surrounded."

"Oh, I'll raise my hands, all right." Lee eased away from Mariah, then held up his hands to show the object he'd been fiddling with since Mariah awakened.

It was a small technical-looking box with a couple of buttons and a digital display. He held a yellow toggle with his thumb, and the digital countdown showed less than seven minutes remaining.

Mariah was no expert, but based on what she little she knew, and the way Gray and the others froze, she had to assume it was a detonator of some sort.

Lee's tone was gloating when he said, "The basement of this place is loaded with explosives. You shoot me and I let go of this trigger, this place goes up immediately. You play along, and you've got three minutes and change to get your girlfriend out of here."

"Define *play along*," Gray said tightly.

"First off, get your agent friends out of here. This is between the two of us."

"Clear the building and push the perimeter back," Gray snapped without looking behind him. There was a mad scramble of bodies. All but one. "You too, Fax," he growled. "Get out of here. For Chelsea's sake, if nothing else."

Fairfax hesitated, then turned and left.

When the three of them were alone, Gray said, "Now what? You know you're not getting out of here alive. We've got the perimeter completely locked up."

"Maybe I don't want to get out." Lee stood and backed across the room, toward the closet he'd used for his clothes and forbidden her from entering when they'd lived there. "Maybe there's something I want to show you, instead."

"Freeze!" Gray barked. "Stop moving right now, or—"

Lee tossed the detonator at him. The trigger snapped open, but instead of an explosion, it brought a gout of choking gray smoke spewing from the handheld unit. Under the cover of that smoke, Lee bolted for the closet, yanking open the door, then stooping to pull up a trapdoor that Mariah hadn't ever seen before.

Shouting for the other agents to get their butts back into the house, Gray fired several rounds into the smoke. Under that cover he lunged forward, grabbing for Lee. He made contact, getting Lee around the waist and throwing him to the ground, but lost hold of his weapon, which went skittering across the floor.

Choking and gagging on the smoke, her eyes watering profusely, Mariah could only lie helpless and watch as the men grappled and struggled. Gray landed two good punches, but then Lee drove his elbow into Gray's temple.

Gray reeled back, dazed. Lee ripped away and leaped into the closet, disappearing down the dark opening revealed beneath the trapdoor.

"Get in here!" Gray bellowed. When Fax appeared at a dead run, Gray waved to the opening. "Down there. Careful, but make it fast. We've got a few minutes to get out of range, assuming the bastard didn't lie about the explosives."

"He didn't," Fax said quietly. "The outside team's fiber optics located them in the basement. And you were right, this was a distraction, too. There's been a riot at the Supermax. The warden's dead, along with two cops. One was the IA detective, Romo Sampson."

"Damn." Gray shook his head. "We can't help them now, though. Get moving."

As Fax palmed his flashlight and dropped through the trapdoor, Gray grabbed his weapon, scooped up the smoke bomb and lobbed it out into the hallway. Then he crouched down beside Mariah and started yanking at her bonds.

Her tears welled up and spilled over. "He's getting away."

"Yes, he is." But although Gray's voice was matter-of-fact, it wasn't the slightest bit cool. In fact, it trembled slightly.

"Go," she urged. "Remember how you said—"

"I remember most of what I've said to you," he interrupted, "and I'm not proud of all of it. Some of it was downright stupid, some of it dead wrong. But what I said just now? That's the truth. It's what matters." He pressed his forehead to hers. "I love you. I'm sorry it took me so long to see that and to say it. You're my priority, you're what matters most. There'll be another chance for us to get Mawadi and al-Jihad. If I leave you here, there won't be another chance for me to save myself and take my life in a new direction."

As he said that, her shackles came undone and she was free.

Sobbing, she threw her arms around his neck. "I love you. Oh, God. I was so afraid you wouldn't come."

"You won't ever have to worry about that again, because I'll always be right there beside you, from now on." His words were muffled against her as he held her close and lifted her, and they turned for the door. Gray raised his voice. "Time to go, Fairfax."

Fax's voice floated up. "There's a tunnel headed north. I'm going to—"

"You're going to get your ass back up here or I'll tell Chelsea on you," Gray said calmly.

There was a brief pause, then Fairfax reappeared, pulling himself out of the hidden tunnel.

Without a word, the men ushered Mariah outside, to a car parked well beyond the blast zone. There was a brief discussion about disarming the bomb, but it was deemed too late. Instead, the other members of the armed response agents hustled to clear the nearby buildings.

As the seconds ticked down, Mariah looked toward the house she'd entered with wonderful dreams and left in the grip of a nightmare.

Gray slipped an arm around her waist. "Let's go."

"No." She shook her head. "I want to see it. Are we far enough back?"

"Yeah."

They were standing there, partially sheltered behind one of the dark SUVs, when there was a *whump* of detonation, a shudder in the ground beneath their feet…and then her house seemed to sag and settle in on itself. The roof tilted, the walls bowed out and everything slid off to one side. Moments later, flames licked from one of the lower windows.

Mariah thought that, in an odd way, it was both anticlimactic and cathartic.

In the distance, a fire engine's siren began to wail. Mariah, though, couldn't find any tears. She couldn't find any joy, either. She was, quite simply, numb. So much had happened so quickly that she couldn't begin to process it.

"He said the hidden files had something to do with al-Jihad's grand strategy, something he'd been planning since long before Lee and I met. I think… I think he meant that marrying me wasn't just about the malls. He made it seem like there was more, that the bombs, and maybe even the jail time, was all part of something bigger, a plan they haven't put into motion yet."

"That plays," Gray agrees. "We'll have you give a full report, go over everything he said or did." He tightened his arm and looked down at her. "I'll be there, and I promise—no browbeating this time around."

Incredibly, she felt a bubble of laughter lodge in her throat. "I think I'm tough enough to hold my own now. Bring on the rubber hoses, Mr. FBI guy."

"Yeah, you're strong enough to make it on your own now." He leaned down and dropped a kiss on her lips. "But you're not going to have to. And neither am I."

And as she closed her eyes and opened herself up to his kiss, and the future that had begun to unreel in front of her, she knew he was absolutely right. Each of them was strong enough to cope with whatever came next, as Bear Claw City dealt with the fallout of the fatal prison riots. But the lovely thing was, she and Gray wouldn't have to handle it alone, not anymore.

They'd deal with everything together.

* * * * *

Cassie Miles, a *USA TODAY* bestselling author, lives in Colorado. After raising two daughters and cooking tons of macaroni and cheese for her family, Cassie is trying to be more adventurous in her culinary efforts. She's discovered that almost anything tastes better with wine. When she's not plotting Harlequin Intrigue books, Cassie likes to hang out at the Denver Botanic Gardens near her high-rise home.

Books by Cassie Miles

Harlequin Intrigue

Visit the Author Profile page
at Harlequin.com for more titles.

UNFORGETTABLE

Cassie Miles

To Sara Hanson, the next writer in the family.

As always, to Rick.

Chapter 1

Morning sunlight sliced into the rocky alcove where he had taken shelter. A blinding glare hit his eyes. The sun was a laser pointed directly into his face. He sank back into the shadows.

If he stayed here, they'd find him. He had to move, to run…to keep running. This wasn't the time for a nap. He shoved himself off the ground where he'd been sleeping and crouched while he got his bearings.

Behind him, the rock wall curved like bent fingers. Another boulder lay before him like a giant thumb. He had spent the night curled up inside this granite fist.

How did I get here?

Craning his neck, he peered over the edge of the thumb. His hideout was halfway up a slope. Around him were shrubs, lodgepole pines, more boulders and leafy green aspen trees. Through the trunks, he saw the opposite wall of a steep, rocky canyon.

Where the hell am I?

His head throbbed. The steady, pulsating pain synchronized with the beating of his heart.

When he raised his hand to his forehead, he saw a smear of dried blood on the sleeve of his plaid, flannel shirt. *My blood?* Other rusty blotches spattered the front of his shirt. *Was I shot?* He took a physical inventory. Apart from the killer headache, he didn't seem to be badly hurt. There were scrapes and bruises but nothing serious.

By his feet, he saw a handgun. A SIG Sauer P-226. He checked the magazine. Four bullets left. *This isn't my gun.* He preferred a Beretta M9, but the SIG would do just fine.

He felt in his pockets for an ammunition clip and found nothing. No wallet. No cell phone. Not a useful packet of aspirin. Nothing. He wasn't wearing a belt or a holster. Though he had on socks, the laces of his steel-toed boots weren't tied. *Must have dressed in a hurry.*

He licked his parched lips. The inside of his mouth tasted like he'd been chewing on a penny. The coppery taste was a symptom, but he didn't know what it meant. *I could ask the paramedics. Oh, wait. Nobody's here. Nobody's coming to help me.*

He was on his own.

His fingers gingerly explored his scalp until he found the source of his pain. When he poked at the knot on the back of his head, his hand came away bloody. Head wounds tended to bleed a lot, but how had that blood gotten on the front of his shirt?

He remembered shots being fired in the night. A fistfight. Running. Riding. On a horse? *That can't be right.* He wasn't a cowboy. Or was he?

No time for speculating. He had to move fast. In four days...

His mind blanked. There was nothing inside his head but a big, fat zero.

In four days, something big was going down, something life-changing and important. Why the hell couldn't he remember? What was wrong with him?

The chirp of a bird screeched in his hypersensitive ears, and he was tempted to go back to sleep. If he waited, the truth would catch up to him. It always did. Can't escape the truth. Can't hide from reality.

He closed his eyes against the sun and gathered his strength. A different memory flashed. He wasn't in a forest but on a city street. He heard traffic noise and the rumble of an overhead train. Tall buildings with starkly lit windows loomed against the night sky. He fell on the pavement. Shadows devoured him. He fought for breath. If he lost consciousness, he would die.

His eyelids snapped open. Was he dead? That was as plausible an explanation as any.

This mountain landscape was the afterlife. Through the treetops, he saw a sky of ethereal blue. One thing was for damn sure. If he was dead, he needed to find an angel to tell him what came next.

Caitlyn Morris stepped onto the wide porch of her cabin and sipped coffee from her U.S. Marine Corps skull-and-crossbones mug. A crisp breeze rustled across the open meadow that stretched to the forested slopes. Looking to the south, she saw distant peaks, still snow-capped in early June.

A lock of straight blond hair blew across her forehead. She probably ought to do something about her messy ponytail. Heather was going to be here any minute, and Caitlyn didn't want to look like she was falling apart.

She leaned her elbows on the porch railing and sighed. She'd moved to the mountains looking for peace and solitude, but this had been a busy little morning.

At daybreak, she'd been awakened by an intruder—a dappled gray mare that stood outside her bedroom window, nickering and snorting, demanding attention. The mare hadn't been wearing a bridle or saddle, but she had seemed tame. Without hesitation, she'd followed Caitlyn to the barn. There, Caitlyn kept the other two horses she was renting for the summer from the Circle L Ranch, which was about eight miles down the winding dirt road that led to Pinedale.

After she'd tended to the wayward horse, sleep had been out of the question. She'd gotten dressed, had breakfast, put in a call to the Circle L and went back to the horse barn to check the inventory slip for the supplies that had been delivered from the hardware store yesterday.

A handyman was supposed to be starting work for her today, even though it was Saturday. Most of her projects didn't require two people, but she needed help to patch the barn roof. She checked her wristwatch. It was almost nine o'clock, and the guy who answered her ad had promised to be here by eight. Had he gotten lost? She really hoped he wasn't going to flake out on her.

When she saw a black truck coming down the road, her spirits lifted. Then she noticed the Circle L logo and the horse trailer. This wasn't her handyman.

The truck pulled into her drive and a tall, rangy brunette—Heather Laurence, half-owner of the Circle L—

climbed out. "Good to see you, Caitlyn. How are you doing?"

There was a note of caution in the other woman's voice. Nobody from this area knew exactly why Caitlyn had come to live at this isolated cabin, which had been a vacation home for her family since she was a little girl with blond pigtails and freckles.

She hadn't wanted to tell her story, and folks from around here—even someone like Heather, whom she considered a friend—didn't push for explanations. They had a genuine respect for privacy.

Caitlyn held up her skull-and-crossbones mug. "Would you like some coffee?"

"Don't mind if I do."

The heels of Heather's cowboy boots clunked on the planks of the porch as they entered the cabin through the screen door.

When Caitlyn arrived here a month ago, it had taken a week to get the cabin clean enough to suit her. She'd scrubbed and dusted and repainted the walls of the front room a soothing sage green. Then she'd hired horses for company. Both were beauties—one palomino and the other roan. Every day since, she'd made a point of riding one in the morning and the other in the afternoon. Though she certainly didn't need two horses, she hadn't wanted to separate one from the others at the Circle L. No need for a horse to be as lonely as she was.

Sunshine through the kitchen windows shone on the clean-but-battered countertops and appliances. If she decided to stay here on a more permanent basis, she would resurface the counters with Turkish tile.

"Looks nice and homey in here," Heather said.

"It had been neglected." When she and her brother

were living at home, the family spent every Christmas vacation and at least a month in the summer at the cabin. "After Mom and Dad moved to Arizona, they stopped coming here as often."

"How are they doing?"

"Good. They're both retired but busy." Caitlyn poured coffee into a plain blue mug. "Cream or sugar?"

"I take it plain and strong." Heather grinned. "Like my men."

"I seem to remember a summer a long time ago when you were in love with Brad Pitt."

"So were you."

"That sneaky Angelina stole him away from us." Heather raised her coffee mug. "To Brad."

"And all the other good men who got away."

They were both single and in their early thirties. Caitlyn's unmarried status was a strategic career decision. She couldn't ask a husband to wait while she pursued her work as a reporter embedded with troops in war zones around the globe.

"That crush on the gorgeous Mr. Pitt must have been fifteen years ago," Heather said. "A simpler time."

Fifteen years ago, September eleventh was just another day. Nobody had heard of Osama bin Laden or the Taliban. "Before the Gulf War. Before Afghanistan."

"You've been to those places."

"And it doesn't look like I'll be going back any time soon." A knot tightened in her throat. Though Caitlyn wasn't ready to spill her guts, it wouldn't hurt to tell her old friend about some of the issues that had been bothering her. "The field office where I was working in the Middle East was closed down due to budget cuts."

"Sorry to hear it. What does that mean for you?"

"I've got a serious case of unemployment." And a lot of traumatic memories. Innumerable horrors she wanted to forget. "I'm not sure I want to continue as a journalist. That was one of the reasons I came here. I'm taking a break from news. No newspaper. No TV. And I haven't turned on my laptop in days."

"Hard to believe. You were always a news junkie, even when we were teenagers."

"Your brother used to call me Little Miss Know-It-All." Her brother was four years older and as cute as Brad Pitt. "I had such a huge crush on him."

"You and everybody else." Heather shook her head. "When Danny finally got married, you could hear hearts breaking all across the county."

Danny was still handsome, especially in his uniform. "Hard to believe he's a deputy sheriff."

"Not really. Remember how he always played cops and robbers?"

"Playing cowboy on a ranch is kind of redundant."

After days of solitude, Caitlyn enjoyed their small talk. At the same time, she felt an edge of anxiety. If she got too comfortable, she might let her guard down, might start welling up with tears, might turn angry. There was so much she had to hold back.

She looked through her kitchen window. "Do you know a guy named Jack Dalton?"

"I don't think so. Why?"

"He answered my ad for a handyman. And he was supposed to be here over an hour ago."

"Caitlyn, if you need help, I'd be happy to send over one of the hands from the ranch."

She wanted to remain independent. "This guy sounded like he'd be perfect. On the phone, he said he had experience as a carpenter, and he's a Gulf War veteran. I'd like to hire a vet."

"You spent a lot of time with the troops."

"And I don't want to talk about it. I don't mean to be rude, but I just can't." Suddenly flustered, she set down her mug on the countertop. "Let's go take a look at the horse that showed up on my doorstep."

After years of being glib and turning in daily reports of horrendous atrocities, she hated to find herself tongue-tied. Somehow, she had to get her life back.

Weaving through the bottom of the canyon was a rushing creek. He sank to his knees beside it and lowered his head to drink. Ice-cold water splashed against his lips and into his mouth. It tasted good.

No doubt there were all kinds of harmful bacteria in this unfiltered water, but he didn't care. The need for hydration overwhelmed other concerns. He splattered the cold liquid into his face. Took off his flannel shirt and washed his hands and arms. His white T-shirt had only a few spots of dried blood.

As far as he could figure, he'd been sleeping in his boxers and undershirt. He'd been startled awake, grabbed his flannel shirt and jeans, jammed his feet into his boots and then…

His scenario was based on logic instead of memory. The remembering part of his brain must have been damaged by the head wound. His mind was like a blackboard that had been partially erased. Faint chalk scribbles taunted him. The more he concentrated, the more they faded. All he knew for sure was that somebody was trying to kill him.

This wasn't the first time he'd been on the run, but

he didn't know why. Was he an innocent victim or an escaped felon? He suspected the latter. If he'd ever rated a guardian angel, that heavenly creature was off duty.

His first need was for transportation. Once he'd gotten away from this place, he could figure out what to do and where to go.

He tied the arms of his flannel shirt around his hips, tucked the SIG into the waistband of his jeans and started hiking on a path beside the creek. Though it would have been easier to walk along the nearby two-lane gravel road, his instincts warned him to avoid contact.

The canyon widened into an uncultivated open field of weeds, wildflowers and sagebrush. This landscape had to be the Rocky Mountains. He'd come to the Rockies as a kid, remembered hiking with a compass that pointed due north. It was a happier time.

A black truck hauling a horse trailer rumbled along the road. He ducked behind a shrub and watched as the truck passed. The logo on the driver's side door read: Circle L Ranch, Pinedale, Colorado.

Good. He had a location. Pinedale. Wherever that was.

He trudged at the edge of the field near the trees. His head still throbbed but he disregarded the pain. No time for self-pity. He only had four days until…

He approached a three-rail corral fence in need of repair. Some of the wood rails had fallen. Two horses stood near a small barn which was also kind of dilapidated. The log cabin appeared to be in good shape, though.

He focused on the dark green SUV parked between the cabin and the horse barn. That would be his way out.

A woman with blond hair in a high ponytail came out of the barn. Around her waist, she wore a tool belt that looked too heavy for her slender frame. At the porch, she paused to take a drink from a water bottle. Her head tilted back. The slender column of her throat was pure feminine loveliness. That image dissolved when she wiped her mouth on the sleeve of her denim shirt.

He didn't want to steal her SUV. But he needed transportation.

Coming around the far end of the corral, he approached.

When she spotted him, she waved and called out, "Hi there. You must be Jack Dalton."

It was as good a name as any. "I must be."

Chapter 2

Caitlyn watched her new handyman as he came closer. Tall, lean, probably in his midthirties. He wasn't limping, but his legs dragged as though he was wading through deep water. Rough around the edges, he hadn't shaved or combed his thick, black hair. His white T-shirt was dirty, and he had a plaid shirt tied around the waistband of his jeans.

When he leaned against the corral fence, he seemed to need the rail for support. Was he drunk? Before ten o'clock in the morning? She hadn't asked for references. All she knew about Jack Dalton was that he was a veteran who needed a job.

"On the phone," she said, "you mentioned that you were in the army."

"Tenth Mountain Division out of Fort Drum, New York."

Colorado natives, like Caitlyn, took pride in the 10th
Mountain Division. Founded during World War II, the
original division was made up of elite skiers and mountain climbers who trained near Aspen. "Where were
you stationed?"

"I'd rather not talk about it."

After the time she'd spent embedded with the troops,
she had a great deal of empathy for what they had experienced. To be completely honest, she had self-diag-
nosed her own low-grade case of post-traumatic stress
disorder. But if Jack Dalton had come home from war
an alcoholic, she had no desire to be his therapist. "Have
you been drinking, Jack?"

"Not a drop, ma'am."

In spite of his sloppy clothes and posture, his gaze
was sharp. He was wary, intense. Maybe dangerous.

She was glad to be wearing her tool belt. Hammers
and screwdrivers were handy weapons. Just in case. She
looked behind him toward the driveway leading up to
her house. "Where's your car?"

"I had an accident. Walked the rest of the way."

"Are you hurt?"

"A bit."

"Oh my God, I'm a jerk!" She'd been treating him
with suspicion, thinking he was a drunk when the poor
guy was struggling to stay on his feet after a car accident. "Let's get you inside. Make sure you're okay."

"I'm fine, ma'am."

"Please, call me Caitlyn. I feel terrible for not realizing—"

"It's all right." He pushed away from the fence, obviously unsteady on his feet. "I was hoping you could

loan me your car and your cell phone so I could go back to my truck and—"

"You're not driving in your condition." She went to him, grabbed his arm and slung it over her shoulder. "Come on, lean on me."

"I'm fine."

He tried to pull away, but she held on, adjusting his position so none of her tools poked into his side. Jack was a good seven or eight inches taller than she was, and he outweighed her by sixty or seventy pounds. But she could support him; she'd done this before.

As they moved toward the back door to her cabin, she flashed on a memory. So real, it felt like it was happening again, happening now.

The second vehicle in their convoy hit a roadside bomb. The thunder of the explosion rang in her ears. Still, she heard a cry for help. A soldier, wounded. Reporters weren't supposed to get involved, but she couldn't ignore his plea, couldn't stand by impartially and watch him suffer. She helped him to his feet, dragged him and his fifty pounds of gear to safety before the second bomb went off.

Her heart beat faster as adrenaline pulsed through her veins. If she closed her eyes, she could see the fiery burst of that explosion. Her nostrils twitched with the remembered stench of smoke, sweat and blood.

At the two stairs leading to the door, Jack separated from her. "I can walk on my own."

With a shudder, she forced her mind back to the present. Her memories were too vivid, too deeply carved into her consciousness. She'd give anything to be able to forget. "Are you sure you're all right?"

His shoulders straightened as he gestured toward the door. "After you."

The back door opened into a smallish kitchen with serviceable but elderly appliances and a beat-up linoleum floor of gray and pink blobs that she would certainly replace if she decided to stay at the cabin through the winter. Mentally, she started listing other projects she'd undertake. Repair roof on the horse barn. Replacing the railing on the porch. Staying busy kept the memories at bay.

She led Jack to the adjoining dining room and pointed to a chair at the oblong oak table. "Sit right there, and I'll bring you some water."

"Something's wrong." It was a statement, not a question.

"I don't know what you mean."

"Yes, you do."

He stood very still, watching her, waiting for her to talk. *Not going to happen.* She knew better than to open the floodgate and allow her nightmare memories to pour into the real world.

Deliberately, she changed the subject. "Are you hungry?"

"I could go for a sandwich."

Up close, he was disturbingly handsome with well-defined features and a dark olive complexion. His eyes were green—dark and deep. Not even his thick, black lashes could soften the fierceness in those eyes. He'd be a formidable enemy.

She noticed a swelling on his jaw and reached toward it. "You have a bruise."

Before her fingers touched his face, he snatched her wrist. His movement was so quick that she gasped in surprise. He had the reflexes of a ninja. Immediately, he released his grasp.

As he moved away from the table, she could see him gathering his strength, pulling himself together. He went through the dining room into the living room. His gaze darted as though assessing the room, taking note of where the furniture was placed. He ran his hand along the mantle above the fireplace. At the front door, which she'd left open, he peered outside.

"Looking for something?" she asked.

"I like to know where I am before I get comfortable."

"Reconnaissance?"

"I guess you could say that."

"Trust me, Jack. There's nothing dangerous in this cabin." He wasn't entering an insurgent hideout, for pity's sake. "I don't even have a dog."

"You live alone."

Women living alone were never supposed to admit that they didn't have anyone else around for protection, especially not to a stranger. Her hand dropped to the hammer on her tool belt. "I'm good at taking care of myself."

"I'm sure you are."

Though he kept his distance, she didn't like the way he was looking at her. Like a predator. "Would you please stop pacing around and sit?"

"Before I do, I need to take something out of my belt." He reached behind his back. "I don't want you to be alarmed."

Too late. "Of course not."

He pulled an automatic pistol from the waistband of his jeans. The sight of his weapon shocked her. She'd made a huge mistake by inviting him into her cabin.

* * *

The throbbing in his head made it hard to think, but he figured he had two options. Either he could shoot Caitlyn and steal her car or he could talk her into handing over the car keys voluntarily.

Shooting her would be easier.

But he didn't think he was that kind of man.

He reassured her again, "Nothing to worry about."

"I'd feel better if you put the gun down."

"Not a problem." He placed the SIG on a red heart-shaped trivet in the center of the table, took a step to his left and sat in the chair closest to the kitchen. From this angle, he had a clear view of the front door.

She asked, "Do you mind if I check your weapon?"

"Knock yourself out."

She wasted no time grabbing the gun. Expertly, she removed the clip. "Good thing you had the safety on. Carrying a gun in your waistband is a good way to shoot your butt off. Why are you carrying?"

There were plenty of lies he could tell her about why he was armed, but an efficient liar knows better than to volunteer information. "It never hurts to be prepared."

She gave a quick nod, accepting his response.

Apparently, he was good at deception. When she'd asked about his military service, he hadn't hesitated to cite the 10th Mountain Division, even though he didn't remember being in the army or being deployed.

His story about the car accident had been a simple and obvious lie. Everybody had car trouble. Claiming an accident prompted automatic sympathy.

If he'd planned to stick around for more than a couple more minutes, he would have felt bad about lying to her. She was a good woman. Kindhearted. When he'd said he was hurt, she'd rushed to help him, offered her shoulder for support.

Taking his gun with her, she headed toward the kitchen. "I hope egg salad is okay."

"Yes, ma'am."

"I told you before, call me Caitlyn. I'm not old enough to be a ma'am."

And you can call me Jack, even though I'm pretty sure that's not who I am. He rolled the name around in his memory. Jack Dalton. Jack. Dalton. Though the syllables didn't resonate, he didn't mind the way they sounded. Henceforth, he would be Jack Dalton.

Caitlyn poked her head into the dining room. "If you want to wash up, the bathroom is the first door on the right when you go through the living room."

He followed her directions, pausing to peek into the closet near the front door. If he was going to be on the run for any period of time, he'd need a jacket. A quick glance showed a couple of parkas and windbreakers. Nothing that appeared to be his size. A rifle stood in the corner next to the vacuum cleaner.

At the bathroom, he hesitated before closing the door. If the men who were chasing him showed up, he didn't want to be trapped in this small room with the claw-footed tub and the freestanding sink. He checked his reflection in the mirror, noting the bruises on the right side of his face and a dark swelling on his jaw. Looked like he'd been in a bar fight. Was that the truth? Just a bar fight? The simplest answer was usually the correct one, but not this time. His problems ran deeper than a brawl. There were people who wanted him dead.

He searched the medicine cabinet. There was a wide selection of medical supplies. Apparently, a woman who swaggered around with a tool belt slung around her hips injured herself on a regular basis. He found a bottle of extra-strength pain reliever and took three.

After trekking through the forest, his white T-shirt was smeared with dirt, and he didn't exactly smell like a bouquet of lilacs. He peeled off the shirt and looked in the mirror again. In addition to patches of black and blue on his upper right arm and rib cage, a faded scar slashed across his chest from his clavicle to his belly button. He had a couple of minor scratches with dried blood. A deeper wound—newly healed—marked his abdomen. *What the hell happened to me?* These scars should have been a road map to unlock his memory.

Still, his mind was blank.

He washed his chest and pits. His worst injury was on the back of his head, but there wasn't much he could do about it. No matter how he turned, he couldn't see the damage.

There was a sound outside the bathroom door. A car approaching? They could be coming, could be getting closer. Damn it, he didn't have time to mess around with bandages or sandwiches. He needed to get the hell away from here.

He slipped through the bathroom and looked out the front window. The scene in front of her house was un-changed. Nobody was coming. Not yet.

Caitlyn called out, "Hey, Jack."

"I'll be right there."

She charged into the living room and stopped when she saw him. A lot of women would be repulsed by his scars. Not Caitlyn. She stared at his chest with frank curiosity before lifting her gaze to his face. "White or rye?"

"Did you get a good look?"

She shrugged. "I've seen worse."

Her attitude intrigued him. If he hadn't been desperate to get away from this area, he wouldn't have minded spending time with her, getting to know what made her tick. "Are you a nurse?"

"I used to be a reporter, embedded with the troops." She moved closer. "I know some basic first aid. I could take care of those cuts and bruises."

He didn't like asking for assistance, but the head wound needed attention. He went to his chair by the table and sat. "I got whacked on the back of my skull."

Without hesitation, she positioned herself behind him. Her fingers gently probed at the wound. "This looks bad, Jack. You should be in the hospital."

"No doctors."

"That's real macho, but not too smart." She stopped poking at his head and pulled a chair around so she was sitting opposite him. Their knees were almost touching. "I want you to look at my forehead. Try to focus."

"You're checking to see if my pupils are dilated."

"If you have a concussion, I'm taking you to the hospital. Head injuries are nothing to fool around with."

He did as she asked, staring at her forehead. Her eyebrows pulled into a scowl that she probably thought was tough and authoritative. But she was too damn cute to be intimidating. A sprinkle of freckles dotted her nose and cheeks. Her wide mouth was made for grinning.

In her blue eyes, he saw a glimmer of genuine concern, and it touched him. Though he couldn't remember his name or what kind of threat brought him to this cabin, he knew that it had been a long time since a woman looked at him this way.

She sat back in her chair. "What really happened to you? You didn't get that head injury in a car accident."

How could he tell her the truth? He didn't have the right to ask for her help; he was a stranger. She didn't owe him a damn thing. "I should go."

"Stay." She rested her hand on his bare shoulder. Her touch was cool, soothing. "I'll patch you up as best I can."

For the first time since he woke up this morning, he had the feeling that everything might turn out all right.

Chapter 3

Caitlyn only knew one thing for sure about Jack. He was stoic—incredibly stoic. His ability to tolerate pain was downright scary.

Moments ago, she'd closed the wound on his head with four stitches. Though she'd used a topical analgesic spray to deaden the area, the effect wasn't like anesthetic. And she wasn't a skilled surgeon. Her clumsy stitching must have hurt a lot.

He hadn't flinched. When she had finished, he turned his head and calmly thanked her.

After that, he had wanted to leave, but she insisted that he stay long enough to eat something and have some water. After sewing him back together, she was invested in his survival.

Also, she was curious—an occupational hazard for a journalist. She wanted to get Jack's true story.

They sat at her dining room table, and she watched as he devoured an egg salad on light rye. She'd found him a faded black T-shirt that belonged to her brother, who wasn't as big as Jack but wore his clothes baggy. The fabric stretched tight across Jack's chest. Underneath were all those scars. How had he gotten wounded? In battle? The long ridge of puckered flesh on his torso was still healing and couldn't have been more than a couple of months old. If he'd been injured in military service, he wouldn't have been discharged so quickly.

She nibbled at her own sandwich, trying to find a nonintrusive angle that might get him talking. In her work, she'd done hundreds of interviews, some with hostiles. The direct question-and-answer approach wouldn't work with Jack.

"You're not from around here," she said, "What brought you to the mountains?"

"Beautiful scenery. Fresh air."

Spare me the travelogue. "Where did you grow up?"

"Chicago."

Was he a kid from the burbs or a product of the mean streets? Instead of pushing, she offered an observation of her own. "One of the best times I had in Chicago was sailing on Lake Michigan at dusk, watching as the lights of the city blinked on."

He continued to eat, moving from the sandwich to a mouthful of the beans she'd heated on the stove.

"Your turn," she said.

"To do what?"

"I tell you something about me, and then you share something about yourself. It's called a conversation."

His gaze was cool, unreadable and fascinating. The

green of his eyes contained dark prisms that drew her closer. "You have questions."

"We're just having a chat. Come on, Jack. Tell me something about growing up in the Windy City."

"The El," he said. "I don't care for underground subways, but I always liked riding the elevated trains. The jostling. The hustle. Made me feel like I was going someplace, like I had a purpose."

"Where were you going?"

"To see Mark." As soon as he spoke, his eyebrows pinched in a frown. He swallowed hard as though he wanted to take back that name.

"Is Mark a friend?"

"A good friend. Mark Santoro. He's dead."

"I'm sorry for your loss."

"Me, too."

His friend's name rang a bell for her. Even though she hadn't been following the news regularly, she knew that the Santoros were an old-time but still notorious crime family. For the first time in weeks, she glanced longingly at her laptop. Given a few minutes to research on the internet, she might be about to solve the mystery of Jack Dalton.

"I haven't been honest with you, Caitlyn."

"I know."

"I didn't have a car accident."

"What else?"

"There are some guys looking for me. They've got a grudge. When I came here, I thought I could use your car for a getaway. But that's not going to work."

"Not that I'm volunteering my SUV for your getaway, but what changed your mind?"

"If I have your car, it connects you to me. I don't want anybody coming after you."

She agreed. Being targeted by the Santoro family wasn't her idea of a good time. "We should call the police. I have a friend, Danny Laurence, who's a deputy sheriff. He's somebody you can trust."

"I'm better off on my own."

He rose from the table, and she knew he was ready to depart. She hated the thought of him being out there, on his own, against powerful enemies. She bounced to her feet. "Let me call Danny. Please."

"You're a good person, Caitlyn." He reached toward her. When his large hand rested on her shoulder, a magnetic pull urged her closer to him. Her weight shifted forward, narrowing the space between them. He leaned down and kissed her forehead. "It's best if you forget you ever saw me."

As if that would happen. There weren't a whole lot of handsome mystery men who appeared on her doorstep. For the past month, she'd been a hermit who barely talked to anyone. "You won't be easy to forget."

"Nor will you."

"For the record, I still think you need to go to the hospital."

"Duly noted."

From outside, she heard the grating of tires on gravel.

Jack had heard it, too. In a few strides, he was at the front window, peering around the edge of the curtain.

A 1957 vintage Ford Fairlane—two-toned in turquoise and cream—was headed down her driveway. She knew the car, and the driver was someone she trusted implicitly. His vehicle was followed by a black SUV with tinted windows. "Do you see the SUV? Are these the people who are after you?"

"Don't know," he said. "They've seen your car so you can't pretend you're not here. Go ahead and talk to them. Don't tell them you've seen me."

"Understood." She gave him a nod. "You stay in the house. I'll get rid of them."

Smoothing her hair back into her ponytail, she went to the front door, aware that she might be coming face-to-face with the enforcers for a powerful crime family. Panic fluttered behind her eyelids, and she blinked it away. This wasn't her first ride on the roller coaster. She'd gotten through war zones, faced terrorists and bloody death. A couple of thugs from Chicago shouldn't be a problem.

From the porch, she watched as the Ford Fairlane parked near her back door. The black SUV pulled up to the rear bumper of her car before it stopped.

She waved to Bob Woodley—a tall, rangy, white-haired man who had been a longtime friend of her family. He was one of the few people she'd seen since moving back to the cabin. A retired English teacher, he had been a mentor to her when she was in her teens. "Hi, Mr. Woodley."

He motioned her toward him. "Get over here, Caitlyn. Give an old man a proper hello."

When she hugged him, he must have sensed her apprehension. He studied her expression. His bushy eyebrows pulled into a scowl. "Something wrong?"

"I'm fine." She forced a smile. "What brings you here?"

"I was visiting Heather at the Circle L when these two gentlemen showed up. Since I'm a state congressman, I figured it was my duty to extend a helping hand to these strangers by showing them how to find your cabin."

She looked past him toward the SUV. The two men walking toward her were a sinister contrast to Mr. Woodley's open honesty. Both wore jeans and sports jackets that didn't quite hide the bulge of shoulder holsters. Dark glasses shaded their eyes.

Woodley performed the introductions. "Caitlyn, I want you to meet Drew Kelso and Greg Reynolds."

When she shook their hands, their flesh was cold—either from the air-conditioning in their car or because they were reptiles. "What can I do for you?"

Woodley said, "We understand that you had a visitor this morning."

How did they know about Jack? Had her cabin been under surveillance? "I'm not sure what you're talking about."

"The dappled gray mare," Woodley said. "You had Heather come over and pick it up."

"Oh, the horse." She rolled her eyes in an attempt to look like a ditzy blonde. She didn't want these men to take her seriously, wanted them to dismiss her as harmless. "Silly me, I'd already forgotten about the horse."

The one named Reynolds said, "It belongs to someone we know."

"Your friend needs to be more careful," she said. "The horse showed up on my property without a saddle or a bridle or anything."

The friendly smiles she offered to the two thugs went unanswered. They meant business.

The taller, Drew, had sandy hair and heavy shoulders. His mouth barely moved when he spoke. "We're looking for the guy who was riding that horse."

"I didn't see anybody." She widened her eyes, even fluttered her lashes. "Like I said, no bridle or saddle."

Drew said, "If you saw him, it'd be smart to tell us."

His comment sounded a bit like a threat. "Who is this person? What's his name?"

"Tony Perez."

With complete honesty, she shook her head. "Never heard of him. But I'll be on the lookout. Is there a number I should call if I see him?"

Drew handed her a business card that contained only his name and a cell phone number.

"I guess that wraps up our business." Woodley checked his wristwatch. "I'd better shove off."

She wanted to cling to him and plead for him to stay until these two men were gone. "Can't you stay for coffee?"

"Sorry, kiddo. I'm running late for an appointment in Pinedale." He strolled toward his vintage Ford Fairlane. "I hope you gents can find your missing friend."

They gave him a nod and headed toward their SUV. Caitlyn breathed a little sigh of relief. They were leaving. The crisis was averted.

Before Woodley climbed behind the steering wheel, he said, "Don't be a stranger, Caitlyn."

He drove down her driveway and turned onto the road. The two men stood beside their SUV talking. With every fiber of her being, she wanted them gone. These were two scary guys. Why hadn't Mr. Woodley been able to see it?

They came back toward her. Drew said, "We want

to take a look around. To make sure he's not hiding around here."

"That's not necessary." She positioned herself between him and her front porch. "There's nobody here but me."

Drew glanced over his shoulder at the other man, Greg Reynolds. He was neat and crisp. His boots were polished. His charcoal sports jacket showed expensive tailoring, and his thick black hair glistened in the sunlight. She guessed that he was a man of expensive tastes, definitely the boss.

Greg gave a slight nod, and Drew walked toward her cabin. Short of tackling him, there was no way Caitlyn could stop him. Still, she had to try.

"Hey." She grasped his arm. "I told you. There's nobody here."

Slowly, he turned toward her and removed his sunglasses. He didn't need to speak; the curl of his upper lip and the flat, angry glare from his eyes told her that he wouldn't hesitate to use violence. And he would most likely enjoy hurting her.

She stepped back. Silently, she prayed that Jack had hidden himself well or had managed to slip out the back door.

"This is for your own safety," Drew said. "Tony Perez is dangerous."

As she entered her cabin, her heart was pumping hard. She shoved her hands into her pockets so no one would notice the trembling.

Jack had cleaned up every trace of his presence. On the dining room table, there was only one plate and one bottled water. She watched as Drew went into the bathroom. Jack's discarded clothing had been in there.

Apparently, his shirt and undershirt were gone because Drew emerged without saying anything.

When Tony brushed past her, she caught a whiff of his expensive cologne. It smelled like newly minted hundred-dollar bills. He rested his hand on the door handle of the front closet and yanked it open. She noticed that her rifle was gone.

In the loft above the stalls in the horse barn, Jack lay on his belly and sighted down the barrel of Caitlyn's rifle. This weapon lacked the sophistication of the sniper equipment he was accustomed to using. Her rifle scope was rudimentary and so poorly mounted that he had removed it. At this range, he trusted his marksmanship. His first shot would show him the correction for this particular weapon, after which he would be accurate.

His plan was simple. Take out the tall man with sandy hair; he was the most deadly. Then the boss.

Holding the rifle felt natural, and he easily comprehended the necessary strategy in an assault situation. These skills weren't inborn. He couldn't remember where he'd learned or who taught him. But he knew how to kill.

When Caitlyn and the men entered the house, Jack adjusted his position, trying to keep track of their movements through the windows. So far they hadn't threatened Caitlyn, except for that moment when she touched the sandy-haired thug. The bastard looked like he wanted to kill her. If he'd hurt her, Jack would have squeezed the trigger. He'd gotten Caitlyn into this mess, but he wouldn't let her be harmed.

The optimum scenario would be for them to make their search and then go. She wasn't a part of this.

Not being able to see what was going on inside the house made him edgy. If they didn't come outside soon, he needed to move in closer to protect her. He started a mental timer for five minutes.

In the corral below him, the two horses—one light and one dark—stood at the railing. Their ears pricked up. They nickered and shifted their hooves. Animals could sense when something was wrong. The horses knew.

He was nearing the end of his countdown when the small group emerged from the back door. Caitlyn looked angry. Earlier, she'd tried to act like a dumb blonde and had failed miserably. Her intelligence showed in every move she made and every word she spoke.

The two men walked ahead of her toward the barn. Jack got ready to shoot. His position gave him an advantage, but he needed to time his shot so there was no chance they could retaliate. He wished there was some way to signal Caitlyn to keep her distance from them.

They walked toward the corral. Coming closer, closer. They were less than fifty yards from his position. The tall man was in front. His hand slid inside his jacket, and he pulled his handgun.

Jack aimed for the center of his chest, the largest target. If he'd been using a more sophisticated weapon, he would have gone for a head shot.

He heard Caitlyn object. "What are you doing? Why do you have a gun?"

The other man assured her, "We have to be prepared. The person we're looking for is extremely dangerous."

Damn right. Jack knew he was capable of lethal action. A trained killer. *Damn it, Caitlyn. Get out of the way.* The slick-looking man with black hair, the boss, stayed close to her. Too close.

Jack adjusted his aim. He'd kill the boss first. As he stared, he realized that he knew this man. Gregorio Rojas. He was the younger son of a drug cartel family that supplied the entire Midwestern United States.

Hatred flared in Jack's gut. His finger tensed on the trigger. Rojas was his sworn enemy. *Take the shot. Rid the world of this bastard whose actions have been responsible for so much misery, so much death.*

Rojas paused, took a cell phone from his pocket. After a brief conversation, he motioned to the other man. They headed back toward their vehicle.

Still, Jack didn't relax his vigilance. Rojas was still within range.

His memory was returning. The blank spaces knitted together in a tapestry of violence. *Take the shot.*

Chapter 4

Jack knew he had killed before. As he stared down the barrel of Caitlyn's rifle, his vision narrowed to his target. The center seam of Rojas's tailored jacket. His hands were steady. He was focused. Cool and calm, as always.

He remembered another time, another place, another killing.

He was in the city, the seedy part of town. On the fourth floor of a dirty brick hotel that rented rooms by the hour, he set up his sniper's nest and assembled his precision rifle with laser scope, silencer and tripod. With high-power, infrared binoculars, he observed the crappy apartment building directly across the street. Fourth floor, corner unit. Nobody home.

He checked into the hotel at sundown. Hours passed. Dusk turned to nightfall when lights flickered on throughout the city. Not that he had a glittering view.

When the lamp in the apartment across the street came on, he eased into position. Though he sat in the dark, the glow from a streetlight reflected dully on the barrel of his rifle and silencer.

He peered through his scope. Through the uncurtained window of the apartment across the street, a man with fiery red hair paced from room to room with his gun in his hand, looking for danger.

"I'm here," Jack whispered. "Come to the window, you bastard."

This man deserved to die.

But his target hadn't been alone. A small woman with brassy blond hair and a child entered Jack's field of vision. Two witnesses.

The killing had to wait.

From the loft in the barn, Jack watched as Rojas and his companion got into the SUV and drove away from Caitlyn's cabin. She turned on her heel and rushed back into her house, moving fast, as though she had something burning on the stove.

When the black SUV was out of sight, he rolled onto his back and stared up at the ceiling in the barn that needed patching.

He knew who he was.

A stone-cold killer.

Inside her cabin, Caitlyn wasted no time. She dove into the swivel chair behind her small desk in the living room and fired up her laptop. It felt good to see the screen come to life. Back when she was a working journalist—especially in the field—her computer had been an ever-present tool, almost an extension of her arm.

Her hands poised over the keyboard. *But I'm not a journalist anymore. Not right now.* She had no assignment, no story to investigate, and she wasn't entirely sure that she wanted to go back into the fray.

Her main reason for moving to this cabin had been to purposely distance herself from the 24-hour-a-day news cycle. During this time of self-imposed seclusion, she hoped to regroup and decide what to do with the rest of her life.

Her parents and nearly everyone else who cared about her had encouraged Caitlyn to seek out a safer occupation. Not that they wanted her to quit writing, but they hoped she would leave the war zones to others. As if she'd be satisfied reporting on garden parties? Writing poetry about sunshine and lollipops?

She wasn't made that way. She thrived on action.

Jack's arrival at her doorstep might be fate. She hadn't gone looking for danger, but here it was. She had armed thugs searching her cabin. If Jack Dalton had a story to tell, she wouldn't turn away.

She jumped on the internet and started a search on the name of Jack's supposed "friend," Mark Santoro. Expertly, she sorted through news stories, mostly from the *Chicago Tribune,* and put together the basic facts.

As Jack had said, Mark Santoro was dead. He and four other members of the Santoro crime family had been killed in a shootout on a city street five months ago. One of the men had his hands cut off. Mark had been decapitated. A gruesome slaughter; it was intended to send a message.

Allegedly, the Santoro family handled narcotics distribution in the Midwest, and they had angered the powerful Rojas drug cartel—the suppliers of illegal drugs.

Agents from the DEA and the Bureau of Alcohol, Tobacco, Firearms and Explosives were all over this incident. They arrested and charged several members of the Rojas cartel, including the top man, Tom Rojas. The federal murder trial was due to start on Tuesday, four days from now, at a district court in Chicago.

Reading between the lines, Caitlyn suspected that much of this story never made it to print. She used to date a reporter who worked at the *Trib*—a sweet guy who had taken her for that romantic sailboat ride on Lake Michigan and begged her to stay in the States. She'd refused to settle down, and he'd moved on. A typical pattern for her relationships. The last she'd heard, her former beau was happily married with an infant daughter. If she needed to find out more about the trial, she could contact him.

Rapid-fire, she typed in the names of the two thugs: Drew Kelso and Greg Reynolds. A quick search showed several people with those names, but nothing stood out. She wasn't surprised. Drug lords and thugs don't generally maintain websites.

Next, she searched for Tony Perez. After digging through a lot of worthless information, she tightened her search and linked it to Mark Santoro. In one of the articles about the shootings, Tony Perez was mentioned as a bodyguard for Santoro. Perez had been killed at the scene.

But Jack Dalton was very much alive.

Slowly, she closed her laptop. Though she hadn't heard him enter the house or walk across the living room floor, she sensed Jack's nearness. She knew that he was standing close, silently watching her.

A shiver prickled down her spine. She wasn't afraid that he would physically harm her. There wasn't a reason, and he was smart enough to avoid unnecessary violence. But she was apprehensive. Jack was pulling her toward a place she didn't want to go.

"Did you find what you were looking for?" he asked.

She swiveled in her desk chair to face him. "You look pretty healthy for a dead man."

He crossed the room and returned her rifle to the front closet. "I brought your gun back."

The smart thing would be to send him on his way and forget she ever saw him. But finding the truth was a compulsion for her. "Those men were looking for Tony Perez. Is that your real name?"

"Tony's dead. Call me Jack."

"They said you stole a horse, and that you're dangerous."

"Half right."

"Which half?"

"I didn't steal the horse. I borrowed it."

He approached her, braced his hands on each of the arms of her swivel chair and leaned down until his face was on a level with hers. "Those men are unpredictable. There's no telling what they might do. I strongly advise that you stay with a friend for a couple of days."

"What about you? Where are you going?"

"Not your problem."

He was so close that she could see the rise and fall of his chest as he breathed. She wanted to rest her hand against his black T-shirt, to feel the beating of his heart. Instead, she picked a piece of straw off his shoulder. "You were hiding in the barn. In the loft."

"I couldn't leave until I knew you were safe."

"Who were those guys?" She searched his eyes for a truth he might never tell her. "They said their names were Drew Kelso and Greg Reynolds."

"Not Reynolds. That was Gregorio Rojas." He reached toward her desk and flipped her computer open. "You know the name. You were reading all about him and his pals."

"And his brother, Tom. His murder trial starts in four days."

He stepped away from her. "I have to go."

"Not yet. I'm still putting the pieces together." She left her chair and stood between him and the front door. "I'm asking myself why Rojas is after you. Something to do with his brother's trial, right?"

"You don't need to know."

"But I do, Jack. I'm a reporter." And she was damn good at her job. He'd thrown out just enough bread crumbs for her to follow this trail. "Let's suppose that you are this Tony Perez and that you survived the attack on the street. That makes you a witness."

"I told you before. Tony is—"

"Dead." *Yeah, sure.* "I'm just supposing here. I can only think of one reason that an eyewitness to a crime in Chicago would be hiding in the Colorado mountains. WitSec."

The Witness Security Program provided protection for those who might be in danger before a trial. There must be a safe house in the area.

"Suppose you're correct," he said. "If a protected witness was attacked at a safe house, it must mean that he was betrayed by the marshals who were supposed to be looking out for him. They gave the location of the safe house to Rojas."

She hated to acknowledge that law enforcement officials—in this case, U.S. Marshals—could be corrupted. But she knew it was possible. While embed-

ded with the troops, she'd run across similar instances.
Somebody taking a payoff. Somebody acting on a
grudge instead of following orders.

With a shrug, she said, "It happens."

"If it did happen that way, there's nobody this witness
can trust. Rojas is after him. And the marshals can't let
him report them. He has to go on the run and find his
own way to make it to the trial in Chicago."

"I can help you."

"I don't want your help."

He stepped around her and went out the front door.

Jack strode away from her house toward the corral
fence. Angry at himself for telling too much. Angry at
her for wanting to know. How the hell could she help
him? And why? Why should she give a damn? As a
reporter with the troops, she was accustomed to being
surrounded by heroes. Not somebody like him.

At the fence, he paused to settle his mind into a
plan. He wasn't sure how he'd make his way out of this
sprawling mountain terrain where a man could disappear and never be seen again. That might be the solution. *Drop out of sight and start over.*

But he had promised to appear in court. His eyewitness testimony would put Tom Rojas and some of his top
men behind bars. Little brother Gregorio didn't have the
guts or the authority to hold the cartel together. Jack's
testimony could make a difference.

He looked toward the road that ran past her house—
the only direct route into and out of this area. His enemies would be watching that road. He'd be better off
taking a cross-country path, walking until… Until he
got to Chicago?

"Jack, wait!" Caitlyn dashed toward him. She thrust a canvas backpack into his hands. "Take this."

Inside the pack, he saw survival supplies: a couple of bottled waters, some energy bars, a sweatshirt and a cell phone. He'd be a fool to refuse these useful items, but he wasn't going to admit that she'd been right about him needing her help.

She dug into the pocket of her jeans and pulled out a wad of cash. "It's a hundred and twenty-seven bucks. That's all I have on hand."

"Caitlyn, why—"

"And this." She handed him a cowboy hat. "To protect the wound on your head."

Jack tried on the battered brown hat with a flat brim. Not a bad fit. "Why are you so determined to help me?"

Her face was as open as a sunflower, deceptively innocent. "Why shouldn't I?"

"You don't know me. You don't know the life I've led."

"You were part of the Santoro crime family," she said. "I'm assuming that you've done a lot of things I wouldn't condone. You could have been a hit man, an assassin or even a drug pusher."

"No," he said, "never a pusher. I hate drugs."

"That's the past, Jack. You made a change. You decided to testify against some very bad men."

"Maybe I didn't have a choice."

"I don't care."

He was surprised to hear a tremble in her voice, an undercurrent of strong emotion. She was feeling something intense. About him? He didn't think she was the kind of woman who formed sudden attachments. Over and over, she'd said she was a reporter. In her profession, she couldn't allow her passions to rule. "What's going on with you?"

"You're risking your life to testify, to do the right thing." She inhaled so deeply that her nostrils flared. As she exhaled, she regained control of herself. "I need to believe that when people fight for the right thing and put their lives on the line, it's not for nothing. Their sacrifice has significance."

Spoken like someone who had been to war and had seen real suffering. His irritation faded behind a new-found admiration. She was one hell of a woman. Strong and principled. For the second time, he wished they had met under different circumstances. "Don't make me into something I'm not."

"Fair enough," she said. "As long as you don't down-play what you're doing. You're giving up your former life to do the right thing."

"I'm no hero."

She cocked her head to one side. A hank of straight blond hair fell across her forehead. "Neither am I."

"I have to go."

"First, let me show you how to use the GPS on the cell phone. It won't give you a detailed topographical map, but you'll have an idea where the roads are."

Instead, he handed the phone back to her. "If the GPS shows me where I am, it'll show other people my location. They can track me from the signal."

"Of course. I knew that." She shoved the phone into her pocket. "You said you didn't want to use my car, but you could take one of the horses."

On horseback, he'd make better time than if he was on foot. He nodded, accepting her offer. "I'll find a way to return the horse to you."

"You should take the stallion. His name is Fabio because of his blond mane. And he's a real stud."

Entering through the corral gate, she motioned to the handsome palomino horse and made a clicking with her tongue. Both animals responded and obediently trotted toward the barn door.

As he followed, he noticed her athletic stride. There was nothing artificial about her. No makeup. No fancy styling to her hair. Her body was well toned, and he suspected that her fitness came from outdoor living rather than a regular workout at a gym. Her jeans fit snugly, tight enough to outline the feminine curve of her ass.

Until now, he hadn't really taken the time to appreciate how attractive she was. When he first stopped at her cabin, he thought he'd be there for only a couple of minutes. He hadn't expected to know anything about her.

While she saddled the stallion and rattled off instructions for the care of the horse, he watched. Her energy impressed him. She was unlike any woman he'd known before. He regretted that after he rode away from her cabin, he would never see her again.

He harbored no illusions about coming back to her after the trial. His life wasn't his own. He'd be stashed away in witness protection, which was probably for the best. Right now, Caitlyn had a high opinion of him. If she knew the reality of his life, she wouldn't want to be in the same room with him.

She finished with the saddle and came toward him. "Fabio is ready to go."

"I'm not."

He placed his hand at the narrowest part of her body and gently pulled her closer.

Chapter 5

When Jack laid his hand possessively on her waist, Caitlyn knew what was coming next. Awareness gusted through her like a moist, sultry breeze that subtly pushed her toward him.

His green eyes shone with an unmistakable invitation, but he gave her plenty of time to back off and say no. During the past several years, she'd spent most of her days in the company of men and had learned how to make it clear that she wanted to spend her nights alone. But she wanted Jack to kiss her. His story had touched the very core of her being and reminded her of important truths. As if she wanted to kiss him because of her principles? *Yeah, right.* There was a whole lot more going on when she looked into Jack's handsome mug. The man was hot. Sexy as hell.

She leaned toward him. Her breasts grazed his chest

as she tilted her head back. Her lips parted. Her eyelids closed.

The firm pressure of his mouth against hers started an earthquake inside her. She gasped, enjoying the tremors. Her arms wrapped around him, her body molded to his and she held on tight. It had been a long time since she felt so totally aroused. Way too long.

His big hands slid down her back and cupped her bottom. He fitted her tightly against his hard body. The natural passion that she usually suppressed raced through her.

If they had more time, she would have gone to bed with him. But that was purely hypothetical. He had to depart immediately. Maybe that was why she could kiss him with such abandon. She knew she'd never see him again.

With obvious reluctance, he ended the kiss and stepped back. "I should go."

Every cell in her body wanted him. She struggled to be cool. "I wish you'd let me call my friend Danny."

"The deputy?"

She nodded vigorously, trying to ignore her intense desire and be logical. "After what you told me, I understand why you don't want to contact anybody in law enforcement. But I've known Danny since we were kids. I trust him."

"That's exactly why you shouldn't call him." He reached toward her and tucked a piece of hair behind her ear. "If he helped me, I'd be putting him and everyone he knows in danger."

"From Rojas," she said.

"You're a reporter. You know how the drug cartels deal with people who get in their way."

Though it was difficult to imagine grisly violence in the Colorado mountains under peaceful blue skies, she knew he was right. Revenge from the drug cartels was equal to the horrors she'd seen in the Middle East. Whole families—women and children—were brutally slaughtered, their bodies dismembered and left to rot.

Those images completely doused her desire. Jack had to go. He had to find his way to safety.

"I'm worried for you," she said. "I don't suppose you'd consider taking me along."

"Not a chance." He grinned, and she realized that it was the first time she'd seen him crack a smile. "Why would you even ask?"

"A federal witness on the run? It's a damn good story."

"Not unless it has a happy ending."

He mounted the palomino stallion. Though Jack wasn't a cowboy, he looked real good on horseback. She hated that he was on the run, couldn't accept that she'd never be with him. There had to be a way to see him again.

Of course there is. She knew where the trial was taking place. If she pulled some strings and used her press credentials, she could wangle a seat inside the courtroom. "I'll see you in Chicago."

"If I make it."

With a wave, he rode from the barn.

She was left standing in the corral, watching as Jack rode into the forest behind her cabin. If she'd been riding beside him, she would have told him to go the other way. Across the meadow, he should have headed southeast. The terrain was less daunting in that direction, and there was water. Eventually, he would have found the Platte River. *What if he doesn't make it?*

Being left behind while someone else charged into danger wasn't the way she operated. She had to do something.

Taking the cell phone from her pocket, she called Heather to get her brother's phone number.

Danny Laurence wasn't as yummy as she remembered from her high school years. Though he looked sharp in his dark blue deputy uniform shirt, he was developing a bit of a paunch—a testament to being settled down and eating home-cooked meals every night.

He took off his cowboy hat as he sat at the head of her dining room table. His short hair made his ears look huge. Had he always had those ears?

"Good to see you," he said. "I've been meaning to drop by and talk about old times."

"Same here. And I want to meet the woman who finally got Danny Laurence to take that long walk down the aisle."

"Sandra." He spoke her name fondly. "You'd like her. She's kind of a goofball."

"Is she Baby Blue or Green Light?"

He laughed. "It's been a long time since I heard those code words you and Heather made up to describe the guys you met. Baby Blue means a sissy, right? And Green Light is good to go."

"And Red Fire means trouble ahead." A particularly apt description. The English translation for *Rojas* was "red."

"My Sandra is Green Light all the way."

She was glad he'd found happiness. Not that a rosy

future was ever in doubt; Danny had always been the most popular guy around—the captain of the football team, the president of the senior class.

Joining him at the table, she set a glass of fresh-squeezed lemonade in front of him. This was exactly the same seating arrangement she'd had with Jack, but the atmosphere was utterly different. With Danny, she felt friendly—as if they should tell dumb jokes and punch each other on the arm. There was none of the dangerous magnetism she experienced with Jack. The thought of him reminded her of their kiss and made the hairs on her arm stand up. Somehow, she had to help him.

She wished that she could come right out and ask Danny the questions she needed answered: Was there a WitSec safe house in the area? Did he know about a federal witness on the run? How could Jack be protected from a drug lord bent on revenge?

The direct approach wasn't an option. If Danny knew nothing, she wouldn't be the one to tell him and bring down the wrath of the Rojas. Caitlyn didn't want to be responsible for a bloodbath in Douglas County.

Danny took a swallow of lemonade. "What's up?"

"I was concerned about that horse I found." Jack had used the gray mare for his escape. Finding the owner meant locating the safe house. "Has anybody claimed her?"

"We haven't had a report of a stolen horse. Which isn't surprising. Livestock gets loose now and then. Nobody wants to make a big fuss only to have the horse come trotting back home."

"Have you checked the brand?"

"Not yet. A runaway horse isn't top priority. I've got other things to do."

"Such as?"

"The usual."

His attitude was way too laid-back to be dealing with the aftermath of a shootout at a WitSec safe house. She doubted that the marshals had reported Jack's disappearance, especially not if they were in collusion with Rojas. As far as she knew, federal marshals weren't required to check in with local law enforcement. It defeated the purpose of a safe house if too many people were aware of its existence.

"I was wondering," she said, "if there's been any kind of unusual activity around here?"

"Like what?"

"Oh, you know. Strangers in town. Suspicious stuff."

"You're working on some kind of news story, aren't you? You haven't changed a bit, Caitlyn. Always have to have the scoop." He sipped his lemonade and licked his lips. "Little Miss Know-It-All."

His teasing annoyed her. "You haven't changed, either. You're still the mean big brother, looking down his nose."

"I remember that time when you and Heather followed me and my date to a party in Bailey and I ended up having to escort you home. You two used to drive me crazy."

"Ditto." She actually did punch him on the arm. "Suppose I was working on a story. I'm not saying I am, just suppose. Would you have anything to tell me?"

"Could you be more specific?"

Not without putting him in danger. "I'm wondering if the FBI or maybe the federal marshals have any current operations in our area."

His expression turned serious. "If you have some kind of inside track on FBI activity, I want to hear about it."

"Nothing. I've got nothing."

"Why did you want me to come over?"

Aware that she'd already said too much, Caitlyn changed directions. "Do you know a guy named Jack Dalton?"

"As a matter of fact, I arrested that sorry son-of-a-gun last night at the Gopher Hole. Drunk and disorderly. He's sleeping it off in jail."

That solved the mystery of her missing handyman—the *real* Jack Dalton. "I almost hired him to work for me."

"Aw, hell, Caitlyn. Don't tell me this Dalton character is some kind of FBI agent."

"He's just another troubled soul." And not her responsibility. "When he wakes up, tell him he lost the job."

"You're acting real weird. You want to tell me what's wrong?"

"I'm just nervous. Because of the horse." She thought about mentioning the two armed thugs and decided against it. There wasn't anything Danny could do about them. "Lately, I've been jumpy."

As he studied her, his expression changed from irritation to something resembling compassion. He reached over and gently patted her arm. "Heather told me that you'd been through a lot, reporting on the war. She's kind of worried about you."

The last thing she wanted was pity. "I'm fine."

"It's okay to be nervous."

"I told you. I'm doing just fine."

"Whatever you say." He drained his glass of lemonade, stood and picked up his hat. "I want you to know, it's all right for you to call me any time."

"If I run into any Red Fire situations, I'll let you know."

He stepped outside onto the porch and waited for her to join him. "The sheriff just hired a new guy who was in Iraq. He happens to be single. If you want to talk, he'd—"

"Whoa." She held up her hand. "I never thought I'd see the day when Danny Laurence started playing matchmaker."

"That's what happens when you get settled down. You want everybody else to pair up."

"When I'm ready to jump into the singles pool, I'll let you know."

"Fair enough."

"Thanks for coming over." She gave him a warm smile. "Be careful, Danny."

"You, too."

She watched as he drove away in his police vehicle with the Douglas County logo on the side. Asking him to come here hadn't given her any new information, except to confirm the identity of Jack Dalton. The *real* Jack Dalton was not the man who had showed up on her doorstep. *Her* Jack Dalton was actually Tony Perez. But he didn't want to use that name. Because he'd changed? She wanted to believe that when Tony Perez agreed to testify, he abandoned his old life.

Her gaze wandered to the hillside where she'd last seen him. By now he'd be miles away from here.

She missed him.

For that matter, she also missed the real Jack Dalton. Without a handyman, patching the barn roof was going to be nearly impossible. *Who cares?* Did it really matter if her barn leaked? Earlier today, she'd thought so.

For the past weeks, she'd filled her waking hours with projects—cleaning, painting, doing chores and making repairs. Those jobs now seemed like wasted energy. Not like when she'd been talking to Jack, figuring out his identity. Tracking down a story made her feel vital and alive. At heart, she was a journalist. That was what she needed to be doing with the rest of her life.

Her decision was made. The time had come for her self-imposed seclusion to end. Looking across the road, she scanned the wide expanse of sagebrush and prairie grass that led to the rugged sweep of forested hillsides. A rich, beautiful landscape, but she didn't belong here.

Her job was to follow the story. Packing a suitcase would take only a couple of minutes; she was accustomed to traveling light. She could be on her way in minutes, driving toward Denver International Airport, where she could catch the next flight to Chicago.

But what if Jack ran into trouble and came back to the cabin? She needed to stay, if only for twenty-four hours. As long as she was here, she might as well patch the barn roof.

She went back into the cabin and picked up her tool belt. Though she never locked her house when she was home, the recent threats emphasized the need for security. After she'd locked the front and back doors, she headed toward the barn.

The midday sun warmed her shoulders. Her life here was idyllic, but it wasn't where she needed to be. Why had she doubted herself? It was so obvious that she was a reporter. What was she afraid of? *Oh, let's see. A million different things.* Not that she was Baby Blue— a sissy. She'd always been brave, and living in a war zone had hardened her to the sight of blood and gore.

She had faced unimaginable horror, and she'd learned to stifle her terror. But those fears never truly went away.

Though she'd never told anyone, she had experienced fits of uncontrolled sobbing, nightmares, even delusions. Once, she'd heard a helicopter passing overhead and panic overwhelmed her. She'd dropped to her knees and curled into a ball. Her mind wasn't right; she wasn't fit to be on the front line.

But she could still be a reporter; not every assignment required her to rush headlong into danger.

Inside the barn, she fastened the tool belt around her hips and looked up at the roof. One of the holes was so big that she could see daylight pouring through.

From the stall nearest the door, the bay mare snorted and pawed at the earthen floor.

"Oh, Lacy." Caitlyn went toward the horse. "I'm sorry. We missed our morning ride. Maybe later, okay?"

Lacy tossed her head as though angry. When she looked sadly at the empty stall beside her, Caitlyn felt guilty. Poor Lacy had been left behind, locked in her stall and deprived of her morning exercise.

"All right," Caitlyn said, "a short ride."

She had just gotten the horse saddled when she looked out the front door of the barn and saw the black SUV approaching her driveway. Rojas was back.

Chapter 6

After Jack left Caitlyn's cabin, he continued to discover more of his innate skills. Horseback riding wasn't one of them. Every time he urged Fabio into a pace faster than a walk, Jack bounced around in the saddle like a broken marionette. How did cowboys do this all day? His ass was already sore.

Lucky for him, Fabio was a genius. The big palomino responded to his clumsy tugging on the reins with impressive intelligence as they wove through the pines and leafy shrubs in the thick forest. They found a creek where the horse could drink, and a couple of rock formations that could be used for hideouts.

After getting repeatedly poked in the arms by branches, Jack put on the sweatshirt Caitlyn had so thoughtfully packed for him. He hadn't expected her help. Her kindness. Or her kiss. It meant something, that kiss. Beyond the pure animal satisfaction of holding a woman in his arms, he'd felt a stirring in his soul as though they were deeply connected. He had a bright fleeting memory of what it was like to be in love, but the thought quickly faded into the darker recesses of his mind.

There could never be anything significant between him and Caitlyn. If he survived the next four days and made it to the trial, he'd have a new life in witness protection. And it wouldn't include her.

Looking up at the sky through scraggly branches, Jack noted the position of the sun and determined which way was north. This ability to get his bearings came from outdoor training in rugged, arid terrain. He remembered a desert. And an instructor who spoke only Spanish and—surprise, surprise—Jack was able to translate. He was bilingual. Another useful skill.

Also, he had a sharp comprehension of strategy. He knew that Rojas and his men were looking for him, as were the marshals at the safe house who had betrayed him. They might have access to advanced technology. Though Jack didn't see or hear a chopper overhead, it was entirely possible that this whole area was under aerial surveillance. His plan was to stay under the cover of the trees until nightfall.

He headed northwest, roughly following the direction of the horse trailer he'd seen on the road to Caitlyn's cabin. The logo on the side of that truck said: Circle L Ranch, Pinedale, Colorado. Locating the nearby population center could prove useful, and Fabio seemed to know where they were going. The big horse moved smoothly through the forest until they came to a ridge overlooking a meadow.

From this vantage point, Jack looked down on a small herd of fat black cattle, twenty-five or thirty head. As he watched, cowboys in a truck pulled up to a feeding area. Another ranch hand on a dirt bike joined them. None of these men were on horseback.

Jack patted Fabio's neck beneath his flowing blond mane. "Don't worry, buddy. A truck will never replace you. You're too pretty."

For a moment, he considered riding down and asking for shelter. On a ranch, there would be a number of places to hide. But he didn't want to put these people in danger. If Rojas suspected they were helping him, he'd gun down every person on the ranch and probably shoot the cattle as well. Fear was how the cartel ran their business; violence was their methodology.

Had Mark Santoro been the same way? Jack had respected Mark. He liked him, but that didn't mean either of them were upstanding citizens.

A clear thought unfurled inside his head. *No crime justifies taking the law into your own hands.* He believed this principle. At the same time, he knew that he had violated it. He had performed an execution. The circumstance wasn't clear, but Jack had killed an unarmed man.

He tugged on Fabio's reins, and they went back into the forest, heading toward Caitlyn's cabin. Thinking about Rojas made him worry. What if the thugs returned to her place? Gregorio Rojas was notorious for taking rash action. He lashed out violently. If he couldn't find another lead, he might return to Caitlyn with the idea that he could make her talk. Even if she didn't know anything. Even if she was innocent.

With Fabio tethered to a tree, Jack settled down to

watch the cabin. An open space in a roughly triangular shape stretched downhill to her back door. The back of the barn was only a couple hundred yards away. Leaning against a sun-warmed boulder, he opened one of the bottled waters and ate a crunchy energy bar. A full meal would be nice. A rare steak with baked potato. Maybe a nice Chianti. And a cigar.

The memory of those rich flavors teased his palate. His mouth watered. The rest of his past was sketchy, but he knew what he wanted for his last meal. He inhaled the remembered fragrance of mellow tobacco. A Cuban cigar, of course.

When he saw the police vehicle arrive at Caitlyn's cabin, he supposed this was the friend she kept talking about. Danny the deputy appeared to be a tall, good-looking guy. Standing on the porch, he gave her a hug that lasted a bit longer than a casual greeting. A boyfriend? Hopefully, she wouldn't feel compelled to tell Danny Boy all about him. The last thing Jack needed was the local cops putting out an APB. There were enough people after him already.

Jack was disappointed to see Danny drive away by himself. If Caitlyn had gone with him, she'd be safe. At least, she'd have an armed cop at her side.

Alone, she was vulnerable.

He considered sneaking down the hill and telling her to come with him. *Bad idea.* With him, she'd be in danger for sure. Without him, she had a chance. *Sit tight. This might all go away.*

Caitlyn seemed to be getting back to her routine. She came out the back door carrying her tool belt. Her single-minded determination made him grin; nothing was going to stop her from patching that roof.

He almost relaxed. Then he saw the black SUV. They were driving too fast on the two-lane gravel road. Reckless. Dangerous.

He had to get Caitlyn out of there. He pushed himself to his feet and ran. Instinctively, he dodged and stooped, staying away from the open area, keeping his approach camouflaged.

The SIG was in his hand. He'd checked the clip and knew he had only four bullets. That should be enough. If he got to the rear of the barn, he'd be in range. First, he'd take out the big bodyguard, the guy who called himself Drew Kelso. Then, he'd shoot Rojas.

The SUV parked in her driveway. Four men and Rojas emerged. Five targets and only four bullets. Jack didn't like the odds.

Kelso led the way. The bodyguard yanked his handgun from the shoulder holster as he stormed toward the cabin. He yelled, "Hey, bitch. Get out here."

The others followed.

The fact that Caitlyn was in the barn might save her. If she moved fast enough, she could get away without having them notice.

Jack crouched at the edge of the trees. There was no cover between him and the back wall of the barn. He stared at the weathered wood. No back door. That would have been too easy.

Caitlyn came through the big door in the front. She was astride the bay mare and, for some reason, wearing her tool belt. If she rode toward the corral gate, it would bring her closer to Rojas. She wheeled the horse in the opposite direction—toward where he was hiding in the trees—and rode across the fenced corral. At the far end was a gate that opened into the field.

She rode straight at it, leaning forward in the saddle and moving fast. Her expertise in handling her mount was obvious, and he admired her skill.

Rojas and his men hadn't spotted her. They were occupied with breaking into her cabin, yelling threats. Jack hoped they would keep up their posturing until she'd gotten safely away.

He sprinted down the rugged hill. When he got to the gate, he'd throw it open. And she'd ride through to safety. Caitlyn was close, almost there. *Come on, baby, you can make it.*

The shouting from the cabin changed in tone. Like hunting dogs on the chase, they'd seen their quarry and reacted. In front of the others, Kelso ran from her house toward the corral. Gunfire exploded in wild bursts.

Caitlyn stiffened in the saddle. She reined her horse. What the hell was she doing?

He reached the gate, unfastened the latch and threw it open. "Caitlyn," he called to her. "This way. Hurry."

She turned her head toward him. All the color had drained from her skin. Her mouth was open, gasping. Had she been hit?

At the other end of the corral, he saw the five men pour through the gate, waving their guns, yelling, shooting.

Jack wanted to return fire, but he only had four bullets. Every shot had to count.

Kelso stopped and spread his legs in a shooter's stance. With both hands, he took aim.

Jack dropped to one knee, pointed the SIG and squeezed the trigger.

His bullet found its mark. Kelso roared in pain,

clutched his thigh and toppled to the dirt inside the corral.

The men behind him stumbled to a halt. They'd thought they were dealing with an unarmed woman. Hadn't expected to be in danger.

Taking advantage of their momentary confusion, Jack fired a second time. Again, he aimed for the legs. Another man screamed and fell.

The others were in retreat. The cowards didn't know he had only two bullets left. He took advantage. Grabbing the reins on Caitlyn's horse, he pulled her toward the open gate.

"Wait." Her voice quavered. "Mount up behind me."

He didn't question her or argue. On horseback, their chances for escape were a hell of a lot better. As she scooted forward and out of the saddle, he stuck his toe into the stirrup and took her place.

Riding like this wouldn't be easy. He would have preferred holding his ground and shooting, picking them off one by one. But he didn't have the firepower. Jack dug in his heels, urging the horse forward. They made it through the gate.

"Where are we going?" she asked.

"Uphill," he said. "Take cover in the trees."

Behind his back, he heard another couple of shots. Leaning forward, he wrapped his arms around her. A screwdriver handle from her tool belt dug into his gut. He noticed that with every blast of gunfire, her body trembled.

They made it into the forest.

When he looked over his shoulder toward the barn, he saw Rojas, staring after them. Revenge was all he lived for. The bastard wouldn't quit until Jack was dead. And now, Caitlyn was another object for his hatred.

Jack felt like hell. It was his fault that she was in danger. Because of him, her peaceful life was torn to shreds. This counted as one of the worst things he'd done in his life as Tony Perez or whoever he was.

"Where's Fabio?" she asked.

"Up here. To the right."

Still within earshot of the shouting from her cabin, they approached the tree where he'd tethered the horse. The big palomino nickered a greeting to the bay mare.

Jack dismounted and went to his horse while she re-adjusted her position. She reached down to the tool belt. "Should I take this off?"

"Keep it." Some of those tools might be modified to use as weapons. "Never can tell when you might need a ratchet."

"I think we should go to the Circle L."

Though her voice was still shaky, the blush had returned to her cheeks. He didn't know what had happened to her when the shooting started, but the intensity of her reaction gave him cause for worry. It was almost like she'd gone into shock.

"We can't involve anyone else," he explained. "If the people at the Circle L help us, they'll be in as much danger as we are. Follow me."

Disappearing in this vast wilderness wouldn't be difficult, but hiding the horses presented a problem. Not only did they need to locate a cave big enough for Fabio and Lacy but they had to figure out a way to keep the animals quiet.

He turned to her and asked, "Do you have your car keys?"

"Why?"

"We might need to use your car."

"The keys are in my pocket. It's weird. I don't usually lock my cabin. For some reason, I did."

"Your instinct was right. The locked doors slowed down Rojas and his men. It gave you more time to escape."

"Oh, damn," she muttered. "I'll bet they kicked in my door. That's going to be a problem. You know, I've gone to a lot of trouble fixing up the place."

Her attitude puzzled him. Earlier, she'd frozen in terror. Now, she seemed more concerned about property damage than the fact that she was running for her life. "A broken door is the least of your problems. Rojas and his men are more likely to burn your cabin to the ground."

"That's terrible. A wildfire would devastate miles of forest." Her blue eyes snapped. "But I guess drug cartels aren't real concerned about environmental damage."

He couldn't believe she was composed enough to make a joke. Every muscle in his body was tense. Their plodding progress along the path beside the creek was driving him crazy. He wanted to fly, but they couldn't go faster without heading into open terrain. It was safer to stay within the shelter of the forest.

Single file, they ascended a ridge leading away from the creek. Direct sunlight hit Fabio's mane. The golden horse glowed like a beacon. "We have to ditch the horses. What will they do if we dismount and continue on foot?"

"They'll probably trot along behind us."

Exactly what he was afraid of. They were approaching an area he'd explored earlier. A rugged granite cliff rose above the tree line. If they climbed those rocks, there were a number of crannies where they could hide until nightfall.

"I have an idea," she said. "Fabio and Lacy don't actually belong to me. They're from the Circle L. If we get within sight of the ranch and shoo them away, they'll probably trot home to their stable."

"I told you before. We can't drag anybody else into danger." Why didn't she understand? "If the horses show up, the people at the ranch will know that something happened to you. They'll report it. Local police will be involved."

"As if that's a bad thing?"

Her sarcasm was the last straw. He wheeled around on Fabio and rode up beside her, confronting her face-to-face. She appeared to be blasé and cool.

"There's a time to be a smart-ass, Caitlyn. This isn't it."

"What do you want me to do? Burst into tears?"

Tears would be more normal than the facade she was putting up. He wanted an honest reaction from her. "Rojas wants us dead. Both you and me. If he gets his hands on us, death won't be painless. This isn't a game. It isn't a tidy little story you're writing for an article."

"You don't know anything about what I do for a living."

"Tell me," he challenged.

"I lived on the front lines of battle." Her eyes darkened. She wasn't joking, not anymore. "I've seen things you couldn't imagine."

"There's a difference between reporting on the shooting and being the target."

"Really? The incoming bombs didn't know the difference. An improvised explosive device couldn't tell that I was a reporter. I know what it's like to be in danger, Jack. I remember every minute, every horrible minute. Sometimes, I wake up at night and…"

He was beginning to understand her earlier reaction. "That's what happened to you when you heard the gunfire. You had a flashback. You froze."

"The only way I can handle the panic is to ignore it, pretend that it's erased. But it won't go away. I can't forget. That fear is branded into my brain."

If they were going to survive, he needed for her to be fully in control. She needed to be smart and conscious. To get beyond the flashbacks.

If they weren't careful, her memories would kill them.

Chapter 7

Caitlyn couldn't help feeling the way she did. Her way of hiding fear was bravado. Cracking jokes and making snide comments gave her a buffer zone. One of the reporters she worked with in Iraq said that when it came to gallows humor she was the executioner. What else could she do? The alternative was to turn as hard as stone.

But the way she'd frozen when she heard gunfire wasn't typical. In other combat situations, she'd been able to respond and follow orders. The attack at her cabin had been unprovoked, unexpected. Because there hadn't been time to prepare herself, fear rushed in and overwhelmed her. She could never let that happen again. Her response had almost gotten them killed.

Jack reached toward her, spanning the space between their horses. She slapped his hand and turned her head away. "I'm fine."

"Listen to me, Caitlyn."

"You don't have to explain again. I've read the news stories. I know the cartels are famous for their vengeance. And brutal. Their victims are dismembered, beheaded, burned alive. I know what Rojas is capable of."

"Look at me."

Reluctantly, she lifted her gaze. His eyes narrowed to jade slits. A muscle twitched in his jaw. He was fierce, a warrior. Quietly, she said, "I'm glad you're on my side."

"I don't make promises lightly." His voice had an edge of steel. "Believe me, Caitlyn. I won't let them hurt you."

How could he stop them? Sure, he was tough, and his marksmanship at the cabin had been nothing short of amazing, but he was only one man. "We need backup."

"Do you really think your friend Danny is a match for Rojas?"

"What do you know about Danny?"

"I'm assuming he's the cop who came to your house."

"You were watching my cabin." She appreciated his concern. Instead of putting miles between himself and Rojas, Jack stuck around to keep an eye on her. "Why?"

"Guilt," he said. "I feel like hell for putting you in danger."

"How did you know they'd come back?"

"I didn't. That was the worst-case scenario." His eyes scanned the forest impatiently. "I have a strategy. Plan for the worst and hope for the best."

"Something you learned while working for Santoro?"

"Santoro wasn't my first job. Let's get back to Danny. You gave him a long hug. Are you close?"

"I've known him since we were teenagers. He's like

a big brother. And why do you care about who I'm hugging? Are you jealous?"

"Hell, no."

His denial came too fast. *He was jealous.* "Danny is happily married."

"Good for him. Now, here's the plan. We'll take the horses down to a field and leave them. Then we come back here, climb the rocks and find a place to hide until nightfall."

"I know this area better than you," she said. "Let me take the lead."

"Move fast."

As she rode down to an open area beyond a grove of aspen, she digested the very interesting fact that Jack cared enough about her to stay and watch her cabin, and he was jealous when he saw another man give her a hug. He must be attracted to her. He'd kissed her, after all.

Frankly, that attraction went both ways. He was handsome, aggressive, masculine and…totally unavailable. It was just her rotten luck to get involved with a guy who worked for a crime family and would be going into witness protection.

When they reached the creek at the edge of the meadow, she dismounted, removed the saddles and used a rope to lightly hobble the front legs of their horses. She didn't like to leave Fabio and Lacy alone for a prolonged period of time, but they'd be all right for a couple of hours. When she and Jack were safely on their way, she'd call Heather and tell her where to find the horses.

Jack slung the little backpack she'd prepared for him over his shoulder. "Give me the tool belt," he said. "We're going to be moving fast, and it's heavy."

She unbuckled the belt and held it toward him. "How much time do we have before they come after us?"

"Not much." While he fastened the belt around his hips, he transferred his gun to his hand. "They had to deal with two injured men and arrange for off-road transportation. Those things take time, but I'm assuming they're already on our trail."

She swallowed the fear that was bubbling inside her. "I suppose that's the worst-case scenario."

"Getting caught is the worst." He looked back toward the rocky cliffs. "Stay under the cover of the trees."

"Why?"

He gestured to the cloudless blue skies overhead. "Possible aerial surveillance."

He really was thinking of every contingency. "Really?"

"Start running," he said.

Though she didn't follow a regular exercise routine, Caitlyn was in good physical condition. She jogged at the edge of the forest, dodging between the tree trunks and ducking under low-hanging branches. The vigorous motion got her heart pumping. Though breathing heavily, she wasn't winded. After a month at the cabin, the altitude didn't bother her. But Jack probably wasn't acclimated to the thin air at this elevation. She glanced over her shoulder to check on him.

With the gun in his hand and ferocious determination written into every line of his face, he showed no indication of being tired. "Faster," he said.

"Need to be careful." She took a breath. "Don't want to trip. Sprain an ankle."

"You can move faster."

She spurred herself forward. When her family spent

summers at the cabin, she and her brother climbed all over these rocks and hills. She knew the perfect place to hide. Her thigh muscles strained as she started the final uphill push.

Pausing, she caught her breath. "We'll climb down this sharp ravine, then up and over those boulders."

"Right behind you."

Her hideout wasn't actually a cave; it was a natural cavern formed by huge chunks of granite piled against each other. The most dangerous part was at the top. She flattened her back against the rock and crept along a ledge. "Be careful here. The drop wouldn't kill you, but it'd hurt."

Even with the tool belt, he managed easily.

At the far side of the ledge, she slipped through a slit between two boulders and climbed down, placing her feet carefully. A cool shadow wrapped around her.

She was inside a low cavern. The waters of the creek trickled through the rocks above and formed a pool, which then spilled down into another cavern that wasn't visible from where she crouched on a rock.

Jack sat beside her. There wasn't enough room for him to stretch his legs out straight without getting his feet wet in the pool. "You did good, Caitlyn. This cave is excellent."

Sunlight through the slit provided enough illumination for her to see him. When she sat on the rock beside the pool, she felt moisture seeping into her jeans. "The only way they can find us is to stick their heads down here. Have you got any bullets left?"

"Two." He unbuckled the tool belt and moved closer to her. "The sound of the creek will cover our voices if we talk quietly."

Her muscles tingled from the run, and his nearness started a whole other spectrum of sensation. In spite of the danger and the fear, she was thinking of how good it would feel to lean against him and have his arm wrapped around her shoulders.

He pointed toward the ledge where the water made a miniature Niagara Falls. "There's another cavern below this one, right?"

"Two others. A large one that can be reached by following the creek. Then another. Then this cubbyhole."

"How visible is the approach to the first cavern?"

"If they come after us on horseback, they'd have to dismount and walk in. Rojas didn't impress me as the kind of man who did that kind of search."

"We have to remember the other men at the safe house," he said, "the federal marshals who betrayed me."

She hated to think of that conspiracy but didn't have trouble believing it had happened the way Jack said. Rojas had plenty of money to use as an enticement. "After you were found dead, how do you think the marshals planned to cover it up?"

"They could say that unidentified men in masks burst into the safe house and grabbed me. Or they could claim that I turned on them and they had to shoot me."

"What about me? How can they explain killing me?"

In the dim light, the rugged lines of his face seemed softer. The rough stubble on his chin faded to a shadow. "Your death wouldn't be explained. You'd just disappear. There's no tangible link between us."

"Yes, there is. The gray mare." The horse that showed up on her doorstep belonged to the men at the safe house. "A good investigator would connect the horse to my disappearance. Plus, Rojas and his men tore up my cabin. Somebody would have to suspect foul play."

"They'd blame it on me." His quiet words blended into the rushing of the creek. "Or on the unidentified men who killed me. The marshals wouldn't necessarily come under suspicion."

Though Rojas and his men represented a direct threat, she was more concerned with those federal marshals. They wouldn't charge through her door with guns blazing. Their approach would be subtle and clever. "What if they contact Danny to help them search for me? He knows about this cavern. He could lead them to us."

"Think it through," Jack said. "In the first place, they won't want to involve local law enforcement. Not while Rojas is in the area."

Wishing that she felt safer, she leaned against him. The warmth of his body contrasted with the cool surface of the rocks. His arm slipped around her.

She looked up at him. Would he kiss her again? Though she wouldn't mind a repeat, she was too nervous to relax and enjoy the sensations. "How long do we wait?"

"After dark," he said, "we'll go to your cabin and take your car."

"Won't they be watching?"

"I'll know if they are."

He sounded so confident that she believed him, even though she had no reason to think that he was a surveillance expert. Being in the employ of the Santoro family meant he knew his way around firearms and was probably good with his fists. But he seemed to have a wider spectrum of experience.

"I don't know much about you." In the subtle light of the cave, she studied him. "You might say I don't know Jack."

"Funny." He touched the tip of her nose with his index finger. "And this is an appropriate time for a joke."

"So glad I can entertain you. Seriously, though. Do you have training in surveillance?"

"I watched your cabin for over an hour, and you didn't know I was there."

"True, but I wasn't looking for you."

"I know how to shadow, how to observe and how to do a stakeout. And I learned from an expert. An old man who lived in Arizona. He was a tracker, a hunter. He showed me how to disappear in plain sight and how to sense when someone was coming after me."

"Sensing a threat? How does that work?"

"Awareness." He pointed to a glow that flickered against the cavern wall. "That patch of light is rising from the cave below us. If I see a shadow, I'll know that someone is approaching and getting too close."

She nodded. Though his method was simple, it hadn't occurred to her. "What else?"

"Listen to the rippling of the water as it slips from this cave to the next. There's a pattern to the sound. A splash indicates an obvious disturbance, but even a stealthy approach can be heard."

Though she concentrated on the sound of the water, she only heard gurgling and dripping. "This awareness thing is a kind of Zen-like approach. Was your teacher a guru?"

"He'd never use that word, but yes." Jack rattled off

a sentence in Spanish, then he translated: "Wisdom comes from an open mind and profound simplicity."

"You speak Spanish. Are you from Mexico?"

"Does it matter?"

"Not really." When she shrugged, her shoulder rubbed against his chest. The moist air in the cavern sank into her pores like a cool sauna. "You make me curious. How did you get those scars on your chest?"

"How do you think?"

"You're being deliberately evasive." And it was beginning to irritate her. "There's no reason for you to be secretive. I already know you're not the real Jack Dalton, because Danny told me he's sleeping off a drunk-and-disorderly charge in jail. I know you're a federal witness on the run. And I'm fairly sure that you're Tony Perez."

"I guess you know it all."

She doubted that she'd even begun to scratch the surface of this complicated and somewhat infuriating man. "When I ask a question, I want an answer. How did you get those scars?"

"I was in a motorcycle accident. And a knife fight. Twice I was shot."

He'd lived a dangerous life, but she'd known that. "What were the circumstances? Why were you injured?"

"I have enemies. They don't place nice."

"Enemies like Gregorio Rojas and his brother," she said.

With his thumb he tilted her chin so she was looking up at his face. Though his expression was unreadable, his eyes glimmered, and that shine was somehow reassuring. A few years ago she had interviewed a mercenary in Afghanistan and had seen a flat coldness in his eyes, as though his soul no longer inhabited his body. Jack wasn't like that. Though she had no doubt that he'd killed people, he still had a conscience.

The tension in his jaw relaxed as he leaned closer to her. She arched her neck and closed her eyes, waiting for his kiss. His lips pressed firmly against hers. He withdrew an inch, then tasted her mouth more thoroughly, nibbling at her lower lip and gliding his tongue across her teeth.

His subtlety tantalized her, and she pressed for a harder, deeper kiss. This wasn't wise. Not profoundly simple. But she experienced a wonderful awareness.

He tensed and pulled away. Without speaking, he pointed to the patch of light on the wall. The pattern had changed. She heard a difference in the splashing of the water.

Someone had entered the cave below them.

Chapter 8

Moving cautiously so he wouldn't betray their hiding place by scraping his boot against the rock, Jack positioned her in the darkest corner of the cavern. He figured that if she froze in panic, he wouldn't have to maneuver around her. Though he didn't dare peek over the ledge overlooking the lower cavern, he stretched out flat on his belly on the rock beside the water. If the searcher got close, Jack could react effectively. The SIG was in his hand.

A voice echoed from the cavern below them. "This is a good hiding place. Not big enough for their horses, though."

Another voice responded from a distance. "Do you see anything?"

A beam from a flashlight reflected on the wall and ceiling of the lower cave. Jack wished that he'd done more reconnaissance. Should have explored the cave below them. Should have been more prepared.

Glancing toward Caitlyn, he saw her tension, but she wasn't frozen as she'd been when she heard the gunfire. She managed a nod. Her eyes were huge. Her hands clenched at her breast.

From below he heard a splash.

"Damn," the voice said, "I got my boots wet."

"Any sign of them?"

"Nothing."

"We'll move on. They're on horseback and would have gone farther away from the cabin than this."

Jack listened carefully to their voices. One of them had a Texas twang that sounded familiar.

The flashlight beam went dark. There was the sound of more splashing from the lower caves. As the searchers moved away from them, his voice faded. "Here's what I don't understand. If he was at that woman's house, he'd have access to a phone. Why didn't he call for backup?"

Jack strained to hear what they were saying. Why did they think he could call for backup? The Santoros were based in Chicago. They couldn't help him from halfway across the country.

"Who knows what's going on in his head," said the other voice. "We're not dealing with an average person. He's a legend."

"Yeah, I've heard. Tall tales," the Texan drawled. "They say he hid out for six weeks in a jungle before he completed his mission."

Though the men were still talking, they were outside the cave. Jack could hear only bits and pieces of their conversation. Something about a "loner" and "killed a man."

He didn't remember surviving in a jungle. What kind

of mission had he been on? Reaching into his memory was like sticking his hand into a grab bag. He didn't know whether he'd pull out a gold medal or a piece of dung.

When he felt Caitlyn touch him, he rolled onto his back and looked up at her. He knew that she'd heard as much as he had. Therefore she'd have questions. Even if he'd known all the answers, Jack figured it wasn't wise to go into details. Some memories were better left unsaid.

He sat up. She was close to him, kneeling on the rock beside his thigh. Her jaw was tight. In a barely audible whisper, she asked, "Are they gone?"

He nodded. "We're safe. For now."

Exhaling in a whoosh, she sat back on her heels. He had the sense that she'd been holding her breath the whole time the searcher had been in the cave below them. Still whispering, she asked, "What did they mean when they said you could call for backup?"

Damned if I know. Hoping he could defuse her curiosity, he grabbed the backpack, unzipped the flap and reached inside. "Energy bar?"

"I'm glad I packed these for you. I'm starving." She tore off the wrapping. "Tell me about this backup."

So much for distracting her. He peered into the backpack. There were two bars left. Like his bullets, their food would have to be rationed. He looked up at the sunlight slanting through the opening above them. "We've probably got three more hours of daylight before we can make our move."

"Were those the federal marshals?"

He shrugged, hoping against hope that she'd drop the topic.

She took a bite of the energy bar and chewed. Her

eyes were suspicious. "Are you going to tell me? Were those the feds or not?"

"I can't say for certain."

"Why not?" Her voice was sharp. "This is getting really annoying."

"I'm not lying to you," he said.

"Hard to believe, Jack. That one guy had a distinct accent. Did you hear his voice at the safe house or not?"

Evading her inquiries wouldn't be easy. She was smart and determined. His glance bounced off the rocky walls of their hiding place. Spending the next couple of hours in this enclosed space with Caitlyn slinging questions every few seconds would make him crazy. Might as well tell her the truth and get it over with.

"I can't remember," he said.

"Can't remember the names of the marshals? Or can't—"

"I don't remember much of anything." He moved away from her, returning to his position against the cavern wall. He felt as if he was literally stuck between a rock and a hard place. "When I got hit on the head, a lot of memories fell out."

"Seriously?" She scrambled around until she was beside him, facing him. Anger sparked in her eyes as she braced her hand against the wall beside his head and leaned in close for her interrogation. "Are you telling me that you have amnesia?"

"Something like that."

"Oh, please. If you don't want to tell me the truth, just say so. Don't insult me by making up a ridiculous excuse."

The irony irritated him. When she'd thought he was a handyman, she'd been more than willing to accept his lies. The truth was harder to swallow. "Believe what you want."

"If you have amnesia, how did you remember Mark Santoro?"

"I watched him die on the street in Chicago. A hell of a vivid memory." Through his shirt he felt the ragged edge of the scar on his belly. He'd been shot on that street. "I was never a soldier, but I understand chain of command. Mark Santoro was my captain. I was supposed to protect him, and I failed. That memory is never going to fade."

"What about the safe house?" she asked. "You remembered being at the safe house."

"I have a recollection of the place." He might even be able to locate the house again. There was a shake shingle roof, a long porch, a red barn. He shook his head. "The only thing I know for certain is that I need to be at the trial on Tuesday."

"Uh-huh."

"True story."

"This amnesia of yours," she said, "it comes and goes. Is that right? You remember whenever it's convenient?"

"I wish." He glared back at her. "If I knew who to call for backup, I'd have been on the phone first thing. Playing hide-and-seek with Rojas isn't my idea of fun."

She backed off, but only a few inches. Her expression remained skeptical as she chomped on her energy bar. "Head injuries can cause all kinds of strange problems. I just don't know whether to believe you."

"I don't give a damn if you trust me or not. There's only one thing that's important—for us to get out of this mess in one piece."

"Why did you tell me about the amnesia?"

"Because you're a pain in the butt." He held her by the shoulders and confronted her directly. "I don't want to spend the next couple of hours being interrogated."

She shoved at his chest. "Get your hands off me."

"Gladly."

He moved around her and picked up the tool belt. There were screwdrivers, a file and a rasp. "I don't suppose there's a knife in this belt. Or a nail gun."

Her voice was quiet but still persistent. "You told me about the wise old man in the desert who taught you about awareness. A memory?"

"I remember him. He trained me, but I don't know why." Without looking at her, he continued, "I'm aware of speaking Spanish, but don't know how I learned the language. I have skills. Seems like I'm a pretty good marksman."

"I'll say. Back at my cabin you made every bullet count."

Though he was pleased that she'd noticed his ability, he didn't let down his guard. "I don't know how I learned to handle a gun. I have no memory of being trained."

"When you said—"

"That's it, Caitlyn. I'm done talking."

His ability to remember was far less important than their immediate problem. They needed to get as far away from Rojas as possible. And they needed to move fast.

No matter how Caitlyn shifted around, she couldn't get comfortable. When she leaned against the wall of the cavern, her backbone rubbed painfully on the hard surface. Her butt was sore and cold from sitting on the damp rocks beside the water. With her knees pulled up, she wrapped her arms around her legs and watched Jack as he sorted through the various implements on her tool belt.

Who was this man? Reluctantly she decided to accept his explanation that he suffered from some form of amnesia. His head injury provided validation for that claim, and she was well aware of the unpredictability of trauma to the brain.

Okay, then. Amnesia.

The only identity that made sense was Tony Perez, member of the Santoro crime family who supposedly died on the streets of Chicago. As Perez, he'd be a witness—a protected witness—whose testimony could convict the elder Rojas brother.

But the searcher who poked around in the lower cave had mentioned a few things that didn't fit. Why would Tony Perez be able to call for backup? And what kind of jungle mission would he have been undertaking? She wished that she'd had more time on her computer to research his background.

Though Jack had made it very clear that he didn't want to answer questions, she wasn't the kind of passive woman who could simply sit back and take orders. She cleared her throat before speaking. "It seems to me that it might be extremely useful to know who you might call for backup."

He grunted in response.

"If you gave me a chance, I might be able to jog your memory. Maybe we could start with the last thing you remember and work backward."

He flipped a Phillips screwdriver in his hand and gripped the handle as if using it to stab. He stared at the tip and frowned. "I know you'd like a simple solution. So would I. But amnesia isn't like misplacing my keys or forgetting where I parked my car. There are empty spaces inside my head."

She didn't want to give up. "We could try. It wouldn't hurt."

"What if I don't like what I remember?" He flipped the screwdriver again. His hands were quick, his coordination excellent. "It might turn out that those blank spots are filled with nasty secrets."

"Are you saying that you'd rather not know?"

"I don't mind being Jack Dalton, a man with no past."

She understood that while he was working for Mark Santoro he might have done things he'd rather forget. But to throw away his entire history? "You're not a bad person. You have a conscience. You agreed to come forward and testify."

"I want Rojas to pay for the murder of Mark Santoro," he said.

"That's a starting place," she said, encouraging him to continue. "What else do you want?"

"To get you to safety."

He focused on her. In the dim light of the cavern, his features weren't clear. She felt rather than saw the heat emanating from him. He smoldered, and she felt herself melting. On a purely visceral level, it didn't matter where he came from or who he was. She knew, without doubt, that he was dedicated to rescuing her. Still, she persisted. "Your memories could help us. There might be someone you could call."

"Someone from the Santoro family?" The corner of his mouth lifted in a wry grin. "That might not be good news for you."

Probably not. The notorious crime family from Chicago wouldn't welcome a reporter into their midst. "Better them than Rojas."

"Leave my past alone, Caitlyn."

He returned his attention to the tool belt. She watched him as he evaluated each implement. In his hands, a paint scraper became a tool for slashing. The hammer was an obvious weapon, as was the crowbar. After discarding wrenches and small screwdrivers, he took the belt apart and reassembled it as a sort of holster.

She couldn't help asking another question. "Have you done this before?"

"Not that I remember. I seem to be good at improvising, using whatever comes to hand."

"Maybe you're MacGyver."

"Anything can be used as a weapon. A belt buckle or a shoelace. A mirror. A rock. It's all about intent."

"And what are your intentions?"

"To be prepared in case we're attacked. Frankly, I'm hoping I won't need a weapon. We'll get to your car and drive to a safe place where I can turn myself in to the authorities. How far are we from Denver?"

"About an hour. If we were going cross-country, we'd actually be closer to Colorado Springs."

He looked up at the sunlight that spilled through the opening in the rocks. "We still have a couple of hours before we can move. Might be smart to catch some shut-eye."

During the time she'd spent embedded with the troops, she'd learned to nap in difficult surroundings. She agreed that it was wise to be rested before they took on the final leg of their escape. "I don't think I can sleep."

Jack settled himself against the cavern wall and beckoned to her. "Lean against me. You'll be more comfortable."

Or not. Whenever she got close to him, her survival instincts were replaced by a surge of pure lust. Why did she have this crazy attraction to him? Sure, he was handsome, with that thick black hair and steamy green eyes. Definitely a manly man, he was her type. But she'd been around plenty of macho guys when she was with the troops. None of them affected her the way Jack did.

He noticed her hesitation. Again, he treated her to that sexy, wry grin. "Scared?"

"Of you?" Was her voice squeaking? "No way."

"Then come here. Use me for a pillow."

Pillows were soft and cuddly. Snuggling up against Jack's muscular body wouldn't be the least bit relaxing. She needed a different plan.

Reaching into her pocket, she took out her cell phone. "We could call the authorities in Denver right now."

"You know that phones can be tracked with a GPS signal."

"You said that before. I get it. But this is a secure phone. It was issued to me by my former employer. It's safe."

"Are you clear on that point?"

"Crystal."

He closed his eyes. "We wait until dark."

Chapter 9

Jack always slept with one eye open. That wasn't a memory but a fact. Being a light sleeper was as indelible as being right-handed.

He leaned against the wall of the cavern. His body slipped into a state of relaxation, allowing his energy to replenish, but part of his mind stayed alert. Even when he was a kid, he knew it was important to be on guard so he would hear the staggering footsteps in the hallway outside the bedroom. His eyes were attuned to deal with the flash of light when that bedroom door crashed open. He knew the smell of the man who meant to hurt him—sweat and whiskey and hate.

Danger was ever present. Survival depended on being ready for the inevitable slap across the face or belt lashing. Or Rojas.

While sleeping, he remained aware of Caitlyn's movements. She tried curling up by herself at the edge of the water. Then she got another energy bar from the backpack. She stood and paced two steps in one direction then the other, like an animal in a cage that was too small. Finally, she settled beside him. Her head rested on his chest, and her slender body curved against him.

He pulled her close. The way she fit into his embrace gave him a sense of warmth and comfort that went beyond the sensual pleasure of holding a beautiful woman. Physically, they were well matched. And there was a deeper connection. Her unflagging curiosity drove him nuts, but he appreciated her intelligence, her wit and her stamina. When he'd given her the clear directive to run, she hadn't complained. Caitlyn wasn't a whiner. She'd been affected by her memories of war but hadn't been broken.

He'd been with other women, many others. One had been special, cherished and adored. He had loved before. Part of him longed to see his lover's face again and to hear her soft, sweet voice. But that was not to be. Without remembering the specifics, he knew his love was gone. Forever.

When Caitlyn moved away from him, he felt the empty space where her head should have been resting. His eyelids opened to slits. The sunlight filtering into the cavern had dimmed to grayish dusk.

He watched as Caitlyn climbed toward the ledge leading out of the cavern. "Where are you going?"

"I'll get better reception here. I need to call Heather at the Circle L Ranch and tell her where the horses are tethered."

"It's best if no one else gets involved. Don't tell her anything else."

"I understand." After she made the call, she looked down at her phone.

"I have a message from Danny. It came through about twenty minutes ago."

He stretched and yawned. The brief sleep had refreshed him enough to continue with his simple plan to get her car and drive to safety. He was aware of potential obstacles, especially since the federal marshals were involved. It might be useful to hear from the local deputy. "Go ahead and play back the message."

As she held the phone to her ear and listened, he watched her posture grow tense and angry. "You need to hear this."

She played back the message on speaker. Danny's voice was low. "Hey, Caitlyn. I found the owners of the gray mare. I thought I remembered seeing that horse."

Danny had stumbled across the safe house. *Bad news.*

The deputy continued, "The owner wants to thank you and maybe give you a reward. Let me tell you where the house is."

He gave directions, starting with "It's not far from where that Arapaho Indian guy lived. I think his name was Red Fire. Yeah, that's it. Red Fire. Turn off the main road at Clover Creek."

After he outlined a couple more twists and turns, he ended the call by saying, "I'll wait here until you arrive. Hurry."

Jack rose and crossed the cavern to stand beside her. Dusky light slid across her stricken face. She whispered, "Danny was warning me. When we were growing up, 'Red Fire' was our code for trouble."

"Even though he made the call, he was telling you to stay away."

"Rojas has him." Her voice quavered. "We can't leave him with that bastard."

The deputy's probability for survival was slim. Neither Rojas nor the feds could afford to release a lawman who would testify against them. Jack knew that the smart move was to drive away and try not to think about what was happening to Caitlyn's friend. It was more important for him to get to that trial and testify.

But Jack wasn't made that way. He couldn't leave someone else to die in his place. "Give me the phone."

"What are you going to do?"

"I'm going to save your friend."

He hit the callback button and waited. With each ring, Jack's hopes sank lower. Danny could already be dead.

The voice that finally answered was unfamiliar. "I'm expecting you."

"I'll be there." As soon as the words left his mouth, Jack knew that he'd done hostage negotiations before. The first step was to give the hostage takers what they wanted. Then demand proof of life. "I need to speak with Danny."

"He's tied up." The cryptic comment was followed by cold laughter. "All tied up."

"If I don't talk to him, you won't see me again. Not until we meet in court."

"Hold on." There were sounds of shuffling and a couple of thuds. Then Danny came on the phone. "It's me. Danny Laurence."

Jack asked, "Have you been harmed?"

"Where's Caitlyn?"

She spoke up. "I'm here, Danny. Are you all right?"

"I'm fine," he said. "The only way we're going to get through this is to do what they say."

Jack assumed that Rojas had threatened Danny's family and friends. He must have told Danny that if he caused trouble, his loved ones would suffer. "I can arrange protection for—"

"No." Danny was adamant. "The less they know, the better."

Jack agreed. He had a new respect for the deputy, who was willing to sacrifice himself to keep others safe.

The other voice came on the phone. "You'd be wise to listen to Danny. Contact no one else."

"Understood."

"Come to the house. You know where it is. And bring the girl."

To do as he said would be suicide. "I want a different meeting place. Neutral ground."

"You have no right to make demands."

"I'm the one you want," Jack said. "I assume I'm talking to Gregorio Rojas. Am I right?"

"Continue."

"If you don't get your hands on me, I'll testify at that trial in Chicago. And your brother will go to jail for the rest of his life. You want me. And the only way you'll get me is if you agree to a meet."

There was a long, very long, pause. "Where?"

"I'll call you back in fifteen minutes with the location. Bring Danny. If he's hurt, the deal is off."

Jack disconnected the call and turned off the phone. As he strapped on the tool belt that had been modified to a holster, he turned to Caitlyn. "How long will it take to get to your house?"

"If we move fast, fifteen minutes. What are we going to do?"

"I need for you to think of a meeting place for the hostage exchange. Somewhere secluded."

He climbed through the slit in the rocks and reached back to help her. The sun had dipped behind the mountains, and the forests were filled with shadow. Though Jack would have preferred waiting for at least an hour when it would be pitch-dark, he knew they didn't have that option. They needed to strike quickly. He started a mental clock, ticking down fifteen minutes until the next phone call.

Rojas had the advantage of superior manpower and weapons. Jack's edge was his mobility and his instincts. And Caitlyn. If Jack had been alone in the forest, he would have wasted precious moments figuring out where he was. She knew the way through the trees and back to her cabin. She leapt from rock to rock. In unobstructed stretches, they ran full out. They were at the long slope leading down to her house within ten minutes.

At the edge of the trees, he crouched beside her. "Good job."

She accepted his compliment with a nod. "I don't see any light from my cabin. Do you think Rojas left a man there?"

His henchmen weren't clever enough to leave the lights turned off. The federal marshals were another story. They'd know better than to betray their position by making themselves at home.

He figured that the marshals would want to distance themselves from the hostage situation as much as possible. They probably weren't at the safe house with Rojas, which left them free to search.

Thinking back to his time in custody, Jack remembered three marshals. Two of them, including the guy with the Texas twang, had been on horseback at the cave. Where was the third man? Hiding in Caitlyn's cabin? In the barn?

"How do we do this?" she asked.

"Give me the car keys."

"I'm driving," she said. "I know my way around this area and you don't. It's logical for me to be behind the wheel."

Logical, but not safe. He didn't want her to be part of the action, but leaving her alone and unguarded in the forest was equally dangerous. "What if you freeze up again?"

"I won't. Not while Danny's life is in danger. I know what's at stake."

There wasn't time to argue, and she was right about knowing the territory. "We'll slip down the hill, run to your car and get in. If we're fired upon, keep your head low and drive fast."

She nodded. "It's been fifteen minutes. You should call them back. The best meeting place I can think of is the old cemetery by Sterling Creek. It's a half mile down a road that nobody ever uses."

"Don't need directions." He took out the phone. "They won't agree to our location anyway."

"How do you know?"

"Apparently, I've done stuff like this before. I'm sure that Rojas will want the advantage of choosing the location."

His phone call took less than a minute. As he predicted, Rojas refused to come to the cemetery and insisted that they use a deserted ranch house. Jack ended the call by saying, "That's too far from where we are. I'll get back to you in ten minutes."

"Wait," she said. "You need to tell them more. They'll hurt Danny."

"Not yet they won't." He shoved her phone into his pocket. "Follow me down the slope. If the third marshal is in your house, he might start shooting. That's your signal to run back to the cave and stay there."

"What about—"

"No more talking."

He started down the hill, keeping to the shadows as much as possible. A twig snapped under his boot. There was no way to muffle the sound of their footsteps. He compensated by moving swiftly. If they got to the car before the marshal had time to pinpoint their location and react, there was a good chance that they could get away clean.

He dove into the passenger seat. Caitlyn was behind the wheel of her dark green SUV. She cranked the key in the ignition and they drove away from her cabin.

No shots were fired. There was no sign of pursuit.

Instead of being relieved, Jack's suspicions were aroused. The marshals were up to something. He was damn sure that Rojas used a threat to Danny's family to get him to cooperate, and he was equally certain that the three traitorous marshals wouldn't allow a blood-bath. If the feds had any hope of protecting their butts, they had to turn the tide in their direction. They needed to look like heroes.

Jack expected the marshals to throw him under the bus.

In the meantime, he and Caitlyn had to get Danny away from Rojas. She was doing her best, driving like a Grand Prix master on the narrow, graded road.

"New car?" he asked. The interior still had the fresh-from-the-showroom smell.

"I'm leasing for a year." Her eyes riveted to the road ahead. "She handles well for a clunky SUV."

"She?"

"All my vehicles are female," she said. "This one is kind of sedate. I'm calling her Ms. Peacock because she's green."

He figured that Ms. Peacock had all the bells and whistles, including GPS mapping and a locator. She wasn't the best car to use for a getaway. "How long until we get to the safe house?"

"At normal speed, twenty minutes. I can do it in fifteen."

"Make it eight," he said.

She shot him a quick glance and juiced the accelerator. "You got it."

When he made the next phone call, his goal was to keep Rojas on the line for as long as possible while they made their approach. Timing was essential to the success of his plan.

Jack had no intention of meeting Rojas at an alternate location. He wanted to be in position for an attack when they were leaving the safe house and not expecting to see him.

After he and Rojas bickered back and forth, Jack said, "I'll agree to a meeting at the place you named. It's going to take us forty-five minutes to get there, but Caitlyn knows where it is."

"Forty-five minutes, then."

"And I've got a couple of conditions," Jack said. "First of all, you can't harm Danny. I need your word of honor that you won't touch him."

"Done." Rojas was terse.

He was lying. Rojas had as much honor as a snake. Jack lied back to him. "I trust you, Gregorio. We can handle this hostage exchange without bloodshed. Here's how it's going to work."

Speaking slowly, Jack rambled through a complicated plan to trade himself for Danny, while Caitlyn careened around a wide curve. They passed the entry gate for the Circle L Ranch and a fenced meadow populated with a herd of cattle. The road narrowed slightly and went through a series of hairpin turns before opening up into a straight line. They were nearing the intersection with a main road.

He talked to Rojas about being set free on a plane to Costa Rica. "And you'll never hear from me again."

"Yes, yes. Whatever you want."

"Well, then. We have an agreement," Jack said. "I'll see you in about forty-five minutes."

He disconnected the call and turned to Caitlyn. "How far are we from the safe house?"

"Within a mile."

"Nice job, Speed Racer."

"You should see me in a Hummer."

This woman had been to war. She knew how to handle herself when she wasn't disabled by fear. "Cut your headlights. Get as close as you can without turning into the driveway."

She nodded. "What do we do when we get there?"

"You park the car and stay with it. I'll get close and grab Danny. We'll run back to you."

When she turned off the headlights, she had to slow her frantic speed; there wasn't enough daylight to see the road clearly. "What if something goes wrong?"

"It won't."

Not if he could help it.

Chapter 10

After her mad race on the twisting gravel roads, Caitlyn was dizzy with emotion. Excited by the speed. Angry about Danny's capture. Grateful that she'd made it to the safe house without careening into a tree or spinning off a hairpin turn into a ditch. Apprehensive about what might happen next. Adrenaline surged through her veins. Her skin prickled with enough electricity to power a small village.

With fingers clenched on the steering wheel, she eased her green SUV into a hidden spot behind a stand of pine trees and killed the engine. Jack had told her to wait. She was unarmed; there was nothing she could do to help rescue Danny.

While embedded with the troops, she'd been in this position before. Watching as the soldiers prepared for a mission. Hearing the determination in their voices. Knowing that some of them would not come back.

But she wasn't an observer anymore. *This is my mission. My friend is in danger.* It would have been reassuring to have a combat helmet and ballistic vest to gird for warfare. Not that the clothing or the weaponry made a difference. Being battle-ready was a state of mind that came from training and experience that she didn't have. Though she'd been to war, she was a civilian.

If saving Danny had depended on writing a thought-provoking essay, Caitlyn would have been helpful. But in this situation? Jack knew better than she did.

She fidgeted in the driver's seat. From where she was parked, she couldn't even see the house. She needed to move. If she didn't take action, the tension building inside her would explode. After turning off the light that automatically came on when the door opened, she quietly unfastened the latch and crept from the vehicle. She approached the barbed-wire fence surrounding the property.

The waning moon hung low in the night sky, but there was enough starlight to see Jack as he darted through the tall brush toward the low, flat ranch house. He stayed parallel to the one-lane asphalt driveway that was roughly the length of a city block.

At the house, Rojas and his men made no attempt to conceal their presence. In addition to light pouring through the front and side windows, the porch was lit. To the right of the house was the horse barn and corral. The black SUV that had earlier visited her house was parked outside. And two other sedans, probably rentals. How many men were inside?

She paced along the fence line, then returned to her SUV, then back to the fence. Squinting hard, she saw Jack as he disappeared into the shadows near the house.

He moved with stealth and confidence. In the natural order of things, she figured Jack was a predator. A dangerous man. The only reason he kept himself hidden was to surprise his prey.

But how could he possibly take on Rojas and his men with nothing more than a tool belt and two bullets? These men were killers, violent and sadistic. She'd read the news stories about the cartel crimes in Mexico. They were as brutal as the Afghani warlord she'd interviewed. Her mind flashed terrifying images. Memories. She had seen the mutilated corpses. *Stop! I can't go there. I can't let myself slip into fear.*

Amnesia would have been a relief. Jack was lucky to have his past erased, but she wouldn't have wished for the same fate. Not all her memories were bad; she'd had a happy childhood. There were many proud moments she never wanted to forget, like the first time she'd seen her byline in print and the thrill of tracking down a story. And Christmas morning. And her sixteenth birthday. And falling in love. Closing her eyes, she forced herself to remember a wonderful time.

Sunset on a beach. Palm trees swayed in the breeze. She held hands with a tall, handsome man as they walked at the water's edge. The cool water lapped at her bare ankles. She looked up at him and saw...

Jack! Shirtless and muscular, the scars on his torso were landmarks to the past he'd forgotten. His grin teased her as he leaned closer. Before they kissed, she opened her eyes.

The night surrounded her. She wanted Jack's embrace. To be honest, she wanted more intimacy than a simple kiss. If they got out of this alive, she would make love to him. Together, they'd create a memory—a moment of passion that was destined to never be repeated.

His destiny was set. After he testified, he'd disappear into the witness protection program. Even if that hadn't been the case, she really didn't see herself in a long-term relationship with a former member of the Santoro family.

She tucked a hank of hair behind her ear and stared toward the house. Why were they taking so long? They had to leave soon to get to the meeting place.

She wished Jack had explained what he was going to do, but she couldn't blame him for not outlining his plan. There hadn't been time to discuss options. And he really couldn't count on her for backup. Not after she'd frozen when fired upon. *That wouldn't happen again. It couldn't.*

Though she trembled, she felt no fear. Anger dominated her mind—white-hot anger. Tension set fire to her rage. She wanted to yell, not whimper.

Consciously, she fed the flame. She despised Rojas and his men, hated the way they victimized Danny and threatened his family. Their cruelty outraged her. She wanted justice and retribution for every criminal act the cartel had committed.

Her anger ran deep. There had been times—while she observed the troops—when she had wondered if she was capable of killing another human being. At this moment, she felt like she could.

The front door to the house opened, and she heard voices. A man stepped onto the porch. He was too far away for her to tell much about him, but she didn't think she'd seen him before. Had Rojas called in reinforcements?

From her vantage point outside the barbed wire, Caitlyn mentally took the measure of the distance between her SUV and the front door to the house. It was over a hundred yards, maybe closer to two hundred. Jack had told her to wait until he rescued Danny and they ran to the car. That plan wouldn't work if Danny wasn't capable of running.

She needed to bring her SUV closer.

From the edge of the house, Jack watched a young man with a buzz cut saunter across the yard between the front door and the vehicles. His path led past the place where Jack was hiding, but Buzz Cut didn't notice him. This guy was oblivious. He flipped car keys into the air and caught them. His casual manner indicated that he wasn't a decision-maker but somebody who obeyed orders. Rojas must have sent Buzz Cut to bring the car around to the front door.

Using implements from the tool belt, Jack armed himself. The claw hammer was in his right hand. A screwdriver in the left. Though Buzz Cut carried a gun in a shoulder holster, Jack's weapons were also lethal. Not many men survived a hammer blow to the skull. Not that he intended to kill this guy. Not unless he had to.

A memory flashed in his brain.

Keeping a half-block distance, he tailed the man with fiery red hair. The bastard walked with his chest out and his arms swinging as though he was king of the world.

Pure hatred churned in Jack's gut. In his pocket his hand held a serrated-edge switchblade, illegal in this state. With one quick slash, he could sever the red-

headed man's carotid artery. Within four minutes, the man would bleed out.

There were too many witnesses on the street. The timing wasn't right. Revenge would have to wait.

Jack shook his head to erase the memory. The past would have to wait; he needed to be one hundred percent focused on the present.

From quick glances through the windows of the house, he had counted seven men, including Rojas and the big guy named Drew, who was nursing his injured leg. He couldn't tell if any of these men were the federal marshals, but he didn't think so.

Danny was slumped over in a chair with his wrists tied to the arms. The black hood that covered his head counted as a positive sign. Rojas was making sure that the deputy wouldn't see too much.

Jack figured that Rojas and his crew would leave soon so they could get to the meeting place first and set up an ambush. They wouldn't be expecting an attack here. Since there were seven plus Danny, they'd need two cars.

When Buzz Cut pointed the automatic lock opener at the black SUV, Jack decided to make his first move. He could eliminate Buzz Cut and take his weapon without anyone being the wiser. Stepping out of the shadows, he sprinted toward the SUV.

By the time Buzz Cut realized that he wasn't alone and turned around, Jack was on top of him, looking into his eyes, seeing his disbelief and surprise. With the hammer tilted sideways, he swung carefully. The glancing blow was enough to knock Buzz Cut unconscious but not hard enough to shatter his skull. He'd live.

Grabbing the gun from the holster, he hauled the

young man into the shadows beside the horse barn and returned to the black SUV. Jack slid behind the wheel and drove to the front door, where he left the engine running while he slid out the passenger-side door and waited on the opposite side of the car.

Two other men lumbered from the house. Both were stocky and muscular. They were gorillas, not the kind of guys you'd want to meet in a dark alley. Walking toward the other car—a dark sedan—they argued.

One of them was limping. He grabbed the other man's wrist and growled, "Give me the keys. I'll drive."

"You're injured. You should sit back and shut up."

"Don't tell me what to do."

The uninjured man shook off the other's grasp and took a couple of quick steps away from him.

Jack hoped these two would drive away before Rojas emerged from the house with Danny. If they left, he had two fewer adversaries to worry about.

"Hey!" The man with the limp rushed forward. The effort of ignoring his pain showed in his clenched jaw. "I'm driving. You'll get lost."

"How can I get lost? We're supposed to follow the SUV."

That wasn't what Jack wanted to hear. With these two armed men in the car behind the SUV, he couldn't pull Danny away from his captors without getting both of them shot.

The threat from these two had to be eliminated, but quietly. If Jack fired a gun, he'd alert Rojas to his presence. That wouldn't be good for Danny.

It took a minimum exertion of stealth to approach the twosome as they fought over the car keys. They were so engrossed in their petty griping that Jack could have announced himself with a coronet fanfare and they wouldn't have noticed.

He aimed for the uninjured man first. A quick blow from the hammer took him down.

The second man reacted. He went for his gun. *Dumb move.*

Jack didn't think he'd been trained in martial arts, but he had experience in street fighting. Striking fast was key. While the other man reached for his gun, closed his fingers around the grip and drew the weapon, Jack made a single move—a backhanded slash with the screwdriver. The edge tore a deep gash. The gorilla gasped, looked down at the blood oozing from his gut. Jack finished him off with a roundhouse right to the jaw.

In a matter of seconds, both men lay unconscious at his feet. Jack took the car keys they'd been arguing about and threw them into the weeds.

Three down, four to go. One of the remaining men was Drew Kelso, the guy who would be slowed down by his leg injury. Another was Rojas who probably wasn't accustomed to doing his own dirty work. That left two armed thugs.

Jack holstered his hammer and screwdriver in the tool belt. His work as Mister Fix-it was over. For this portion of the rescue, he needed firepower. He gripped one of the semiautomatic handguns and ran toward the SUV that still had the engine running.

He resumed his position at the front of the SUV and crouched between the headlights. The bad thing about street fighting was that you couldn't plan ahead. Winning the fight was all about instinct and reaction. His only goal was to get Danny away from here unharmed.

Looking up the road, he tried to see where Caitlyn had parked her car. The outline was barely visible through a stand of trees. It wasn't going to be easy to get Danny all the way up that driveway, but he didn't want Caitlyn to come closer. He wanted her to stay safe, untouched. When he was done here, he wanted to be able to look into her clear blue eyes and assure her that the world wasn't a terrible place. Sometimes, the good guys came out on top.

The last group appeared in the doorway of the safe house. One man escorted Danny, holding his arm and shoving him forward. The black hood still covered Danny's head, and his wrists were handcuffed in front of him. He stumbled, and his escort yanked him upright.

Kelso and Rojas had not yet appeared.

Another man went to open the back door of the SUV.

Jack made his move. Using the butt of the gun, he smacked the guy holding Danny on the head. The guy staggered a step forward, leaning against the car. His legs folded.

"Danny," Jack whispered, "I'm on your side. Don't resist."

With one hand he yanked the hood off the deputy's head. With the other he pulled him out of the line of fire.

The guy who had been opening the car door grabbed for his holster. He was out of reach; Jack had to shoot. At this point-blank range, he'd blow a hole six inches wide in the guy's gut.

Though the automatic handgun was unfamiliar, Jack aimed for the thug's weapon and squeezed off a single shot. The thug's gun went flying. He screamed in pain and clutched his hand to his chest. Then he took off running.

Rojas and Kelso came onto the porch. They looked

surprised by the chaos in the yard. These men weren't accustomed to being hunted. They considered themselves to be the attackers, the predators at the top of the food chain. Not this time.

Rojas stared into his face. "You. Nick Racine."

The name stopped him short. Echoes of memory surged inside him. An angry voice, his father, yelled the name. A woman whispered it in soft, sultry tones. A teacher took roll call. *Racine, Racine, Racine.*

"No." That wasn't him. He unleashed a spray of bullets toward the porch. Too late.

His few seconds of hesitation cost him dearly. It had been just enough time for Kelso and Rojas to retreat into the house.

Though Jack cursed himself for his lapse, he wasn't entirely sure that he would have shot them. It was his duty to take them into custody. Death was too easy for these bastards; they deserved a life sentence in a small, gray cell. *His duty?* What the hell was he thinking?

He pulled Danny around to the opposite side of the car. If he could maneuver them into the vehicle, he might be able to drive away. As he reached for the door handle, a burst of gunfire exploded from inside the house. Bullets pinged against the black SUV. A window shattered. Using this vehicle wasn't a good option. It was directly in the line of fire. There had to be another way.

He looked at Danny. His face was battered and swollen. His eyes seemed unfocused. When he leaned against the car, he slid to the ground. His cuffed hands fell into his lap.

"Danny, can you hear me?"

He nodded slowly.

"Do you think you can run?"

He raised his hand to wipe the blood from his split lip. "I'll do whatever it takes."

His fighting spirit was admirable. But was he physically capable of moving fast? If Jack was alone, he could have easily escaped, but he couldn't make a dash across the open meadow while dragging an injured man. Peering around the front end of the car, he returned fire. Should have killed Rojas and Kelso when he had the chance. Shouldn't have held back.

He and Danny were trapped, pinned down.

He turned his head and saw Caitlyn's green SUV zooming down the driveway. She was driving in reverse, coming to their rescue.

For once in his life, he wasn't alone. He had Caitlyn for a partner, and she was one hell of a good woman.

Chapter 11

Driving backward down a long driveway wasn't easy. Caitlyn slipped off the asphalt and heard the slap of brush against the side of her SUV. Her tires skittered on the loose gravel at the edge of the drive.

The bursts of gunfire rattled inside her brain, but she didn't succumb to a paralyzed PTSD flashback. When she'd been standing at the barbed-wire fence and had seen Jack and Danny pinned down by gunfire, she knew she had to rescue them. Nothing else mattered.

Looking over her shoulder, she saw the headlights of the black SUV. There was plenty of time to hit her brakes, but she decided to use Ms. Peacock as a battering ram, putting the other vehicle out of commission.

Her rear end smacked the front grille of the black SUV with a satisfying crash that jolted her back against the seat. Good thing she'd buckled up. Bullets snapped against her car. The rear windows splintered. Ducking low in her seat, she should have been terrified, but her focus was on the rescue. *Please, God, let them get away unharmed. Don't let anything happen to...*

The back door to her SUV swung open. Danny crawled inside. He'd been beaten. His face was red as raw meat. She'd never been so glad to see him.

"Caitlyn, I didn't mean for you to come after me. When I gave you the 'Red Fire' signal, I thought you'd call the sheriff and—"

"Shut up, Danny."

Looking over her shoulder, she saw Jack take aim and blast the tires of the black SUV before he dove in beside Danny. As soon as his door closed, she slipped into Drive and took off. At the turn to the main road, the tail end of her SUV fishtailed, but she maintained control. Ms. Peacock was doing a fine job. Caitlyn might have to change her name to something less ladylike and more daring. Maybe she should be the Green Hornet.

Jack reached between the seats and rested his hand on her shoulder. His fingers tightened in a gentle squeeze. "Thanks."

"You told me not to move, but when I saw you and Danny trapped, I had to help you."

"You did exactly the right thing, babe."

Usually when a man called her "babe" or "honey" or "sweetheart," she snapped at him. "Babe" sounded sexy when Jack said it. "Where are we going?"

From the backseat, Danny said, "Circle L. We were supposed to go there for dinner, Sandra and me. I've got to make sure she's okay. And Heather, too."

"It's going to be okay," Jack said calmly. "Let's see if we can get those cuffs off."

"Not important." Danny's voice was hoarse with urgency. "I have to see them. You don't understand."

"Sure, I do," Jack said. "Rojas threatened you. He told you that your wife and sister would be harmed if you didn't cooperate. Is that right?"

"Yes."

"I expect that he went into brutal details because that's the kind of man he is. Sadistic bastard." Though Jack kept his tone low and controlled, she heard the steely echo of his anger. "Those look like they might be your own cuffs. Got a key?"

"There's an extra key in my wallet. Back pocket."

Keeping her eyes on the road, Caitlyn said, "We can telephone Heather if you want."

"Good idea," Jack said. "We won't be bothered by Rojas for a little while. His big, black SUV isn't going anywhere. Why don't you pull over, Caitlyn. You can take care of Danny, and I'll drive."

She guided the car to a stop on the shoulder. When she turned in her seat, she saw that Jack had removed the tool belt and was unlocking Danny's cuffs. She took out her cell phone and hit the speed dial for the Circle L Ranch. Heather answered in a brisk, no-nonsense tone.

"It's Caitlyn. Are you all right?"

"Sure am."

"And Sandra? Is she there?"

"I'm fine. Sandra's fine. I picked up your tethered horses, and they're fine." Her voice dropped. "What's going on? What kind of trouble have you gotten yourself into?"

Caitlyn was satisfied. If Heather had been in danger, she would have found a way to tell her. "There's somebody here who wants to talk to you."

She passed the phone to Danny. His hand was shaking so much that he could barely hold it. "I love you, sis. I don't tell you enough. But I do." He gasped out a sob. "Put my wife on the phone."

Giving Danny some privacy, Caitlyn left the car and circled around to the back. She winced as she observed the amount of damage she'd done. One fender and the taillight were smashed. The rear door to her SUV was beyond repair. Three windows were broken, and there were bullet holes along the driver's side. Explaining this incident to her insurance company wasn't going to be easy.

Jack stepped around the other side of the car and stood facing her. His hand slid down her arm in a caress, and he took the car keys from her. "If anything happens to me, there's something I want you to know."

"What do you mean?" As far as she was concerned, they were out of danger. Almost. "Nothing is going to happen to you."

His mouth curved in that teasing grin that made her want to kiss him. "Just in case."

"Damn it, Jack. Do you always have to look on the dark side?"

"Like I told you before, I always plan for the worst."

Reaching up, she stroked the rough stubble on his jaw. The light from the waning moon and the stars outlined the rugged planes of his face. "I couldn't tell exactly what you did at the safe house, but from what I saw, you were amazing. You caused enough concussions to keep a brain specialist busy for weeks."

"Assuming those guys had functional brains."

One thing she had observed didn't make sense. "It

looked like you had the drop on Rojas. But you didn't shoot."

"Not my job," he said.

As far as she knew, he'd been an enforcer for the Santoro family. In that line of work, she was fairly sure that his duties included murder. When she thought about it, she realized that Jack hadn't killed anyone. Not at the safe house. Not at her cabin. "I'd like to know more about this job of yours."

"So would I." He tapped the side of his head. "Amnesia."

"Convenient."

"Not really."

His large hand slipped around her neck, and he pulled her closer. His lips were warm against hers. As she leaned toward him, the tips of her breasts grazed his chest. A shiver of awareness washed through her, leaving a tingling sensation.

When they kissed, she was hungry for more. Especially now. She knew her time with Jack was limited. Her torso pressed firmly against him. Her arms encircled him.

"Caitlyn," Danny bellowed from inside the car.

She tore herself away from Jack's embrace. As guilty as a teenager caught in the act, she put a polite distance between them. "I guess we have places to go."

"Here's what I want you to know," he said. "You're going to be all right."

Why was he telling her this? She cocked her head to one side. "Explain."

"You have doubts about yourself and your career. That's why you're living in the mountains like a hermit."

Though his characterization irked her, she didn't deny it. "Go on."

"You're scared. But you don't have to be. You're tough, Caitlyn. You're strong enough to take whatever life throws at you. If we had more time together, I'd—"

"Caitlyn," Danny called again. "We need to get going."

Jack shrugged. "I believe in you. Whatever happens, you're going to be fine."

As he walked past her on his way to the driver's seat, he patted her butt. Again, this wasn't a gesture she would usually accept without complaint, but she said nothing.

His reassurance was shockingly perceptive. It didn't seem fair that a man who was so good-looking and capable would also be wise.

In spite of the time she'd spent alone—time that was supposed to be for reflection and renewal—she hadn't made the connection between her PTSD fear and her doubts about her career. She'd been afraid of just about everything. Until now.

When she'd realized that Jack and Danny needed her, she'd been able to overcome her fear and do what had to be done. *I'm going to be all right.*

She was damaged but not broken. Her life would mend. All the energy she'd poured into fixing up the cabin could be turned into something she was actually good at.

In her heart, she'd always known what she was meant to do. She was a journalist, a seeker of truth. Losing her assignment in the Middle East didn't negate her skill or her talent. There were plenty of other stories to write…starting with Jack. He had a story she was itching to write.

As she settled into the backseat next to Danny, she asked Jack, "Do you need directions to the Circle L?"

"I remember the way."

Of course he would. He did everything well. When she turned her attention to Danny, her mood darkened. She was accustomed to seeing her old friend as a cool, confident leader—the most popular guy in the county, the local hero. Being held hostage had devastated him, and she feared that these wounds went deeper than the bruises on his face. His shoulders slumped. His uniform was stained with blood, torn and disheveled. The acrid smell of sweat clung to him.

Gently, she took his hand. Instead of offering false reassurances, she said the only positive thing she could think of. "We're almost at the Circle L. You'll be with your wife soon."

"I called the sheriff," he said. "He'll arrange for bodyguards for Sandra and Heather until that sick bastard is in custody."

From the front seat, Jack said, "Arresting Rojas will be dangerous."

"You don't have to tell me." With an effort, Danny lifted his head and looked toward the front seat. "You're the man they're looking for, aren't you? The witness."

"That's right," Caitlyn informed him. "He's also the guy who saved your butt."

"And I thank you for that," Danny said. "I didn't think I'd get away in one piece. Thought I was a dead man."

She didn't like seeing him this way. She missed his

natural arrogance. "I wish there was something I could do for you. I don't have any first-aid stuff in the car."

"It's all right." He exhaled slowly and spoke to the back of Jack's head. "You did a good job negotiating. I only heard one side, but you convinced them to do what you wanted."

"I had an advantage," Jack said. "I knew Rojas would lie. He'd try to set up a meet where he could get there first and set up an ambush. I just had to stall him long enough so that I could beat him to the punch."

"What's your name?" Danny asked.

Caitlyn answered, "You can call him Jack."

"As in Jack Dalton?" Danny turned toward her. "I thought we established that Jack Dalton was in jail sleeping off a drunk and disorderly."

There was no simple way to explain how she'd gotten involved with Jack and how he had amnesia. "Just call him Jack for now."

Danny sank back against the seat and closed his eyes. His lips barely moved as he spoke. "You were always good at getting yourself into trouble, Caitlyn. Remember? And you thought you were so smart. A regular Little Miss Know-It-All."

"I don't just think I'm smart," she said. "I really am."

"Not always."

He seemed to be implying that she'd made a mistake. "Is there something you need to tell me?"

He spoke in a barely audible whisper. "How well do you know Jack?"

"Well enough to trust him with my life. Why do you ask?"

"There were eight men at the house, not including me. One of them was a federal marshal. He was dead."

Danny looked down at his hands. "I knew he was a lawman because they pinned his badge to his forehead. He was…mutilated."

She glanced toward the front seat. Jack had worried about the whereabouts of the third marshal. Apparently, he wasn't in on the scheme with Rojas and the other two. And he had paid the ultimate price. "I'm sorry."

"How about you, Jack?" Danny's tone turned hostile. "Are you sorry about the marshal's death?"

"Stop it, Danny." What was wrong with him? She reached forward and tapped Jack on the shoulder. "We're here. This is the turn for the Circle L."

He drove through the open gate toward a well-lit, two-story ranch house that was painted white with slate-gray trim. A tall, thick cottonwood tree stood as high as the roof. Though there were no children at the Circle L, a tire swing hung from one of the branches.

The ranch looked like a peaceful sanctuary, but Caitlyn had the sense that something wasn't right. "Danny, what's going on?"

"There are my girls." The hint of a smile touched his lips as he gazed toward the wraparound porch where Heather stood with her arms braced against the railing. Beside her was a delicate-looking blonde who had to be Sandra. "They're safe. That's all that matters."

Jack pulled up close to the porch and parked. As soon as he turned off the engine, two men emerged from the shadows. They moved quickly and with purpose, flanking the vehicle. The one who stood at the driver's side window pointed a rifle at Jack's head.

"U.S. marshal," he said with an unmistakably Texan twang. "I'm taking you into custody."

Chapter 12

If the marshals got their way, Jack would be cuffed and carted off, never to be seen again. Caitlyn refused to let that happen.

Her experience as a reporter in the world's hot spots had taught her to talk her way around just about anything. She'd been the first journalist to wrangle an interview with an aging Afghani warlord who fought with the mujahideen. She'd interviewed politicians and generals, even faced a serial killer on death row. Argument was her battlefield. Words were her weapons.

She bolted from the car and launched her verbal attack at the two marshals. Though she spoke with authority, she wasn't sure exactly what she'd said—something along the lines of legal and jurisdictional issues. "Danny was first deputy on the scene, which means he has custody. The Douglas County sheriff is responsible for this man."

Still holding his rifle on Jack, the Texan drawled, "What in hell are you yapping about?"

"He's ours," she said.

Brandishing the handcuffs she'd removed from Danny's wrists only moments ago, she opened the driver-side door and leaned inside. She whispered, "Let me handle this."

Staring straight ahead, Jack sat with both hands gripping the steering wheel. He turned his head and met her gaze. A bond of trust stretched between them. He believed in her; he'd told her so. It was time for her to justify his confidence.

As she snapped a cuff on his right wrist, he muttered under his breath, "You'd better be right about this."

"You should know by now. I'm almost always right."

"Little Miss Know-It-All."

When he stepped out of the car, she fastened the other cuff. Though she considered pressing the key into his palm so he could escape, she decided against it. Jack unchained was a force of nature, and she preferred a little finesse. The fewer bodies he left in his wake, the better.

Whirling, she faced the marshal from Texas. "Lower your weapon."

Danny—the big, fat traitor—was out of the car and appeared to be gathering his strength to object, but his wife, Heather and a couple of ranch hands swarmed around him, determined to help him whether or not he wanted to be helped.

One of the ranch hands bumped the rifle, and Heather snapped at the marshal, "You heard Caitlyn. Put down your weapon before you accidentally shoot yourself in the foot."

The Texan scowled but did as she said. His partner stalked around to their side of the car and spoke up.

"Thanks for your help, folks. We've got it. This man is in our custody."

"Where's your warrant?" Caitlyn demanded.

"Don't need one." The gray-haired marshal produced his wallet and showed her his five-point star badge and his marshal credentials.

Caitlyn inspected his documents. "You're Marshal Steven Patterson."

"Correct." His jaw was speckled with bristly white stubble, and his gray eyes were red-rimmed with exhaustion. "I'd appreciate if you'd step aside and let us do our job."

"Is this man a criminal?"

"No."

"Then why are you taking him?"

"He's a witness," Patterson said.

"A protected witness?"

"Correct."

"Pointing a rifle in his face doesn't seem like the best way to keep your witness safe," she said. "Maybe he doesn't want your so-called protection."

"He's in our custody. That's all you need to know."

Caitlyn nudged Heather's arm. "Does that sound right to you?"

Heather drew herself up to her full height. In her boots, she was nearly as tall as Jack, and she towered over Patterson. She hooked her thumb in her belt, right next to her revolver.

Caitlyn noticed that all the ranch hands were armed; they must have heard that there was danger, and they all watched Heather for her cues. She said, "Nobody does anything until my brother is taken care of. Sandra, you get Danny inside and call the doc."

Danny's petite blonde wife didn't need instruction;

she was focused one hundred percent on her husband. Her devotion touched Caitlyn, and she would have been happy that Danny had found the perfect mate if she hadn't wanted to kill him for leading them into this trap.

Patterson spoke to Heather, "Looks like you have everything under control, ma'am. We'll be going now."

"Hold on," she said. "The Circle L is *my* ranch. *My* property. We do things *my* way. On *my* schedule."

"What are you saying?"

"I want you to answer Caitlyn's questions," Heather said.

"I don't answer to you." Patterson's polite veneer was worn thin. "I'm a federal officer, and your ranch isn't some kind of sovereign nation."

He couldn't have picked a worse argument, and Caitlyn was glad to see him digging his own grave. In this part of the world, respect for ownership of the land was as deeply engrained as the brands on the cattle. "Marshal Patterson, I can tell that you haven't spent much time in the West." To his partner, she said, "Explain it to him, Tex. Tell him how we feel about our land."

"The name's Bryant," said the younger marshal. "And I promise you, Miss Heather, we ain't here to cause trouble."

"I'll be the judge of that." Heather watched Sandra and the ranch hands escort her brother into the house, then she swung back toward Caitlyn. "What were you saying?"

"According to Marshal Patterson, he can take a witness into custody whether he wants to be protected or not. Now, that doesn't seem fair, especially since Patterson is a U.S. Marshal. The *U* and the *S* stand for *us,* as in you and me. He works for us. And I'm pretty sure I wouldn't want to be dragged off without my permission."

"She's got a point," Heather said.

"And I've got a job," Patterson said.

Caitlyn pulled out her cell phone. "Before you proceed, I need to make sure I have the facts right. I want to verify with the director of the Marshals Service or the attorney general."

"You can't."

"Oh, I think I can. I'm a journalist for a national news service." A little white lie since she wasn't actually employed at the moment. Using her cell, she snapped a photo of Patterson and his partner. "As a reporter, it's my job to raise holy hell if this situation isn't handled properly. Will you call the director? Or should I?"

Bryant asked his partner, "Can she do that?"

"Damn right I can."

Jack spoke up. "I'd advise you to listen to her."

"Why's that?"

"She might look like a Barbie doll, but this woman is G.I. Jane. She was embedded with the troops. Just came back from a war zone."

Patterson regarded her with a little more respect and a lot more loathing. "Is that so?"

"She knows people," Jack said. "Important people. The kind of people who could end the careers of a couple of marshals who screwed up."

"Bad luck for you," she said to Patterson. "I'm guessing that you're close to retirement. It would be a shame to lose your pension."

Two police vehicles careened down the driveway and parked, effectively blocking the exit. Four deputies rushed toward them, firing questions about what had happened to Danny and who was responsible. The confusion rose to the edge of chaos.

"Enough," Patterson said loudly. "All of you. Back off."

Frustration turned his complexion an unhealthy shade of brick red. He grasped Jack's upper arm—a move that Caitlyn saw as a huge mistake. The muscles in Jack's shoulders bunched as though he was preparing to throw off Patterson's hand. Even unarmed and in cuffs, he was capable of annihilating the two marshals. He might even be able to defeat the deputies, grab a vehicle and run.

But she didn't like the odds. There were too many guns. Too many nervous trigger fingers.

"Marshal Patterson," she said, "I have a suggestion."

He was desperate enough to listen. "Go on."

"You and your partner could step into the house. I'm sure Heather would let you use her office. And you could contact your superior officer for further instructions. When you produce verification that you have jurisdictional custody of this witness, we'll all be satisfied."

"Fine," he said, "but we're taking this man with us into the den while we make our phone calls."

It wasn't exactly the outcome Caitlyn had hoped for. The marshals weren't going to give up easily, and she'd have to come up with another ruse to get Jack away from them. But she'd bought some time. And nobody had gotten killed.

Ever since Danny mentioned the marshal who had been murdered and mutilated, Jack had been remembering details of what had happened to him at the safe house when Rojas came after him. How many times had he asked himself about the third marshal? At a deep, subconscious level, he had sensed the importance of the third man.

His name, Jack clearly remembered, was Hank Perry. His age, forty-two. He stood five feet ten inches. Brown hair and eyes. He was divorced, and his oldest son had just graduated from high school.

Hank Perry was dead. He'd given his life to protect Jack. Somehow, Jack would make sure that Perry's ultimate sacrifice would not be in vain. Somehow, he had to escape and make it back to Chicago for the trial.

Sitting on the floor in the den, he rested his back against a wall of bookshelves with his cuffed wrists in his lap. No doubt the two marshals in the room with him would have liked to hogtie him and pull a hood over his head, but they had to treat him humanely or Caitlyn would raise a stink.

Though he kept his face expressionless, Jack smiled inside when he thought of how she'd leapt to his defense. In spite of her dirty clothes and tangled blond hair, she'd transformed into a person of stature. With gravitas equal to Lady Justice herself, Caitlyn had created a wall of obstacles. Using wild-eyed logic and aggressive questions, she'd backed the marshals into a corner.

With grim satisfaction, he was glad that he'd taken a moment before they got to the ranch to tell her how he felt about her. Life experience had shaken her determination, but she'd made a full recovery. They made a good team. With her mouth and his muscle, they could have done great things together.

He looked over at Patterson, who slouched in the swivel chair behind the desk. He'd been on his cell phone for the past fifteen minutes. His side of the conversation was a lame explanation of how he and Bryant had been attacked, lost their witness and had their colleague murdered by Rojas.

Patterson admitted, over and over, that they'd made a mistake in not calling for backup. His excuse was that he feared a showdown with Rojas would give the cartel gang a reason to commit wholesale murder in this peaceful Colorado mountain community.

While he talked on his phone, Patterson juggled the SIG Sauer P-226 that he'd confiscated along with all the other weapons Jack had taken from Rojas. The SIG had belonged to Perry. Watching Patterson play with that honorable man's gun made Jack's blood boil.

The tall Texan marshal with the hundred-mile stare sauntered across the den and stood in front of Jack. With the toe of his cowboy boot, he nudged Jack's foot. "You're kind of quiet."

Brilliant observation, genius. Since they'd entered the den, Jack hadn't said a word. He'd been too consumed with memories of the midnight assault on the safe house. His mind echoed with the blast of semiautomatic gunfire and Perry's shout of warning. In the dark, he hadn't been able to identify the men who came after them. And he couldn't exactly recall how he'd gotten his head wound. But he'd seen Perry take a bullet and stagger back to his feet. With his last breath, he'd fought.

All of Patterson's talk about "doing his job" turned Jack's stomach. Patterson didn't have a clue about the real responsibility of being a U.S. marshal. He was a coward. A traitor.

Bryant squatted down to Jack's level. "We didn't get much chance to talk when you were at the safe house. I'm low man on the totem pole, so my assignment was to patrol outdoors."

Except for when Rojas showed up. Jack didn't remember seeing Patterson or Bryant during the attack. Their plan had probably been to leave him alone and unguarded.

Bryant continued, "Is all the stuff they say about you true? About the legendary Nick Racine?"

There was that name again. Racine, Nick Racine. Rojas had shouted it out, distracting him. If that was his real name, he ought to remember, but he couldn't make the connection. "What have you heard?"

"That you killed twelve men using nothing more than your belt buckle and your bare hands."

Though Jack was sure that hadn't happened, he nodded. If he impressed Bryant, he might convince the young man to take his side against Patterson. "What else?"

"You survived for a month in the desert with no food or water."

That was legendary, all right. "I had a good teacher, a wise old man who lived in Arizona. I owe it to him to pass on this knowledge. You could learn."

"Me?" Bryant shook his head. "I've never exactly been at the top of the class."

"It's not book learning. It's instinct."

"I got instincts." His brow lowered as he concentrated. "Seems like a damn shame to kill you, but we can't have you telling the truth to the Marshals Service."

In a low voice, Jack said, "It wasn't your fault. You were just following orders. It was Patterson who told Rojas the location of the safe house, wasn't it?"

"That's right. The old man arranged for the money, told me all we had to do was leave the house for an hour. Rojas was supposed to swoop in, grab you and take off. Slick and easy."

"Except for Perry," Jack said.

"Oh man, that was a big mistake. Rojas promised that Perry wasn't going to get hurt."

Yeah, sure, and then the Easter Bunny would leave them all pretty-colored eggs. Bryant was young, but he wasn't naive enough to trust a man like Rojas. At some point, the marshal had made a deliberate decision to turn his head and look the other way. "What was supposed to happen to me?"

"Guess I didn't think that far ahead."

Thinking wasn't Bryant's strong suit. "You can make up for your mistake. I'll take care of it."

"You're trying to trick me. That's part of the legend, too. You can change your identity like a shape-shifter."

"I'm not lying."

"I still don't believe you. The way Patterson tells it, you've gone rogue. You know what that means? Being a rogue?"

Jack said nothing. The question was too ridiculous to answer. Though Bryant was a moron, he knew enough to follow orders from Patterson. A dangerous combination—stupidity and loyalty.

"One time," Bryant said, "I saw a television show about rogue elephants in Africa. My gal likes to watch that educational stuff. Anyway, there was this big, old elephant with giant tusks. We got a forty-six-inch flatscreen, and I'm telling you, that elephant was big. You might even say he was legendary. Like you."

"I'm an elephant?"

"A rogue," Bryant said. "The safari guy said the only way to handle a rogue was to kill him before he killed you."

I'm a dead man.

Chapter 13

In the front room of the ranch house, Caitlyn positioned herself so she could keep an eye on the closed door to the den. Her mind raced as she tried to come up with a plan. Though she wanted to believe that the marshals wouldn't dare hurt Jack while he was in their custody, she knew better. They couldn't let him live. He had witnessed their treachery.

She could insist on accompanying them while they took Jack, but that might mean they'd kill her, too.

Looking down at the cell phone in her hand, she willed it to ring. She'd left a message for her former lover in Chicago, but she hadn't talked to him in years and didn't know if he was still employed at the newspaper. Her stateside contacts had dried up after she'd been stationed in the Middle East for so long. The only highly placed individuals she could call for a favor were in the military, and they couldn't help with this problem. If Patterson got the go-ahead from his superior officer, there wasn't much she could do to stop him from taking Jack.

When Heather handed her a steaming mug of coffee, Caitlyn grinned at her friend and said, "Thanks for taking my side."

"I didn't like those marshals when they showed up here and said they were supposed to protect us. Everybody who works at the Circle L has at least one gun. We take care of ourselves."

Considering the viciousness of Rojas and his men, Caitlyn was glad it hadn't come to a showdown. "Your instincts are right about the marshals. They're working with the bad guys."

"Fill me in."

Caitlyn glanced around at the other people in the room—ranch hands and a couple of deputies who were making phone calls. Since she didn't want to broadcast her story, she spoke in a quiet tone. "Jack is a federal witness who's supposed to testify on Tuesday in Chicago. He was in protective custody at a safe house that was attacked last night. He escaped, riding the gray mare that showed up on my doorstep. Here's the important thing, those marshals were supposed to be guarding him, but they stepped aside and let the bad guys go after him."

"Not all of them." Danny limped into the room, leaning on his pretty little wife for support. "One of the marshals died a heroic death in the line of duty."

Though he'd changed into a fresh shirt and his face was cleaned up, he still looked like hell. Caitlyn didn't feel sorry for him; Danny had betrayed them. "You knew the marshals were waiting here for Jack."

"They came here to protect my family."

"How did they know?" she demanded. "If they weren't working with Rojas, how did they know your family was in danger?"

"They were keeping an eye on the safe house," Danny said, defending them. "They must have seen what happened to me."

"And yet, they did nothing to rescue you. They didn't contact the sheriff, didn't call for backup. What kind of lawmen operate like that?"

"If they'd called for an assault on the safe house, I'd be dead right now."

His wife shuddered. "Don't say that."

"I'm okay, Sandra." He patted her arm. "There's nothing to worry about."

"You should be resting until the doc gets here. Let me take you upstairs to bed."

"Not until this is settled."

Her lips pulled into a tight, disapproving line, but she said nothing else. Caitlyn sympathized with her dilemma. It wasn't easy to love a stubborn man who wouldn't let anyone fight his battles for him. A man like Jack? Though she couldn't compare her relationship with Jack to a marriage or even to being in love, she cared about him. How could she not care? He'd saved her life. She thought of how he'd rescued her when she froze and his quiet heroics when at the safe house. He was a one-man strike force. But that wasn't why she cared so much. He'd seen inside her. He brought out the best in her. And, oh my, the man knew how to kiss.

She glared at Danny. "You don't know the whole

story, but I'm not saying another word until you sit down. You look like you're about to collapse."

"She's right." Sandra gave her a grateful nod. "Let's all get settled and figure this out."

While Sandra made her husband comfortable in a leather armchair near the fireplace, Caitlyn perched on the edge of a rocking chair beside him. In as calm a tone as she could manage, she said, "You've got to admit that the actions of those two marshals were questionable. They had a whole day to track down Rojas and his men. What the hell were they doing?"

"Their job," Danny said. "They were tracking down their runaway witness."

At the cave, they'd come close. "They almost found us."

"Hold on." Heather held up her hand, signaling a halt. "It sounds like you and Jack were hiding from the marshals. Why would you do that?"

"We were on the run." When Caitlyn thought back, the afternoon seemed like a lifetime ago. "Rojas and his men showed up at my cabin. Because the gray horse came to my place, they must have figured that Jack had also been there. When they showed up, I was in the barn. They had guns. They were yelling. I've never been so scared in my life."

A residual wave of fear washed through her as she remembered turning to stone. "Jack had been watching my house. He rescued me. We took off on horseback."

"It's a damn good thing he was there," Heather said, "or else you'd be as beat up as my brother."

"We were hiding in that cavern that's not far from my cabin—the one with the water that runs all the way through it. Those two marshals nearly found us. I didn't see them, but I recognized the Texas accent."

"What did they say?" Heather asked.

She was tempted to lie and tell them that the marshals talked about murdering her and Jack, but she needed to stay on the high road. "Nothing incriminating."

"You should have spoken up," Danny said. "If you'd turned Jack in, this whole thing would have been over."

"Why are you so dead set against him?" Her anger flared. "He's a good man."

"He's a witness in a mob crime, probably a criminal himself who agreed to testify in exchange for immunity. I said it before, Caitlyn, and I'll say it again. You don't know anything about this guy."

Unable to sit still, she rose from the rocking chair so quickly that it almost overturned. "I haven't finished telling what happened. If you don't mind, I'd like to continue."

"Go right ahead."

"While Jack and I were hiding, we got a message from Danny that told us he'd been captured by Rojas and was being held at the safe house. Jack didn't hesitate. Not for one minute. He knew he had to get Danny out of there."

Sandra's eyes widened. "Jack saved Danny?"

"If it weren't for Jack, you'd be a dead man. Right, Danny?"

He nodded slowly. "Right."

"I don't understand," Sandra said. "This man risked his life for you, and you're willing to sit back and watch while he gets dragged off in handcuffs."

"You're not seeing the big picture," he said.

"What's bigger than saving your life? Oh, Danny, you're not thinking straight."

He shifted in the big leather chair. "As far as I'm concerned, Jack could be working with Rojas. He might be responsible for the death of that marshal."

Caitlyn scoffed. "That's crazy."

"Yeah? Well, explain this for me. Jack had the drop on Rojas and that other guy. He could have pulled the trigger and taken them out. Why didn't he shoot?"

She didn't have a logical response. "I don't know."

"Because he's part of this scheme," Danny said. "He let Rojas get away. On purpose."

"Or maybe Jack isn't a murderer. Maybe he didn't want to shoot a man in the back."

"I'm sure he's got a smooth-talking answer," Danny said. "He's slick enough to convince you that he's some kind of hero, but I don't believe him. I'll take the word of a federal marshal over that of a criminal turned witness."

"Even when he saved you," Heather said, as she rose from her chair and stood beside Caitlyn. "I hate to say this because you're my brother, but Danny, you're a jerk. And just about as perceptive as a fence post."

He frowned and looked toward his wife.

Sandra arched an eyebrow. "I'm with Heather on this. Caitlyn, what do you need?"

She was glad for these two votes of confidence. Before this was over, she'd need all the allies she could get. "I don't object to Jack being taken into protective custody. He wants to testify and break up the Rojas cartel. It's important to him. But I don't want those two marshals to be alone with him. They can't be trusted."

The front door swung open and Bob Woodley

marched inside. He wasn't even pretending to be a docile, law-abiding citizen. In his right hand, he held his hunting rifle. In spite of his age, he emanated vitality and energy. His clothes were as disheveled as if he'd just gotten out of bed. His thick, white hair looked like he'd combed it with an eggbeater. As soon as he spotted Caitlyn, he charged toward her and pulled her into a bone-crunching hug.

"I'm sorry," he said. "I brought those bastards to your house. I put you in danger."

"You didn't know," she said.

"If anything had happened to you, I'd never forgive myself. Your mother would never forgive me."

"I'm fine." She separated from his ferocious hug and smiled up at him. "How did you hear about what happened?"

"Being an elected official, I have an inside track. Half the lawmen in Colorado—state patrol, SWAT teams, cops and deputies—are involved in a manhunt, looking for Rojas. I assume he's the fellow who told me his name was Reynolds."

"He lied to you, lied to everybody."

Danny struggled to get out of his chair. "Everybody else is mobilized. I should—"

"Sit down," Sandra said. "You've done enough."

Woodley took a look at him. "What the hell happened to your face?"

"Long story," he said. "Tell me what else is going on."

"I don't know much. As soon as I heard Caitlyn was in trouble, I jumped in my Ford Fairlane and raced over here." He turned back to her. "You're not hurt, are you?"

"I'm worried. Something terrible is about to happen, and I can't stop it."

Woodley drew himself up. "Tell me how I can help."

"That goes for me, too," Heather said. "I don't want to see the man who saved my brother's life get into any more trouble."

"All of you," Danny said, "stop it. You need to back off and let the marshals do their job. That's the law."

Caitlyn confronted him. "Sometimes, the law isn't right. Jack saved you. The marshals were willing to let you die."

"But I'm an officer of the law."

"That means you're sworn to enforce justice," she said, "even if it means stepping outside the law."

He winced. The bruises on his face were a crude reminder of what he'd suffered at the hands of Rojas. His gaze rested on his sister, then on his wife. "I wanted to keep you both safe."

"I know," Sandra said. She rested her small hand gently on his cheek. "Now, we have to do the right thing."

When they looked to her for direction, Caitlyn felt warm inside. Her heart expanded. These people were her friends, as loyal to her as the troops in combat.

The beginnings of a plan tickled the inside of her head. "There might be something we can do."

Negotiating with Bryant or Patterson was futile. Jack's only option was to fight. He had the vague outline of a plan. He'd wait until they left the Circle L Ranch; no point in having anyone else hurt in the crossfire. He'd go after Bryant first. Though the younger marshal wasn't quick-witted, his reflexes were good. Then he'd take out Patterson. Vague, extremely vague.

This version of planning fell mostly into the category of wishful thinking.

Though Jack could hear people coming and going outside the door to the den, this room was quiet, except for Bryant's tuneless humming of a country-western song and Patterson's urgent phone conversations.

The old man was kidding himself if he thought he'd get out of this mess with his job intact. Another marshal had been brutally murdered, and that kind of error wouldn't be excused with a slap on the wrist. Jack wondered how much Rojas had paid for their treachery; he hoped it wasn't nearly enough to make up for their lost pensions.

Wearily, Patterson stood behind the desk. In the past half hour, he'd aged ten years. His jowls sagged and his eyes sunk deep in their sockets. He concluded his conversation with a crisp "Yes, sir." When he turned toward Bryant, a cold smile twisted his thin, bloodless lips. "They bought it."

Eager as a puppy, Bryant bounded toward the desk. "Are you telling me that we ain't going to get blamed for Perry being killed?"

"We'll be fine," Patterson said, "as long as you stick to the story. All you have to say is that we were asleep at the safe house, and Perry was on watch. Rojas killed him and went after Jack. Before we had time to react, it was over."

"Got it." Bryant nodded, easily satisfied. "What do we do right now?"

"We have our orders." He held his cell phone so Jack could see. "I've got a couple of emailed verifications from on high. That ought to keep your girlfriend happy."

"She's not my girlfriend," Jack said. No way did

he want any repercussions to bounce back on Caitlyn. "She's just a woman who happened to be in the wrong place at the wrong time."

"But she's a reporter, and that means trouble. Not that she'll get any answers after we're gone. Everything about this case is going to turn top secret."

Jack thought he was seriously underestimating Caitlyn's abilities but said nothing. He wanted Patterson to think he was getting away clean.

Bryant asked, "What are our orders?"

"We go to a private airfield not far from here. A chopper picks us up and flies us to Colorado Springs. From there, we get a flight to Chicago."

Jack didn't like the sound of these orders. A short drive didn't give him much time to act. "How do you rate a private chopper?"

"Since Rojas is still on the loose, our situation is considered eminently dangerous." There was a flash of anger in his dulled eyes. "But you won't be riding on that chopper. Rojas is my excuse for you to be dead before we even get to the airfield."

There was a knock on the door. Danny stepped inside. Though he moved stiffly, he looked like he was well on the way to recovery. "Marshal Patterson, we have a problem."

"Now what?"

"There's an FBI agent on his way to talk to you."

"FBI," Bryant yelped.

"Our local congressman, Bob Woodley, showed up, and he's pretty peeved. He called an FBI agent he's worked with. I'm afraid if you don't humor Woodley, he'll be on the phone to the governor."

"Let him." Patterson waved his cell phone. "I have authorization to take this man into custody."

"Great," Danny said. "All you need to do is talk to Woodley. It'll only take a minute. He wants to see both of you. I'll keep an eye on your witness."

As soon as Patterson and Bryant left the room, Danny went to the window and yanked it open. "Get the hell out of here."

"Why are you doing this?" Jack asked.

"Let's just say this makes us even."

He didn't waste another second wondering why Danny had a change of heart. Jack knew the answer. Caitlyn.

Chapter 14

Caitlyn was impressed with Jack's agility as he slipped through the den window into the shrubs at the side of the house. His cuffed wrists didn't hamper his movements in the least.

Without speaking, she motioned to him. As soon as he reached her side, she whispered, "Duck down and stay low. We're going to weave through these cars."

He glanced over his shoulder. "I'd rather run for open terrain. I can make it to the barn."

"No time to explain. We do it my way."

She'd already arranged with Heather to lay down a couple of false trails. Moments ago, Heather had instructed two of the ranch hands to saddle up and ride to the far pasture to check on the couple hundred head of cattle grazing in that area. Another guy was driving one of the four-wheelers toward the south end of the ranch. Caitlyn figured the marshals would be distracted by those tracks while she and Jack got away.

He followed as she crept around the eight or nine vehicles that were parked helter-skelter at the front door of the Circle L ranch house. She moved stealthily, being careful not to attract attention from the ranch hands who had gathered near the barn or the two deputies on the porch. Though she couldn't make out the words in specific conversations, she heard tension in their voices. By now, everyone was aware of the threat from Rojas.

When she got to Woodley's huge, finned, turquoise-and-cream-colored 1957 Ford Fairlane, she unlocked the trunk and pointed to the inside.

He shot her a look that was half anger and half disbelief. Then he glanced around. With all these people, he couldn't run without being seen. Grumbling, he climbed inside.

She joined him and pulled the trunk closed. The dark covered them as tightly as shrink wrap. The air smelled of gas, grease and grit. Even though this space was big for a car trunk, they were jammed together. Her legs twined with his. She couldn't find a good place to put her arms without embracing him.

"The cuffs," he said.

She dug in her jeans pocket for the key. After a bit of clumsy groping, she used the flashlight function on her cell phone so she could see well enough to unlock the cuffs.

As soon as he was free, he caught hold of her hand and turned the cell phone light so he could see her. "You combed your hair," he said, "and changed your clothes."

"Thanks for noticing."

"You look nice in blue," he whispered.

"What is this? A first date?"

Before he turned the light off, she caught a glimpse of his sexy grin. Being this close to Jack was already having a sensual effect on her. She tucked her arms over her breasts so she wouldn't be rubbing against his chest.

His upper arm draped around her with his hand resting on the small of her back. He asked, "How is Danny going to explain my escape?"

"By the time the marshals get back to the den, Danny will be upstairs in bed with his wife standing guard over him. None of the local guys are going to give him a hard time. They all think he's a hero."

Keeping her voice low, she told him about the decoy trails they'd set out for the marshals to follow. "Assuming that they're able to track in the dark. Patterson doesn't strike me as somebody who knows his way around the outdoors, but I'll bet the Texan has done his share of hunting."

"That's possible," Jack said. "There has to be something Bryant is good at."

The voices from the ranch house took on a note of urgency. There were sounds of footsteps hustling and doors being slammed. She guessed that the marshals had discovered Jack's escape. The arm he'd wrapped around her tightened protectively. She knew that they needed to be silent.

With her eyes closed, she pressed her face into the crook of his neck. His musky scent teased her nostrils. After a day on the run, he definitely didn't smell like cologne. But she didn't mind the earthy odor; it was masculine and somehow attractive. Heat radiated from his pores. His chest rose and fell as he breathed, and even that action was sexy. If she relaxed and allowed her body to melt into his, she knew she'd be overwhelmed.

Mentally, she distanced herself from him. More than once, she'd asked herself why she was so invested in Jack's rescue. The big reason was utterly apparent. He was a good man, trying to do the right thing, and he didn't deserve to be threatened, especially not by the men who were assigned to protect him. She had to fight for Jack because it was the right thing to do. Her motivations were based on truth, justice and the American way.

And it didn't hurt that he was hot. Being close to him set off a fiery chemistry that was anything but high-minded. She didn't want to lose him, didn't want this feeling of passion to dissipate into nothingness.

Trying to get comfortable, she wriggled her legs, and he reacted with a twitch. They needed to be careful. If the Ford Fairlane started bouncing, they'd be found for sure.

The voices came closer. She thought she heard Patterson shouting angry orders. Car doors creaked open and slammed shut, but she didn't hear anyone driving away. Were they searching the cars? Someone bumped into the fender of the Fairlane, and she caught her breath to keep from making noise.

Until now, she'd been too busy planning and thinking to acknowledge the undercurrent of fear that started earlier today. If they were found, the consequences would be disastrous. She never should have gotten all these other people involved. Danny could lose his job for helping Jack escape. There might be legal charges against Heather and Woodley. As for Jack? If the marshals took him, they'd kill him. She trembled. *What have I done?*

Jack whispered in her ear, "Scared?"

Though he couldn't see her in the dark, she nodded.

"Think of something else," he said. "Something good."

That was a childish solution, like whistling in a graveyard to show the ghosts you weren't afraid. Tension squeezed her lungs. She felt a scream rising in the back of her throat.

"You have some good memories." His voice was one step up from silence. "Think of your childhood."

She remembered a summer afternoon. She was sixteen and had just gotten her driver's license. Her mom asked her to deliver a basket of muffins to Mr. Woodley's house.

Determined not to have an accident, she drove very carefully past the Circle L and went to Mr. Woodley's house. He sat on a rocker on the front porch, waiting for her. Most of her parents' friends ignored her or regarded her with the sort of suspicion and disdain adults reserved for teenagers. Mr. Woodley was different—a high school English teacher who actually enjoyed his students.

He accepted the muffins and told her to thank her mom. "Now let's get to the real reason you came to visit."

He escorted her to the computer in his spare bedroom. While they were staying at the cabin, her parents banned all use of electronics, especially the internet. Her brother and she were supposed to spend the summer appreciating nature, but she had more on her mind than gathering pinecones and wading in creeks.

A few days before, she had been at the Circle L when a mare birthed her foal. She needed to write about the experience. While she waited for the computer to boot up, she pulled a small spiral notebook from her back pocket. The pages were densely scribbled with notes, which she held up for Mr. Woodley to see. "I interviewed the veterinarian."

"That will give some depth to your story."

"And I want to talk to the ranch hands so I can get an idea of what life is going to hold for the baby horse."

"I thought you had the makings of a poet, but I see I

was wrong." Mr. Woodley placed his hand on her shoulder. *"Someday, you're going to be a fine journalist."*

Her memory soothed the panic that had threatened to overwhelm her. Her breathing settled into a regular pattern. Caitlyn was a long way from calm, but she wasn't about to explode.

When she felt someone yanking on the door handle of the Fairlane, she was jerked back to the present. Whoever had been tugging let go with a string of curses.

Woodley's voice boomed from nearby. "Be careful, Patterson. This is a classic vehicle."

"Unlock it." Patterson's voice was terse.

"Sure thing," Woodley said. "But nobody's in there. I always keep my car locked. It's a habit."

She heard the door open. The car rocked, and she assumed that Patterson had climbed inside to look into the backseat. Silently, she prayed that he'd move on. Their hiding place in the trunk seemed as obvious as a wrapped birthday present with a big red bow.

Patterson growled, "You've caused me a lot of trouble, old man."

"Let's talk it over with my friend from the FBI. He ought to be here any minute."

"I don't have time to waste with the FBI." He raised his voice. "Bryant, I'm over here."

In a breathless rush, the Texan said, "I was in the barn. Think we got a trail to follow. There's a couple of horses gone from their stalls."

"I should have known," Patterson muttered. "He took off on horseback. Again."

A moment passed. The sounds of the searchers became more distant. The door of the Ford Fairlane opened. The car jostled as someone got behind the steering wheel. The engine started. As the car went in reverse, she heard Mr. Woodley say, "On our way. Over the river and through the woods."

They'd pulled it off. A clean getaway.

Hiding in the trunk of a car wasn't the most manly way to escape, but Jack didn't mind. The ancient suspension system in the old Ford bounced Caitlyn against him with every bump they hit, and there were a lot of bumps on the graded gravel roads. They probably hadn't traveled a mile before her clenched arms loosened up, and she accidentally smacked him with the handcuffs she still held.

"Give me those," he said.

"Can't see where you are. I'll stick them in the pocket of this lovely blue jacket that's probably going to be filthy by the time I get out of the trunk."

"That'd be a shame." He hadn't been lying when he told her she looked pretty.

After one huge jolt, she started to giggle. Her unbridled laughter was as bright as the inside of the trunk was dark. Her legs tangled with his, accidentally rubbing against his thighs and groin. They were bumping apart and grinding together. It was like making love in a blender.

On a relatively smooth stretch of road, he asked, "Do you mind telling me where we're going?"

"I considered riding all the way to Denver," she said. "But there's too much going on in this area. The manhunt for Rojas is massive. The police have heavy-duty surveillance and roadblocks. The car could be stopped and searched."

And he didn't dare turn himself over to anyone in law enforcement. No matter what they thought, they'd be obliged to take him into custody and turn him over to Patterson. "I don't expect the cops are going to be happy about my escape from the Circle L."

She bumped against his chest. "Probably not."

"You never answered my question."

"Do you really want to know where we're going?" she teased. "Wouldn't you rather sit back and let me take care of every little thing?"

He had to admit that she'd done a good job of springing him from Patterson's custody. She was a problem solver, smart and competent. But he liked being the one in charge. "Tell me."

"Or else? How are you going to make me talk?"

He knew what he'd like to do. With her body rubbing up against him in many inappropriate places, there was one predominant thought in his mind. He held her tight.

"Here's what I'll do to you, babe. First, I'm going to kiss you until your lips are numb. Then I'm going to take off that blue jacket and unbutton your shirt. And I'm going to grab you here." He lowered his hand and squeezed her butt. "You're going to be putty. You'll tell me everything I want to know."

"Bob Woodley's house," she peeped. "That's where we're headed."

"Woodley? The guy who owns this car?" If the Ford Fairlane was any indication, he didn't think Woodley's house would be safe. People who lived in the past tended to be less than vigilant when it came to the present.

"He told me that he was robbed last year, and he put in a state-of-the-art security system."

Jack doubted that good old Bob Woodley could guarantee their safety, but he needed a place to rest, recuperate and eat something more substantial than energy bars. Since last night, he'd caught only a few hours' sleep in the cavern. His body still ached with old bruises. Whenever he recalled the wound on the back of his head, it answered him with a quiet throb.

The car stopped and the engine went quiet. He heard the sound of a mechanical garage door closing.

The trunk opened. After being in darkness, the overhead bulb in the two-car garage glared like a klieg light. Untangling himself from Caitlyn took a moment and unleashed another burst of giggles from her.

Finally, Jack was on his feet. The first thing he noticed was that the second car in the garage was a Land Rover that couldn't have been more than two or three years old—a sensible vehicle for someone who lived in the mountains. A tool bench at the back of the garage displayed a neat array of power tools. Apparently, the old man had an organized side to his personality. Caitlyn had spoken fondly of Woodley. A retired English teacher. A friend of her parents.

He faced the rangy, white-haired stranger who had played a pivotal role in his rescue. Though there weren't sufficient words to thank him, Jack said, "I appreciate what you've done."

Woodley assessed him with a stern gaze. "You're the fellow who caused all this trouble."

Jack held out his hand. "Call me Jack."

"That's not your real name." With a firm grip, Woodley shook his hand. "I don't cotton to men who hide behind aliases. Let's use your real name. Nick Racine."

Chapter 15

Jack wasn't often caught off guard. His natural wariness kept him on his toes, ready to react to any threat. The name Nick Racine was dangerous. As soon as Woodley spoke it, Jack thought of plausible excuses for the alias. Deception was second nature to him, but he couldn't look this good man in the eye and lie to him. More important, Jack wanted—no, needed—to be truthful with Caitlyn.

She eyed him suspiciously then focused on Woodley. "Where did you hear that name?"

"From my friend in the FBI. He's one of my former students, and he doesn't have any reason to lie to me."

"What did he say?"

"He spoke to the marshal on the phone." Woodley scowled. "By the way, that Patterson fellow is rude and unpleasant. I try to see the best in people, but that guy was shifty."

"Agreed," Caitlyn said briskly. "And then?"

"My young FBI friend warned me that there wasn't much he could do to stop the marshals. That was when he mentioned the name Nick Racine." He stared hard at Jack. "I thought it strange because Caitlyn called you something else."

When she turned her gaze on Jack, she'd switched into her journalist persona. Her eyes were clear. Her attitude, cool. She was nothing like the soft woman who had been giggling in the trunk of the Ford Fairlane and rubbing up against him. "Have you ever heard the name Nick Racine before?"

He didn't connect with that identity and he sure as hell didn't believe the stories Bryant had been spouting about his supposedly legendary deeds. If he truly was a one-man strike force, shouldn't he be able to remember? "Bryant and Patterson said I was Nick Racine."

"I thought you were Tony Perez."

So did I. He shrugged. There wasn't anything he could say to clarify his identity.

"We need to look into this." She pivoted and marched toward the side door in the garage. "I'll need to use the computer."

"Hold on," Woodley said. "Who's Tony Perez? Why in blazes doesn't this man know his own name?"

She came back and stood before him. "The important thing for you to know is that this man—I'm going to call him Jack—is a decent human being. He risked his life to rescue Danny, and he saved me from a gang of men with guns." She took both of Woodley's hands in hers. "I trust Jack. And I'm asking you to do the same."

The way he looked at Caitlyn reminded Jack of an affectionate uncle with his fair-haired niece. The old man was proud of her accomplishments. "You've grown up to be quite a woman. I always knew you'd turn out okay."

"You were one of the first people who believed in me. You encouraged me to be a journalist."

"It's not hard to pick out a diamond in a bowl of sand." He gave her a wink and turned to Jack. "All right, young man. If Caitlyn vouches for you, I've got to accept you. With all your fake names."

"Thank you, sir."

"Now," she said, "lead me to the computer."

Woodley circled around the car and went to the door. "Are you two hungry?"

"Starved," Caitlyn said. "You know what I really want? When you used to come over to our cabin and play Scrabble with Mom and Dad, you always made grilled cheese sandwiches and tomato soup for me and my brother. Comfort food."

"Coming right up," he said, "but I don't want you two in the kitchen with me. There are too many lights, too many windows and too many people looking for you."

Jack appreciated Woodley's caution. Rojas was still at large. And Patterson might decide to come here after he was done with his wild goose chase. Jack followed Caitlyn and Woodley through the door that led directly into the house.

Woodley said, "I don't want to turn on any lights."

Again, Jack approved. Moonlight through the windows provided enough illumination to find their way through a living room and down a hallway. In a small bedroom, Woodley turned on the overhead light.

The windows were covered with shades and curtains. The decor was a mixture of antique and high-tech. A laptop computer rested on a carved oak, rolltop desk with a matching office chair. Wooden bookshelves held the eclectic collection of an avid reader, ranging from poetry to electronics manuals. A patchwork quilt covered the double bed with a curlicue brass frame. One corner was devoted to surveillance and security.

"Here's where you'll be sleeping, Jack." The old man went to the security equipment and flipped a couple of switches. "These four infrared screens show the outdoor views of my property. The garage, front door, northern side and western. The back of the house butts up to a hillside and is inaccessible. I've activated the motion sensors at a twenty-yard perimeter around the house and the burglar alarm in case anybody jiggles the door or busts a window."

In the unformed memories of his past, Jack knew he'd seen similar security arrangements. "This is a sophisticated system. Did you install it yourself?"

"It's overkill," Woodley admitted. "When I got robbed, I was so ticked off that I set this place up as a fortress, mostly because I enjoyed fiddling around with the electronics."

"He's always been that way," Caitlyn said. She'd already positioned herself at the desk where she opened the laptop. "If he hadn't been an English teacher, Mr. Woodley would have been a mechanic."

"And a damn good one—good enough to keep my 1957 Ford Fairlane in running condition."

Jack liked the old guy—a man who could work with his hands and with his mind. "I'm impressed."

"And you're going to be even more excited by my grilled cheese sandwiches. Before I head out to the kitchen, there's one more thing I need to show you." He stepped into the hallway and pointed at a closed door. "This is going to be Caitlyn's bedroom. Understand?"

"Yes, sir." Jack had been hoping they'd have to sleep in the same room, preferably in the same bed. No such luck.

He closed the door behind Woodley and went to the rolltop desk, where Caitlyn sat hunched over the computer. Her fingers skipped across the keyboard as she started her identity search. "Should I look for Nicholas Racine or Nick?"

"Neither. I'm not Nick Racine."

"Other people seem to think you are. We need to research the possibilities."

Buried deep in the back of his mind was something akin to dread; he didn't want to be Nick Racine. Uncovering that identity would cause no end of pain. "I have a better idea. Look up Tony Perez."

In a couple of minutes, she'd accessed a site that showed his mug shot. His hair was longer, as were his sideburns, and he had a soul patch on his chin.

"That's you," Caitlyn said. "Love the facial hair."

He massaged the spot between his lower lip and his chin that was now rough with stubble. "That settles it. We know my real identity."

"Do you remember being Tony Perez?"

He had a crystal clear memory of watching Mark Santoro die and of being shot. "I remember some things."

She pointed to the computer screen. "This is your address in Chicago. Tell me about the place where you lived."

Her voice was firm and demanding. Bossy, in fact.

And he wasn't inclined to take orders. "Are you interviewing me?"

"I'm looking for answers, yes."

"What's the point? We know Rojas wants to kill me to keep me from testifying. He paid off the marshals, and they need me dead so they can keep their jobs. Those are the facts. My name isn't going to change them."

She rose from the desk chair and faced him. Curiosity shone in her eyes. The color of her jacket emphasized the deep blue of her irises. "Don't you want to know who you are?"

"I like being Jack Dalton." A man without a past had no regrets.

"Please cooperate."

"Are you asking because you care or because you're a reporter?"

"I'll admit that you're a damn good story. And I suppose I could say that I care about you." With her thumb and index finger she measured an inch. "Maybe this much."

"Not much incentive."

She rolled her eyes. "Has anyone ever told you that you're a giant pain in the butt?"

"I'd like to answer that question but, damn…" He shot her a grin. "I just don't remember."

"Tell me about the place where you lived in Chicago," she repeated.

He tore his gaze away from her and paced as though moving around would jog his memory. "It was a one-bedroom apartment in an older building with an ancient elevator. I was on the third floor." A picture took shape in his mind. "Brown sofa. Television. Wood table full of clutter. I had a king-size bed. I like big beds."

"Did you have a girlfriend to share that bed?"

In his mind, he saw a woman with long hair and too much eye makeup. "A blonde. That's my type. Blondes with long legs. Kind of like you."

"Lucky me," she said. "Keep talking."

"The woman in Chicago wasn't anything special. We dated." And she had spent a few hours in his king-size bed. "She was no big deal."

"Where did you live before that?"

In the corner of the room, he stared at the surveillance screens that surrounded the house. In infrared view, the trunks of pine trees were ghostly shadows. "There isn't time for us to work backward through my rental history. What do you really want to know?"

"I've never interviewed someone with amnesia. I'm trying to find the key that makes you remember."

"Tony Perez. I grew up in southern California." His biography flashed before him as clearly and neatly as though it had been written out on a sheet of paper. He filled in details about growing up in foster care and never knowing his parents. He'd gotten in trouble as a kid for stealing cars and shoplifting. "I lived in Arizona for a while. How am I doing?"

"Considering that you started from zero, I'm surprised. You remember a lot."

He had details. He could visualize his driver's license and recite his Social Security number. But none of it seemed real. His identity as Tony Perez seemed like something he'd seen in a movie, but he wasn't making it up. "Remembering isn't the kind of relief I thought it would be."

"How did you make a living?"

He recited a string of menial jobs. "Then I hooked up with Santoro. I collected his debts."

"An enforcer," she said. "That makes sense. I've seen you in action, and you can be very intimidating."

"I'm not a thug." He didn't want her to think of him that way. "Getting people to do what you want is more about attitude than actual violence. I developed a reputation. People were scared of me. That threat was enough."

"There had to be a reason why they were afraid. What was your reputation based on?"

"Word of mouth and a couple of well-placed lies."

He went to the bed, propped the dark blue pillows against the headboard and took off his boots so he wouldn't get the patchwork quilt dirty. Then he leaned back against the pillows with his legs stretched out straight in front of him. For the first time today, he allowed himself to relax. God, he was tired.

Caitlyn perched on the edge of the bed beside his legs, positioning herself so she wasn't touching him. "I'm interested in how you set yourself up as a dangerous person."

"First you've got to build a reputation. Other people have to say you're tough. In Chicago, I used a snitch and a couple of cops. The stories they told made me sound like a cold-blooded sadist."

"Cops? How did you get them to lie for you?"

"Give them something they want. A bribe. A promise. A gift. Just like Rojas got Patterson to work for him."

"Then what?" she asked.

"You need to prove yourself. I picked the biggest,

toughest guy in the gang and took him down. I didn't kill him or do any permanent damage, but I hurt him enough that he knew I could have killed him. In a way, he owed me his life."

"Keep your enemies close." She regarded him thoughtfully. "This is beginning to sound like Sun Tzu, *The Art of War*."

"All warfare is deception," he quoted.

"Your life as Tony Perez sounds complicated. Why would you go through such an elaborate setup?"

A good question. "I was in a new town. I needed to get close to power. That's what I do." He laced his fingers behind his head and leaned back. Exhaustion tugged at his eyelids.

"Okay, you established your reputation and you proved yourself," she said. "What next?"

"I needed an ally. Somebody who had my back. That was Mark Santoro. When I first met him, I was using him. But he became a friend."

Santoro wasn't a saint. Pretty much the opposite. He was a head man in a drug-running crime family, but he was loyal to his crew and strong-willed. He had a family—twin girls who would grow up without their father.

"You still grieve for him," she said.

"His death was unnecessary and pointless," he said. "I should have seen the attack coming, should have known what Rojas was planning."

"How could you know?"

"It was my job."

"Protecting your boss?" she asked.

Though he nodded, he knew there was something more. Only a few hours ago, Greg Rojas looked him in the eye and called him Nick Racine. Jack had been so startled that he lost his chance to shoot in spite of his need for revenge. He wanted Rojas to suffer for the part he'd played in the death of Mark Santoro and for… There was another name, another person.

An intense rage exploded behind his eyelids in a blinding fireball. Someone else had been murdered. He had to remember. Until he knew that name, his soul was empty. His life had no meaning.

There was a reason he had played this complicated charade with Mark Santoro.

"Jack?" He heard Caitlyn calling him back to reality. "Jack, are you all right?"

He had to find the answers, and he knew where to start. "We need more information on Nick Racine."

Chapter 16

Near midnight, Jack lay on his back and stared up at the ceiling above the bed. His body floated in a sea of exhaustion, but his mind wouldn't succumb to sleep. The surveillance screens in the corner cast an eerie, gray light across the flat surface. His memories took shape.

He saw the number eight on the scuffed beige door of the motel room. The night was heavy, dark and cold. The red-haired man unlocked door number eight and walked inside carrying a black gym bag.

Jack blinked. He knew what came next, knew he should close his eyes, but he couldn't stop himself from staring as the scene played out. He watched himself.

He parked a block away and crept toward a clump of leafless shrubs at the edge of the motel parking lot. There, he waited impatiently with his Beretta M9 au-

tomatic. This wasn't murder; it was an execution for a man who lived outside the law. His name was Eric Deaver. He'd done unspeakable things.

The curtains in room number eight didn't close all the way. Through the gap, he saw the flicker from a television screen. Was Eric Deaver lying on the bed? Laughing at lame jokes from late-night talk-show hosts?

The door flung open. Red-haired Deaver was silhouetted in the frame. He gripped guns with both hands. He bellowed, "I know you're here."

One shot. One bullet. In the center of his forehead. It was over. Justice was served.

Still caught up in his memory, Jack heard the knob on his bedroom door click. He bolted from the bed, ready to fight to the death.

Caitlyn paused with her hand on the doorknob. Entering Jack's bedroom might be a really foolish move. She shifted her weight, and the floorboards creaked. Maybe she should trot back to her bedroom and put on more clothes. Not that the oversize T-shirt and terry-cloth bathrobe she'd borrowed from Woodley counted as a seductive negligee, but she didn't want Jack to get the wrong idea.

I'm not going to have sex with him. She'd known Jack for only a day. From the little he'd told her about his past, he was a scary guy. And there was absolutely no chance of any future relationship. She didn't want him to think that appearing at his bedroom door was some kind of booty call. There would be no lovemaking. She did, however, intend to sleep in the same room as him.

If she left him alone, she was certain that he wouldn't be here in the morning. He'd made it clear that he didn't want to work with a partner because of the unknown, the intensity, the danger, blah, blah, blah. She wasn't going to be shuffled aside. If he was going to run, she'd be at his side. He was her story, and she intended to follow him to the conclusion.

Twisting the knob, she opened the door and poked her head inside. Before she had a chance to whisper his name, he'd grabbed her around the throat. His arm was steel. She couldn't move, couldn't breathe, felt herself losing consciousness.

When he suddenly released his grip, she fell to the floor, gasping.

"Never," he said, "never sneak up on me like that."

She coughed. "What was I supposed to do?"

"Knock."

Though he was right and she really didn't expect an apology, he could have at least helped her to her feet. Instead, he went to the security corner and stared at the screens. Unspeaking, he kept his back toward her. Hostility rolled off from his wide, muscular shoulders in waves.

She stood, turned on the overhead light and padded to his bed where she sat on the edge. She adjusted her bathrobe to cover her breasts. As extra protection, she was still wearing her sports bra. "I'm sorry I couldn't find anything about Nick Racine on the internet."

"Not your fault," he muttered.

She'd tried. As a journalist, she'd learned how to use the computer to track down leads, and she'd employed every bit of her skill to locate information on Nick Racine. She'd hopscotched through databases, scanned websites and probed blogs. Though she'd found plenty of people named Nick Racine, none fit his description.

"The identity should have showed up somewhere. In a credit file or bank record or work history. It's almost like Nick Racine was erased."

"It's possible," he said without turning around.

Glaring at his backside, she got distracted by the snug fit of his black jersey boxer shorts. His legs were long, muscular and masculine, with just the right amount of black hair. His bare feet and long toes looked oddly vulnerable.

She tucked her own feet—in sensible white cotton socks—up under her. "We need to make plans for tomorrow. I'm sure Mr. Woodley won't kick us out, but the marshals are going to be canvassing the area."

"I'll be gone before first light."

She noticed that he hadn't included her in his plans. "I'm coming with you."

He pivoted and came toward her. The fact that he wasn't wearing a lot of clothing made him seem bigger and more intimidating. Stubble outlined his jaw. His black eyebrows pulled down in an angry scowl. "There's no reason for you to be in danger."

"I was embedded with the troops. I can handle it."

"This is different," he said. "Use Woodley's contact at the FBI. Put yourself in his protection until Rojas is under lock and key."

An hour ago, Woodley had gotten an update on the police activity. The safe house had been secured and four men arrested after a shoot-out. Rojas and two of his men had escaped. "What if he isn't caught?"

"That means he's out of the country, and you'll never see him again."

"What are you going to do?"

His chin lifted. "It's better if you don't know."

She wasn't ready to let go. There were too many un-answered questions. "I'll decide what's best for me."

There was something different about him, but she couldn't exactly put her finger on it. A heaviness? A dark, brooding anger? He said, "This isn't your fight."

"Earlier, you asked if I was interested in you be-cause you're a good story. Well, you're right. You're on the run, a witness in a gangland murder and a victim of unscrupulous federal officers. And let's not forget the amnesia angle. Jack, if I can get inside your head and write your story, I could be looking at a Pulitzer."

"You want inside my head?"

"That's right," she said.

"You're not going to like what you find." He lowered himself into the desk chair and leaned forward, his el-bows resting on his knees. The focus in his green eyes was painfully sharp. "I killed a man."

A murder confession? That wasn't what she wanted to hear. She held herself tightly under control, refusing to flinch. "Are you sure? What did you remember?"

"I saw the bullet pierce his skull, saw the light go out in his eyes. And I was glad to execute the bastard. I felt no guilt, no regret."

This memory wasn't consistent with what she'd seen of Jack. In dealing with the men at the safe house, he hadn't opened fire and gunned them down. His behav-ior was logical and precise; he didn't act like a killer. "Who was he?"

"I know his name," he said, "but I don't know why I needed to end his life. I believe the reason is tied to Rojas."

"Why?"

Though he was looking right at her, his gaze was

distant. "I keep replaying that moment when I had the drop on Rojas and didn't shoot. It wasn't an ethical concern that kept me from pulling the trigger. I could have winged him without killing him."

From what she'd seen, he was a good marksman and his reflexes were lightning fast. No doubt he could have disabled Rojas and Kelso with surgical precision. "Why didn't you shoot?"

"He yelled out the name Nick Racine, as though he recognized me. And something clicked inside my head. Everything was clear. The confusion and sorrow and rage I'd been carrying around for years vanished in a puff of smoke. I knew. Knew the answer."

His voice had fallen to a hush. If she hadn't already been intrigued by him, this moment would have captured her interest. What had become clear to him? What truth had he learned? She dared not speak and break the profound silence.

"Gregorio Rojas is the answer," he said, "but I don't know the question. I need to figure it out."

"You seem to be remembering more pieces of your past all the time. If you're patient, it'll come to you."

He shook his head. "I was on this quest long before I lost my memory. It's the reason I went to work for Santoro, the reason I agreed to testify. Somehow, all of what's happened ties together."

She had to get to the bottom of this. Never in her career had she been issued such a clear challenge. "Where should we start?"

He rose from the chair, took her hand and pulled her to her feet. With gallantry unbefitting a man dressed only in jockey shorts and a T-shirt, he escorted her to the door. "Go back to bed. We both need our sleep."

"Promise you won't leave without me."

"I won't lie to you." For a moment, the hint of a smile touched his mouth and she thought he was going to kiss her, but he turned and went to his bed. As he stretched out on the sheets, he said, "Good night, Caitlyn."

Trying to get rid of me? It's not that easy, Jack. She went to the bed and leaned over him, close enough to kiss but not touching. "I'm glad you won't lie to me."

"I owe you that much."

"Actually, quite a bit more." She reached into the pocket of her bathrobe and took out the handcuffs. In one swift click, she fastened one around his right wrist and the other around her left. "You won't be going anywhere without me."

His gaze went to the steel cuffs, then to her face. His sexy grin spread slowly. "If you wanted to sleep with me, all you had to do was ask."

"We're only going to sleep." It took an effort to hold on to that resolution while she was this close to him, but she was determined.

"I don't believe you." His voice was warm, intimate, seductive. "If you wanted to keep me here, you could have handcuffed me to this fancy brass bed frame."

"As if you couldn't pick the lock? No way. Hooking us together is the only way I can be sure where you are."

She showed him the key to the cuffs. Then she stuck her hand inside her bathrobe and T-shirt, tucking the key safely into her sports bra.

"Do you really think that's going to stop me?"

"I know you won't hurt me."

"You're right, babe." He caught hold of her right arm and pulled her down on top on him. "This won't hurt a bit."

The bathrobe tangled around her legs as she struggled to get away from him, and she was reminded of how their bodies bounced against each other during that crazy ride in the trunk of the Ford Fairlane. There was no way to avoid touching him. She knew this would happen. How could she not know? What had she been thinking?

The answer was obvious. Maybe, just maybe, she didn't want to escape. Maybe she'd come to him hoping that he'd make love to her. The magnetism between them was undeniable. Why shouldn't she relent?

"No," she said, speaking as much to herself as to him.

"This is what you want."

He undid the tie on the bathrobe and pushed it out of the way. He was on top of her. Through the thin fabric of her T-shirt, she felt his body heat, and the warmth tempted her. She felt herself melting.

His face was inches away from hers. If she kissed him, she knew this battle would be over. She wouldn't be able to stop herself.

She twisted her head on the pillow so she was looking away from him, staring at the wall beside the bed. Through clenched teeth, she said, "Stop it. I mean now."

He rolled off her. They were lying beside each other with their cuffed wrists in the middle.

"Can't blame me for getting the wrong idea," he said. "When a woman comes into your bedroom in the middle of the night with a set of handcuffs—"

"I know what this looks like." Excitement made her voice shaky; she couldn't stop her heart from throbbing. "I'm using the handcuffs for professional reasons."

"And what profession might that be?"

"I'm a reporter, and you're a story. If I want to get my career in order, I need to show that I can be an effective investigative journalist. You understand what I'm saying, I know you do. You're the one who told me I was going to be okay, that all I needed was to believe in myself."

"That wasn't much of a deduction," he said. "Anybody who's met you knows you're smart enough to accomplish great things."

"But I was scared. Paralyzed. I didn't believe in myself."

She'd hidden at her cabin like a hermit. When her position in the Middle East was cut, she knew it wasn't because she was doing a bad job. The decision was based on budgets and revenue. Still, she couldn't help feeling that she'd failed. Not anymore.

Jack's story had all the hooks that readers love, from involvement with a crime family to being on the run to corruption within the marshals. Not to mention his mysterious past. His story was worth a whole book or a miniseries, and she'd be the one to write it. She'd be damned if she would miss a single minute.

"You're right, Caitlyn. I believe in you."

His surprising moments of sensitivity made it even harder to resist him. "If we're going to get a good night's sleep, we should turn off the lights."

She climbed out of the bed, pulling him behind her with the handcuffs. She hit the light switch, and the bedroom faded into the half darkness. The glow from the surveillance screens lit their way back to the bed.

Finding a comfortable position with their hands cuffed together wasn't easy. They both ended up on their sides, facing each other. In the dim light, she saw that his eyes were closed. His lashes were long, thick and black. Any woman would kill for eyelashes like that. But there was nothing feminine about his face. Not with the stubble that outlined his sexy mouth. Not with his strong cheekbones and jaw.

Sleep was the furthest thing from her mind. She asked, "Do we have a plan for tomorrow?"

"No particular plan, just a couple of ideas. I figured I'd stick around this area. Do some investigating."

"Shouldn't you be focused on escape?"

"There's still three days before the trial. I want to use that time."

"How did you plan on getting around?"

"Woodley has a nice little ATV in a shed behind the garage and I—"

"You can't steal his four-wheeler," she said firmly. "After the risk he took for you, how could you even think of hijacking his property?"

His eyelids opened. "Woodley and I already talked about it. He gave me the keys."

"Well, good." She shouldn't have accused him. No matter what had happened in his past, Jack was far too loyal to betray the people who treated him right. "I can ride on the back of the ATV. You'll be glad you brought me along. I can guide you through the backcountry."

For a long moment, he gazed at her. A deep sense of yearning urged her toward him. She wanted to touch him, to glide into his embrace. Physically, he was everything she wanted in a man—tall, lean and muscular. She even liked the scars she knew were under his T-shirt.

"Tell me the reason," he said, "that we can't make love."

"I don't know who you are—Tony or Nick or some-one else altogether."

"You know me as Jack."

She certainly did. He was the stranger who showed up on her doorstep, the man who saved her life and be-lieved in her. "It's only been a day."

"A matter of timing."

Though she didn't have silly rules, such as not kiss-ing on the first date, she didn't want to rush into love-making. Intimacy was a risk she wasn't ready to take. "Timing is important."

"Tomorrow," he said, "we'll have known each other twice as long. That should be enough."

She closed her eyes and pretended to sleep.

Chapter 17

Though the curtains and shades over the bedroom windows blocked out the light, Jack sensed that it was close to dawn. His inner alarm clock, which he considered more accurate than a Swiss timepiece, told him that he'd been in bed for five hours. He lifted his head from the pillow and craned his neck to see the digital clock on the desk. Four forty-seven. Time to get moving.

In spite of the handcuffs, he'd slept well. The cozy presence of a woman in his bed reminded him of what normal life was all about. Her scent, the little kitten sounds she made in her sleep and the way her body occasionally rubbed against him made him feel alive. He looked over at Caitlyn. His eyes had become accustomed to the dim light from the surveillance screens, and he could see fairly well. Her bathrobe was open and her long T-shirt had hiked up, giving him an unfettered view of her long, firm legs. One knee was bent, and her toes pointed like a ballerina midleap. Her free arm arched above her head. For a slender woman, she took up a lot of space. He grinned. *Bed hog.*

Leaning over her, he studied the delicate angles of her face from the sweep of her eyebrows to the tip of her chin. Her straight blond hair fell in wisps across her cheeks. Her lips parted slightly, and her breathing was slow and steady. She was still asleep.

Her need to follow him and get his whole story was understandable, and he appreciated her dedication to her career. But he'd rather work alone. If he could unfasten the handcuff and slip away before she missed him, that would be all for the best. The trick would be to retrieve the key from her bra without waking her up.

He lightly touched the bare skin below her collarbone. Her breathing didn't change. Beneath her shapeless T-shirt, her chest rose and fell in a steady pattern.

Slowly, slowly, he moved his fingertips toward the valley between her breasts. He'd been in custody since he was shot, hadn't been anywhere near a woman for five months. Her skin was soft and warm, enticing him. He wanted to touch her all over, to taste her mouth, her throat, the tips of her breasts. He wanted her legs wrapped around him. Her arms, clinging to him. Her idea of waiting for a specific number of hours or days or weeks before making love was ridiculous. They were consenting adults, obviously attracted to each other. Why the hell shouldn't they seize the moment?

Under her T-shirt, he felt the edge of her sports bra. Just a little lower…

Her eyelids snapped open. "Are you trying to cop a feel or grab the key?"

"Both."

"How about neither?" She pushed his hand away. "Go back to sleep."

"It's time to go. Unless you want to watch me pee, you should unlock the cuffs."

"Ew. I'm not following you into the bathroom." As she fished the key from her bra, she glanced at the clock. "It's not even five o'clock."

"You could stay here and sleep in."

"Not an option," she said. "But this is really, really early. Do we have to leave now?"

"I promised Woodley I'd be gone before he got out of bed. If the police come knocking, he can honestly say that he has no idea where I went."

"Fine." She unlocked the cuffs and rubbed the red circle on her wrist. "I get the bathroom first."

"Hurry."

"Less than five minutes," she promised.

"Don't turn on any lights," he warned. Though Woodley's security system hadn't sounded an alert, it didn't hurt to be careful. *Always plan for the worst-case scenario.* The marshals could be staking out the house.

Jack doubted that Rojas was still in the area. A wealthy man like him was able to pay for an arranged escape. He probably had a private chopper on call.

After her allotted five minutes, Caitlyn peeked in to tell him she was done, and he took his turn. Though he would have liked to shave, he followed his own warning and kept the lights in the bathroom off. Back in his bedroom, he dressed in a fresh T-shirt and jeans provided by Woodley. The old man had also given Jack a lightweight canvas jacket in khaki. The keys to the ATV were in the front pocket.

Caitlyn joined him. She'd yanked her hair into a ponytail and thrown on the clothes she'd worn last night. The blue jacket was grungy from being in the car trunk, but she still looked fresh and awake.

Together, they went down the hallway, pretending that they hadn't made enough noise to wake their host. Jack hoped Woodley's taste in all-terrain vehicles didn't mirror his love of vintage cars.

Circling the house, they entered the shed behind the garage, closed the door and turned on the light. The two-person ATV wasn't brand-new but probably less than ten years old. The dents and scratches on the frame indicated that Woodley had ridden this four-wheeler hard, but Jack trusted the man who liked mechanics to keep all his vehicles in good running order. A blue helmet rested on the well-worn front seat. The lid on the storage container behind the second seat was propped open, and Caitlyn looked inside.

"This is so sweet," she said. "He packed a sleeping bag, a canteen and some food for you."

"Woodley's a good man."

She started searching thought the other outdoor gear in the shed. "He didn't know I'd be coming along. We need to find another sleeping bag and helmet. Maybe a tent in case we need to set up camp."

"We're not going on a field trip."

"Which brings up an important question," she said. "Where exactly are we going?"

The best way for him to figure out why he'd executed the red-haired man was to learn more about Nick Racine. The name still didn't resonate with him. He had hoped the hours of sleep might heal the holes in his memory, but no such luck. He needed to investigate.

Since Patterson and Bryant had identified him as Racine when he was in their custody, Jack thought he might find clues at the place where they'd held him. "We're going back to the safe house."

She found a second blue helmet which she plopped on her head. "But it's a crime scene. Mr. Woodley said the police had their shoot-out with the Rojas men there. Won't the area be closed off?"

"We'll see."

She stuffed a second sleeping bag into the carrier and closed the lid. "Have you ever driven an ATV before?"

"Oh, yeah."

During the time he spent in the desert with his mentor, they used dune buggies to get around. This ATV—with its solid frame and seriously heavy-duty tires—was the muscular big brother of those dune buggies. Jack was looking forward to riding over the hillsides. Pushing hard, he wheeled the ATV out of the shed and locked the door behind him.

"Don't forget your helmet," she said.

"Colorado doesn't have a helmet law."

"Humor me." She shoved the helmet into his hands. "We're in enough danger without getting into a crash and busting our heads open."

Helmet in place, he climbed onto the seat. Caitlyn mounted behind him. Her arms weren't wrapped around him like they'd be on a dirt bike, but she was close enough to lean forward and tap the back of his helmet.

He turned his head. "What was that for?"

"Just excited," she said. "Let her rip."

He turned the key in the ignition. The engine roared as he drove away, threading his way through the tree trunks, heading uphill and away from the road. In the thin light before the dawn, he couldn't see clearly and had to move at a slow pace through the forest. It was difficult to gauge distances, and he added a couple more dents to the frame of the ATV.

At the crest of the ridge above Woodley's house, she flicked her fingers against his helmet and said, "You should go east. That's to your right. And head downhill."

He might have guessed as much, but he was glad to have her confirmation. The ATV rumbled along a narrow path, louder than a Harley. This vehicle wasn't made for stealth; they'd have to park a distance away from the safe house and approach on foot.

As they meandered through the trees, the rising sun painted the sky in tones of pale pink and yellow, streaked with the long wisps of cirrus clouds. The dawn light gave form to the rising hills and dark forests.

When they came to a meadow, the wide-open space beckoned to him. After picking his way cautiously, he wanted to go fast. He gunned the engine and floored it. They were flying, careening over the uneven terrain with the fresh wind whipping around them. He felt free. Behind him, Caitlyn yelped and laughed in sheer exhilaration.

At the far side of the meadow, she tapped his helmet again. "Jack, you need to stop."

He pulled onto a flat space and killed the engine.

Immediately, she jumped off the back seat and took off her helmet. She winced and rubbed at her tailbone. "Ow, ow, ow."

"Are you okay?"

"Going over those ruts, I really whacked my bottom." She stretched and groaned and stretched again. "I'm fine. It's nothing a good massage won't fix."

"I'd volunteer for that job."

"I bet you would."

The light of a new day glimmered in her blond hair, and she beamed a smile. The combination of nature's awesome beauty and Caitlyn's lively energy delighted him. His blood was still rushing with the sensation of speed. He was…happy.

He dropped his gaze, knowing that he'd felt this way before. As Nick or Tony or Jack or whoever the hell he was, he had experienced happiness. A dangerous emotion often followed by despair. "How far are we from the safe house?"

She approached him. "What's wrong?"

"I want to get there before it's too late."

"We're not far," she said. "I can't give you exact coordinates, but the safe house and Mr. Woodley's place are both to the east of Pinedale. From the top of that ridge, we ought to be able to get our bearings."

After she got back onto the ATV, he headed toward the high point. His skill in maneuvering had improved to the extent that he only ran over one small shrub on the way.

She tapped his helmet. "Park here."

He turned off the engine, dismounted and took off the helmet. "You've got to stop flicking my helmet."

She shrugged. "I used to do that with one of my drivers in the Middle East. We were covered in protective gear, and tapping his helmet was the best way to get his attention."

"I don't like it." He hiked uphill to the edge of the cliff. A long view spread before him. To the south, he saw the main road and the turnoff to the safe house. Surrounding trees blocked his view of the house itself.

Standing beside him, Caitlyn bragged, "Am I good or what?"

Without her knowledge of the area, he could have been wandering these mountains for hours. "You have an impressive sense of direction."

"I used to ride over here to visit Mr. Woodley and then go exploring. Never once did I get lost."

That dangerous happiness lingered inside him, and he realized that she was a big part of that feeling. Though she could be irritating and aggressive, she challenged him in a good way. He wanted to pull her into his arms for a hug. Instead, he teased, "You have the instincts of a bloodhound."

"Are you calling me a dog?"

"I'm saying that it's no wonder you turned out to be a reporter. You always find your way."

She leaned her back against a boulder and folded her arms below her breasts. "Getting close to the safe house is going to be a problem. We can't muffle the engine noise. And it's getting lighter by the minute."

Though it couldn't have been much past five-thirty, the sun was rising fast. "If anybody's at the safe house, we'll turn back. If not, the noise won't matter."

"I can't believe the police left the place abandoned," she said. "Don't they need to process the crime scene?"

"Real life isn't like the movies. In most cases, there isn't a crack team of CSI investigators on hand. I'd expect the local law enforcement to be occupied with their manhunt. The search for Rojas."

"And for you." She pushed herself away from the boulder and came closer to him. "I've been thinking. Would it be so bad to turn yourself in?"

"I'm not going anywhere with the marshals."

"You don't have to," she said. "After the sheriff has taken a look at the safe house, Patterson and Bryant won't have much credibility. No matter what their excuse, it's obvious that they fouled up royally."

"True."

"Anybody would understand why you refused to be in their custody."

"True again."

Her gaze searched his face. "If you turn yourself in, you'll be taken to Chicago and sequestered before the trial. After that, you'll probably be in the witness protection program. I might not see you again."

He couldn't resist her any longer. His arm slipped around her waist, and he pulled her against him. "If you want to find me, you will."

"But there are rules."

"Since when did the rules stand in your way?"

She was a fighter, doing what she thought was right in spite of conventions and restrictions. She'd arranged to spring him from the custody of the marshals.

Her head tilted back. Her lips parted. He kissed her long and hard. They needed to be on the move. Didn't have a moment to spare. Still, he took his time, savoring this moment when her body melted against him. He wanted to make love to her in the soft light of dawn, and he could feel her yearning. She wanted it, too.

He murmured, "Have we known each other long enough?"

"Not yet." She exhaled a sigh. "Soon."

They were meant to be together. He knew it.

Chapter 18

Jack saw only one vehicle outside the safe house: the black SUV with the demolished front end and the flat tires. Since there was no reason for the police to conceal their presence, he assumed no one was here guarding the place. Still, he used caution, parking about a hundred yards away in a forested area and camouflaging their ATV with loose brush.

As they approached the house, Caitlyn said, "They didn't even put up yellow crime scene tape. This doesn't seem right."

"I'm guessing the sheriff has his hands full." Last night, local law enforcement had taken five dangerous men into custody, dealt with the death of U.S. Marshal Hank Perry and started a manhunt. There would be jurisdictional considerations. Not to mention dealing with the media. "I expect they'll call in CSI's from Denver or even from the FBI."

"But shouldn't a deputy be here to make sure people like us don't come in and mess up the scene?"

He didn't sense a trap, but he'd been wrong before. "Let's not question our good luck. We'll get in and out ASAP."

The front door was locked, but enough of the windows had been shot out that it wasn't a problem to shove one open and climb inside. In spite of the devastation caused by last night's firefight, Jack recognized the front room and the adjoining kitchen with pine paneling on two of the walls. He remembered sitting at the table, playing penny-ante poker with the marshals; he had suspected Patterson of cheating.

In the middle of the hallway, he went into the room where he'd been sleeping and turned on the overhead light. Shutters were closed and locked over the only window. The simple furnishings included a single bed, dresser and desk.

"Charming," Caitlyn said sarcastically. "This looks like a pine-paneled prison cell."

"The Marshals Service doesn't use interior decorators. The idea is to keep the witness safe. That's why the windows are shuttered."

"It wouldn't hurt to hang a couple of pictures or stick a ficus in the corner." She went to the desk and pulled open the middle drawer. "What are we looking for?"

"I'd like to find my wallet." He rifled through the dresser. His T-shirts and clothing were bland and familiar, nothing special. "I didn't have time to grab anything when we were under assault."

She held up a paperback book. "Science fiction?"

"I like androids. And don't bother reading anything into that."

"But it's so accurate," she said. "It totally makes sense that you'd be attracted to a human-looking creature with super-abilities and no real emotions."

He had emotions, plenty of them. They pressed at the edge of his peripheral vision like certain blindness. When he had slept in this room, his name was Nick Racine. Pieces of that identity were drawing together, threatening to overwhelm him. "It was a mistake to come here."

"What are you remembering?"

Too much. Not enough. "We should go."

She stepped in front of the door, blocking his retreat. "You can't run away from this. Sooner or later, you'll have to quit using the name of some poor guy who wanted to be my handyman."

She was right, damn it. "Where do I start?"

"With something you remember. Tell me what happened when you were attacked. It was close to midnight, right?"

"Yes." He didn't want to remember.

"You were in bed," she said.

"That's right." He pivoted and went to the unmade bed. In the paneling above the headboard, he spotted six bullet holes in a close pattern, probably fired from a semiautomatic.

"What did you hear?" she asked.

"I was asleep. A noise woke me. The sound of a door slamming or a distant shout. I didn't know exactly what it was, but I got up, pulled on my pants and flannel shirt. Stuck my feet into my boots. Then all hell broke loose. I heard gunfire."

"Did someone come into the room?"

"The door crashed open. Perry shoved me down on

the floor. Everything happened fast." The vision inside his head was chaos. Bullets flying. The flash of a knife blade. A burst of pain. "Perry was shot, but he got back up. We made it to the door at the end of the hallway. We were outside. Fighting for our lives."

"What about Patterson and Bryant?"

"Didn't see them. Perry must have told me they deserted us because I was mad." A sudden realization occurred to him. "I didn't have my gun, didn't have time to get my gun."

"Why is that important?" she asked.

He looked down into her bright blue eyes. "You're good at this interviewing stuff."

"It's kind of my job, Jack. And don't change the subject. Why is your gun important?"

"For one thing, I wasn't supposed to be armed. That's not the way witness protection works."

"I don't suppose it is," she said.

"If I hadn't been trying to hide my weapon, I would have slept with the gun beside the bed. Within easy reach." A mistake he'd never make again. "My response would have been faster. Perry wouldn't have died."

He crossed the room. The closet door was open. Hanging inside were a couple of shirts, a jacket and the charcoal-gray suit he intended to wear at the trial. He closed the door, knelt and pulled at the edge of the paneling near the floor. A foot-long section came off in his hand. He had created a cache inside the wall. Inside was a gray flannel bag.

"Very cool," she said. "Those are some serious precautions you took."

He opened the drawstring on the bag, reached inside and removed the Beretta M9. This gun belonged to Nick Racine; it carried a lot of memories. The grip felt like shaking hands with an old friend. His identity was coming back to him.

Something else was in the bag. Through the cloth, he felt a round object that was probably about an inch in diameter. He shook the bag, and it fell onto the floor by his feet. The gleam of silver caught his gaze.

"An earring," Caitlyn said.

Holding the post between his thumb and forefinger, he lifted the earring to eye level. Delicate threads wove a weblike pattern inside the circle. A dream catcher.

He sat on the floor, holding his gun in one hand and the silver earring in the other. Memory overpowered him.

He saw her from afar—lovely as an oasis in the rugged desert terrain. She stood in the open doorway of an adobe house. Her thick, black hair fell in loose curls to her shoulders. When he parked his car and got out, she ran to greet him. The closer she came, the more beautiful she was. Her dark eyes lit from the inside.

She threw herself into his arms. "Oh, Nick. I missed you so much."

He loved this woman. Elena. His wife.

A sob caught in the back of his throat, and he swallowed his sorrow. Oceans of tears wouldn't bring her back. He stared at the earring. "She didn't like jewelry. Rings got in the way when she was working with clay. Necklaces were too fancy. But she wore these earrings. Do you know the legend behind the dream catcher?"

In a quiet voice, Caitlyn said, "The web allows good dreams to filter through and stops the nightmares."

"I gave her these earrings so she'd sleep easy when I wasn't around to protect her." He remembered the silver dream catcher glimmering against her shining black hair. "Nothing could keep her safe. When I found her body, she was wearing only one of these earrings."

It had been his hope to bury her with the earrings, and he'd searched long and hard for the mate to this one. He'd gone through her closet, checked the box of jewelry she never wore, had felt along every inch of floor in the house, and he'd come up empty-handed.

Someone had taken the earring. The murderer.

But the red-haired man didn't have it.

With a sigh, he continued, "I lost them both. My wife and her father, my mentor. It was almost four years ago. I blamed myself for not being there, but Elena wasn't killed because of me. She was staying with her father, and he had enemies."

"Did Rojas kill them?" she asked.

"Someone hired the red-haired man. I wasn't sure who and I needed to know. That's why I created the identity of Tony Perez. Through Santoro, I thought I'd get close enough to the Rojas brothers to find out who was responsible." But he'd failed. The old familiar emptiness spread through him. He didn't care if he lived or died. "That's the life story of Nick Racine."

An identity he never wished to resume.

Caitlyn knelt beside him on the floor with her hands in her lap, itching to reach out to him and hold him. She was there for him, supporting him. If he wanted to talk, she'd listen. If he needed to cry, her shoulder was ready and waiting.

But he didn't reach out. His gaze averted, he withdrew into himself.

She'd seen this reaction from others. No stranger

to tragedy, she had experienced the aftermath of violent death while embedded with the troops. Everyone dealt with the pain of sudden loss in their own way, and his grief was deep, intense, almost unimaginable. His wife had been murdered. At the same time, he'd lost his mentor—a man who not only taught him but was his father-in-law.

No wonder Jack had retreated into amnesia. It must have been a relief to shed the burden of being Nick Racine.

He stared at the dream catcher earring. The delicate silver strands contrasted with his rough hands. What was he thinking? What memories haunted him?

From outside, she heard the grating of tires on the gravel driveway. Someone was approaching the safe house. Though she thought this might be a good time for him to turn himself in, that wasn't her decision to make.

Softly, she spoke his name. "Nick?"

He didn't seem to hear her.

"Nick, there's a car coming."

Immobile, he continued to stare at the memento from his dead wife.

More loudly, she said, "Jack."

He looked at her as though he was seeing her for the first time. He pressed the dream catcher against his lips and slipped it into his pocket. Slowly, he rose to his feet. "We'll see who it is before we decide what to do."

He directed her down the hallway to the rear door, unfastened the lock and stepped outside. She followed as he rounded the house and stopped. From this vantage point, they could see the front of the house.

Jack peeked around the edge. Under his breath, he cursed.

Caitlyn looked past his shoulder and saw Bryant and Patterson emerge from their vehicle. Until now, she and Jack had been riding on a wave of good luck. They'd escaped from the ranch and hidden at Woodley's without anyone coming after them. Apparently, that positive trend had reversed. The two marshals were the last people she wanted to meet.

"What should we do?" She looked to Jack for an answer, but he'd sunk back into a daze of sorrow. He leaned against the wall of the house, staring blankly into the distance.

This apathy didn't work for her. They were in trouble, and she needed for him to be sharp and focused. She needed for him to be Jack.

Bryant took off his cowboy hat and dragged his hand through his hair. "I still don't get it. Why the hell did you make such a big stink about this place being our jurisdiction?"

"Because it is." Patterson dragged his feet. The older man's exhaustion was evident. "This safe house belongs to the U.S. Marshals Service. Besides, I need to keep the CSI's away. When they start prowling around, they'll find clues."

"They're going to figure out what we did, especially when the men they've got in custody start talking."

"Rojas's men? They won't talk. They're too afraid of their boss to make a peep."

"It's over. We ain't going to get out of this." The tall Texan leaned against the side of the vehicle. "I don't want to go to prison, man. I say we make a run for it."

"There's another option."

She watched as Patterson opened the back door of the vehicle and reached inside. Jack had roused himself enough to observe, and she was glad that he'd decided to pay attention.

When Patterson emerged from the car, he held an automatic gun in his hand.

"It's the SIG Sauer," Jack whispered. "Perry's gun."

Jack had also been using that gun. He'd spent all but two bullets defending her when Rojas and his men came after her at her house.

Patterson rounded the front of the car and raised the gun, aiming at the center of Bryant's chest. "Sorry, kid."

The tall Texan turned toward his partner. His back was to them as he held up both hands. "What are you doing?"

"Don't worry. I'm not going to kill you."

"Kill me? What?"

"My God, you're dumb." She saw disgust in Patterson's weary face. "I'm so damned tired of having to explain every tiny detail to you. This is simple. I need to convince our supervisor that Nick Racine went off the rails and is dangerous."

"By shooting me?"

"I'll tell them that Nick shot you," Patterson said. "This gun is proof. Nick used it. When ballistics compares bullets, it proves that he's dangerous."

"Don't do it," Bryant pleaded. "We can go on the run. Rojas will protect us. He'll give us more money and—"

"Shut up," Patterson snapped. "I'm not going into hiding. I have a family. I have a pension. I'm not giving those things up."

Quietly, Jack said, "Patterson can't trust the kid to keep his mouth shut. He's going to kill him."

Apparently, Bryant had come to the same conclusion. He reached for the gun on his belt.

Jack stepped clear of the house, took aim and fired.

His marksmanship was nothing short of amazing. His bullet hit Patterson's arm. He clutched at the wound near his shoulder and staggered backward. The SIG fell from his hand.

Bryant reacted. He whirled, gun in hand, and faced Jack.

"Drop it," Jack said.

The Texan looked back at the partner who had intended to kill him. Then at Jack. Caitlyn could almost see the wheels turning inside his head as he made his decision. *The wrong decision.*

He fired at Jack.

She heard the bullet smack into the house just above her head.

Jack returned fire. Two shots. Two hits.

The Texan fell to the dirt.

Chapter 19

There was a lot of blood, but both marshals were still moving. Not dead. Caitlyn wondered why she wasn't shrinking into the shadows at the side of the house, paralyzed by terror, and then she realized that she wasn't afraid; she trusted Jack to protect her.

Patterson lurched backward and braced himself against the car. With his good arm, he reached across his body toward the gun on his hip.

"Don't try it," Jack warned. "You make one more move, and my next bullet goes through the center of your forehead."

The gray-haired marshal dropped his arm. His left hand was bloody from the wound on his right arm. His dark windbreaker with U.S. Marshal stenciled across the back was slick with gore.

On the ground, Bryant struggled to sit up. His face

contorted in pain, and he was groaning, almost sobbing. In his beige jacket, his injuries were more obvious. One of Jack's bullets had ripped through his right
shoulder. He'd also been shot in the right thigh. His gun
was out of his reach, and he seemed to be suffering too
much to go after it.

Caitlyn asked, "What are you going to do with
them?"

"First, I'll make sure they're completely disarmed.
They're both wearing ankle holsters and probably have
a couple of other weapons stashed. Next, I'll get rid of
their cell phones."

"Will you kill them?"

"Not unless it's necessary," he said. "I want you to
go back to the ATV and wait for me."

Her natural curiosity told her to stay and observe.
She wanted to see how Jack got these men to give up
their weapons and to hear what they said to each other.
By leaving, she'd be walking out before the story was
finished.

But she was well aware that she and Jack had no
backup. This situation wasn't like anything she'd en-
countered in the Middle East. Replacement troops
weren't going to be riding over the hill to help them out.
The smartest thing she could do was to follow Jack's
orders. "I'll be waiting."

She jogged around the house and the barn to the
forest where they'd hidden the four-wheeler. Was Jack
going to finish what he'd started? With her out of the
way, would he kill the marshals? She remembered what
he'd told her about executing the man who'd murdered
his wife. In her frame of reference, an execution meant

killing in cold blood. In his identity as Nick Racine, he was a murderer.

But Jack wasn't. Though he didn't hesitate to use physical violence, he hadn't killed anyone. He'd said it wasn't his job. Had he been talking about an occupation? Clearly, he had training in marksmanship, and his hand-to-hand combat skills were finely honed.

At the ATV, she pulled away the brush that camouflaged the vehicle. There was a lot she didn't know about Nick Racine. A lot she needed to find out.

Right now, there was a more pressing issue. By shooting the marshals, Jack had—ironically—given credence to Patterson's plan to discredit him. When the marshals were rescued, they would accuse Jack of ambushing them. Every law-enforcement person involved in the search for Rojas would shift their focus toward Jack. And toward her.

There was no way they could turn themselves in with any guarantee of safety. Not unless she could negotiate the terms with someone she trusted, someone like Danny or Mr. Woodley. She wished she'd kept up with her contacts stateside. At one time, she'd known people in high places. There were still a few. A plan began to form in her mind.

She saw Jack running toward her. Since she hadn't heard any other gunfire, she assumed he hadn't shot Patterson and Bryant. There wasn't any blood on his clothes, so he hadn't knifed them. She might have thought less of him if he'd murdered the marshals, even though they were despicable men who deserved punishment.

He climbed onto the front seat of the ATV. "Let's roll."

"I know exactly which way to go."

Their first challenge would be to get across the main highway without being seen. Since it was early on a Sunday, there wouldn't be much traffic, but law enforcement would be watching the roads. Leaning forward and shouting over the noise of the engine, she directed him to a ridge overlooking a section of road that wasn't fenced. "Stop here."

He killed the engine. "Use your cell phone. Call 911 and get an ambulance out to the safe house."

"Are you sure?"

"I don't like those two morons, but they're still marshals. They must have done something useful in their lives."

As far as she was concerned, that was an awfully generous assumption. Still, she made the call and turned off her phone.

To Jack she said, "You could have killed them."

"That's not who I am."

"Nick Racine?"

He pulled off his helmet and turned in his seat. She studied his face, searching for the terrible sadness that consumed him when he held the silver dream catcher. His expression was grim and as unreadable as granite.

"I've committed murder," he said, "but I'm not a killer. If there's another way, that's the path I'll chose."

"Why?"

"Death is permanent. If you make a mistake, there's no chance for a do-over."

She knew they needed to get moving. There wasn't time for him to answer all the questions that boiled inside her brain. "I want to know about Nick Racine."

Like the sun coming out from behind a cloud, the sexy grin slid onto his face. "Call me Jack."

She answered with a smile of her own. "As if you were born in the moment you walked up to my cabin?"

"Something like that."

What an amazing fantasy! Yesterday morning, the only thought in her mind had been repairing the roof on her barn. She certainly hadn't been thinking about a mate, but if she had imagined the perfect man, he'd be strong, handsome and capable. He'd be complex and interesting. He'd be sexy. He'd be… Jack.

Her heart gave a hard thump against her rib cage. There was no denying her attraction to him. Did it really matter who he was or what he'd done? Fate had dropped him into her life. She was meant to be with him.

She picked up her helmet. "We need to get across the road without anybody seeing us."

"Hang on."

He turned the key in the ignition and maneuvered down the hill. This stretch of road was relatively straight, with good visibility in either direction. There were no other vehicles in sight. The ATV bounced over a ditch, onto the shoulder and across the pavement. It seemed that they'd made it safely across this hurdle, but she wanted to be sure.

"Go into the trees and stop," she said.

He followed her instructions and parked again. He must have been following her line of thinking because he quickly dismounted and moved to a position where he could see the road which was a couple of hundred yards from where they were standing. His gaze scanned from left to right. "We're not being followed."

A beat-up Dodge truck rumbled along the road,

traveling a lot faster than the limit. She saw nothing suspicious about his speed; people who lived in the mountains treated the posted limits as guidelines rather than laws.

She heard the wail of an emergency vehicle. As they watched, an ambulance raced past. It was followed by an SUV with the sheriff's logo on the door. In just a few minutes, Patterson would be spewing his lies to the local officers.

"We're in big trouble," she murmured.

His arm encircled her waist. With the thumb of his other hand, he lifted her chin so she was looking up at him. "This might be the right time for you to turn yourself in. After Patterson tells the cops how I went berserk and shot them both, the search is going to get intense. Dangerous."

"I'm pretty sure he's going to implicate me in his lies." She slipped her arm around him. Their bodies had become accustomed to each other; they fit together perfectly. "Besides, you need me. I have a plan that's nothing short of brilliant."

"Brilliant, huh?"

When he combed his fingers through her hair, she realized that her ponytail had come undone. She shook her head. "I must look awful. Do I have helmet hair?"

"Tell me about this plan."

"The way I figure, being taken into custody isn't really the problem. You want to make it to the trial to testify."

"Correct." He kissed the center of her forehead.

"We need to find someone in authority who can facilitate the process and get you to court." Though his kiss distracted her, she kept talking. "I actually do have a contact I can call upon. Someone who knows me and trusts me."

"Who?"

"He's a full-bird colonel, and he's stationed at the Air Force Academy. Once we're on the base, we're under the jurisdiction of the military. Nobody else can touch us, neither the police nor the marshals."

Jack pulled his head back and looked at her with a combination of surprise and appreciation that made her feel warm inside. "How did you get to be so smart?"

"You have your talents," she said, "and I have mine."

"And what makes you think he won't throw us into the brig?"

"He's a fair man," she said. "He'll at least listen to what I have to say. We spent enough time together in the Middle East for him to know that I'm trustworthy."

"Let's contact him and put an end to this. Give him a call on your cell phone."

"I can't really do that. Technically, he doesn't have jurisdiction if we're not on the base. We have to go there. But the Academy isn't that far, only about forty-five miles."

"So all we have to do is make it across forty-five miles through rugged mountain terrain. On a four-wheeler. With deputies, cops, the Marshals Service and the FBI looking for us."

"And possibly Rojas," she said.

He snugged her tightly against him. "Piece of cake."

His kiss was quick and urgent. There wasn't time for a delicate building of passion; they needed to put miles between themselves and the search parties.

They took their places on the four-wheeler, and he asked, "Any instructions?"

"Keep going in a southeastern direction. Avoid the roads, the fences and cabins."

Turning invisible would have been a handy trick, but neither she nor Jack was magical. To find their way through the mountains, they would have to rely on her sense of direction and her memory.

During the summers when her family stayed at the cabin, she and her brother had taken daylong horse rides to Colorado Springs. Mostly, they'd followed marked trails and roads—an option that she and Jack didn't have. Still, she figured that she wasn't plunging into an altogether unfamiliar wilderness.

Instead of going deeper into the forested area, Jack drove at the edge of the trees, putting distance between them and the safe house. Their route was parallel to a barbed-wire fence with a rugged dirt path beside it. Other four-wheelers probably used that path. Following it would have allowed them to go faster, but she didn't want to risk running into anyone else.

When the distance between the trees and the fence narrowed, Jack veered into the trees. Their progress was slow and bumpy. This vehicle wasn't built for comfort or for long-distance travel. Her already-bruised tail-bone ached.

After what seemed like an eternity, Jack found a space without cabins or road and came to a stop. She immediately hopped off, stretched and walked stiffly.

Jack looked up toward the sun. "It's getting close to noon. Do you have any idea where we are?"

"My butt is in hell," she muttered. "All I can say for sure is that we're in the front range of the Rockies."

"A while back, I spotted a road sign. It said something about Roxborough State Park and Sedalia."

"Great," she muttered.

"We've been headed south and mostly east."

"I know."

She'd been pointing him that way. Their route would have been easier if they'd followed South Platte River Road, but she knew there would be fishermen—witnesses who might feel compelled to report a noisy ATV that was scaring the trout.

Jack went to a storage container behind the second seat and opened the lid. "You said Woodley packed some food."

Dear, sweet Mr. Woodley. She hoped he wouldn't be fooled by Patterson's lies, wouldn't think the worst of her. Sooner or later, he'd probably contact her parents. She shuddered to think of what they'd say. Mom hadn't been at all happy when she'd taken the assignment in the Middle East. Now Caitlyn was on the run with a desperate fugitive.

She took out her cell phone. "I should give Mr. Woodley a call."

"Don't turn it on."

She paused with the phone in her hand, watching as he held the quart-size canteen to his lips and took a long glug. He wiped his mouth with the back of his hand and said, "Even if your phone is supposedly untraceable, we can't take a chance. It's likely the FBI is involved in the manhunt. They might have equipment to track the signal."

Morosely, she shoved the phone back into her pocket. "I suppose using the GPS function to get our bearings is out of the question."

He held out a sandwich. "Eat something. It'll make your butt feel better."

Though his logic left a lot to be desired, she took the food. Her mouth was so dry that she nearly choked, but the ham-and-cheese sandwich tasted good. A hot cup of coffee would have been heaven, but she settled for water.

Jack ate his sandwich in a couple of giant bites and started digging through their supplies. "There are a couple of oranges and bananas. And a whole box of energy bars. What is it with you mountain people and granola?"

"Easy to carry and yummy to eat. Give me one."

After taking in food and water, she felt immeasurably better—nearly human, in fact. When Jack suggested hiking to the top of the rise to get their bearings, she was ready. Any activity that didn't involve sitting sounded good.

Her muscles stretched as she hiked. She swung her arms and wiggled her hips. Walking the rest of the way to the Air Force Academy seemed preferable to more hours on the back of the ATV.

She joined Jack on the rocky crest devoid of trees. The wind brushed through the tangles in her hair, which undoubtedly resembled a bird's nest, but she didn't care. An incredible panorama filled her vision and gave her strength. In the distance, she saw Pike's Peak, capped with snow.

Energizing her body seemed to help her brain. As she gazed across the rugged landscape, she knew where they were and where they should be headed. She pointed. "We go that way."

"Any particular reason why?"

"The best place to hide is in plain sight," she said. "We're close to the Rampart Range Recreational Area. It's full of trails that are sanctioned for ATVs. With our helmets, we'll blend in with the other off-roaders."

He didn't answer immediately. Preoccupied, he stared into the sky. "I see a chopper."

"And there will be a lot more planes and gliders and such as we get closer to the Academy. It's nothing to worry about."

"You're probably right." He shrugged but still looked worried. "I like your plan. If we're on a trail, we can move faster."

"Okay," she said. "Let's hit the road, Jack."

He raised an eyebrow. "How long have you been waiting to say that?"

"Hours."

Not all of her thinking was about escape. Sometimes, they just needed a chuckle.

Chapter 20

Though Jack made several more rest stops in the afternoon, the constant vibration of the four-wheeler was getting to him. Navigating this machine through the wilderness was like crashing through a maze on a bucking bronco.

When they found the groomed trails of the Rampart Range Recreational Area, the ride was a hundred times smoother. In comparison to open terrain, these trails were like cruising on polished marble. Finally, they were getting somewhere. Approaching the last step in their journey.

As soon as he was taken into custody by Caitlyn's colonel, he'd be swept into the system and transported to Chicago to testify. His time with her would be over. Sure, they'd promise to see each other again after the trial. They'd make plans. Maybe even meet for coffee.

But she'd be charging back into her career. And he'd likely be in witness protection.

He didn't want to lose her.

Other ATVs and dirt bikes buzzed along the trails around them, careening around sharp turns and flying over bumps in the road. Woodley's four-wheeler was more utilitarian than recreational, not designed for stunts. Their top speed was about forty or forty-five, and Jack was moving considerably slower.

A skinny teenager in a flame helmet zipped past them and shouted, "Step on it, Grandpa."

"I'll step on you," he muttered. He cranked the accelerator. Then he backed off. This was no time for a motocross race.

At a fork in the trail, he stopped at a carved wooden marker with arrows pointing the way to different trails. Behind him, Caitlyn was quick to choose. "Left," she said. "It's a camping area."

He didn't much care for organized campsites; having other people around ruined the experience. "What if we have to register? Neither of us have wallets or IDs."

"We don't have to stay there," she said. "But we can fill our water bottle. And maybe there's a bathroom. Oh, God, I'd love to find a bathroom. Even an outhouse."

A half mile down the trail was a large camping area with several separate sites, two of which were occupied by other ATV riders. Their campfires tinted the air with pungent smoke. His concern about registering was unfounded. There wasn't a ranger station, just a couple of restrooms in a small house designed to look like a log cabin. He parked behind the restrooms and watched as Caitlyn went inside.

He stood for a minute and waited before he decided

it wasn't necessary to stand guard. If anyone had been following them, they'd have made their move long before now. He glanced around the area. *Were they safe?* More than once, he'd seen choppers swooping like giant dragonflies across the skies. *Aerial surveillance?* It was possible. But the helicopters hadn't come closer or hovered above them.

He took his helmet with him as he strolled through the groomed area surrounded by a thick forest of lodgepole pine and Douglas fir. This land had been untouched by wildfires, and the foliage grew in robust clumps. A narrow creek trickled beyond the edge of the campground. He stood beside it and listened to the sound of rippling water mingled with the distant voices of the other campers.

The late afternoon sunlight reflected on the water as it rushed to join with a wider river or a lake or, perhaps, to flow all the way to the Gulf of Mexico. Everything had a destination. Every person had a future, even a man with no past.

He used to be Nick Racine. Not anymore. Though the full picture of his past was hazy, he vividly remembered the soul-deep devastation after Elena's murder. The single earring in his pocket reminded him of broken dreams—a future he'd lost. Tragedy had consumed him. Then rage. Then he'd embarked on the quest for revenge that turned him into a murderer.

When amnesia wiped the slate clean, he was freed from his past. He didn't know what fate had directed him to Caitlyn's cabin, but he was grateful. She had refused to give up on him. She'd believed in him. Literally, she knew Jack Dalton better than anyone else.

She came up beside him. "I found a brochure in a box at the bathroom. There's a trail map."

The squiggly lines marking the trails resembled a tangle of yarn, but he zoomed in on the important part. "Here's where we come out. Woodland Park."

"From there, it's a straight shot to the back entrance to the Air Force Academy," she said. "We're close. But it's late. I think we should stop for the night."

It wasn't necessary to stop. Their vehicle had headlights, and Jack knew he could push his endurance and reach the Academy tonight. But he was in favor of camping tonight; he didn't want his time with her to end. He pointed to a location on the map. "We'll camp here."

She squinted to read the tiny name beside the dot. "Devil's Spike? The code says there's no bathroom or water."

"It's not far from here. Looks like a couple of squiggly miles up the road we're on."

"Why can't we stay right here?"

"Witnesses," he said.

He turned on his heel and walked back to the four-wheeler. His reason for choosing the most remote location on the map was simple: he wanted to be alone, completely alone, with her.

Grumbling, she climbed onto the back of the ATV. In less than fifteen minutes, they'd climbed a zigzag trail to the Devil's Spike area. Each campsite consisted of a cleared space, a table and a fire ring. Each was separated from the others by trees and rocks. All were deserted. It was Sunday night, not a time when many people were camping.

While Caitlyn climbed onto the top of the wood picnic table and sat with her feet on the bench, he took the sleeping bags from the storage container. Since they didn't have a tent or any other gear, setting up camp was simply a matter of spreading the bags on the flattest part of the clearing.

He took the freshly filled water bottle and joined her on the table. Devil's Spike was higher than the other campground. From this vantage point, they overlooked rolling hills covered with trees and dotted with jagged rock formations—one of which was probably supposed to be the Spike. In the west, the sun had begun to set, coloring the sky a brilliant magenta and gilding the underbellies of clouds with molten gold.

For a change, Caitlyn was quiet. And so was he.

After spending the entire day with the roar of the ATV motor, the stillness of the mountains was a relief. The wind was cool enough to be refreshing without making him shiver.

He gazed toward her. The glow of the sunset touched her cheekbones and picked out strands of gold in her hair. He'd told her several times that she was smart, tough and brave, but he'd forgotten the most important thing. She was a beautiful woman.

She exhaled a sigh and stretched, rotating her shoulders and turning her head from side to side.

"Sore?" he asked.

"From my toes to the top of my head. My butt is killing me."

"I've got a cure." He brushed the twigs and pine cones from the surface of the table. "Lie down. I'll give you a massage."

She hesitated for a nanosecond before stripping off her jacket, which she folded into a makeshift pillow. She lay down on her stomach on the table. "Be gentle," she said. "I'm not a big fan of the deep tissue stuff."

He started by lightly kneading the tense muscles of her shoulders and neck. The fabric of her T-shirt bunched under his fingers. "You really should be nude."

"If I was naked on this table, I'd come away with a belly full of splinters."

He stroked lower on her back. He could count her ribs, but her body was soft and feminine, with a slim waist and a sensual flare of her hips. *Really beautiful.* He needed to tell her.

When he returned to her shoulders, she gave a soft moan—the kind of sound that lovers made. For several minutes, he continued to massage, and her moans got deeper and more sensual. "Oh, Jack. That's amazing."

He agreed. It felt pretty damned good to him, too.

As he rubbed near her tailbone, she tensed. "Be careful, that hurts."

"Let me take a look."

Before she could object, he reached around to unbutton her jeans. He slid the denim down her hips. A patch of black and blue colored the milky skin above her bottom.

She grumbled, "Are you staring at my butt?"

"You've got a nice little bruise back here."

"Really?" She twisted her torso, trying to look over her shoulder. "Where?"

"Without a mirror, you aren't going to be able to see it."

"Are you sure it's bruised?"

"How does this feel?" With two fingers, he pressed against bruise.

"Hurts," she said. "What should I do about it?"

"I could kiss it and make it better."

She rolled onto her back and looked up at him. Her eyes were the purest blue he'd ever seen. Now was the time to give her his sincere compliments about her beauty, but he found himself tongue-tied. What the hell was wrong with him? He wasn't inexperienced with women, but this felt like his first time.

"There's something," he blurted, "something I need to say."

Her eyebrows pulled down. "What is it?"

He couldn't blame her for being worried. Every time she turned around, he threw some giant revelation at her. She probably though he was going to confess to the crime of the century. "It's nothing bad."

"Okay," she said hesitantly.

"I wanted you to know that I appreciate you." *Real smooth, Jack.*

"And I appreciate you, too."

They sounded less intimate than coworkers discussing a business project. He took a breath and started over. "I like the way your hair slips out of the ponytail and falls across your cheek. And the way you squint when you're thinking. And the little gasping noise you make when you laugh."

"I don't snort," she said.

"You catch your breath, as though laughter surprises you. It's a happy sound." Feeling more confident, he glided his hand along her arm. "I like the proportion of your shoulders and your hips. And your long legs. What I'm trying to say is that you're beautiful, Caitlyn."

She reached up and touched his cheek. "Last night, I didn't think we'd known each other long enough to make love."

"And now?"

"It's time."

That was all he needed to hear. He kissed the smile from her lips.

Finally! He was kissing her. Caitlyn clung to him. His massage had lit her fuse, and she was certain that she'd explode into a million pieces if they didn't make love now, right now.

She expected Jack to show his passion with the same skill he showed in every other physical activity, but he had seemed unsure of himself. His clumsiness was endearing, but not what she was looking for. She wanted him to sweep her off her feet.

As he deepened the kiss, she felt his attitude change. He went from boyish to manly. Dominating and powerful, he took charge. With a surge of strength, he yanked her off the picnic table.

"You're so damn beautiful," he said.

"So are you."

"Men aren't."

"You are."

He carried her across the clearing. She knew he wouldn't stumble or drop her; she trusted him. In his arms, she felt completely safe.

His step was sure as he bent his legs and lowered her onto the smooth fabric of the sleeping bag on the ground. Not exactly a feather bed, but she was accustomed to sleeping in rough conditions.

Impatient, she tried to pull him down on top of her, but he sat back on his heels. Twilight wrapped around him. His eyes glistened as he consumed her with a gaze.

Then he went to her feet and removed her shoes and socks.

She looked down the length of her body, watching him as he stroked her instep and pressed on her toes. Another massage. Incredible! Most men required hours of pleading before they'd rub your feet. A burst of sensual tremors slithered up her legs, rising from her bare feet to her groin. She exhaled a low moan of sheer pleasure.

He moved up her body to her already unfastened jeans. His hand slid inside her waistband. Her thighs spread, welcoming his touch. Quivering in anticipation, she arched her back, inadvertently putting pressure on her bruised tailbone. Pain shot through her. "Ouch."

He stopped what he was doing and stretched out beside her. "Does it hurt?"

"Yes, but I don't want to stop."

"There's only one thing to do." He held her tightly and flipped onto his back. The move was so unexpected that she gasped. She loved the way he manhandled her.

"I get it," she said. "I have to be on top."

She liked this plan. As they undressed each other, she felt like she had some control. She decided the moment when their bare flesh would make contact. Lying naked on top of him, she reveled in the head-to-toe sensation. The cool mountain breeze that flowed down her spine contrasted the heat generated by their joined bodies.

Even though Jack was on the bottom, he remained the aggressor. He directed her with gentle shifts in position and not-so-subtle touches. Her thighs spread. As she straddled him, he moved her hips up and down, rubbing hard.

They were both breathless when he said, "You know I don't have a condom."

"I'm on the pill." Though she craved him, she hesitated. In his life as Racine and as Perez the mob enforcer, he'd been exposed to a lot of bad things. "Do you have any issues I should know about?"

"I'm clean. Haven't made love since I was in the hospital."

Her fingers ran along the edge of the scar on his torso. "You were Tony Perez when you were shot."

"A lifetime ago."

When he pulled her against his body, she knew that one night with him wasn't enough. She couldn't imagine a lifetime without Jack.

Chapter 21

Caitlyn had been right to assume that Jack would be a great lover. He knew all the right moves and some unusual twists that had surprised and delighted her. Their first bout of lovemaking had been fierce and hungry. The second time was more about gentleness and finesse.

On her side, she curled up inside the sleeping bags they'd zipped together. No other campers had chosen Devil's Spike, and she was glad for the privacy as she watched Jack—naked except for his boots—as he started a fire in the rock-lined pit.

Though she was enjoying the show, she said, "We don't really need a fire. We don't have anything to cook."

Crouched in the darkness, he coaxed the flames. "It's a primal thing. Like a caveman."

His long, lean body was far too sculpted to be that of a primitive man. She'd told him that he was beautiful, and she'd meant it. He reminded her of a perfect sculpture.

"We don't need the fire for warmth," she said. The early summer night was chilly, but the thermal sleeping bag would keep them warm enough.

He stepped away from the pit and looked down on the tiny dancing flames. "Call it ambience. Or protection from bears. Every campsite needs a fire."

When he crawled into the sleeping bag beside her, his skin was cold. It took a couple minute of giggling and wrestling for them both to get comfortable. They ended up in a spooning position, facing the fire with his arms snuggled around her.

Turning her head, she looked up through the tracery of pine boughs into a brilliant, starry night. She should have been perfectly content, but the wheels in the back of her mind had started turning. She was thinking about tomorrow. Turning to the colonel for help was the right thing to do, and she was sure he'd get Jack where he needed to be for the trial. And then what would happen?

As a journalist, she could use her press credentials to stay in touch with him until she'd written her story. But she couldn't violate the rules of witness protection to be with him unless she was willing to give up her own identity and disappear. She couldn't do that, couldn't sever her ties with her family and friends. The most important thing she'd learned from this experience was the value of friendship. She and Jack never would have escaped if it hadn't been for Heather, Danny and Mr. Woodley.

"After you testify," she said, "do you have to go into the WitSec program?"

"I was wondering how long it would take."

"How long what would take?"

He nuzzled her ear. "Until you started asking questions again."

"I don't want to say goodbye to you tomorrow." They had forged a bond, made a connection unlike anything she'd ever known. She might actually be falling in love with him. "We need to spend more time together."

"I wonder how much money I have."

"What?" She wriggled around until she was facing him. "What are you thinking?"

"When I was Nick Racine, I wonder if I was rich or poor or somewhere in between."

They hadn't had much luck researching his finances or his identity on the computer. "I couldn't find Nick Racine in any of the usual credit databases. Online, you don't exist."

"Which brings up a couple of possibilities," he said. "I might be someone who lived completely off the grid. Or I might have a numbered Swiss bank account."

"Those are the choices? Either you were a criminal or a mogul?"

"I vote for mogul. Then I wouldn't have to worry about WitSec. I'd buy an island in the tropics with a waterfall, and we could live there, eating coconuts and mangos."

"Not the best location for a reporter," she said.

"You'd adjust, and I'd buy you a newspaper of your own. *The Caitlyn Daily News*." With the firelight glimmering in his tousled black hair, he was disconcertingly gorgeous.

"Unfortunately, we don't know if you're a crook or a billionaire. We need more information. Seems like we're back to the beginning. We need to know more about your past."

"Blank," he said. "Not being able to remember isn't entirely due to amnesia. I consciously erased Nick Racine. Couldn't live with the tragedy. Or with the way I handled my revenge."

She was tired and hungry. Having him naked beside her made her want to spend the rest of the night making love. But this was important; the future depended on it. "Let's try to figure out the easy stuff. Like your occupation."

"Nothing comes to mind."

With the tip of her finger, she traced the jagged scar from his bullet wound. Other injuries had left their marks on his body. Obviously, he'd lived a physically active, dangerous life. "I think we can rule out Sunday school teacher and peace activist."

"I could be a peace activist," he protested. "I have a gentle side. I like flowers."

"Flowers, huh?" She supposed that any memory was good. "What kind of flowers?"

"Orchids." His sexy grin slid into place. "That's a good sign, right? Orchids are expensive."

He was the furthest thing from a hothouse flower that she could imagine. "Let's go with your skills. What kind of work requires you to be a marksman? Why would you be trained in hand-to-hand combat?"

"The military," he said, "but that doesn't fit. I have no memory of basic training or being on a base, can't imagine myself in a uniform. Besides, you checked military data and didn't find a record of Nick Racine."

Some jobs in the military weren't part of the records. He could have been trained in a special operation—the kind that didn't leave a paper trail. Or he could have been working for an outside organization. "You might be a mercenary."

"Maybe."

She'd never interviewed a mercenary but had met a few. They were cruel, emotionless men with cold eyes and even colder hearts. "You have the skills but not the temperament. If you were a mercenary, you would have slit the throats of Rojas's men at the safe house."

"That's not how I roll." He caressed the line of her throat. "I'm a lover, not a fighter."

She caught his hand. "You're both."

"There's no point in figuring out my past. Tomorrow, when I turn myself in, the federal prosecutors in charge of the trial in Chicago will fill in the blanks. I'm sure they have a fat dossier on Nick Racine and Tony Perez." He raised their hands to his lips and brushed a kiss on her knuckles. "On Tuesday, I'll testify."

She hated this neat, logical package. "What about me? What happens to us?"

"I won't let you go." Though he spoke softly, his voice rang with determination. "Before I met you and became Jack Dalton, I didn't give a damn about my future. I was empty. Didn't care if I lived or died. You changed that."

She'd never been anyone's reason for living. Unexpected tears welled up behind her eyelids. "What next?"

"The possibilities are endless, babe."

A tear slipped down her cheek, and he kissed it away. She never wanted him to leave. She wouldn't say goodbye to him. No matter what.

The next morning, Jack studied the trail map to find the most direct route to Woodland Park. The ATV was running low on fuel, and he didn't want their plan to be derailed by something as mundane as running out of gas.

His focus was clear. He wanted to get this thing over with so he could start his new life. No longer consumed by his past, he was ready for the future.

Caitlyn sat gingerly on the backseat of the four-wheeler. "Know what I want?"

He draped an arm around her shoulder and gave her a quick but thorough kiss. "Some of this?"

She glided her hand down his chest and tugged on the waistband of his jeans. With a grin, she released the fabric and patted his gut. "I really, really want steak and eggs. A medium-rare T-bone. And hash browns."

"When we get to the Academy, I'm sure your colonel friend can arrange it."

"I'm starved." She put on her helmet. "I burned off a lot of calories last night."

"It was a good workout." Their lovemaking hadn't been overly athletic but it had been sustained. He couldn't get enough of her, and he was pretty sure that feeling went both ways. "A lot more fun than when I was training for the triathlon."

She whipped her helmet off and stared at him. "You were in a triathlon?"

He remembered swimming, biking and running with the sun blistering down on his head and shoulders. "My goal was to finish in the top twenty."

"Did you?"

"Sixteenth."

"This is a positive sign, Jack. Your memories are falling back into place."

He wasn't sure how much he wanted to remember.

The triathlon had been a proud achievement, but he couldn't help thinking that something in his past would come between them. "It's good to know I don't have permanent brain damage."

When he mounted the ATV and drove away from their campsite, the fuel gauge dipped into the reserve tank. How many more miles did they have before it died? Caitlyn had told him that Woodland Park was only ten miles from the Academy, but she'd been iffy on distances.

The trails were clearly marked, and it didn't take long to find the main road—the most direct route. Barely two lanes, the graded dirt had the reddish color of sandstone. There wasn't much traffic, but the vehicles varied from dirt bikes and ATVs to regular two-wheel drive cars. When a slick, cherry-red, top-down Jeep Wrangler passed them, he watched with envy. The Jeep was a nice ride that made sense on this scenic road. In contrast, Woodley's utilitarian ATV was like driving a lawn mower; it would be virtually useless in a chase.

Being around other vehicles reminded him that they weren't on a pleasure outing. He and Caitlyn were still the center of a manhunt. Last night, he'd felt safer. Nobody could have tracked their bizarre cross-country route from Pinedale.

Today was different. On this road, they weren't hidden by forest. They could be picked out in aerial surveillance. Patterson had talked about hitching a ride on a helicopter. What if that chopper stayed around? What if the marshals had an eye in the sky?

The dirt road snaked along the side of a mountain. Every twisting turn revealed another panorama. At a high point, he pulled onto the shoulder and stopped.

"Something wrong?" Caitlyn asked.

"Not yet."

He walked to the edge of the cliff. In the distance was Pike's Peak, glistening in the morning sunshine. A ribbon of road twisted through the trees below them.

"Nobody can recognize us in our helmets," she said.

It was in his nature to plan for the worst possible outcome. If they were pursued, the dramatic views on a high road without a guardrail would turn into a death trap. Too easily, they could be forced over the edge.

A dark SUV whipped along the road below them. The driver was going too fast, kicking up swirls of dust when he skidded onto the shoulder. "What does that car make you think of?"

"The black SUV," she said. "Rojas."

Gregorio Rojas was wealthy enough to pay for his own aerial surveillance. One of those choppers or gliders had been looking for them, and Rojas himself had come to finish the job.

He climbed onto the ATV and maneuvered if off the road where he hid behind a fat boulder. He and Caitlyn removed their helmets and waited. His Beretta was in his hand.

The SUV zoomed past their hiding place. Its dark-tinted windows made it impossible to see who was inside, but the passengers in this car weren't taking the time to enjoy the mountain scenery.

"They're going too fast," Caitlyn said. "If they meet anybody on this narrow road, they're going to scare the hell out of them."

"Or force them off the road," he said. "And the people they want to meet are us."

"How did they find us?"

"By now the sheriff has probably figured out how we escaped from the ranch. They'll know we took Woodley's four-wheeler. Aerial surveillance will be looking for a two-seat ATV ridden by people in bright blue helmets."

"But how does Rojas know?"

"Patterson." The marshal would have told his lies about how Jack attacked them and shot them. Patterson would still be in the law enforcement loop. "He's feeding information to Rojas."

Any doubt Jack might have had about who was in the SUV vanished when the car came roaring back down the road in the opposite direction. Rojas was searching for them, pinpointing their position. And he wasn't known for leaving survivors.

Chapter 22

Jack knew he'd been in similar situations when he was on the run. Memories flashed: hiding in a dry ravine waiting for the sun to set, being chased across a rooftop in San Diego, jumping from an overpass onto a ledge.

In each memory he was alone. The only life he'd risked was his own. He refused to put Caitlyn in danger.

"We can't outrun them in the four-wheeler," he said.

"Do we keep going on foot?"

"Not safe. They'll be armed with sniper rifles. As soon as they spot us, we're dead."

She took out her cell phone. "We need reinforcements. I'm calling the colonel at the Academy."

"What are you going to tell him?"

"The truth," she said. "I'm in danger, and I need his help."

It couldn't hurt to have backup on the way, but Jack

needed to do something now. He had to level the playing field. That meant disabling the SUV. Shooting the tires with a handgun was nearly impossible, even for him. But he had to try.

As they watched from their hiding place, the SUV drove past again, moving more slowly this time. At the wide end of the road where he'd pulled off, they turned and went back up the hill and disappeared behind a curve.

"I want you to stay hidden," he said. "If anything happens to me, run."

"Forget it. I'm not leaving you."

He gazed into her clear blue eyes. She'd come a long way from being the woman who froze in terror, but she didn't have his experience or skill. "They're not after you. Rojas wants me dead so I can't testify against his brother."

"But we're a team." Her chin jutted stubbornly. "There's got to be something I can do to help."

"Survive," he said. "That's what I ask of you, Caitlyn. I need for you to get through this in one piece."

"Without you?"

There were worse things than death.

"I lost my wife," he said. "If anything happened to you, I might as well hang it up. I couldn't live with the pain, can't bear to lose another woman I love."

Caitlyn heard the words, but it took a moment for them to sink in. *He loved her.*

She'd been telling herself that she was with him because he was a good story, but she'd violated the cardinal rule of journalism by getting involved with her subject. Involved? Wasn't that a mild way of describing their mind-blowing sex last night? She gave up the pretense. When it came to Jack, she wasn't objective.

"I love you, too."

His sexy grin mesmerized her. "This is going to work out, babe. You stay hidden. Stay safe."

He turned away from her and grabbed his helmet. In a crouch, he dodged through the trees and rocks.

She still held her cell phone, but she couldn't make the call until she knew what Jack was doing. Being careful to stay where she couldn't be seen from the road, she moved to a position beside a tall boulder. Peering through the trunks of trees, she caught a glimpse of his khaki jacket before he ducked behind a shrub at the edge of the cliff where the road made a sharp, hairpin curve.

She saw the SUV coming down the hill toward him.

Many of the people she'd interviewed over the years had told her that the moments before a disaster were so intense that everything happened in slow motion. She'd never experienced that sensation until now. The SUV with dark-tinted windows seemed to be creeping forward an inch at a time.

As she watched, Jack rose from his hiding place. On the edge of the cliff, he stood straight and tall. A gust of wind blew his jacket open. She thought she could see his jaw clench as he raised his gun and sighted down the barrel.

The windows on the SUV descended. A man leaned from the passenger seat. Rojas himself? He had a gun.

A scream crawled up the back of her throat, and she pressed her hands over her mouth to keep from making a noise. *Oh, God. Jack, what are you doing?*

The SUV lurched forward, coming at Jack.

The driver would be forced to turn. If he tried to hit Jack, the car would fly over the edge of the cliff.

She heard two gunshots.

The windshield cracked, but the car kept coming.

The front grille was only a few feet away from Jack. He fired again and again with both hands bracing his gun.

He dived out of the way as the big vehicle swerved into a turn. It was sideways on the corner of the road when the front tire slipped over the loose gravel on the shoulder. Off balance, the car flipped onto its side as it plummeted over the edge.

"Jack." She screamed his name. "Jack, are you all right?"

She couldn't see him.

Clinging to the trunk of a scraggly little pine to keep from sliding down the steep incline, Jack ducked his head to avoid the flying shards of rock. A few feet from him, the SUV crashed down the cliff on its side. The drop was close to vertical for about sixty feet. Then the vehicle smashed into an outcropping of rock. Forward momentum flipped the SUV onto the roof, and it slid. The terrain leveled out, but the SUV kept going until it plowed into two tall pine trees.

The upper branches of the trees trembled. Dirt churned in the air. In the aftermath, there was silence, swirling dust and the stink of gasoline.

With his Beretta in his hand, Jack climbed down the craggy rocks toward the SUV that had come to rest upside down.

Nothing moved. The roof was caved in but not flattened. Rojas could have survived. Even if he was injured, he'd shoot to kill.

Keeping his distance, Jack watched and waited.

"Jack!"

Looking up, he saw Caitlyn standing at the top of the cliff. She looked like an angel—a very worried angel.

Waving, he called to her. "I'm all right. Stay where you are."

But she was already climbing over the ledge.

An arm thrust through the open passenger window of the SUV. Rojas clawed his way forward until he was halfway out. One side of his face was raw and bloody. His right arm twisted at an unnatural angle. "Help me."

"Throw out your guns," Jack said.

"Get me out of here. Before the damn car explodes."

"Where's your driver?"

"Dead. His neck broke. Dead." Rojas dragged himself forward an inch at a time. His hips were through the window. "I know it's you. Nick Racine. You son of a bitch."

Jack approached, keeping his Beretta aimed at Rojas, not taking any chances. A wounded man could be dangerous; he had nothing to lose.

Rojas hauled himself free of the car. His left leg, like his arm, was in bad shape. Breathing hard, he rolled onto his back. His face screwed into a knot, fighting the pain.

As far as Jack could tell, he was unarmed.

Caitlyn was all the way down the hill. Not taking his eyes off his enemy, Jack said to her, "Don't come any closer."

"Ambulance," Rojas said. "Get me an ambulance."

"I have my phone," she said.

"Make the 911 call." Jack stood over the injured man. "Make one false move, and I'll shoot."

Rojas glared up with pure hatred in his dark eyes. Deep abrasions had shredded the right side of his face. "You wanted to ruin my family. You and the other damned feds."

What other feds? "Who?"

"DEA."

That was the answer that had eluded him. Three little letters: DEA. In his mind he saw his badge and his official identification papers. He was a DEA agent, an officer of the law. Huge chunks of memory fell into place.

"Bastard." Rojas turned his head and spat. "You sent my brother to jail. You tried to destroy me."

"That's what happens when you're running a drug cartel. You get caught."

With his good hand, Rojas reached into his jacket pocket.

Jack tensed, ready to shoot.

Rojas withdrew a fist. He held his arm toward Jack and opened his hand. "I still win."

In his bloody hand he held a delicate silver dream catcher, the mate of the one Jack had found at the safe house. That earring was as good as a confession. Rojas was responsible for Elena's murder; he had hired the hit man.

Jack stood and aimed his gun at the center of Rojas's chest. If any man deserved killing, it was him. "Why?"

"Her papa was my enemy." His eyelids closed. "Didn't know she was your woman. But I'm glad."

"Rot in hell." He could have pulled the trigger, but it would be more painful for Rojas to survive. He took the earring from the unconscious man's hand, turned his back and walked toward Caitlyn.

She ran to him and threw herself into his arms. "Never do anything like that again. Never."

"I can't make that promise."

She stepped back. Her eyes filled with questions, but she said, "We'd better hurry. I called for an ambulance. That means the police will be here any minute."

"We don't have to run anymore. I remembered. Everything." He took a breath, accepting his identity. "I'm a DEA agent. Most of my work is undercover. I was taught by Elena's father, based in Arizona."

"DEA?" She cocked her head to one side. "You're an undercover agent?"

"That's why I don't have a presence on the internet. I have to keep my identity hidden. It's also how I knew how to turn myself into Tony Perez."

"It's also how you became Jack Dalton."

He didn't want her to think that she was nothing more than another project. "I haven't lied to you. Okay, I did at first when I claimed somebody else's identity. But after that I've told you as much of the truth as I could remember."

"It fits," she said. "When the marshals nearly found us in the cave, they said something about backup. Why didn't you call the DEA for backup?"

"If it hadn't been for the amnesia, I could have contacted my superiors. We wouldn't have gone through all this. Listen, Caitlyn, I'm sorry for scaring the hell out of you. Sorry I put you in danger. Sorry I dragged your friends into this mess. But there's a silver lining."

She gazed past his shoulder to the wreckage of the SUV. "There is?"

He took her hand. "I fell in love with you."

Her lips pinched together. "Is that Jack Dalton talking? Or Nick Racine?"

"Does it matter? They're all me."

Her eyes grew brighter. "Does this mean you won't have to go into witness protection after you testify?"

"If I remember correctly, the agreement I made with the federal prosecutors has me testifying in closed court as Tony Perez. After the trial, Tony disappears. And I go back to my life."

"We can be together?"

"That's right." He caught hold of her hand and pulled her into an easy embrace. "We're together. Until you get sick of me."

"Not going to happen." She rested her head on his chest. "No way can I leave you before I have my Pulitzer-winning story written. It just keeps getting better and better. I start out with the story of a federal witness on the run, and then you turn out to be an undercover agent with amnesia."

His heart sank. This was going to be an obstacle. "You can't write this story."

No matter how many times he explained it to her, Caitlyn still didn't understand. In the hangar of the small airport where they were waiting for the private jet that would take Jack to Chicago, she paced back and forth in front of him.

"What if I don't use your real name or any of your aliases?"

"You'd still be in danger." He shifted on the worn leather sofa that was pushed up against the metal wall of the hangar. "People who have a problem with me—

cartels like Rojas—would know they could find me through you."

She flung herself onto the sofa beside him. Though she would have preferred having this conversation in private, he had two marshals and another DEA agent keeping an eye on him. They stood in a clump by the open door of the hangar. All of them wore sunglasses. All of them were armed.

Her time with Jack was limited. The plane had already landed and was taxiing toward the hangar.

"What happens," she asked, "when we're together and somebody wants to know what you do for a living?"

"Tell them I'm a Sunday school teacher. Or an independently wealthy mogul."

"Even my friends?"

"Especially your friends."

"I hate this." Her life as a journalist was based on ferreting out the truth. How could she live a lie?

He leaned forward, resting his elbows on his knees. "There is a solution. You could have your story published under someone else's name."

"Then who's going to pick up my Pulitzer?"

The main purpose of writing this story was to reestablish herself as an investigative reporter. If she gave the writing credit to someone else, she'd be back to zero. "I have a better idea. You could quit your job."

He shook his head. "I'm pretty good at what I do."

"So am I."

She'd never anticipated this kind of impasse. Before she got involved with Jack, her main project was fixing the roof on the barn. She'd been thinking about giving up her career. It was his belief in her that reminded her how much she loved being a journalist. She couldn't turn her back on a story like this.

The DEA agent approached them. "Time to go."

"Give me a minute," Jack said.

They both stood, and she looked up at him. "You know, I could just write the story, anyway."

"That's your choice."

Her decision was clear. She could be with him and live a lie. Or she could write her story and say goodbye. "I want both."

He rested his hands on her shoulders and gave her a quick kiss. "I hope I'll see you when the trial is over."

As she watched him walk away, her vision blurred with tears. Love wasn't supposed to be this hard.

Chapter 23

Nick Racine, aka Tony Perez, was under close protection for the two-week duration of the Rojas trial in Chicago. No phone calls. No emails. No meetings. If he'd insisted, he could have made some kind of arrangement to contact Caitlyn, but he wanted to give her space.

He missed her. It wasn't the same kind of devastating pain he'd felt after Elena's murder. Caitlyn's absence was a gnawing ache that grew sharper with every hour they were apart. There was so much he wanted to tell her, so many things he'd learned about himself.

His childhood was something he never wanted to clearly remember. An alcoholic father. A mother who deserted him. And years in foster care. The only positive was that he'd learned how to fight at an early age.

His financial situation didn't elevate him to mogul status, but he was well-set. He didn't own property, but he did have a numbered Swiss bank account in a different name.

There were dozens of identities he'd used, but the only person he wanted to be was Jack Dalton, the man who was loved by Caitlyn Morris.

At the Federal Courthouse in Chicago, he waited in the hallway outside the courtroom where the trail had taken place. The jury had finished their deliberations.

As a witness, he wasn't allowed inside the room where he could see the look on Tom Rojas's face, but he wanted to know the verdict as soon as it was announced. Gregorio Rojas hadn't survived the car crash. If his brother was found guilty, the cartel was dead. Jack's revenge was complete.

Mentally, he corrected himself. Nick Racine had lived for revenge and allowed his grief to poison his life. As Jack, he had much more to live for. The future was within his grasp. He just had to make Caitlyn see things his way.

He sensed her presence and turned his head. There she was, striding confidently down the hallway toward him. Her newly trimmed blond hair fell to her shoulders in a smooth curtain. The skirt on her white linen suit was short enough to be interesting. Her high heels were red.

He stood to meet her, and when she stopped a few feet away from him, he was itching to yank her into his arms, to mess up her coiffed hair and kiss the lipstick off her mouth.

With a grin, he said, "You clean up good."

"So do you." She reached toward him and glided her fingers along the lapel of his jacket. "A designer suit."

"It turns out that I've got good taste."

"I knew that. After all, you like me."

Having her this close was driving him crazy. She was everything he wanted. "The way I feel about you goes a lot deeper than liking."

The door to the courtroom swung open. They were about to hear what the jury had decided. This was the moment Jack had been waiting for, the reason he'd taken the Tony Perez identity, the culmination of his revenge.

A woman stepped into the hall. "He's guilty."

Jack should have felt elation, but all he could do was stare into Caitlyn's blue eyes and hope. "It's over. I'm a free man."

She placed a newspaper in his hand. "The front-page article is about corruption in the U.S. Marshals Service. Patterson and Bryant don't come off well."

They were already in jail, and he hoped they would stay there for a long time. Jack glanced at the article, then back at her. "I guess you made your decision."

"I did." With a manicured fingernail she pointed to the byline. "That's my friend. There's no mention of you or me in the article. I'm just an unnamed source."

"You chose me."

"I chose both," she said. "As a matter of fact, I sold a four-part series to a magazine based on something I learned about when I was with you. Amnesia."

"Is the story about what happened?"

"Not everything is about you, big guy." She grinned. "I've been interviewing shrinks and experts. There's a guy who lost his memory for thirteen years, started a new life and got married. Then he woke up one day and remembered who he was. And a woman who—"

"Little Miss Know-It-All."

"I had to write about it," she said. "Because of you. Because you're unforgettable."

He pulled her into his arms and kissed her. The reality of holding her was better than his memories.

No matter what it took, he would never let her go.

* * * * *

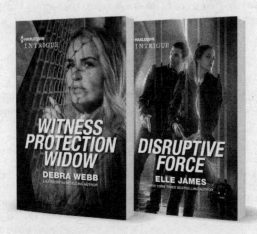

"What happens next?" Naomi had an awful, awful feeling that this was not going away anytime soon.

There were parts of no less than three people out there—of course it wasn't going away quickly.

"I've put in a call to the FBI office in Nashville. They're going to send a team to have a look around. Their crime scene investigators have far more experience and far more state-of-the-art equipment. If there's anything to be found, they'll find it."

The FBI.

The ability to breathe escaped her for a moment.

The sheriff held up a hand. "Don't get unnerved by the federal authority becoming involved. I know the agent they're sending, Casey Duncan. He's a good guy and he knows his stuff. The case will be in good hands with him."

"But why the FBI? Why not the Tennessee Bureau of Investigations?" Seemed far more logical to her, but then she knew little about police work beyond what she saw on television shows and in movies.

"Considering we have three victims," he explained, "there's a possibility we're looking at a repeat offender."

He didn't say the words, but she knew what he meant. Serial killer.